Praise for *New York Times* bestselling author
LORI FOSTER

"Foster hits every note (or power chord) of the true
alpha male hero…a compelling read from start to finish."
—*Publishers Weekly* on *Bare It All*

"A sexy, believable roller coaster of action and romance."
—*Kirkus Reviews* on *Run the Risk*

"Bestseller Foster…has an amazing ability to capture a
man's emotions and lust with sizzling sex scenes and meld
it with a strong woman's point of view."
—*Publishers Weekly* on *A Perfect Storm*

"Foster rounds out her searing trilogy with a story that tilts
toward the sizzling and sexy side of the genre."
—*RT Book Reviews* on *Savor the Danger*

"The fast-paced thriller keeps these well-developed
characters moving… Foster's series will continue to garner
fans with this exciting installment."
—*Publishers Weekly* on *Trace of Fever*

"Steamy, edgy, and taut."
—*Library Journal* on *When You Dare*

"Intense, edgy and hot. Lori Foster delivers everything
you're looking for in a romance."
—*New York Times* bestselling author Jayne Ann Krentz
on *Hard to Handle*

"Lori Foster delivers the goods."
—*Publishers Weekly*

LORI
FOSTER

GETTING ROWDY

Recycling programs
for this product may
not exist in your area.

ISBN-13: 978-0-373-60214-8

Getting Rowdy

Copyright © 2013 by Lori Foster

This edition published by arrangement with Harlequin Books S.A.

For questions and comments about the quality of this book,
please contact us at CustomerService@Harlequin.com.

® and TM are trademarks of Harlequin Enterprises Limited or its
corporate affiliates. Trademarks indicated with ® are registered in the
United States Patent and Trademark Office, the Canadian Intellectual
Property Office and in other countries.

www.Harlequin.com

Printed in U.S.A.

Dear Reader,

I am so pleased to bring you *Getting Rowdy*, Rowdy Yates's story! From the moment he showed up on the page in *Run the Risk*, the first book in my Love Undercover series, he's been one of my all-time favorite characters. Rowdy is loyal through and through, tougher than nails, dangerous, dark and edgy—but still sexy and sweet with a lot of mystery surrounding him.

I loved how he protected his sister at all costs in *Run the Risk*. I equally loved how he befriended Alice, the troubled heroine of *Bare It All*. But mostly, I loved how Avery, the tough-talking waitress at the bar Rowdy now owns, drew him beyond mere sexual attraction—even when he tried to resist.

There's something to be said for "broken wing" alphas.

Please let me know what you think of Rowdy and Avery. I sincerely hope you end up loving their story as much as I do!

All my best,

Lori Foster

When writing, I often ask for quick information on Facebook and Twitter. For all the many reader friends who so generously share their expertise in various fields, THANK YOU. You are my favorite form of research!

For those extraspecial reader friends who went above and beyond in supplying feedback:

To Jenna Scott,

Thank you for passing along my many law enforcement questions to your father, and please thank him for taking the time to answer. My favorite bit of feedback, when asking about the situation for my fictionalized criminals, was your dad's very succinct "These guys are screwed."

To Rhonda Copley,

A key feature of this story was understanding what happens to a child caught in the untenable situation of having bad parents who also happen to be criminals. I told you what I *needed* to happen, and you told me how it could work. I can't thank you enough for your patience in helping me with the details.

And last, to Amy Miles-Bowman,

If not for your help, I'd have been trolling the bars for info. As a teetotaler. That would have been pretty uncomfortable for me. ::grin:: Your knowledge of owning and running a bar helped guide my Muse through a few plot points, and I'll be forever grateful.

CHAPTER ONE

AVERY MULLINS HESITATED outside the entrance of the newly renovated bar. This early in the day, only a dim interior showed beyond the locked, glass-and-oak double entry doors—new doors that had just been installed two weeks ago.

Doors she'd helped to pick out.

Freshly painted signs crowded the big front window, advertising food, two pool tables, dancing and drinks. Overhead neon lights showcased the name of the bar: Getting Rowdy. It made her smile, remembering how she'd suggested the name, and how he'd followed through.

In such a short time, so much had changed. The business had gone from a failing, run-down dump of a place known mostly for its cheap drinks and availability of illicit drugs to a promising, fresh new bar with a fast-growing crowd. Even more notable was her switch of positions, from struggling waitress to head bartender.

Satisfaction had her smiling through most of her days. Thanks to the tips she made along with the raise she'd gotten, she no longer had the grind of two jobs just to make ends meet.

She'd kept the same apartment that could only be called modest if someone felt generous. And for the sake of anonymity, she still took the bus to and from work, rather than drive. But…

She had changed.

Before meeting Rowdy Yates—bar owner, boss and scalding-hot temptation—before being swept up in his enthusiasm for turning around a broke-dick bar, she'd… survived. No more, no less. She hadn't been unhappy, really. Or rather, there'd been no time to dwell on ideas like happiness.

But she hadn't enjoyed her life, either. Not like she did now.

She loved how Rowdy so often included her in decisions concerning the bar, almost as an equal partner instead of simply an employee. He had final say in all things, but he welcomed her input. He was proud, but not too stubborn to listen. Strong, but never a bully. He made her feel important again.

And of course, every woman who laid eyes on him noticed his appeal—her included.

They got along great, working to make the bar as successful as it could be. Associates, and she liked to think friends, as well.

Rowdy wanted more. God knew he hadn't been shy in sharing his interest.

And though he didn't know it, she returned those sentiments. But…did she dare to get intimately involved with a heartbreaker like Rowdy? He was honest with her; she didn't worry about what he wanted because he spelled it out. His honesty could sometimes be so brutal that it took her breath away.

He wanted sex.

Preferably with her, but every time she refused—and she'd refused every time—he easily found "company" elsewhere. With the way the female patrons came on to him, she doubted he ever had to spend a night alone.

Yet he always asked her first before moving on to second choice—his words, not hers.

Who did that?

Why did he do that?

If she really mattered to him, wouldn't he wait until he got her agreement?

But, being honest with herself, Avery had to admit that went both ways. If he mattered to her, why make him wait? After the year she'd had, she deserved some fun.

Bad-boy Rowdy Yates, with his scrumptious bod, brazen attitude and overactive libido, would be *so* much fun.

A brisk October wind cut through Avery's jacket and sent shivers up her spine, bringing her back to the here and now. Daydreaming about Rowdy had become her prime preoccupation. Seldom did a minute pass that he didn't plague her mind.

Maybe tonight, before he hooked up with someone else, she'd clue him in to how she felt.

With that decision made, Avery unlocked the door. Only she and Rowdy had keys. It still amazed and pleased her that he trusted her so much. She would never do anything to make him regret that.

Without turning on lights, she made her way through the dim interior of the bar. The early-morning sunshine barely penetrated the shadows. Usually she arrived around two o'clock, an hour or so before her shift so she could get set up. But she had errands to run today, as well as an important phone call to make, and she'd forgotten her phone near the register. She figured she may as well combine the trips.

After locating her cell phone behind the bar—right where she'd left it—she started to leave. She'd taken only a few steps when she heard the first noise.

Heart going heavy, alarm prickling, Avery stopped to listen.

There! She heard it again. A slight rustling, a low... groan?

She swallowed hard. Had someone gotten in through the back door? A drunk? A vagrant?

A robber?

Or worse?

No. She shook her head, denying that possibility. No one from her past would ever think to look for her here. There were times when she still couldn't believe the differences in her life. Differences that, since meeting Rowdy, she no longer regretted.

Besides, Rowdy's ongoing renovations to the bar had started with updating all the security, installing sturdy new locks to both the front and back door and all the windows that opened. No one could easily break in.

Before her transformation, she'd been an utter coward. Oh, sure, some might have called it circumspect, but she knew the truth. For far too long she'd relied on others...for everything.

A year ago, when faced with an unknown noise, she would have slunk back out the front door and called the police to investigate. If it turned out to be nothing, well, she didn't mind the possible inconvenience to others.

But a year in hiding had taught her to be more self-reliant, to handle her own problems. Independence had freed her, so she wouldn't backslide now.

Trying to be utterly silent, Avery crept toward the sound, her ears straining. She heard another groan that appeared to come from Rowdy's office. Maybe a radio? The creak of the wind outside?

Rowdy's door stood ajar, when he usually kept it closed. Daring took her only so far, but never beyond common sense. Just in case someone had found a way in, Avery pushed 9-1-1 on her cell and put her thumb on the call button. Inching along the wall, she held her breath until she stood right beside the door.

"Yeah, that's it."

Recognizing Rowdy's rough, whispered voice, Avery relaxed. Thinking he spoke on the phone, probably to one of his lady friends, she rolled her eyes, stepped around the door frame…

And her stomach did a free fall.

Slouched in the big padded chair behind his desk, his hands gripping the armrests, his blond head tipped back, Rowdy released another low groan, this one deeper, more gravelly. Avery saw him in profile, the large desk hiding most of his lower body—but not the top of the woman's head moving over him, precisely in the general area of his lap.

Good God, she knew what they were doing; even an idiot wouldn't misunderstand. Jealousy, hurt, resentment rose up to choke her. Avery wanted to move, she really did, but her feet stayed glued to the spot.

She wanted to look away, too, but…she didn't.

Rowdy's body went taut, straining, his expression bordering on acute pleasure. Then, with a final sound of repletion, he released a breath and eased again, his every muscle going lax. With a deep exhalation, he stroked the woman's hair and said, "Ease up, honey, I'm spent."

Oh. My. God.

Avery tried to swallow, but she couldn't find any spit. She tried to close her eyes, but couldn't even manage a blink.

On her knees before him, the redhead gave her own sound of satisfaction and slowly rose up over Rowdy's thighs. "My turn."

Whoa. No way did she want to hang around to witness that. Horrified, Avery shifted to sneak off—and the floor squeaked.

Rowdy's gaze swung around to pinpoint her there in the doorway. His light brown eyes went from mellow satisfaction to razor-sharp focus. He didn't straighten, didn't take his big hand from the woman's hair.

Maybe he didn't even breathe.

Their gazes clashed for two heavy heartbeats before Avery got it together and lurched away. Heat scalded her face. Her heart punched against her ribs. *Please don't let him follow me. Please don't.*

From behind her, she heard Rowdy's low curse, and then the high-pitched laughter of the woman.

No, no, *no.* Humiliation chased Avery to the front door. Once there, breathless in a confusing mix of emotions, she paused and glanced back over her shoulder.

No one followed. In fact, she could now hear the quiet conversation between Rowdy and the woman.

Fury tightened her chest and burned her eyes. *Damn you, Rowdy Yates.*

Forcing her chin up, Avery pushed through the door, out of the bar and away from the first man who'd interested her in over a year.

ROWDY FOUGHT THE urge to call Avery back, to chase after her and say…what? *Sorry you busted me getting a blow job.* Hardly. She'd annihilate him if he even tried.

He could tell her the truth. *I wish it had been you on your knees instead.* He snorted at the idiocy of that thought.

Avery already knew he wanted her. Hell, he'd been so open and up front with her that his pursuit bordered on infatuation, as asinine as that seemed.

Growing uneasiness obliterated the pleasure from release. Damn it, he didn't owe Avery any explanations. She was his employee. Period.

That's how she wanted it.

But what if she didn't come back?

No, he wouldn't think that way. In the short time he'd known her, Avery had proved to have a backbone of iron, an overload of pride and possibly a chip on her shoulder bigger than the one he carried.

She'd be back, if for no other reason than to fry him with her disapproval.

Besides, she loved her job, and she was good at it. He checked his watch. Why was she here so early?

Whatever her reason, it didn't matter. She had seen him, and that destroyed all the ground he'd gained with her. For a little while there, she'd been softening to him. Sort of.

Maybe not.

With Avery Mullins, it was hard to tell.

From the first time he'd spotted her in the bar, he'd wanted her. She had amazing red hair, a killer attitude and tons of energy contained in a petite and enticing body. Smart, savvy, observant.

And sexy as hell, though she denied that truth, just as she denied wanting him.

The contrast of her personal pride and work ethic, compared to where she chose to work—with him—intrigued Rowdy. He'd met her before buying the bar, back when it was no more than a dump filled with creeps and criminals. He still wasn't sure if she'd factored into his desire to have the bar.

Eventually he'd win her over. He refused to accept any other outcome. But even to him, this current transgression looked bad.

The long, lonely night had ended, so he had no reason to continue lingering with…shit. What was her name?

Feeling the sting of Avery's censure, even though she hadn't stuck around to share it with him, Rowdy caught the woman's arms and tugged her to her feet. "C'mon, honey. Fun's over."

"For you," she complained, and tried to crawl into his lap.

"As I recall, you had your turn at least twice already."

"At least." She gave him a sultry, satisfied smile and rubbed up against him.

Her hair, red but not the rich, natural red of Avery's, trailed over his arm. She was a small woman also, but without the same proud stature as Avery.

And when it came to outlook, the two women were worlds apart.

Had he really imagined a similarity of any kind? Dumb. Maybe even desperate, but he didn't like that idea, so he snuffed it from his mind.

Holding the woman away, Rowdy stood and then turned from her so he could refasten his jeans. "It's later than I realized. Time for you to go."

"Because of her?"

On the nose. "No."

Snuggling up to his back, she rubbed her breasts against him. "I had an incredible time."

Now, after seeing Avery, the purring tone and brush of body on body left him cold. "Glad to hear it." Though he felt like a bastard, he skirted around his desk and went to the door to wait, his impatience plain.

She pouted before accepting the inevitable. With a slow lick to her lips, she sauntered toward him, tried to kiss him—but he dodged that—and started to head through the bar.

Rowdy caught her arm and redirected her. "Back door is closer." On the off chance that Avery lingered out front, best not to push his luck.

"Did you have fun?"

"Yeah, sure." He'd tried to win Avery over last night but as usual, she'd turned him down in her no-nonsense way.

He hadn't wanted to, but he'd accepted an alternate.

"I need cab fare."

"Not a problem." The lady was from out of town and staying with her family, which meant going to her place hadn't been an option. Rowdy hadn't wanted her in his new apartment, either…so he'd taken her to his office instead.

Not good. He should have just rented a room for the night. Next time he would.

Because the nightmares never went away for long, he knew there *would* be a next time, and a time after that.

He was a twenty-nine-year-old man, and he'd been on his own for most of his life. But sometimes the ugliness of long ago closed in around him with the suffocating discomfort of a boy's desperation.

Damn it, he hated his own weakness.

Disgusted, Rowdy dug out his wallet and retrieved two twenty-dollar bills. Now, with a new day ahead, he craved a few hours' sleep. "Will that do it?"

"Thanks." She curled her manicured fingers around the money and said with suggestion, "I get into town every couple of weeks."

Rowdy unlocked the back door while saying, "Sorry, honey, but I already told you this was a onetime deal."

"It doesn't have to be."

"Yeah." His thoughts already moving ahead to what had to be done before he opened the bar, he held the door wide-open for her. "It does."

"If you change your mind…"

As gently as he could, he nudged her along. "I won't." She'd been a nice distraction, but nothing more. At the moment, he wanted to concentrate on the bar…and on Avery.

The woman left reluctantly—but she did leave.

Just as they all did.

And that's the way he wanted it. Usually. But odd as it seemed, even though they hadn't yet hit the sheets, he enjoyed Avery's company.

Hell, he liked it so much that he'd made her the bartender as soon as he'd bought the bar. If he wanted her to stick around—and he did—there'd have to be no more sex in the office.

Unless it was sex with Avery.

And wasn't that one hell of a nice idea?

IN THE PAST YEAR, Avery had learned all sorts of things about herself. She was stronger than she'd ever realized. More determined. More resilient.

But it took every bit of her confidence to walk back into that bar before her shift. She couldn't rid her brain of the darkly sensual image of Rowdy involved in such an intimate act. How he'd looked, how he'd sounded. *So hot.*

Being honest with herself, she knew that jealousy ran hand in hand with curiosity. They didn't have an agreement, so he hadn't betrayed her in any way. But she still felt…a lot.

Rowdy lived life by his own rules. How freeing might that be?

He took care of his business and accepted his responsibilities, but when it came to personal relationships, he avoided commitments and instead indulged a healthy sexual appetite. She wasn't as pathetically naive now as she'd been a year ago, but she knew a badass bad boy like Rowdy was so far out of her realm of experience that it left her dizzy.

She couldn't play with him without getting burned. She couldn't indulge him without risking a broken heart.

Sadly, there wasn't anything she could do with him—except work—so she might as well put anything more intimate from her mind.

But now that she'd seen him during a release…

No, Avery told herself, *stop thinking about it!*

Not even Rowdy was around when she returned and began rushing through her setup. She had enough to do that for a while, she managed not to stew.

At 3:00 p.m., only half an hour before he needed to open the doors, Rowdy strode in. Wearing faded jeans and a black T-shirt, freshly showered and with his hair still damp, he looked as delicious as ever.

She braced herself for the inevitable awkwardness, what Rowdy would say, what she would say.

It didn't happen.

Rowdy went right to work setting up. Jones, the newly hired cook, and Ella, one of the three waitresses, also bustled about. The prep work kept them all too busy for chitchat.

She looked away as Rowdy stocked the cash register with small bills and change. She occupied herself elsewhere when he set up the dry-erase board with the day's specials. She chatted up Ella while Rowdy did a general run-through of the bar.

But all the while, she was far too aware of him.

Rowdy, damn him, acted as if nothing had happened.

Maybe, for him, it hadn't been a big deal at all. Maybe getting busted in an intimate sex act was something he took in stride.

He did repeatedly look her way. Avery knew because she felt it every time. The man had a way of looking that felt more like a hot, physical touch.

As the night wore on and customers crowded in, Avery's tension grew. She'd expected Rowdy to confront her, at the very least to ask her why she'd been in the bar so early.

But he didn't.

Was *he* avoiding *her?* Well, he'd have to eventually talk with her, but she wanted to put it off as long as possible. She still had to figure out what to say.

Best-case scenario, she'd follow his lead and play it off like it hardly had an impact at all.

During the dinner hour, while much of the crowd ordered off the limited menu, Avery took the time to tidy her work area. She didn't have a barback so keeping the bar prepared was one of her main responsibilities. Whenever possible, she reorganized things.

Hustling along the length of the countertop, she grabbed up empty straw wrappers and cocktail napkins and wiped up a few spills. When she turned toward the sink, she almost plowed into Rowdy. Stumbling back two steps, taken off guard, she scowled up at him. "What?"

He didn't seem to mind her acerbic tone. "Going to ignore me all night?"

A deep inhalation didn't help. She said without thinking, "You were ignoring me."

"No." He turned them both so that he blocked her from view of the customers. "But every time I looked at you, you got so red faced I thought you might faint."

Yeah, and now that he mentioned it, heat scalded her cheeks. Hoping to exude disinterest, Avery tried to elbow him out of her way. He was so rock solid that she didn't budge him a single inch, so she stepped around him with haste. "I don't know what you're talking about."

"Bull." He crossed his arms and leaned back on the bar. "We have to talk about it."

At the breaking point, she started to blast him, but instead got caught up in the flex of his biceps, how his soft cotton T-shirt stretched over his chest, how the denim of his jeans had faded over his…fly.

Stifling a groan, she set out more napkins and clean glasses just to give her hands something to do—other than reach for him. "About what?"

"Avery," he chastised. "You know what I'm talking about."

A spark of temper smashed through some of her

embarrassment. She gave a quick glance around, but no one was close enough to overhear. "Are you talking about your inappropriate behavior in your office?"

"Yeah." The corner of his mouth lifted in a smile. "That."

Well, if he could be so blasé, she would be, too. "Sorry about interrupting. Hope you didn't—" she almost choked "—stop on my account."

"I'd just finished anyway—but then, you know that, don't you?"

Breath strangled in her throat.

He lowered his voice to a husky rumble. "I mean, since you watched."

Shooting up to her tiptoes, Avery growled, "I was *shocked!* And actually, I figured you two had stayed at it for hours after I fled the scene."

"No." His humor faded until he looked far too serious. "I'm sorry you walked in on that."

Before she could censor her mouth, she heard herself say, "But you're not sorry you did it?"

As if sizing her up, Rowdy watched her without replying.

Good grief. Rushing, Avery pulled out the bags of peanuts and pretzels to refill the bowls. "Forget I said that. Not my business."

"I've asked you—"

"I know you have," she said, a little too loud and way too fast. Her rusty laugh wouldn't convince anyone. "And if not me, then someone else, right?" Anyone else.

Way to make her feel special.

"Avery—"

She plopped the bowl up on the bar so hard that peanuts jumped out. "Believe me, Rowdy, I get it."

"I don't think you do."

For whatever reason, that really annoyed her. Hands on her hips, her cheeks hot, she faced him. "You want sex. Constantly."

He glanced around, then took her arm and pulled her aside again. "Keep it down, why don't you?"

Already on a roll, she continued. "With any willing woman. I'm not ready, so you—"

"It's not like that."

"No?" *Just shut up, Avery.* But of course she didn't. Around Rowdy, she lost much of her control. "Then how exactly is it?"

He dismissed that question with a shake of his head and asked one of his own. "What do you mean you're not ready?"

Oh, crap.

Shifting closer, his gaze bored into hers. "You haven't asked me to wait, Avery. Not once. All I've heard from you is a flat no."

She stared up at him—and badly wanted to say, *Wait.*

As if he knew her thoughts, he whispered, "Avery—" and the bar's landline phone rang, cutting off whatever Rowdy had planned to say.

She started to reach for it, but he beat her to it.

Watching her, he said into the phone, "Rowdy's bar and grill." He might have adopted her suggested name for the place, but he rarely referred to it that way. "How can I help you?" His eyes narrowed. "Yes, she's here. Hold on." He held the phone out to her.

Avery lifted her brows. "For me?"

"You're Avery Mullins, right?"

She stepped back so fast she bumped into the bar.

Someone had asked for her by name? An invisible fist squeezed her lungs. "Who is it?"

Concern and suspicion narrowed Rowdy's gaze. "He didn't say."

He. Thoughts churning, unreasonable worry blooming, Avery tried to decide what to do, how to act.

Rowdy covered the phone. "What's the problem?"

She chewed her bottom lip. Surely it was just a customer, a bar question maybe. The caller couldn't know that the owner himself had picked up and could share any info needed....

Rowdy moved so close, they almost touched. "Want me to take the call for you?"

He was so big, so impressively male, that he inadvertently emphasized the differences in their sizes, making her feel even smaller and far too vulnerable.

Feelings she'd tried to bury deep.

"No." She was an independent adult—time to act like one. "No, of course not." She tried to smile, but didn't feel real successful. Taking the phone from him, she said with only a modicum of caution, "Hello?"

The cold silence sounded louder than a shout.

Her heart started pounding a wild tattoo. The way Rowdy studied her didn't help. She said again, a little louder, "Hello?"

She heard a faint laugh—and the line went dead.

Worry burned into real alarm.

"Avery?"

From now on, she'd have to be more careful. No more walking out to the bus alone. No more getting to her apartment unprepared for the worst.

"All right, enough." Rowdy took her shoulders. "Tell me what's wrong."

And no reason to share her absurd past with Rowdy. "Nothing is wrong." Nothing that he could fix. Not that she'd let him anyway.

She'd gotten along well enough before meeting Rowdy.

And since he didn't want to get tied down, well, she'd get along fine and dandy without him still.

"Nothing, huh? That's why you're strangling the phone?" He took the receiver from her, put it to his ear.

"He hung up." Avery turned to do a few refills along the bar. When she finished, Rowdy still stood there. Waiting. Maybe she'd misunderstood. "You say he asked for me? Like, he asked to speak to the bartender?"

"Actually, he asked if Avery Mullins was working."

Well…that sucked. Not many ways she could spin that, except for assuming the worst.

Someone had found her.

Rowdy caught her arm and gently pulled her around. "You work for me."

"Seriously? How did I miss that?"

His gaze narrowed with bad attitude. "Don't be a smart-ass."

"Sorry. Right, I work for you." She loved her job, so she should really be tending customers instead of fretting. "If you'd get out of my way, I could get more done."

He searched her face, realized she wouldn't be swayed and growled a sound of exasperation. "Stick around tonight after we close. I need to talk to you."

She opened her mouth to refuse him, but he cut her off before she could say a single word.

"Work related." The bad attitude remained. "Ella will be there, too."

Oh. Well, then…"I can only stay till two-thirty."

After that, she'd miss the bus, and no way did she want to pay for cab fare.

He nodded his acceptance of that. "Won't take long."

"Okay, then."

Still holding her arm, he brushed his thumb over her skin. "You're sure you're okay?"

Ahhh. Rowdy had his faults, sure, but he was also caring, protective.

And he possessed more raw masculine appeal than should be legal.

"I'm absolutely positive." She'd worked hard to get her life together. No way would she backslide now.

Someone said, "Rowdy!" with far too much familiarity. They both turned to look, seeking out the voice.

Two blondes and a brunette waved at him, but Avery didn't see a redhead anywhere. She crossed her arms and curled her lip. "If you decide to use your office again, I suggest you lock the door."

Rowdy touched her chin, lifting her face. "We'll talk after work."

"About work," she clarified, but he'd already left her, circling out from behind the bar to greet the trio of women.

THE MOON AND a flickering lamppost illuminated the dark night. A cold wind cut through his coat. He turned up his collar and, shoes crunching on the gravel lot, paced away from the pay phone. Churning satisfaction almost brought him to a laugh.

He had her now.

Avery Mullins might have thought herself well hidden, but with enough money he could uncover anyone—or hide the darkest secret. It had taken a year, but soon it'd all be over.

He couldn't wait to see her again. Everyone would be happier when she returned to her rightful place. Never again would he be so careless. They'd both miscalculated in a big way: he'd underestimated her resourcefulness, she'd misjudged his determination.

He'd match his bank account to her gumption any day.

Soon, he'd right the wrongs. Avery would never again play him for a fool.

CHAPTER TWO

AVERY LOCKED HER teeth together and tried to ignore them. Impossible. The women hanging on Rowdy were pretty, sexy and on the make. If Rowdy started for his office with them, she'd…what? Quit? Not likely.

She could just throw cold water on them. She eyed the seltzer water under the bar. It had possibilities.

But as she waited on customers, Rowdy disengaged from the women and then had to dodge others who tried to cling to him. He was polite to them all, but only polite.

Not that it mattered, she reminded herself. Not to her.

He glanced up and caught her scowl. With a wink and a small smile, he went about greeting customers.

Since they'd opened a few weeks ago, Rowdy made a point of doing every job, overseeing every aspect of the operation and mingling with the crowd. The men enjoyed the casual setup of the bar, but Avery suspected the women came as much for Rowdy as for anything else the bar offered.

It had taken a while to get the interior refurbished. A lot of the equipment had to be repaired, and what couldn't be fixed Rowdy had replaced with used. To save money, he'd done much of the work himself, putting fresh paint on the walls, scrubbing the floors and windows, making sure everything was as shiny and clean as he could make it.

Whenever possible, Avery had pitched in, working side by side with him…and falling harder every second.

She couldn't pinpoint what it was about Rowdy, but from the day she'd met him, she'd been sinking under his rough-edged charm. Add his gorgeous face to that strong, honed body, and he made spectacular eye candy.

But it was so much more than his physical appeal. Rowdy smiled as if he knew all her secrets, looked at her as if they'd already been intimate. He had confidence down to a fine art, and faced each day with a fearless type of daring.

She knew he did his best to hide it, but there was something supersensitive and attentive in the way he treated life—his own and others.

When Rowdy's sister had married Detective Logan Riske, Rowdy had inherited a cop as a brother-in-law. She smiled, thinking of how he'd reacted to that. Overall, he didn't trust the police. But from what she'd seen, he got along well with Logan, and with Detective Reese Bareden, Logan's partner.

The majority of Rowdy's background remained a mystery to her, but it didn't take a psychic to know he'd had a rough life, that he was street-smart and survival savvy. Odds were he'd spent some time on the wrong side of the law, and that accounted for his feelings toward police officers.

Busy washing glasses, Avery didn't see Rowdy when he came around the back of the bar with her. She turned and ran into him.

Blast the man. "Why do you keep sneaking up on me?"

"Wasn't sneaking." Gaze dark with suggestion, he shifted past her. "I'm refilling drinks."

"Oh. Thanks." Using chitchat as a cover, Avery tried not to think about seeing him in such a compromising situation earlier. "It's busy tonight."

"We're getting there." He gave her a quick once-over. "How are you holding up?"

Avery froze. "What do you mean?"

"Like you said, it's busy. You need any help?"

Oh. *Get it together, Avery.* Rowdy didn't care that she had seen him in such a private situation, and that said a lot. "I can handle it. No problem."

"Let me know if it gets to be too much." He picked up the tray and started back out to the floor. "I'll be over in a little while to give you a break."

"Okay." Seeing the shift of muscles as he walked away curled her toes in her shoes. Not an uncommon reaction to the sight of him.

A rush of customers kept her too busy to daydream. She liked when things got hopping because it put her in a zone. She found a rhythm and lost herself in the work. She felt... Zen.

When things eased up again, she spotted Rowdy at the back of the bar, inserting himself into an escalating argument between two men and a woman. A chair tipped over. Voices rose.

Before things got out of hand, Rowdy had it back under control. The men subsided. Rowdy had that type of "don't mess with me" influence. The woman flounced off angrily, and neither of the men attempted to stop her.

Half smiling, Avery watched Rowdy right the chair, which had her recalling how he'd looked during off-hours while working on the bar. The way his biceps bulged when toting heavy equipment. How his thighs flexed when he bent. Those ripped abs when he'd lifted his T-shirt to wipe sweat from his brow.

The sheer pleasure on his face each time he completed a task.

Though Rowdy hadn't been entirely comfortable with it, he'd gotten help from his new family and friends, too. Seeing them together had taken a little getting used to.

Standing six feet four inches tall, she considered Rowdy supersized. His brother-in-law, Logan, was a few inches shorter, their friend Reese a few inches taller and Logan's brother, Dash, was a similar height to Rowdy. But physical differences aside, the men couldn't be more different.

As cops, Logan and Reese were watchful, serious. But Rowdy had a vigilant, even expectant edge to his nature that made him more so. The detectives would relax; Rowdy never seemed to let down his guard.

Logan's brother, Dash, owned a construction company. From what Avery could tell, he took pride in his work, but once the workday ended, he was all about pleasure. He charmed women with ease.

But again, Rowdy had him beat. An air of danger sharpened everything about Rowdy: his appeal, his looks, his attitude and his capability.

His success with women.

It seemed to her that Rowdy either worked or indulged in female company. Overall he seemed tireless, and very determined to make the bar a success. He stayed after she left, and was almost always there when she arrived.

Today... Well, he'd been there, all right. *Really* early.

Did he often stay the night at the bar? Had he indulged in other liaisons in his office?

Ella approached for a drink order. "Crisis averted," she quipped, talking about how Rowdy had defused the situation. "He's the whole package, isn't he?"

"He does a great job," Avery agreed.

At thirty-four, Ella was eight years older than her. Unlike Avery, the waitress wore heeled shoes and a low-cut top, and she never stopped smiling. Forever flirting, she called everyone "sweetie" or "sugar," and she liked to touch. Nothing too intimate, at least not while working. But she did like to get close.

On some women, that barhop personality might seem clichéd, but not on Ella, who was too sincere and far too caring to be anything other than original.

Twining a long lock of her dark brown hair around a finger, Ella leaned on the bar while Avery filled three whiskey shots. "What do you think the meeting is about tonight?"

Avery shrugged. "Rowdy didn't say, so who knows?"

"Jones was hoping he'd finally get some help in the back. That poor baby works up a sweat every night."

While Avery would never call the midsixties, lean-and-mean cook a "baby," she agreed that he had his hands full. Jones, like Ella, was a happy guy. He wore his long graying hair in a ponytail, had more tats than Avery could count, and cursed while cooking—especially during the busier nights.

When possible, one of the waitresses lent him a hand, but those times were few and far between. Rowdy had hoped to keep three waitresses full-time, but only Ella had accepted. The other two, who enjoyed the tips they'd made while dancing the pole, hadn't appreciated Rowdy's decision to remove it. They'd dropped to part-time, their schedules rotating so they could pick up work at a club.

"I doubt it has anything to do with the kitchen since we're getting together late." With some remodeling still underway, Rowdy often called meetings. If it involved the cook, he'd have collected them before work because the kitchen closed at eleven.

"Well, no matter. He always pays us well when he keeps us over, so I don't mind." Ella picked up her tray. "Rowdy sure is something."

Yeah, he was something all right. Big. Macho. Oversexed.

Sashaying with each step, Ella strolled away.

Even without the pole, Ella made a killing in tips. But then, it was a busy night, so Avery didn't do so badly, either.

At 1:00 a.m., when Rowdy gave the last call, Avery was more than ready to call it a night. Twice Rowdy had given her a break, but she'd yet to see him off his feet.

Finally, when the last guest was out the door and Rowdy had locked up, they gathered in the break room. As soon as Avery and Ella took a seat at the round table, Rowdy said, "Sorry, Ella, but we're switching to a uniform."

"Why are you sorry, sugar?" Ella crossed her long legs. "I've worn uniforms before. Some of them are real cute."

"Not this kind." Rowdy laid out the black, unisex, crew neck T-shirt with the bar name on the front in neon yellow. "Nothing sexy, Ella. I want everyone wearing the shirt with jeans." He shook an apron from a bag. "And one of these."

Avery eyed the black utilitarian aprons with the same logo as the T-shirts. "I like them."

Ella looked horrified.

"You get three each. If I could, I'd pony up one for each day of the week, but hopefully, for now, these'll get you through."

"You'll look incredible, Ella," Avery told her. "It'll be like a tease. All the men will wonder what they're not seeing."

"It's not the same." She located her size, hesitated, then put the shirts back and took a size smaller. "I better not lose tips because of this."

"I doubt you will," Rowdy said, "because the customers love you. But all the same, I'm giving you a raise. Additional buck an hour."

That got her smiling again. "Really?"

"We're doing better than I'd expected, and you've really given a hundred percent."

"Aren't you the sweetest ever?" Ella dropped the shirts and left her seat to give Rowdy an enthusiastic hug.

Clearly thankful for that reaction, Rowdy hugged her off her feet and kissed the top of her head.

He looked so relieved that Avery assumed he must have been expecting more of an argument.

Over the top of Ella's head he met her gaze, and slowly eased the other waitress away.

Did he think she'd be jealous of Ella? No. She knew Rowdy valued Ella as an employee, nothing more.

Ella beamed up at him. "Is there anything else, sugar?"

"Nope. That's it." He put her shirts and aprons in a bag for her. "Here you go."

"Thank you." Ella gave him a loud kiss on the cheek,

stroked his chest once and headed for the back door with her share of the new garments.

From her chair, Avery could see out the break room, through the kitchen to the back door. She watched Rowdy lock the door and then return to her. He dropped into a chair. "One down," he muttered.

Grinning, Avery asked, "She had you worried?"

"A little." He rolled his shoulders, rubbed the back of his neck. "I like Ella. She's a hard worker with a great outlook. Never complains. Smiles at all the customers. But man, she does like to put it out there on display."

"And here I thought you enjoyed that sort of thing."

"Somewhere else, sure. But we're trying to be a different type of bar, remember."

Realization hit. "So the uniform shirts were your way of downplaying Ella's assets without hurting her feelings?"

He shrugged. "It seemed better than telling her that she was showing too much boob."

Avery laughed. "An ingenious move." She picked up a shirt to better examine the logo. "And I like this. Casual but classy."

"It'll go with your jeans."

Since that's all she wore while working, she appreciated the effort. "Thanks for that. Just so you know, if you'd produced some cheesy uni that either looked ridiculous or like a fetish, I would have refused."

"I figured." Rowdy watched her as she gathered up three shirts and the aprons. "Looks like you're doing the opposite of Ella."

"How's that?"

"A size larger than you need, versus her size smaller.

You hide your figure. Ella flaunts hers. But I guess it balances out."

"It's not that I'm hiding anything." Though she had stopped dressing to attract attention a while ago. "It can get pretty fast paced behind the bar. I need freedom of movement. Comfort is more important to me than anything else."

"Avery?"

She folded the shirts. "Hmm?"

He didn't move from his seat, didn't change his tone, so it took her by surprise when he asked, "Why were you early today?"

Pausing, Avery felt the memories flood back in on her.

Rowdy's deep, rough groan.

His taut expression while coming.

Flustered, she avoided his gaze while fussing with the garments. "I left my phone here last night."

Slowly, Rowdy leaned forward in his seat and crossed his arms on the tabletop. "You could have gotten it when you got here."

And instead she'd caught him getting his jollies in the office. "I needed to make a call before my shift started."

"Yeah? Who did you call?"

No way would she tell him she'd planned to set a doctor's appointment to get on the pill…because she'd wanted him to get his jollies with her.

But definitely *not* in the office. "It doesn't matter now."

He picked up that bad attitude again. "A boyfriend?"

Avery did a double take. "Where in the world did you come up with that?"

"You got a call from a man. Someone you're seeing?"

"I… No. That was probably a wrong call or something." She hoped. Waving off the question, she admitted, "I'm not seeing anyone."

There was a heavy pause before Rowdy asked softly, "No?"

Refusing to admit it again, she checked the clock on the wall. "I need to go or I'll miss the bus."

His gaze searching her face, he came to his feet with her. "Bus?"

"Did you think I walked?"

"No, but I assumed…" He shook his head. "I'll drive you home."

"Nooo, you will not." It was difficult enough being with him in a break room; a closed car would be too much temptation. "Thanks anyway."

Irritation honed his tone. "Damn it, Avery, this is a tricky situation for me."

For *him?* "That has to be a joke, right?"

The muscles of his jaw flexed. "I wish you hadn't walked in on me today."

"That makes two of us!"

"But you did," he stated, "and I think we should talk about it."

Oh, no, she would not let that intimate tone and determined expression win her over. "I'm not your keeper, Rowdy. And believe me, even without the peep show today, I wasn't ignorant about your…overactive sex drive. I just hadn't expected to trip over it at work."

"It was before work, and an isolated incident."

Of all the nerve! "You're saying it's never happened before?"

"Sure it has."

Her stomach cramped—until he continued.

"But not *here*."

Sputtering, Avery snapped, "*Here* is what I was talking about!"

"Yeah?"

He left her so disconcerted, she could barely find words. "I wasn't suggesting that you had *never*...that you *hadn't*..." No, she couldn't spell it out for his amusement. She squared her shoulders. "I've never met a more uninhibited person."

Male arrogance curled his mouth. "So it was just the location that upset you?"

"I'm not upset!"

At her raised voice, he lifted a brow.

Inhaling in a bid to regain control, Avery said more calmly, "What you do in your own time is your own business."

"That was my own time—time I wanted to spend with you, but you weren't interested."

Dropping the shirts, Avery propped her hands on her hips. "That's your excuse?"

He eased closer. "Sorry, honey, but I don't need an excuse." Oh-so-gently, he smoothed back a curl that had escaped her ponytail. "I'm a grown man, it's my bar and I wasn't expecting anyone to show up so early, especially not you."

"Perfect!" She snatched up the shirts again, anxious to be on her way. "I guess that's settled then."

Rowdy caught her arm. "Hold up." She started to jerk free, until he said, "Come on, Avery, give me a chance to explain."

It wasn't the smartest move, because every second with him chipped away at her resistance, but she paused anyway.

"All right, let's hear it." This ought to be good.

But then again, maybe not.

To GIVE HIMSELF a moment to think, Rowdy took the garments from Avery and tossed them back on the table. With her looking so mulish—and so damned cute—he would have preferred backing her up to the wall and following his instincts instead of talking.

But he could just imagine how she'd react to that.

Rubbing a hand over the back of his neck, he tried to figure out what to say, and how to say it.

Overflowing with belligerence, Avery crossed her arms. "Any day now."

"Give me a second, will you?" He propped a hip on the tabletop and scrutinized her. "You might not know this, but I've never explained myself to a woman before. That is, a woman other than my sister. But even with Pepper, it was generalizations. Never anything detailed about when, where or with who I had sex."

Avery bristled. "You don't have to explain to me, either."

"I think I do, but it's complicated by the fact that you work for me."

When he said no more, she lifted her chin. "How so?"

Rowdy had never had a problem with plain speaking. He saw no reason to start complicating things now. "I have a major jones for you, Avery. You know that."

Her jaw loosened. "Oh, my God. You are so—"

"But as your employer," he interrupted, "I could cross a line here if I'm not careful."

She choked. "Seriously, Rowdy? This is you being *careful?*"

To hell with it. Brushing his knuckles over her cheek,

down her throat, he said, "I want you. All the fucking time." *Even when I'm with other women.* He opened his hand on her shoulder, urged her closer. "And it's not going away anytime soon."

She softened the tiniest bit, but still said, "Looked to me like it went away just fine this morning."

Seeing the hurt she tried to hide with sarcasm, he shook his head. "No, honey, not even close."

Her mouth tightened. "So your date was just—"

"You're confusing things now. I don't date. What you saw was sex, plain and simple."

"Oh, my God." She pressed her hands to his chest, but not with any real conviction at pushing him away. "I don't want to hear this."

"She knew what it was." Rowdy easily held on to her. "I didn't sugarcoat things, and she agreed one hundred percent."

Anger darkened her blue eyes and lowered her voice to a rasp. "I can't imagine why you're telling me this."

Because what you think of me matters. Rowdy slid his hand to the back of her neck, keeping her near. "I get the feeling you saw me with her and you took it personally."

"Your ego is showing."

Knowing he'd hit a nerve, Rowdy dipped his head, brushed his nose over her hair. "You think it was a rejection or something." He inhaled her scent, and tightened all over. God Almighty, the way she stirred him...

"Honestly," Avery whispered, "I don't know what to think."

"Think about saying yes instead of no."

She drew back a small fist and punched his ribs.

Grinning, Rowdy hugged her. After the long day at

work, it felt better than good to hold her. "I shouldn't tease?"

"Definitely not."

"Okay." He kissed her temple and leaned her back so he could see her face. "Seriously then, I'm sorry if it hurt you in any way. Never my intent, believe me."

She looked up at him, her blue eyes big and soft, her hands now curled into his shirt—holding on to him. "Then why did you do it?"

At least she wasn't storming off, Rowdy told himself. She sounded far more reasonable than he could have hoped for. "I didn't want her in my new place, and she didn't have any privacy in hers."

Eyes flaring, Avery finally shoved him away. "Ass!"

To be on the safe side, Rowdy moved to lean in the doorway, but she didn't try to leave.

She only went to the other side of the table—out of his reach. "That's not what I meant. Yes, I'm surprised you'd do such a thing here at work. But I was asking..." She shook her head. "Never mind."

No, he wouldn't let her do that. "Why was I with her in the first place?"

After a long hesitation, she gave one sharp nod.

He didn't want to detail the extent of his own failings, but he also didn't want to end the night with her pissed off. He considered making up a believable story, but he knew he wouldn't lie to her.

What he saw in her beautiful eyes touched him.

She wanted him to have a good excuse because she wanted a reason to give in to him.

To chase off his personal demons, he'd spent the night in a sexual marathon. He should have been well spent, and he had been.

Before Avery.

But now, with her so close, being alone with her, seeing that particular look in her eyes, he instead felt like he'd spent a month being celibate.

He'd tell her the basics and it'd have to be enough. "Women have usually come easy to me."

"There's a news flash."

From the day they'd met, before he'd bought the bar, Avery had seen him picking up women. Not something he was proud of, but not really anything he'd try to hide, either. He was a grown man and he more than enjoyed sex.

Determined to stay on track, Rowdy ignored the gibe. "When I get turned down, it doesn't matter."

"Why would it?" Like an accusation, she said, "There's always another woman waiting."

He shrugged, accepting the inaccurate claim. "That's not the point." Once again, he moved toward her. He couldn't seem to help himself. From day one, Avery had drawn him, not just physically but in other, more disturbing ways—ways he didn't want to analyze too closely. "I'll try to explain if you let me."

She crossed her arms. "I'm all ears."

No, she was all backbone and pride and, even when trying to conceal it, hot sensuality. "When I get turned down, and believe me, I do, it doesn't matter because I don't care enough for it to matter."

She half turned away. "Guess I should remember that, huh?"

Rowdy brought her back around, and though it unnerved him, he admitted the truth. "With you, it matters."

She searched his face, but wasn't convinced. "That'd

be easier to believe if I hadn't busted you just this morning."

He needed to get her past that. "I needed a distraction, that's all."

Dubious, she asked, "Sex?"

"Best distraction I've ever found." He'd still been in his early teens when he'd learned that girls brought light to the darkest shadows. He'd always been big for his age, always looked older, and girls had taken his quiet, cautious nature as maturity.

While other boys were busy playing ball or...fuck, maybe G.I. Joe for all he knew, he'd been running interference for his little sister. He'd defended her verbally, and when that didn't work, he'd protected her physically. For as long as he could remember, he'd done his best to shelter Pepper from the reality of their lives—which often meant accepting the brunt of the abuse himself. As a result, turmoil sometimes exploded inside him.

Thanks to a high school cheerleader, he'd lost his virginity at fifteen. What an eye-opener that had been. He'd learned that grinding release had a profound way of emptying his mind and body of pent-up tension. With sex as a stress reliever, he could cope with whatever life threw at him.

But none of that had anything to do with Avery.

"Rowdy?"

That gentler tone set him on edge. She'd watched him get lost in thought, and damn it, he never did that. Definitely not with women. "What?"

"Is something wrong with the bar?" Concern softened her expression. She touched his arm. "With you?"

"No." Did she honestly think he'd go mewling to a woman if he did have a problem?

"Then why did you need a distraction?"

Damn it. He'd said too much. "It's getting late." He checked the time. "You're going to miss that bus if we don't get moving."

"Oh, shoot!" Jumping away from him, she shrugged into her lightweight jacket and gathered the new shirts and aprons together. After slinging her purse strap over her shoulder, she rushed to the break room door and… hesitated. "Are you leaving now, too?"

Right behind her, Rowdy took the shirts from her. "I'll walk you out."

Her shoulders loosened. "Great. Thanks."

Expecting an argument more than easy acceptance, Rowdy asked with suspicion, "How often do you take the bus?"

"Always."

So night after night she left on her own? *At two in the morning?* And here he'd always thought her so sensible. Had he known, he'd have been walking her out every night.

They weren't in the best area, and even though the street never completely emptied of passersby, it could still be dangerous for a woman alone. There were a lot of alleyways, parked cars and deserted buildings where a woman could disappear.

Since he'd locked up earlier, Rowdy turned off the remaining lights as they went to the back door. He couldn't quite keep the irritation out of his tone when he asked, "Is there a reason you take the bus?"

"Yup."

While waiting for her to expound on that, he opened the door, stepped out with her and then locked it up again. When she said nothing more, he prompted, "Care to share?"

"Sure." Already striding ahead, she said over her shoulder, "Soon as you tell me why you needed a distraction."

So he hadn't thrown her off the track at all, huh? Avery wasn't like other women. She wouldn't take a hint, and she sure as hell didn't defer to his wishes.

Taking several long steps, Rowdy reached her as she headed to the bus stop at the front of the bar. Unfortunately, at least from her point of view, the bus had just turned a corner and was disappearing from sight.

"Great." She glanced around in what looked like worry, then dropped onto a bench, opened her purse and started digging around.

Rowdy stood over her. "What are you doing?"

"Finding my phone so I can call a cab."

Not happening. "Why don't you be reasonable instead and let me drive you home?"

She found her phone and lifted it out.

"Avery." Crouching down in front of her, Rowdy took her small hands in his. She was so petite, so fine-boned and feminine.

"What?" Something showed in her eyes, maybe anxiety. Possibly even fear.

Protective instincts jumped to the forefront of his brain. "You don't trust me?"

"It's not that."

"Then what?"

Slumping back, she gave him a narrow-eyed glare. "If you have to know, I'm not sure I trust myself."

Now, that was interesting. "You mean with me?"

Grudgingly, she muttered, "You are a temptation."

Still? Even after she'd busted him getting head from a one-night stand? That surprised Rowdy, and sent a rush of lust through his bloodstream. "Then..."

She got huffy. "Get real, Rowdy. All the women want you."

Her perceptions of him were a bit skewed, but why disillusion her? "Not *all*."

Chin up, she stated, "I won't be just another body in a long line of one-night stands."

Like one night would even come close to taking the edge off. And yeah, that was unusual. One night was normally more than enough...with other women.

Apparently not with Avery.

As independent as she might be, his little bartender had a very old-fashioned way of looking at things. "Why not look at it as mutual fun?" He gave her his most wolfish smile. "We both know eventually you'll be in my bed."

"Really?" Never one to disappoint, Avery said, "Why don't you hold your breath waiting for that to happen?"

He laughed, kissed her knuckles and said, "Just for that, I'm going to make you ask real pretty."

"That," she said, "isn't going to happen. The other... Well, I have enough common sense to know I don't want to go there." Her gaze dipped to his mouth, and she sighed. "Not yet."

Not yet? Meaning... "Maybe soon?"

She shrugged.

Well, that had his dick perking up. In some instances, a shrug was as good as a resounding affirmation. His shoulders knotted with restraint, but he managed to say, "Okay, then," without too much satisfaction.

He'd sort through things, figure out her reasons for

waiting and find a way around them. But until then, he didn't want to scare her off. "Let's agree that there's no reason for you to splurge on a cab. I made you miss the bus, so I'll see you home."

She studied the moon shadows lurking between buildings, frowned at a few dark cars parked near the curb. A stranger walked up the street, head down, hands in his pockets.

On a deep breath, Avery checked her watch—and bit her lip.

Taking that as another sign of agreement, Rowdy rose to his feet again. "It's late. No way will I leave you out here alone, so run up to my apartment with me, okay? I'll grab my car keys." He took one step off the curb, ready to cross the street—and realized that Avery hadn't moved. He turned back to her. "Coming?"

Clutching her purse, she stared at him with confusion. "I don't understand."

With anticipation surging, he turned to face her. "About?"

"So many things..." She looked up and down the street again, at a few people loitering on the corner, back at the bar. After palpable hesitation, she rose from the bench and approached him.

"Like?" He watched her eyes and saw her sort through a dozen issues before settling on one.

"Where exactly is your apartment?"

"Right here." Rowdy indicated the big brick building on the opposite side of the street from the bar. "I just moved in a week ago."

CHAPTER THREE

It HAD BEEN a very long day, but Avery wasn't tired. Not anymore. While watching the bus leave her behind, she'd experienced an odd disquiet.

Not because of Rowdy. Even when he tried to be intimidating, his presence provided only reassurance. He wouldn't hurt her, and he wouldn't let anyone else hurt her.

But someone had been nearby, watching her, waiting. She shivered in dread. She wanted to blame it on bad memories, on dread from that earlier phone call, but she knew better. She'd learned to trust her instincts.

And her instincts told her the night wasn't safe.

Now, trailing behind Rowdy, her hand held in his, she worried that she might be leading trouble to his door. He could handle it, of that she had no doubt.

But her problems were her own, and she didn't want them dumped on him.

Looking back again, she still saw nothing.

"Worried someone will see you with me?" He shifted his hand to the small of her back and urged her inside.

She was, but not for the reasons he thought. "I heard something," she lied. She'd heard only her own turbulent thoughts.

Taking her seriously, he glanced back, his gaze searching everywhere. A few doors down, a couple got into a car and pulled away. Across the street, three men laughed drunkenly as they made their way down the sidewalk. In the distance, a siren whined and a dog barked.

Seeming distracted, he murmured, "The night echoes everything and makes it sound closer than it is." After another scrutiny of the area, he turned back to her. "You don't need to be nervous with me."

"If you say so."

The building they entered used to be a warehouse, but had since been divided into four rental units. It had a certain industrial appeal, with concrete interior walls, metal stairs and open ceilings. Overall, it suited Rowdy, being strong and sturdy like him, but also polished in a nice way.

"I'm on the second floor."

Avery looked up to a huge skylight in the very high ceiling. "Wow." Holding on to the welded handrails, she went ahead of Rowdy up the open, diamond-plate stair treads. Everywhere she looked, she saw something cool, like the exposed ductwork and pipes.

"This way." Rowdy took her to a thick steel door, opened several locks, pushed the heavy door open and flipped on overhead fluorescent lights.

They stepped into a small landing above the rest of the living area. Following Rowdy down four clattering metal steps brought her to a sparse sitting area that held a worn couch and chair, one table and lamp, and a moderately sized flat-screen television on an entertainment stand.

Only the television looked new.

Beyond that, at the far side of the room, freestanding L-shaped bookshelves formed a wall to separate the kitchen and laundry area on the left from the bed, dresser and nightstand on the right. Avery assumed the one and only closed door led to a bathroom.

She took in the wall of tall arched windows that would overlook his bar, then to the polished wood-plank floors.

"It was close," Rowdy said, as if defending his choice.

"It's pretty impressive actually." Especially compared to where she now lived. She touched a thick round metal support beam in the middle of the floor. "Doing a little pole dancing of your own?"

He crossed his arms. "No, but if you feel like giving it a try, go ahead. I'll wait."

She fought off a grin. "No thanks."

"Spoilsport." He headed off to the kitchen area.

Still taking in the uniqueness of his apartment, Avery said, "Know what I don't understand?"

"I can guess." His boots made little noise on the thick floors. "You're wondering why I didn't just hook up here, instead of in my office."

It did make her very curious. "Wouldn't it have been a lot more…convenient?" He had a bed at his disposal instead of a desk chair. Not that he'd let it hinder him, from what she'd seen.

"Probably," he agreed. "But I didn't want her in my place." He flipped a switch and more light spilled from the kitchen.

Avery realized that not only could he see his bar, but now, with the bright lights on inside, anyone on the street would be able to see him, too. She made sure to stay out of view. "Why not?"

From the counter, he lifted a set of keys. "I'm private, that's why."

Unbelievable. "You could have been a lot more private here than in your office!" While Avery found his living space pretty awesome, it was bare-bones, not a single personal item on display. No photos, not even of his sister. That disappointed her. She'd never met Pepper, and she was very curious.

He did have a nice display of books on his bookshelves.

"I told you, I wasn't expecting anyone to show up." He returned to her, the keys jangling in his hand. "This is the first permanent place I've had. Before this, it was rotating motel rooms. If I took a woman there, no big deal because by the next day I'd be gone."

So no woman would be able to track him down? That attitude concerned her, but wondering where he'd moved, and why, took precedence. "Gone where?"

"It's a long story." He tried to steer her back to the stairs.

Avery held on to the pole, resisting him.

He eyed her, worked his jaw and said, "You're not going to let it go, are you?"

This might be her best chance to get insight into his background. How could she pass that up? "Is it a big secret?" she teased. "Were you on the run from the law? Dodging child support? A transient?"

Rowdy narrowed his eyes—and stalked toward her. "On the run, yeah. But not from the law."

"Seriously?" That so surprised her that it took her a moment to see that particular look in his eyes. She'd only seen it a few times—right before he'd kissed her. One of those times happened while hiding him in a storage closet at the bar because a gang of ruffians wanted to take him apart.

Since then, he'd only stolen a kiss or two—and she always craved more. *Dangerous.*

But maybe that incident was indicative of his life. "Do you always have people after you?"

"Often enough."

He said that without jest! Hastily, Avery back-stepped behind the pole, considered going farther, but really, where did she have to go? The couch was against the wall, the chair too far away....

Catching her wrist and pulling her around to him, Rowdy said softly, "Don't run from me."

"I wasn't." But her heart pumped as if she'd been on a five-minute sprint.

With the back of one finger, he caressed the pulse in her throat. "Fibber."

"I'm not afraid of you." Whatever secrets Rowdy had in his history, he wasn't a threat to her. She'd known dishonorable men, and she knew Rowdy was differ-ent. "Maybe you're the one who should stop running."

"From you?"

Was she chasing him? Mmm...pretty much. Until now, she just hadn't realized it. "Yes."

His gaze warmed. "I don't run from anyone."

Knowing it would spur him on, she whispered, "Good."

But when he started to pull her against him, she flat-tened both hands to his chest.

He drew in a breath. "No?"

Disappointment kept her voice low. "You were with another woman just this morning."

He looked struck, almost like he'd forgotten. "Yeah, sorry." Releasing her, he stepped away. "Guess for a woman like you, that puts a damper on things?"

For other women it wouldn't? She curled her lip. "Yeah, afraid so." But she wished it was otherwise. "Why were you on the run?"

Resigned, he said, "It had nothing to do with dodging my duty, so forget that."

"No little Rowdys running around?"

"Hell, no. I'm always careful, but if it did happen, you can bet I wouldn't bail on them."

She believed him. From what she'd seen so far, Rowdy never shirked his responsibility, whatever he decided his responsibility might be. "Okay."

Maybe thinking she mocked him, he studied her a moment before being satisfied with her sincerity. "I would never do that to a kid."

Hands behind her, she leaned back against the pole. "So…why did you move around?"

"Mostly because the idea of settling down never appealed to me."

"Wanderlust?" Before her life had taken such a drastic turn, she'd enjoyed traveling everywhere in the States and often around the world. Before she was twenty, she'd already been to more than two dozen hot tourist spots.

"Hardly. I stayed in the area."

"The area being Ohio?"

He shrugged. "My sister was here. Still is, but now she's with Logan and she doesn't need…" He stopped, cursed low and let out a long breath. Indicating the couch, he said, "If we're going to do this, you want to sit down?"

"This, meaning talk?"

His mouth quirked. "Unless you have something else on your mind."

She had all kinds of things on her mind, but none of them were appropriate. "Talk it is."

"Then I'll give you my bare-bones history."

Jumping on that promise, Avery headed for the couch. "Why only the bare bones?"

Rowdy sat close beside her and stretched out one arm along the back of the couch. "It's a long story, it'll be morning soon and I don't feel like rehashing it all."

"I suppose you're tired." From what she could tell, he'd been up all night. If he'd slept at all, it would only have been for a few hours before coming in to work again. That should have made her feel guilty for keeping him awake, but she remembered why he hadn't slept and it irked her.

As if he knew her thoughts, Rowdy smiled. "We can talk until the sun rises if that's what you really want to do."

It wouldn't be the worst way to spend the night. "You don't need to sleep?"

His attention moved over her face, her throat, her shoulders. "I've never needed much sleep."

Given the intensity of his gaze, she almost felt naked. "You're sure?"

His fingers trailed down her ponytail. "Fire away, honey, before I forget my promise."

Avery tried to relax. It wasn't easy, not with her thigh touching his, his heat surrounding her, his presence so… overwhelming—as usual.

To start, she went back a little in history. "That time I hid you in the pantry at the bar, I asked if you were in trouble, and you said pretty much always."

"I have no problem making up shit when necessary, but for some reason I didn't want to lie to you."

Had he never lived aboveboard? What type of up-bringing made him so casually accepting of difficulty? "There were five men searching the bar for you. Why?"

His hand stilled. "Because I'd asked too many questions, and I was getting too close."

"Too close to what?"

"A trafficking operation." She started to ask, but he shook his head. "No, not drugs. Women."

Her throat tightened. "That's..."

He agreed with a nod. "Totally fucked up, I know. I hid because there were too many of them. Three or four I could handle." He held up a hand for her to see. "I'm a big man with big fists. When I hit someone, he feels it." He rested his hand on her thigh. "I know how to fight dirty, and I know how to win. But five men at once? That would be pushing it."

Of course, she recalled another time when he'd taken apart the goons who'd been involved in forcing women to transport drugs. It had all transpired in the bar just prior to Rowdy buying it. He'd fought with such ease, walking through the men as if they were nothing at all. "I've seen you fight. You're dangerous."

"You learn to be when it's necessary."

Sitting more or less snuggled into his side, she inhaled the warm musk of his skin with every breath. That, combined with the idea of him playing defender for so many women in need, left her liquid with desire. Rowdy used his size and strength to protect.

Such an admirable trait to have.

So different from her own personal experience.

Without even trying that hard—just by being himself—Rowdy pulled her from her self-imposed exile. "You're a regular white knight, aren't you?"

He eased closer. "Want to see my sword?"

A hero and a comedian. "You're outrageous." Avery smoothed a hand over his shoulder, enjoying the contrast of the soft T-shirt stretched taut over his solid frame. "Why was it necessary for you to learn?"

Her touch caused a brief pause and the tensing of his muscles. "What?"

"To fight." She knew very few people who ever engaged in physical confrontations. While growing up, the only fights she'd ever witnessed had been in sporting matches. In her world, men had ruled with money and prestige, not brute strength.

Her one and only experience with physical anger had sent her running away and into hiding. "You're so good, you make it look…effortless."

He studied her, his attention far too intuitive. "You know I have a younger sister."

And that explained his need to fight? One day, Avery would love to meet Pepper. "You two are close?"

His concentrated attention strayed from her mouth to her collarbone to her hair. "Our folks died in a car crash a long time ago, so it's just the two of us."

Oh, God, so tragic. In sympathy, Avery reached for his hand. "I'm sorry."

"Don't be." As if it didn't matter at all, he laced his fingers with hers and said, "They were a waste of breath."

The harsh words threw her, leaving her wide-eyed and speechless. She still grieved for her father, who'd died years past.

She mourned what would never again be, and for how everything had irrevocably changed—not for the better.

Rowdy turned her hand over, brushed his thumb over her palm. "My parents were both miserable drunks." He explored the thrumming pulse in her wrist. "That's how I got my name."

Her stomach dipped when he put a damp, warm kiss to her wrist, followed by the soft touch of his tongue.

She needed to get him back on track, and fast—before she forgot her reasons for waiting. "I think you told me once that your mom was a Clint Eastwood fan. I assume that's why she named you after one of his characters."

Sardonic humor curved his mouth. "She claimed that she went into labor during a three-day drinking binge and couldn't remember any other names. She and Dad would laugh about the good times, which usually led to a rip-roaring drunk and a lot of bitching about how kids got in the way of having fun."

The insensitivity of his parents both angered and saddened her. "They actually told you that?"

His mellow gaze showed total disregard for the cruelty. "The night they wrecked, they took out six other cars. Luckily no one else died, but a lot of people got banged up pretty good."

Emotion squeezed the air out of her lungs, making her chest hurt. "You weren't with them?"

He shook his head. "I was pretty young still when I learned to recognize the signs. Mom would get giddy, or Dad would smile a certain way, and I knew they planned to tie one on. I'd hide with Pepper so they couldn't take us." Looking beyond her, he drew in two slow breaths. "When I got big enough, around the time I turned twelve or so, I just flat out refused to go. They figured leaving me behind was easier than the fight it took to take us along."

So young! Her eyes burned with the idea of how he'd lived his youth. "Pepper..."

"I kept her with me."

She was glad to hear it, but how much strength had it taken for a boy at that young age to defy alcoholic parents?

Rowdy traced the lines in her palm. "I was home with Pepper when we got the news they were dead." His hand tightened on hers. "She cried for two days straight."

That poor girl. "How old was she?"

"Fifteen. Plenty old enough to understand that we'd been on the radar for children's services for years. She figured with our folks gone, she'd end up in a foster home."

A vise of sorrow closed around Avery's heart. Now she understood what had forged Rowdy's hard edge— pure survival. "How old were you?"

"Just turned eighteen."

On the run. Avery already knew, but asked anyway. "You took off with your sister, didn't you?"

"That seemed better than being separated. And we did okay for a few years. At times, it was even kind of fun."

Because he no longer had abuse to deal with? She fought the unbearable urge to hug him tightly, knowing he wouldn't appreciate it.

Not for the reasons motivating her.

Without her realizing it, Rowdy tugged the cloth-covered band from her hair, freeing it.

"Rowdy..." She reached back to gather the unruly

mass, but he already had his fingers tangled in it, spreading it out, bringing it forward over her shoulder.

As if fascinated with her hair, he watched his hand instead of meeting her gaze. "Pepper had grown up without much, so she didn't feel like we were missing anything. Long as we had a roof over our heads and enough to eat, she was happy."

Gently, Avery said, "I think being happy had more to do with having her big brother around."

"Maybe." He gave a gruff laugh of disgust. "I screwed up a lot of stuff, but most of all when I got us both jobs in a high-end club. The pay was great. I was able to save up some money and keep Pepper close at hand."

Had he been protecting Pepper his whole life? First from his parents, and then from well-meaning authorities?

If so, where did that leave Rowdy?

Who had looked out for *him?*

Avery tried to imagine him as a little boy stuck in a bar while his parents drank themselves into oblivion. At thirteen, hiding with his sister. At eighteen, on the run from the establishment.

"You did the best you could." Always.

Something shifted in his demeanor, the sadness replaced with iron will—yet his touch remained gentle as he toyed with a long lock of her red hair. "By the time I realized the club owner was a murdering bastard, it was too late."

Oh, no. Visions of horrible scenarios played out in her head. "You were hurt?"

"That would have been easier."

Meaning he'd been hurt before? The thought crushed her, making it even more impossible to resist him.

Concern robbed her voice of strength. "Your sister?"

He nodded. "It's a convoluted story, but the gist of it is that Pepper saw a city commissioner take a bullet to the brain."

Stunned, Avery forgot about her hair and barely noticed when Rowdy lifted it to his face.

"She stuck to the shadows, so they didn't at first know that she'd seen anything. I was working the floor as a bouncer, and Pepper didn't want to chance telling me. Before I knew what had happened, she'd shared the details with a reporter."

It took Avery a moment to find her voice. "Why not the police?"

As if it made perfect sense, and was to be expected, he said, "Powerful men have powerful contacts."

Sadly, she knew something about powerful men. "Police?"

"Yeah. More than a few of the boys in blue hung out in the club. So many of them were on the take, Pepper didn't know which ones, if any, were honest."

That explained Rowdy's distrust of the law. "A terrible situation."

The back of his knuckles brushed her cheek, down the side of her neck. "Unfortunately, the boss also employed a few people at the newspaper. When the reporter tried calling in his 'big story from Yates,' he ended up with his throat cut. The only upside was that everyone figured me as the snitch."

Covering her mouth with both hands, Avery waited to hear the rest of the story. She knew it wouldn't be good.

He slid a hand around her jaw, tipped up her face. "We had few options, and no one to trust."

Because they were all alone in the world. *How tragically heartbreaking.* "You became a target?"

He shrugged as if it didn't matter. "For once, being a street rat came in handy. I had my own contacts, so I got Pepper a new identity and tucked her away in an apartment building I won in a card game. I stayed mobile, moving around so no one could get a bead on me. I was the one they remembered, the one they wanted. I figured without me, they wouldn't find her."

Meaning they'd ended up separated after all? It felt like her heart shattered. "I'm so sorry."

"I covered our trails the best I could..." He locked his jaw and turned away. "But not good enough, since Logan Riske still found us."

Logan, the detective his sister fell in love with, and vice versa. "I thought that was a good thing."

"They're in love. But it could have easily gone south, without the happy ending."

Avery tried to take it in, but it wasn't easy. "You said you won a building in a card game?"

"I have all kinds of talents." He slid a finger along the neckline of her shirt, seducing her almost out of habit. "Want me to show you a few?"

His resourcefulness, his dedication to his sister, astounded her. She tipped her head. "Have you ever been arrested?"

He blew out a breath, and for the moment at least gave up on his seduction. "A few times when I was underage. Shoplifting and stuff like that."

She wanted to ask him what he'd stolen, but it didn't matter. *Survival.* Somehow she knew whatever he'd taken had been inspired by need, not greed. "And since then?"

His smile hardened. "I've gotten better—at everything I do."

Knowing the outrageous comment was meant to distract her, Avery snorted. She had a feeling Rowdy was more honest than most. "What sort of illegal stuff do you do now?"

He opened his hand on the side of her neck, bent to kiss her temple. "Whatever I have to."

"To protect the people you love?"

"What the hell, Avery?" He sat back from her. "Don't make me out a saint, okay?"

"I would never make that mistake." Rowdy was better than a saint, more solid and real. An honest-to-God tough guy, here in the flesh. She'd take that over an ethereal saint any day.

No longer caring what Rowdy thought, Avery slipped her arms around his neck and nestled against him.

"Damn it." He stiffened without returning her embrace. "Here I am, getting more turned on by the second, and you want to slap a halo on my head."

With her nose pressed close to the skin of his throat, she breathed deep, filling herself with his potent scent. He smelled so good, felt even better, and she admired him so much. "A halo would never fit over your massive ego."

It'd be so easy to fall in love with him—and that was a problem. Rowdy wasn't an emotional man looking for commitment. For the most part, he was a loner with an overactive sex drive and a lack of respect for boundaries of any kind.

"True, so don't act like I was noble or something." He

caught her shoulders and tried to pry her loose. Avery held on until he finally gave up. Tangling a hand in her hair, he gently drew her head back. "I fucked up, you know. Pepper and I ended up living off the grid for more than two years. It was hard on her—"

Avery touched her mouth to his, saying, "She's alive."

His breathing quickened. "Thank God."

"Thank *Rowdy.*" Smiling, she brushed her mouth over his again. Her fingertips touched his now-bristly jaw, moved down to the side of his hot neck then under the neckline of his shirt to his solid shoulder. Need unfurled, but she sat back before she got carried away.

Rowdy looked stunned.

And interested.

She wanted more. So much more.

Did she dare take a walk on the wild side?

She had a feeling that Rowdy would be more than worth the risk. As long as she kept her heart safe, what was the worst that could happen?

No, she didn't want to think about the worst. Not now.

With Rowdy watching her warily, she forced herself back on track. "Since your sister is happily settled here, you're going to settle down, too?"

Apparently uneasy with the idea of settling down, he shifted his shoulders and glanced around at the apartment. "For now, at least."

He didn't sound entirely set on the idea. But he'd bought the bar, and she knew he loved working it. He couldn't pick up and disappear without her knowing. "Can I ask you one more question before we go?"

"Do I actually have a choice?"

Beneath his teasing tone, she heard the agitation. He

worried that she'd dig too deep, that something he said would drive her away.

He couldn't know how much she wanted him, because she'd taken pains to hide it from him. Maybe it was time to stop doing that.

"I want to know everything about you." For most of his life, choices had been taken away from him. She'd never do that to him. "But I won't pry anymore if it bothers you."

That surprised him, too. He scowled at her. "Let's hear it."

Enjoying him like this, in this particular humble, grumbling mood, she rested against his chest again. "You said you didn't want to bring a casual hookup here."

"It's bad enough that the ladies in the building keep bugging me. Some women don't know how to take no for an answer."

Few men would complain about that situation. "So... why is it okay if I'm here?"

Avery felt his sudden stillness, heard the heavy thumping of his strong heart along with his softly muttered curse.

She stayed close, waiting.

He let out a strained breath. "With you, Avery, I never really know what the hell I'm doing."

THE COLD NIGHT started to seep into his bones. All around him he heard unsettling noises that made him jumpy. He wouldn't be surprised if murder and mayhem happened on a regular basis in such a downtrodden area. It was time for him to go home. He had what he needed now.

He knew where she worked, and he knew who she fucked.

Putting a plan in place would be oh-so-easy.

Soon, Avery, he silently promised. Very, very soon.

CHAPTER FOUR

THE MOON, COMBINED WITH dashboard lights, sent a soft glow over Avery's profile as he drove her home. His awareness of this one particular woman throbbed through his veins, leaving him on the ragged edge. It wouldn't take more than a single agreeable look from her to get him hard.

Again.

That damned torturous episode on his couch had nearly done him in. He couldn't keep from touching her, even if he was the only one to combust.

No one had ever touched him so...*gently* before. That kiss hadn't been sexual. It didn't say, "Fuck me, Rowdy." Actually, he didn't know what the hell it said, and he wasn't at all sure he liked it.

The uncertainty hadn't kept him from getting turned on, though.

Why is it okay if I'm here? she'd wanted to know. So many reasons...

Instead of reacting as most women would, Avery had looked at him with empathy, sadness, maybe understanding. Because he'd spilled his guts to her. He flexed his hands on the steering wheel and tried to shrug off the uncomfortable sense of vulnerability.

It pissed him off that he'd said so much. Hell, he didn't confide in anyone. Not even his sister. Definitely not a woman he planned to have under him as soon as humanly possible.

Why is it okay if I'm here?

Then again, Avery was different from other women. He wanted her, no mistaking that, but even when he knew he wouldn't have her, he enjoyed talking to her and just…being with her. She made him feel things, unfamiliar stuff he'd never dealt with before.

And that was saying something, since he'd had more than his share of shit to manage.

"You're so quiet," she said with unsettling understanding. "Everything okay?"

"Why wouldn't it be?" Just because she asked him questions he couldn't answer.

"I don't know," she said. "You seem bothered."

"I'm thinking, that's all." He had no idea about Avery's background. He knew enough about false impressions that he refused to draw conclusions just because she worked in a shit bar and rode a bus instead of driving.

"About my question?" She turned defensive. "Relax, Rowdy. I won't make assumptions just because I was granted entrance to your private domain."

Defensive and dramatic. Did she really have no clue how differently he felt with her? "A smart person never assumes."

She crossed her arms and huddled farther into the corner of the front seat. "If it's that much of a problem, forget I asked about it."

He glanced at her, but she kept her face averted, watching the landscape pass by her window. Her beautiful red hair, now freed from the band thanks to him, flowed over her shoulders and helped to keep her concealed.

"Never said it was a problem." He just didn't have an easy answer.

"Yet, ten minutes later, you're still stewing."

Her prickly attitude amused him, and maybe that's what he liked most about her. No matter his mood, she lightened it just by being near at hand, by being herself—quirky and honest and so damned unique. "I had to figure it out."

That got her attention. Like a warm touch, her gaze moved over him. "And did you?"

"I think so." Following her directions, he took a right down a quiet side street. "I don't like having women chase after me."

She snorted. "And that's why you do *so* much to discourage them?"

"I meant after I've already slept with them," he clarified. "Doesn't matter how I spell things out up front, too often they're looking for a repeat."

She smirked in annoyance. "One and done, huh?"

Feeling her scrutiny, he gave a noncommittal lift of his shoulder. With Avery, he had his doubts that even a dozen times would be enough. "Living out of my car, using motels just as a place to crash—"

"Or have sex."

He agreed with a nod. "That's not really the type of setup where you want to get cozy with someone. I didn't date. I didn't do romance. I hooked up long enough to take care of business—"

"To get laid?"

Having her break it down like that annoyed him.

"Are you going to paraphrase everything I say? I can be more blunt if that's what you want."

She shook her hair behind her shoulders and lifted her chin. "I'm listening."

"All right, fine. I'm set in my ways. I like to fuck and move on. No reason to make more out of it than that."

The silence became so heavy, he felt like a dick. And really, why had he shared that with her? Avery was unique, so the usual didn't apply to her.

He still hadn't answered her question, but she let it go and instead cleared her throat.

"I guess that helped pass the time?"

Rowdy laughed. He glanced at her, and laughed again. "That's one way to put it." He'd already said too much to her; no way would he tell her that occasionally, casual sex was all that got him through the night. "What about you?"

"What about me?"

"Ever had any one-night stands?"

She wrinkled her nose. "Not my thing."

"Only serious monogamy, huh?" That could be a big problem for him, but somehow he'd get around it.

"I've dated casually, just for fun."

"With a handshake at the end of the night?"

She swatted his shoulder. "I'm not that bad." Looking away and going introspective, she added, "But I had to know the guy and at least like him a lot to want to get involved."

The idea of her "being involved" bugged him more than it should have. "Ever been engaged? Married?"

He felt her withdraw. Hell, it got so quiet he could hear her breathing, could almost hear her heartbeats.

"Avery?" What the hell? Was she still hung up on someone? Was she nursing a broken heart?

"My life was different from yours."

"Glad to hear it." But what did that have to do with anything?

"I almost feel guilty now. While you were dealing with so much, I was pampered."

"Good." Headlights showed in his rearview mirror, distracting Rowdy. "I wouldn't wish my folks on anyone, much less another kid." Definitely not Avery.

Slowly she inhaled, exhaled, inhaled again. "My parents were well-off. Growing up, I can't remember wanting anything that I didn't get."

"Were well-off? They're not now?" The car pulled closer behind them. Too close for safety.

Close enough for him to read the license plate and commit the number to his memory.

Oblivious to their tail, Avery worried her hands together for a different reason. When she realized what she was doing, she flattened them on her thighs. "Actually, I think Mom has even more wealth now. After my dad died a few years ago, she married one of the partners in his company."

She'd lost her dad? Bummer. Somehow he figured the loss was a whole lot different for her than it had been for him. "I'm sorry."

"Me, too. Dad was everything your dad wasn't. I saw him drink wine occasionally, but I don't remember him ever getting drunk. Mom, either. It's just not done. Even though Dad traveled a few times a month, we had a lot of time together. Vacations and holidays. He'd set his schedule around my life so he could be there for all the important stuff."

Still aware of the car behind them, Rowdy took another turn, this one not part of Avery's directions. She didn't notice. "That's how it should be, right? In a real family, I mean." What the hell did he know of real families? Jack shit.

"I suppose." Melancholy tinged her soft voice. "I've never been in love."

"That's a problem for you?" Because it sure wasn't a problem for him. In fact, he liked it that she hadn't fallen for anyone.

Avery shook her head. "Dad wanted to see me settled down. But it never happened. I traveled a lot after college. I wanted to see the world and my parents indulged me. Getting a job, marriage and all that…it didn't seem that important."

So why was she working for him now? Still seeing the world? Maybe experiencing the other side of life?

He'd met women who wanted to try slumming it. Didn't matter to him. In his bed, rich or poor, they all screamed out the same during a hard climax.

If Avery wanted a walk on the wild side, he'd show her just how hot the wild side could be.

He was curious about Avery's motives, but digging into her psyche would have to wait. "We have a tail."

Confused, she stared at him. "What?"

"We're being followed."

"Oh, my God!" She twisted to look out the rearview mirror. "Who is it?"

"No idea." Her reaction dumbfounded him. He'd half expected her to laugh, to say he was being paranoid. Instead, she'd shot straight into panic mode. "Hang on, babe. I'm going to lose him."

She said "Wha—" as he accelerated around a corner, and the word ended in a gasp.

Grabbing the door, she braced herself as he took another right, then a sharp left. His tires squealed obscenely loud in the dark, quiet hours of the night.

He stepped on the gas, barreling through a yellow light on the empty street and turning again down a narrow road. Killing the car lights, he pulled into a parking lot and stopped, but kept the car idling just in case he had to gun it out of there.

Arm on the back of the seat, Rowdy looked over his shoulder, watching.

Voice trembling, Avery whispered, "What are we waiting for?"

Concentrating, Rowdy didn't answer her, and half a minute later, the car sped past them on the main road. A fancy new model, silver, four-door hybrid. Facing forward again, lights still out, he put the car in Drive and turned.

Who the hell would be following him, and why? It was bad enough that it happened, but with Avery along for the ride? Heads would roll.

In a killing mood, he asked, "You okay?"

She stared at him for too long before saying, "Yes. You?"

"I'm fine." Why wouldn't he be? Taking back roads, he got them on track again. She still looked shaken, her eyes a little too wide, her shoulders stiff. He remembered how nervous she'd been outside the bar, watching the darkness as if the boogeyman might jump from the shadows.

He didn't take Avery for a timid woman easily spooked. Something else was going on.

When he reached over and put a hand on her knee, she didn't pull away. "Sorry about that."

She hugged herself. "You're sure the car was following us?"

"Afraid so." He'd spot a tail every time. It was like his senses kicked into gear, alerting him. "Hazard of my life. You can't live as I have and not make a few enemies along the way. 'Course, it could've just been someone who recognized the car. It has a previous history all its own."

Avery looked around at the late-model Ford. It ran well, but the interior had seen better days. "What does that mean? Did you win the car in a card game, too?"

"No, but I bought it cheap from a guy who lost in a card game and needed some fast cash before he got beat with a tire iron."

She stared at him agog. "You're not joking."

"No." A million stars lightened the skies to a smoky gray and more traffic joined him on the road, but no one else followed. "Who knows what else he was into?"

Not that it mattered. Whoever had been behind them didn't realize what he'd started. He'd find the bastard and put an end to the cat-and-mouse game before Avery was further upset.

"Fascinating."

"You don't sound scared." Not anymore. He gave her knee one final squeeze and returned both hands to the wheel. Avery wasn't the typical frail cookie who fainted at the first sign of danger. She wasn't a hardened ballbuster, either, immune to the plight of others.

In so many ways, under so many situations, she surprised him again and again.

"I was scared."

"I know." And still she'd handled it well. No real hysterics. She hadn't freaked out and distracted him. She hadn't even complained about the insane way he drove.

"Not *that* scared," she said, sounding peeved. "Mostly I'm curious."

"Now, why doesn't that surprise me?" So far she'd wanted to know everything about him. And wasn't that a kicker? Women usually only wanted to know how to get him into bed, and occasionally how to keep him afterward. They cared no more about his past, his motivations or aspirations, than he cared about theirs.

With still-trembling fingers, she tucked her hair behind her ears. "I know I said I wouldn't keep grilling you...."

"We'll be at your place in another five minutes." He could have made it in two, but no way in hell would he risk having his past follow her there. He'd continue with the jumbled route just in case. "Ask whatever you want until then."

"You're sure?"

Being frank with her, Rowdy said, "If I don't want to answer, I won't."

His honesty brought her brows down in a frown. "You won't lie to me?"

"Nope." At least, not this time. If it ever became necessary, well then...

"What about the bar?" She pulled one knee up to the bench seat and twisted toward him. "How'd you get it? You did a quick turnaround with the sale."

And here it had felt unending to him, waiting to see if he'd get the liquor license, if he'd pass the background check. He knew he'd gotten lucky, and that having a cop for a brother-in-law had helped expedite things. "I made the owner a cash offer he couldn't refuse."

She tipped her head. "Cash?"

"It's not like I've had a lot of need to spend what I make." In the past, he'd kept Pepper as comfortable as he could, bought the most basic necessities and paid as he went for everything else. "When you have little, you spend little to maintain."

Her tone, her mood, her expression, all turn tender. "Now that you've put down roots, you have insurance and utility bills, upkeep and employment, supplies and—"

"Set down roots?" Jesus, that idea made him jumpy. "Don't remind me."

"Why not? You do an amazing job. You've already turned things around. Everyone loves the bar, and everyone loves working for you."

She was playing fast and loose with the *L* word all of a sudden. *Did Avery love working for him?*

"You made Ella pretty happy with that raise."

"She deserved it." Truthfully, he enjoyed handling the books, working a budget. He'd been fortunate with employees, too. Avery made a terrific bartender, even if it drove him nuts to see other guys hit on her. All he really needed now was someone to help Jones in the kitchen. "In some ways, it's a lot like a high-stakes card game. I've always been a cautious gambler, but I still play to win."

"Cautious?" She gave an incredulous laugh. "You forget that I know how much trouble the bar was in when you took over."

He grinned. "Yeah, but I got it cheap." Someone would even call it a steal. "As a legit business it was hemorrhaging cash. It was only the drug trade bringing in money, and even the idiot who'd been running it knew that was about to come to an end."

"You told him that the cops were on to him?"

Rowdy shook his head. "I let him think rival competition was moving in."

"You?"

"I've known plenty of thugs and how they work, enough to make it believable." Hell, he'd been hustling the street since he was a kid.

Rather than be disgusted with his low associations, Avery looked awed. "That's ingenious."

So far, the only thing that seemed to upset her was him getting a blow job. It'd be best if he didn't share that thought with her, though. "The dumbass cut his losses and bailed. Good riddance."

"Given he let women be abused, I'd say you let him off easy."

When Avery looked at him like that, like maybe he was more than trouble, more than a speed bump in life, it...hell, it both bugged him and made him feel a foot taller.

And she'd called him dangerous.

"I used him, Avery." She deserved the bare truth. "I used that whole fucked-up scenario to get what I wanted."

As if the circumstances didn't matter at all, she nodded. "You also lent a hand to the police."

"Yeah, so?" Helping the cops was just a side effect of doing what *he* wanted.

"And now that your sister has married, you have the law in your family."

Did she have to twist his guts with his newly changed

status? He cringed, still unused to the idea. "Logan's all right. He's not like most cops."

She put her small, cool hand on his forearm. "Or maybe he is, and it's just that you haven't known the standard."

No reason to argue the point. "Maybe." He pulled onto her street—and got a new focus for his discontent. Streetlamps were broken, some buildings vacant with the windows boarded up, graffiti everywhere. The muscles of his neck knotted, and he murmured with sarcasm, "Home sweet home."

"Don't judge."

Oh, he'd judge all right. Something didn't add up. He knew all about dirt-poor, and he knew about disappearing. If Avery only wanted cheap rent, there were more secure places.

His little bartender wanted to hide, probably where no one would ever think to look for her.

He'd honed his instincts on a cutthroat society that ate the weak. He recognized the signs on a gut level.

Now he had to decide what to do about it.

Unaware of his darkening mood, Avery pointed. "Last apartment on the left." She picked up her purse from the floor and began digging for her keys. "You can go in the second driveway and pull around back."

Worse and worse. The back of the two-story structure butted up to the parking lot of an all-night convenience store. Three scruffy men hung around, drinking, smoking and talking too loud. No good ever came from a scenario like this. Even as Rowdy parked, he heard the breaking of a glass bottle, followed by loud guffaws and a few rank curses.

The stiffness of his neck crawled all the way down

to his toes. He clenched his jaw. "I'll walk you in." A statement, not an offer.

Avery didn't argue. "Thanks. I appreciate it." She gripped her keys tightly in one hand.

He noticed a small can of mace hanging from the key ring. *Did she honestly think that'd do her any good?*

Circling the hood of the car, he reached her just as she stepped out. He took the bag holding the T-shirts and apron.

"Usually," she said, "the fast-food restaurants and liquor store are still open when I get here, and they help to light up the lot. I've never gotten in this late, though."

And she never would again, not if he could help it. "Where does the bus drop you off?" He looked around and saw nothing but trouble waiting to happen.

"One block down. Not far. It's only a pain if it's raining."

For the love of… He'd gotten through a lot of ugliness in his lifetime, but right now, seeing how Avery lived, he was about as grim as a man could get. "Come on."

Hooking her purse strap over her shoulder, she looked around with apprehension, not at the men—who Rowdy considered the obvious threat—but again at the shadows. "Guess I should pick up a flashlight, huh?"

Or a gun. Maybe a bodyguard or two.

But with him nearby, she didn't need anything or anyone else. He would protect her.

"Doesn't matter." More often than not, the dark had been Rowdy's friend. In so many ways, he was still more comfortable in it than in the light. As he walked with her to the back entrance of the tall, narrow brick building, he eyed the motley trio hanging out. Given the way they watched Avery, he wondered if he should talk with them, make sure they understood—

"Behave, Rowdy."

Yeah, she picked up on his cues as easily as he picked up on hers. "I am behaving." *And weighing my options.*

"I don't want any trouble, so ignore them, please."

He had a feeling there'd be trouble regardless of her wants. "Are they always there?"

She kept her attention on the apartment building. "Or their ilk. It's not like we've had introductions so I can't say for sure if it's always the same men." She sorted through her keys. "So far it's been fine. No big problems."

Little problems, he knew, could sometimes escalate into a tsunami of threats. While Rowdy waited impatiently, Avery struggled to get the key to work the old rusted lock.

One of the men must've been feeling brave, because he took a few steps closer and called out to them in a drunken slur. "Ain't had no ponytail in a while. Maybe I can be up next?"

The other two chortled, offering their encouragement and egging on the drunken bum. The comments continued, going from Avery's hair to her ass, getting more crude by the second.

When another bottle broke, that one too close to be an accident, Avery nearly dropped her keys.

"Let me." Rowdy took the keys from her and opened both locks, then pushed the warped door open.

The guy moved closer, probably no more than three or four yards behind them. "What will five bucks get me?"

More hilarity, some cheering on. "Might get you a handy," his buddy called out.

"Or a least a flash peek of that bod."

"Yeah," the nearest man demanded. "Five bucks for a peep show! Prove you're a real redhead."

And Rowdy decided aloud, "Fuck it."

Oftentimes it was better to confront a problem head-on instead of trying to avoid it. This was one of those problems.

As he shoved the bag of apparel back at Avery, she said, "Don't you dare!"

He gave her one stern look. "Get inside. Lock the door behind you."

"Damn you, Rowdy Yates—"

Shaking off her clutching hands, he moved farther away from her while assessing the group.

What he saw was no challenge at all, not as long as Avery went in and secured the door so he'd know she was safe.

The group looked to be late thirties, early forties.

Drunk and dumb.

He understood both firsthand.

Staring at the leader with dead eyes, Rowdy walked toward him. "Got something to say?"

Too wasted to understand his precarious position, the fool gave a loud laugh. "If the honey is taking on customers, I've got some change I can spare."

Eyes narrowed, Rowdy kept up a steady but unhurried approach. As he drew closer, the man balked, dropping his hands from his hips, looking back at his buddies. As one, they crowded in with silent support, chins out, shoulders squared, mouths sneering—and strides staggered.

Rowdy curled his mouth in a mean, provoking smile. "I know you're firing on liquid courage, but you really might want to rethink this. Whatever bullshit you're considering, I've been there and done it better."

"I'm thinking it's three against one."

"Lousy odds for you." Rowdy stopped only inches in front of the other man. "You've shown your ass and had your fun. But nothing else is happening here. Not this time. Not ever with her."

One of the men, heavily bearded like a damned yeti, tried to move to Rowdy's side. Rowdy stopped him with a look. "I wouldn't if I were you."

The brazen one laughed. "You seriously want to fight all of us?"

"There wouldn't be a fight." The burning urge for violence uncoiled inside him. "I can prove it if you need me to, but it'd be easier on all of us if you just moved on." Easier on Avery, for sure. He knew when this ended, she'd give him all kinds of hell.

Soured beer breath assaulted Rowdy when the man bumped closer to him. "We're allowed to be here."

Rowdy didn't budge an inch. Sometimes men just needed to let off steam. He got that.

Hell, he felt it himself right now.

"Here in the lot, sure." He leaned in—forcing the shorter man to lean back. "But you're not allowed to disrespect her or bother her, and you sure as hell aren't allowed to get near her."

In a belated bid for control, the guy lifted both hands to shove Rowdy back.

Bad move.

Using his momentum against him, Rowdy pulled the fool forward, off balance, and clipped him in the face with his elbow. The drunk sprawled to the ground, landing on the rough gravel with a painful curse.

The yeti swung but Rowdy dodged the fist, then delivered one short jab to the bloated beer gut. On a sharp exhalation, the bigfoot went down hard over his buddy.

"Fucking asshole," the third man said, charging forward.

Rowdy leaned to the left and brought up his knee, catching the shorter man in the chin. He stumbled backward, stood frozen for a second and then crumpled to the ground.

The first man showed signs of life, groaning from beneath the ape. Rowdy stood there, fists clenched, wanting him to get up. He still sizzled with unspent tension.

He wanted, needed, a real fight.

What happened instead left him very dissatisfied.

The third guy slid on the gravel until his feet found purchase, then he lurched away, a hand to his nose to stem the flow of blood. He literally fled the scene and never once looked back.

Well, hell.

The second guy sat up, grumbling and holding his big gut. Calling Rowdy names in a low, whiny voice, he got to his feet. Meaty arms wrapped around his belly, he staggered off after his buddy.

The first man down stay sprawled on his back.

Rowdy crouched beside him. "You're a disappointment, man. I really wanted to take you apart, but you're drunker than I realized."

"Fuck you," he grumbled in a very slurred voice. Unbelievably, he curled to his side and stopped moving.

Narrowing his gaze, Rowdy waited—and heard the drunk's breathing even out. "No way." He nudged the guy, but only got a snuffling groan that went back into a near snore. Rowdy shot to his feet. *"Goddamn it."*

"I take it you wanted more sport?"

Jerking around, Rowdy found himself facing three other guys. This group was younger than the first, physically fit and from all appearances, clearheaded.

A slow smile lifted his mouth.

Maybe he'd get the fight he wanted after all.

CHAPTER FIVE

THE YOUNG MAN who'd spoken smiled right back. Watching the drunks retreat, he said, "Relax, man. We're innocent bystanders, just taking in the show." Stance relaxed, he shrugged. "Not that there was all that much to see."

"Unfortunately." Rowdy did a quick evaluation. This guy looked to be early twenties, maybe six-two. Dressed in jeans, sneakers and a flannel shirt, with a stocking cap pulled over his hair.

The worn clothes didn't hide a ripped physique.

The smile showed confidence, and maybe even amusement, which meant he wasn't worried about handling himself.

The two behind him looked more ragtag, and while also fit, more on the average side. One of them held a cola can and an expression of boredom. The other crossed his arms over his chest in a show of antagonism.

They weren't intimidated by the pathetic beat down they'd just witnessed, and why should they be?

Rowdy hoped like hell that Avery stayed put in the apartment building. "Out for an evening stroll, huh?"

Cockiness widened his smile even more. "Something like that." He shoved his hands into his jeans pockets and nudged aside a broken bottle with the toe of his shoes. "Loudmouths and litterbugs. What's the world coming to?"

Poverty had carved false daring into many personalities, maybe even his own. Rowdy would disabuse the young men of any forward intent right now. "They can be as loud as they want, and trash the place for all I care. But they won't—"

"Go near the lady? Yeah, I got that." He looked over his shoulder at his pals. "You guys mind picking up these bottles? Some kid will come through here and shred his feet."

To Rowdy's surprise, the backup came forward and began picking up broken glass.

"I'm Cannon Colter." The talker gestured with his shoulder to the apartment building. "You live around here?"

The door to the apartment squeaked like a horror movie when Avery tried to sneak it open. Shit, shit, shit. Should he lie? Should he say he was with Avery each night to deter any thoughts of bugging her?

Cannon leaned forward. "We don't do that, so relax."

Feeling like an unscripted extra in a very bad play, Rowdy said, "Do what?"

"Hassle women." Cannon shook his head. "Not our thing."

"So what is your thing?"

He withdrew a little, looking up at the lightening sky, then the convenience store, before giving Rowdy a direct stare. "We grew up here. I hate seeing those creeps foul the place up more than it already is."

"Is that so?"

"And I have a little sis." He lifted his brows as if that explained everything.

Being a big brother himself, Rowdy supposed it did. Cannon—*and here he thought Rowdy was an odd name*—didn't want his sister bothered by the scum. He dared a quick glance back, but luckily, even though Avery had poked her head out the door, she'd stayed inside as he'd…asked. Okay, so it'd been more of an order. He'd apologize for that as soon as he got this wrapped up.

Cannon looked at Avery, too. "Sorry, man, but she sticks out like a sore thumb."

"Yeah, I know."

"She's gonna draw drunks like flies to manure."

Glad that Avery hadn't caught that comment, Rowdy fought off a grin. He could only imagine how she'd react if she heard that particular comparison. "Yup."

"You're the first guy she's brought here."

Good info, even if it wasn't any of his business. "You noticed?"

"I pay attention." His brows lifted. "And she's pretty noticeable."

Rowdy couldn't help but be curious. "How long has she lived here?"

"About a year or so. Something like that."

"She's always on the lookout, too," another offered.

"Yeah. She is," said the smallest of the three, which didn't really make him small. "She's real cautious."

Rowdy would call that smart, given the area. "Have you actually seen anyone bother her?"

"Nah, but if you want, we can keep an eye out."

Cannon grinned. "She keeps that li'l bottle of pepper spray in her hand and she mean mugs anyone who looks her way."

"You?"

Cannon lifted both hands. "Not me. We already settled that, right? But I've seen other dudes looking her over."

Rowdy scowled. It took him less than three seconds to make up his mind. Pulling out his wallet, he took out three twenties, one for each of them, with an equal number of business cards for the bar. His cell was listed below the bar number.

Holding out the bills and cards, he said, "Think of this as a down payment. You ever see anyone bothering her, call either of the numbers. Ask for Rowdy. I'll pay you for the trouble."

The temperature dropped about ten degrees in Cannon's expression. "Keep your money." He took all three cards. "I don't need to be paid not to be an asshole."

Slowly, Rowdy withdrew the offered bills. "All right." He'd rather bust his knuckles on a hardheaded bully than insult an honest man's pride. "Sorry for the misunderstanding."

"Forget it." He studied the card. "You're Rowdy? As in the owner of the bar?"

"You know it?"

"I know you kicked a bunch of dope dealers to the curb when you took over." He met his gaze. "Appreciate that."

"It was my pleasure." Rowdy got the feeling that Cannon took the cleanup of the bar as a personal favor. For a young guy, he had his nose in a lot of business. Interesting. "If you're ever in the area, stop in for a drink on the house."

"I just might take you up on that." He shoved one card into his back pocket and went to his friends to hand out the other two. "See you around, Rowdy."

Watching the three of them cut across the lot and disappear into an alley, Rowdy decided he'd do a little research on Cannon, as well as the car that had tailed him.

Funny that making a smidge of headway with Avery had unearthed more questions than answers.

Walking off, Rowdy wondered if Avery had locked him out or if he'd be able to tell her good-night. She surprised him by opening the door again before he reached it.

Brows pinched, she greeted him with, "Are you *insane?*"

Could be. She had that effect on him. "Calm down, honey. Everything's fine."

"*Fine?* You could have been killed!"

He snorted, which only seemed to infuriate her more. "Those guys could barely stay on their feet." He stepped in and secured the door behind him, noting again what a crappy lock it was.

"What if one of them had been armed?"

Apparently a shrug wasn't the right answer.

"Ohmigod," she said dramatically. "You *are* insane. And that second group was not inebriated."

"They weren't hostile, either."

"Something you didn't know until *after* you'd faced off with them." She thrust up her chin. "What did you and the hottie talk about for so long?"

Oh, hell, no. Slowly, Rowdy gave up his inspection of the lock to face her.

Bristling head to toe, he stiffened his shoulders and stared down at her with intimidating heat. "Hottie?" he whispered.

The glare was wasted on her. "You know who I

mean. The good-looking kid? The one built like an athlete."

Jealousy sucked, adding pure gravel to his tone. "He's only a few years younger than you, so hardly a kid."

Her turn to shrug, and damn it, he didn't like it much more than she had. But when she patted his chest—presumably to reassure him—Rowdy felt compelled to let it go.

"I gave him a card and told him to come by the bar sometime." Before he made an even bigger ass of himself, Rowdy put an arm around her and steered her away from the front door. "If he does show up, let me know immediately." Rowdy didn't have reason to distrust Cannon, but he didn't take chances unnecessarily.

And with the way Avery had described the guy, he was even less inclined to risk leaving her alone with him.

"Okay."

"By the way." He kissed her temple. "Thanks for staying inside."

"I'm not an idiot." She lifted her hand with the cell phone in it. "But I almost called the police."

Definitely not what he needed. "Don't ever do that."

Stubbornness sharpened her expression and launched her to her tiptoes. "I will if I think it's necessary!"

Damn it. Again Rowdy tried to stare her down, but it didn't even come close to working. On a tight exhalation, he took her phone from her, saying, "If *you* ever need the cops, call 9-1-1. But if it's for me, just call Logan or Reese." He pressed several buttons. "Their numbers are now saved in your contacts." He dropped her phone back in her purse.

"Really?"

"Sure. Why not?"

For some reason Rowdy couldn't understand, Avery smiled in pleasure. "Thank you."

That smile of hers could work magic. Forcing himself to look away, Rowdy took in the main floor of the building. He now understood the reason she came in the back door instead of the better-lit front. The house had literally been divided in two with a wall erected in the middle to separate the halves.

A door to his right led to the first apartment, with stairs leading up the second. He assumed the layout would be the same in the front. "Do you know your neighbors?" *Please let her say no.*

She shook her head. "I keep to myself."

Just as Cannon had claimed. "Glad to hear it." Even here in the foyer, the building looked run-down with chipped, dirty paint and carpet so gross he hated to walk on it even in his shoes. Praying it'd be the latter, Rowdy asked, "First floor or second?"

"I'm up." She started ahead of him, her keys in hand. "I understood the first exchange easily enough. But you did more than exchange cards with that second group of guys, right? So what did you talk about?"

Fudging the truth just a little, Rowdy said, "I told them you were off-limits." At the top of the stairs, he took her arm. "You'll let me know if anyone bothers you, okay?"

"No one will, but thank you."

Though it'd soon be morning and her eyes were a little tired, she was still so incredibly sexy to him. That abundance of red hair trailed around her shoulders and over her breasts.

He brushed it back. "Let me have your keys."

Suddenly shy, her gaze dropped away from his. "What are you going to do?"

"Check it out, make sure you're alone."

That brought her attention back with startled worry. "You think someone could have gotten in?"

He squeezed her shoulders. "Probably not, but I'll feel better once I see how safe your place is."

A pulse fluttered in her throat as she stared at his mouth. "I'm not sure..."

Damn but she could tempt a saint, so what chance did a sinner like him have? "I'll look around, check on things and then leave."

"I suppose you're good at picking out security problems." Looking at the door again, she made up her mind. "Okay, thank you. I appreciate it." She handed over her keys.

Rowdy was so used to her stubborn streak of independence, he didn't quite trust her when she was like this. She hid something—but what?

The setup of the building sucked. Here on the landing, she was trapped. No window, no door but into her apartment. He unlocked and opened the door, reached inside and found a light switch. Unlike at his place, lamps came on beside a stuffed couch.

Rowdy brought her in with him, left the door open and said, "Wait here." Before she could protest, he went through the apartment, glancing long enough at the small open kitchen to see a box of Cocoa Puffs sitting on the counter. Cold, sugary cereal, huh? Somehow that fit.

The first door led to a miniscule bathroom with a cluttered counter. Makeup, blow-dryer, a basket of

girlie-looking headbands and hair ties. He pushed back
the shower curtain and found an array of bottles surrounding the narrow tub—shampoo, conditioner, body
wash, lotion, bubble bath.

The woman took her bathing very seriously.

He left that room and glanced into a hall closet that
held her towels, extra blanket and pillow and more toi-
letries. Avery said not a single word as he went into
her bedroom.

First things first, he checked her closet, moving her
clothes around to look behind them. She had a wardrobe
of T-shirts, sweatshirts, sweaters and jeans, with only
a few dresses and skirts thrown in. A pile of shoes and
boots littered the floor of the closet. He never would
have pegged Avery to be so messy, but he kind of liked
it.

He didn't see any real dirt, just a whole bunch of
disorganization.

Her bedroom window overlooked the convenience
store and the now-empty lot. After checking the lock
on her window, he closed the curtains and bent to peek
under her unmade bed. Nothing but dust bunnies, a
stray sock and a suitcase. Too curious to let it go, Rowdy
tugged at the luggage handle.

It wasn't empty.

So Avery kept a packed suitcase under her bed. For
an emergency exit?

Straightening again, he took a moment to look over
her room. Not as utilitarian as his; she had knickknacks
everywhere. Change and a few pieces of jewelry littered
the single dresser. A scented candle and a book rested
on her nightstand. He touched the fluffy comforter and
supersoft sheets on her bed. She had three pillows.

"Rowdy?"

"Be right there." Trying to remove the image of her curled up all warm and sleepy in that bed, he walked out feeling strangely...enlightened.

His bartender didn't live like a woman from a pampered upbringing. In fact, her messy apartment didn't look much different from where his sister used to hide out.

Secrets. Avery had them in spades. How hard would it be for him to uncover them?

WITH A STRANGE sensation of anticipation humming in her veins, Avery watched as Rowdy prowled her apartment. She shouldn't have left it so cluttered, but there never seemed to be enough hours in the day to do everything that needed to be done.

She had Sundays off, but usually slept late and then spent the day running errands and doing laundry. Who had time to clean?

When Rowdy emerged from her bedroom, her heart thumped harder. "Done snooping?"

"Almost." He checked out the window in the main living area, and then the smaller window behind her kitchen sink.

She checked out the flex of muscles in his shoulders and the way his butt looked in those threadbare jeans. He had such strong thighs, and such a terrifically muscled backside.

He met her gaze. "They're locked."

She knew it, because she kept them that way. In the summer, when it had gotten hot as Hades, she'd run a portable room air conditioner that hadn't quite cut through the humidity, but at least offered a little relief. "It's okay?"

"As good as it can be here, but if you don't mind, I'd like to talk to your landlord about changing the lock on the entry door."

"I already did." She felt a little out of control. Surely she wasn't one of those women turned on by a macho display of violence? Not that there'd been much violence, not with the expedient way Rowdy had handled the bullies. "He told me to go for it."

From across the room, Rowdy looked at her mouth, then her throat and finally her breasts. In a distracted way, he said, "I'll take care of it before work."

Her breath caught when she inhaled. "You don't have to do that."

Holding up his hands to prove that he'd keep his promise, he stalked toward her. "I want to do it."

Oh, the way he said that. Her mind conjured all kinds of things other than replacing an old lock. "Okay, then."

Casually, he leaned a shoulder on the door frame next to where she stood. "So."

She started to thank him again, but he cut her off.

"You didn't like seeing me with another woman."

She stepped away from the open door—and away from temptation. "Seriously, Rowdy, I see that every night." Lying through her teeth, she said, "Not a biggie."

He thought about that, nodded. "You didn't like seeing a woman with her mouth on my—"

"No!" Jerking back around, Avery broke her own rule. She stretched up to smash two fingertips against his mouth. "Don't you dare say it."

Slowly, Rowdy wrapped his much-larger fingers around her wrist and lowered her hand to his chest.

And, oh, God, that wasn't much better than touching his mouth. He felt so hot.

His thumb brushed over the back of her hand. "I can promise you that it won't happen again."

She curled her fingers against him, a little embarrassed that her nails were clipped so short, her hands rough from so many washings during work. The smell of the bar probably clung to her.

Then she remembered that it didn't matter; she'd never again be that manicured woman from her past. "At work, you mean?"

His mouth tightened. "I won't lie to you, Avery. I'm not going to become a monk."

Thank God. That would be such a waste of raw sensuality. Unsure what his point might be, Avery said, "I wouldn't expect you to."

"Good, because now I have a question for you." He released her, took a step back so that he stood outside the door and asked, "How long do I have to wait, honey?"

Avery's heart jumped. She could have pretended that she didn't understand, but she knew exactly what he meant.

Rowdy didn't rush her, and he didn't joke. That told her he was serious, so she gave him a real answer.

"I don't want to be an available convenience. I don't want to be interchangeable."

His gaze darkened, grew more intense.

"So…" She screwed up her courage. Not to say it, but to mean it. To commit to it. "I guess you have to wait long enough that I know you want me, specifically, more than you want easy sex."

He touched her jaw, the side of her throat, and opened

his hand on the back of her neck. "I think I can handle that."

He *thought* he could? That was the best reassurance he could give? She started to protest, but he put his mouth over hers in a kiss that was deep, soft and consuming. His warm tongue lightly teased, and his hard body stole her breath.

When he ended the kiss, she more or less hung limp in his arms right outside her door. "Damn, woman, you do know how to drag out the suspense." He kissed her once more, firm and quick—then lifted her over the doorjamb and back into her apartment. "Lock up behind me. I'll see you tomorrow. And remember, anything at all happens, I want to know, no matter what time it is. You call me."

She nodded. What in the world did he think would happen? "Thank you for…well, everything."

He had such a gorgeous smile. "My pleasure, Avery. Always."

Always…until he got what he wanted, and then he'd probably be done with her.

She closed and locked the door, and then she started grinning. Holy cow. Rowdy Yates had packed a wallop in that kiss.

No matter how long it lasted, Avery knew her world would never be the same.

She supposed she should call the doctor, since it appeared she'd be needing the pill after all.

FOR THE FIRST TIME since buying the bar, Rowdy couldn't concentrate on business. He'd kissed Avery on her doorstep three days ago. The next day when he'd gone back to change out the lock, she'd given him a key and insisted on repaying him what he'd spent at the hardware store. He'd taken that one on the chin because she'd been so insistent about it.

But since then, she'd also been working extra hard, almost as if she wanted to make sure she didn't get any special favors just because she'd admitted her interest.

Not like he could show favoritism anyway. She was the only bartender—a situation he'd need to remedy if he ever hoped to spend much time with her. When she needed a break, he was the one to give it to her. If she needed a day off, he worked the bar. The bar was closed on Sundays, but he often used that day to work on more renovations to the unused areas. He wouldn't be satisfied until every inch of the bar was used wisely.

Each night he'd wanted to drive Avery home, but she always refused. So instead he had to stand there and watch her get on a bus.

Avery didn't know that he followed in his car to make sure she got in without being bothered. On one of those nights he'd spotted Cannon and his buddies hanging around again, but other than watching Avery go into her apartment, Cannon hadn't approached her.

The hours they kept made it tough for Rowdy to work a seduction. And damn it, with every hour that passed, he wanted her more.

As he cleared a table to help Ella with the remaining customers, a sexy blonde leaned into his view. "Hey, Rowdy."

Her cleavage just naturally drew his attention. "Hey..." He racked his brain...something with an *S,* if he recalled right. "Sheila, isn't it?"

"You remembered!"

More like he'd gotten lucky with guessing. She came

into the bar several times a week, and each time she hit on him. He'd planned to take her up on her not-so-subtle offers—until Avery had laid out her stipulations. Now, knowing Avery would eventually be his, Sheila held little interest for him. "Of course I did. You've turned into a regular." He went back to cleaning the table.

"You know," she said suggestively, "I live close by." Her hand smoothed up his arm to his shoulder. She leaned in to whisper, "We could get there in under twenty minutes."

He couldn't help but grin. It was nice to be wanted, especially with Avery all but avoiding him. And thinking of Avery, he straightened again and glanced her way.

Even from across the room, her fierce glower torched him. She looked like she expected him to haul Sheila off to his office any second. Apparently, his little bartender still didn't understand just how much he wanted her specifically, not just any willing body.

Rowdy saluted Avery before saying to Sheila, "I appreciate the offer, hon, I really do. But I'm slammed."

"Tomorrow, then." She trailed a painted fingernail over her collarbone, and then dipped it into her cleavage.

Which, of course, ensured that his gaze followed.

Nice rack. Big and heavy and pale. She'd be a handful.

He wasn't tempted even a little. "Can't. I'm out of commission until…" Until when, damn it? How long would it take for Avery to realize how good they'd be together? Whether she felt the chemistry or not, he knew they'd burn up the sheets.

Deciding it didn't matter because Sheila wasn't doing it for him anyway, Rowdy said, "Until further notice.

The bar is really growing, and as it is, I'm only squeaking in a few hours of sleep a day."

"I could make it worth your while."

"I didn't have a doubt." He nodded at a tableful of young men behind them. "They know it, too. They haven't been able to take their eyes off you."

Sheila wasn't fooled. She knew a rejection when she heard it, regardless of how he'd tried to pretty it up. "It's your loss." With a smile, she went off to easier game.

Rowdy shook his head, always amused by women and their antics. It'd be nice if Avery were so predictable.

Then again, it was her uniqueness that he lo—

Whoa. No fucking way. He stomped that thought right out of his head real fast.

He tried focusing on the bar instead, on the many tasks that still needed to be done. But on his way to the kitchen with some dirty dishes, he again sought out Avery. She bustled along the busy bar, filling drink orders and smiling at customers—all of them men.

In many ways he felt like a possessive ape around her, but this he took in stride. He knew Avery well enough to know she wouldn't flirt with a customer, and beyond that, she wasn't interested in hard drinkers.

He was just about to push into the kitchen when the phone rang. Avery answered it. No big deal. With the only phones behind the bar and in his office, she took the calls more often than not.

He went on through the kitchen doors and deposited the dirty dishes into the sink. Even with the dinner hour long over, Jones still hadn't finished up. Rowdy knew he had to find him some help soon or Jones would quit on him.

"Leave those if you want," Rowdy told the cook.

"You paying me for the time I'm here?"

"Don't I always?"

"Yeah, and it'll only take me another hour, so I'll stay." He pointed a scrub brush at Rowdy. "But stop being so choosy and hire someone already, will you?"

"Working on it." Hell, he'd interviewed a dozen people. "It's not as easy as you'd think." Especially with the bar's reputation. He'd had a few druggies show up, a hooker, a drunk and a barely of-age kid who'd quailed at the idea of putting in eight hours.

Suddenly Ella stuck her head into the kitchen. "Rowdy?" Her usual smile was missing, her tone nononsense. "Avery's in trouble."

Instead of asking questions, Rowdy dropped the dish towel and strode through the doors and into the main room. He sensed Jones and Ella right on his heels.

His gaze locked on Avery. She looked more annoyed than hurt or afraid, but a big bruiser had her half pulled over the bar thanks to a grip on her wrist. Rowdy barely remembered moving before he had the heavy man by the front of his shirt. "Let. Her. Go."

The guy released Avery with a shove and she stumbled back, fetching up against the ice chest.

Rowdy saw red. Back in the good old days, before he was a fucking proprietor, he'd have taken the guy apart and been done with it. Now...well, now he had boundaries, so he'd try it the "nice" way—and hope the guy gave him a reason to demolish him. "Get out and don't come back."

"Who the hell are you?" the man demanded.

Righting herself, Avery said, "Rowdy, don't do it."

Vibrating with the surge of anger, Rowdy kept one

fist knotted in the man's shirt, the other held down at his side.

As the man tried to jerk free, his shirt ripped.

Rowdy wanted to rip out his heart, too. It wasn't easy, but he managed to say with controlled fury, "Don't ever put your hands on my employees."

Realizing he had the attention of the owner, the man shoved his face close. "I've been here for hours. She made me lose my temper."

Rowdy didn't blink; it took all his concentration to fight his natural instinct to defend what was his—and he didn't mean the bar.

"Ever touch her again and you'll lose a hell of a lot more. Now *leave.*"

Frustrated, the man shoved both hands through his dark, greasy hair. He drew in a deep breath. "I don't have time for this shit." Belatedly, he looked around, realized he was drawing attention and leaned in for privacy.

The foul stench of sweat and desperation almost caused Rowdy to flinch.

"I made a deal," the man said through wet lips, "and I never got paid. The owner traded me some of the equipment to even things up and avoid retaliation."

"I'm the owner," Rowdy enjoyed telling him. "And I don't trade with drug dealers."

"Before you!"

"Before me is none of my concern."

The man locked his large hands into boulder-size fists. "Look, buddy, my day has been shit already, okay? I have my own debts to pay, the junker truck I borrowed barely runs and to top it off, the old lady shoved the kid off on me."

Ice ran down Rowdy's spine... *Shoved the kid off on me...* His thoughts scrambled, tripping over ugly possibilities.

"So now I'm done playing nice." The man ground his teeth together and lowered his voice to a snarl. "Either give me the equipment or give me my money."

Rowdy swallowed hard, but sickness continued to crawl up his throat. A Mack truck parked on his chest, making a deep breath impossible. Ugly memories sharpened everything he felt. "Where are you parked?"

Thinking he'd won, the bruiser rubbed his hands together. "Out back. I'll take the jukebox and the—"

"We'll discuss it." Rowdy clamped a hand on his arm and propelled him forward. "Let's go somewhere private."

A soft, feminine voice reached out to him. "Rowdy?"

He didn't look at Avery. He didn't dare. The last thing he needed was her interference. "I'll be right back," he told a narrow-eyed Jones and a pale Ella. "Back to work."

Avery said nothing else, and that should have made him suspicious, but he was too busy concentrating on the man in front of him. Big, dirty, a bully used to getting his own way, scum who didn't mind making a scene or using his strength against those who were smaller or weaker. Rowdy might've just met the bastard, but he knew him.

Far too well.

Rowdy wasn't small and he wasn't weak, not now, not ever again. Each step he took narrowed his focus until it became a single laser beam of driving purpose.

People shifted out of the way as the two of them went through the bar and out the front door. Chill evening air filled Rowdy's lungs, helping to clear away the haze of blistering rage. A restless breeze played over his fevered muscles, reminding him to relax.

Battles were always best fought with a cool head and limber muscles.

"I'll take the jukebox," the bully said again, "and a few cases of whiskey. That's a bargain for you."

Keeping a tight leash on his emotions, Rowdy stayed two steps behind. "We'll talk about it near your truck." And if he found what he thought he would, then God help the man.

At the alley beside the bar, they turned to head around back. The security lights Rowdy had installed helped to light the dark alleyway, which had discouraged hookers, dopers and gangs from hanging out there.

He had a clear path to the back lot—a lot where only employees should have been parked.

Rowdy stepped out of the alley and faced a nightmare, his worst suspicions confirmed.

The fucking bully had sealed his own fate.

He'd brought along a kid.

CHAPTER SIX

SITTING ON THE ground outside the open truck door, his knees pulled up to his skinny chest, wearing only a T-shirt and jeans too short, the boy huddled against a rear tire. Rowdy guessed him to be eight, maybe nine years old. When the boy saw them, he jumped to his feet, his skinny chest working, his gaze filled with wariness.

"Who's this?" Rowdy asked.

"He's nobody. Don't worry about it."

Nobody. Rowdy forced himself to breathe calmly. "Is he your son?"

"That's what the bitch says." Not realizing his own peril, the guy laughed. "The runt don't really look like me though, does he?"

A strange sort of peace settled over Rowdy. He knew what it was, because he'd felt it before. A defense mechanism. A way to push aside emotion so that only cold, lethal intent remained. It was how he'd coped back then, and how he would cope right now. "Where's his coat?"

"How the fuck do I know?"

Chills had the boy trembling. And damn it, Rowdy shook with him. "What's your name, kid?"

The boy put up his chin, silent, miserable. Afraid to speak.

Impatient, the thug barked, "Get back in the truck, Marcus." And then to Rowdy, "I told you, his mom had shit to do so I had to drag him along. He won't be a problem. He knows to stay out of the way. Now forget about him, will you?"

"No, actually, I won't." Despite the man's order, Marcus didn't move, and damn, Rowdy wanted to make him understand. He met the boy's gaze. "Sorry, Marcus." *I'm about to shake up your world.*

Maybe Marcus did catch on, because his eyes went wide—and suddenly Avery opened the back door of the bar. She looked…he didn't know. He'd never seen her look like that before.

She flashed an uncertain and very false smile. "I'm sorry to intrude. I figured the young man should come in with me while you two…negotiate your business."

Was that her nice way of saying, *While you kill that no-good SOB?*

Belligerence amplified the man's bloodshot eyes. "He's staying with me."

Before Rowdy could bury his fist in the man's face, Avery half stepped out, not so far as to put herself at risk, but far enough to intrude and make the bully want her to back off. "Oh, but you know what they say. Little pitchers have big ears. I'm sure you men would like to keep this conversation private."

The man's eyes narrowed on the kid. "He knows to keep his trap shut."

Volcanic rage expanded Rowdy's chest. He pushed past the man and put a hand on Marcus's narrow shoulder. "Go on in, okay? She'll get you something to drink."

The boy dug in. "I'm not thirsty."

Rowdy had expected that answer, because long, long ago, he'd given it a few times himself. To expedite things before his fragile thread of control snapped, he hardened his tone. "In."

"Do what you're told!" The man drew back a hand, ready to belt the boy.

Rowdy flattened one hand to the bastard's chest and shoved him back hard. The single-word command cut through the night: *"Don't."*

Taken by surprise, the man floundered. "What the fuck?"

"Oh, and Rowdy?" Avery got the boy inside and leaned out again. "In case you needed help moving the jukebox, I called Logan." And with that parting shot, she closed the door.

Rowdy narrowed his eyes. He finally had the man alone, and here Avery had snatched away his opportunity by calling in the law.

Had she known all along what he planned to do? Probably. Avery was cagey that way. Very little got by her.

The man shoved back from Rowdy's hold. "I'm owed more than the jukebox for all my trouble. Like I said, a few cases of whiskey will help, but—"

Fury closed in, narrowing his vision. "All you'll get from me is the beating you deserve."

"What are you talking about?"

Egging him on, Rowdy said, "You're a coward, a sloppy drunk and I'm going to enjoy taking you apart." Rarely did he ever hit first. He'd learned that in the legal world, words were allowed, but first contact was frowned upon.

Predictably, what he said enraged the man enough that he threw a big, meaty punch. Rowdy ducked, but not in time. The blow connected with his shoulder and knocked him off balance. He dropped to one knee, then braced for the impact of a tackle.

They went into the sharp gravel; it cut into Rowdy's spine and shoulders before he rolled, shoving the heavier man to the side. Now with the gravel assaulting his knees, Rowdy pounded the other man with several heavy hits, catching him in his fat gut, his solar plexus, his chin.

The smell of blood blinded him to everything else. He hit harder and heard the bully's nose break. His knuckles hurt, but it was a small price to pay for the pleasure he got in his retaliation.

When Rowdy got back to his feet, the big man rolled, trying to grab for his legs. Rowdy kicked out and got him in the nuts.

That took the fight right out of him.

Out of the shadows, a man said, "Jesus, Darrell, you fucking puke. If you can't hold your own, then don't start this shit."

Breathing hard and fast, Rowdy turned, and another man appeared. He flashed a grin—and a big tactical knife with a serrated blade.

"You should have given me my money," Darrell grunted as he struggled up to his knees.

"Fuck you." Rowdy didn't know the second man, but he knew Darrell, the abusive prick.

He kicked him in the chin, rendering him flat on his back, out cold.

Immediately Rowdy turned to fend off the knife wielder, but the second guy was on him too fast. As Rowdy lunged away, he felt the blade slice over his shoulder and down his back. Liquid heat ran along his nerve endings.

Not that he'd let it slow him down. A lifetime of hatred kept the pain at bay. Any man who abused his kid deserved a beating—and so much more.

With singular purpose, Rowdy dodged the next thrust of the knife and got in a solid punch that staggered the man. It didn't take him down, though; it only pissed him off, wiping that smirking grin right off his face.

Keeping the knife at the ready, he spit blood to the side. "You're dead meat, asshole."

Coiled, ready, Rowdy smiled and beckoned him forward. "Let's go, then."

Sirens pierced the night, not an unfamiliar occurrence, but Rowdy figured this time it was Logan sticking his cop nose in where it wasn't wanted.

Time to wrap this up.

The man circled to the side, but Rowdy moved with him, slowly closing the space between them. "You've got the knife," Rowdy taunted. "What are you waiting for?"

The fool charged at the same time that Rowdy adjusted his stance to kick out—and he broke the man's elbow. The knife fell from his hand and into the rough gravel. Rowdy moved in, punching him in the face, once, twice, a third time.

Dropping to his knees, the man swayed.

With one final kick to the chin, Rowdy sent him backward in a heap.

Behind Rowdy, someone applauded.

He spun around, and there was Cannon leaning against the side of the brick exterior wall of the bar. "Now that was more like it."

Dumbfounded, Rowdy said, "I didn't hear you."

Which had to mean the younger man was good, because no way was Rowdy slipping.

"Just got here," Cannon said. "I would have helped out, but looked like you had it handled. Mostly, anyway."

Rowdy opened and closed his fists, not quite satisfied with the damage he'd done.

Not sure he could ever be satisfied when it came to child abuse.

Struggling to get his shit together, Rowdy forced a deep breath. "What are you doing here?"

"I was curious." Cannon *accidentally* kicked Darrell as he stepped forward. "And you did offer me a free drink."

Rowdy looked at Cannon, then at Darrell sprawled on the ground, a hand at his gushing nose, bruises swelling his face and the side of his head. Darrell's cohort gave a faint moan, still out but starting to come around.

The black cloud of destructive anger continued to swim before Rowdy's eyes. He blinked to clear things up, then rotated his head, doing what he could to flex out the coiled tension.

The sirens grew louder before suddenly stopping. Great. Just the type of advertisement his place didn't need. He worked his fists again. "That drink will have to wait."

"Yeah?" Cannon shook his head at Darrell when he started to move. "Why's that?"

Logan stepped out of the alley, gun drawn. When he saw Rowdy standing there—doing his damnedest to look relaxed—he relaxed, too. "You're okay?"

"Yeah, sure." But he knew he wasn't.

From the other side of the bar, Reese cursed. "Pigheaded fool. How can you be okay when your back is covered in blood?"

"Knife," Cannon said, apparently not discomfited by the bloodshed or the appearance of cops. He nodded at Darrell's backup. "If Rowdy hadn't gotten so sloppy, it would have been a perfect performance."

"And you are?" Reese asked, while lifting Rowdy's shirt to survey the damage.

Rowdy did the introductions. "Cannon Colter, meet Detectives Logan Riske and Reese Bareden."

"Huh." Cannon moved to inspect Rowdy's back, too. "Somehow I didn't figure you for the type to hang with cops."

"I'm not." Rowdy tried to shrug Reese away. "My sister married Logan." He glared at Reese. "This big oaf came along as part of a package deal or something."

"Can't you just feel the love?" At six feet six inches, Reese towered over almost everyone. He glanced at Cannon. "I take it you aren't part of the trouble?"

"He's not." Rowdy's knees started to feel wobbly, meaning he'd lost too much blood. Shit. "They attacked me."

"Yeah," Logan said. "Avery told me when she called."

Two uniformed cops joined them. With a quick order from Logan, they cuffed the goons and began reading them their rights.

Logan looked at Rowdy, a brow cocked. "Wanna tell me why?"

Why not? He had a lot to say, and maybe not a lot of time to say it before he just might pass out. "These two wanted to shake me down. Something to do with a drug deal they'd made with the previous owner."

"It was bound to happen." Reese holstered his weapon and grabbed Rowdy's arm. "Sit down."

"I think I will." Rowdy's legs more or less collapsed under him. The rough gravel dug through the denim of his jeans to his backside, but he refused to complain.

"I'll call for an ambulance," Logan stated, and although he had his "I'm in charge" voice going, Rowdy heard the concern.

"Don't even think it." Rowdy tipped his head toward the bar. "There's a kid in there with Avery. Darrell brought him here, and I'm pretty sure he's his son."

Sensing there was more, Logan waited.

"Don't let him go anywhere. I mean it, Logan. He's..." *He's me, when I was a kid, and I know just how fucked that can be.* Rowdy blew out a breath. "I'll take care of it. Of him, I mean." *Somehow.*

"We have people for that," Reese said, and he ripped Rowdy's shirt in two. Thankfully, his back was mostly numb. He barely felt it when Reese used the shredded shirt to clean up some of the blood so he could see the actual cut. "Jesus, was he trying to fillet you?"

Unconcerned, Cannon checked it out for himself. He touched, prodded and, somewhat satisfied, said, "You know how to move, so it's not that deep, but you're bleeding like a stuck pig."

"He'll live." This time Reese was pulling Rowdy back to his feet.

Why, Rowdy didn't know. He only knew that he didn't want Marcus caught up in the system. "Listen to me, Logan. I'll help the boy myself. I'll get a few stitches and be right back—"

"The emergency room takes forever," Cannon informed him. "Looks like you'll only need one layer of stitches. I think you avoided muscle damage. But still, you'll be lucky if it only takes four or five hours."

Reese lifted his brows. "You don't look like a doctor to me."

"Fighter." Cannon shrugged. "We see our fair share of serious injuries."

All three men paused. Rowdy was the first to speak. "Professional?"

"I'm working on it." Cannon pulled off his stocking cap, ran a hand over his black hair, then tugged it on again. "But I don't yet make enough to get by."

"Which is why you came here?" Even with the blood loss, it started to click for Rowdy. "You're looking for a job?"

"If you're hiring."

Perfect timing. Rowdy turned to Logan and stopped him before he made the call. "Don't do it, Logan."

"Sorry, but you have to trust me on this one." Logan finished pushing in a number. "You know me. Would I abandon a kid?"

There were all kinds of abandonment.

The door opened and Avery strode out. Her stern expression held a wealth of emotion, and even more resolve. As if she knew Rowdy's most immediate concerns, she said, "Ella has Marcus. He's worried, way too silent, but now that we got him started, he's eating like there's no tomorrow." She had a couple of fresh dish towels in her hand, and one of the new black aprons.

Rowdy tried to catch her gaze, but she stepped behind him. He twisted to look at her over his shoulder. "You saw?"

"Watched most of it through the window. Thank God

I'd already called Logan before things got out of hand." She tsked at the sight of his back.

Not exactly the hysterics he'd expected.

"I'll take Rowdy to the hospital," she announced.

"On the bus?" Rowdy asked, just because he felt that snarky.

She shouldered Reese away and gently placed the clean cloths against his wound. "I have my car with me." Using the long apron strings, she tied the cloths in place to stop the bleeding.

"You have a car?" He bit off a grunt of pain when she tightened the makeshift bandage around him.

"Sorry."

"Pepper would have my head." With his call complete, Logan closed the phone and put it away. "Reese can stay here with the kid to wait for the social worker and to make sure no more trouble shows up. I'll drive you to the hospital, but Avery can come along if she wants."

"Damn, you're bossy in cop mode." Rowdy frowned at Avery. "And in case you've forgotten, you have a job—"

She cut him off. "I am going with you, Rowdy Yates, and that's that!"

Okay, he heard the near hysteria that time. So she'd only been holding it together for him? Considerate.

Now what to do? He eyed Cannon. "You know anything about working in a bar?"

"My dad used to own one."

Perfect. "Think you can start right now?"

"Let me check my calendar…." He held out his empty hands and grinned. "You're in luck. I'm free."

"Good. You're hired." Next he narrowed his eyes at

Reese. "Sorry, man, but you have to play bartender for me. I don't close for another two hours."

Reese, the big lug, lit up with excitement. "Go get stitches or whatever." He took off his coat and started rolling up his sleeves. "I've got it covered."

AVERY WANTED TO coddle Rowdy so badly. She wanted to stroke his head and hug him and somehow make his life different.

Instead she sat in silence beside him in the backseat while Logan drove—with Rowdy holding *her* hand as if to offer comfort.

Such an amazing man.

Darrell had downed four whiskeys at the bar before he'd started making his demands. At first she hadn't understood, and when she did catch on to what he wanted, Avery had tried to dissuade him. She knew Rowdy wouldn't give him a thing, and she hated to see an ugly confrontation take place.

But the more the man drank, the nastier he got, and then, right after the breather had called again, she'd gotten lost in thought and Darrell had used that moment to grab her wrist.

She flattened her mouth, remembering again the discomfort, the fear, the…memories.

"Hey." Rowdy lifted her hand to his mouth. "You okay?"

From the front seat, Logan snorted.

Rightfully so. Rowdy had a nearly two-foot cut from the top of his right shoulder all the way to the bottom of his left shoulder blade. He sat slightly forward, his left forearm braced on a thigh to keep his back from making contact with the seat.

But other than that, no one would know he'd been hurt.

She wasn't even sure Rowdy knew it; he seemed so immune to pain.

Yes, she'd fretfully watched much of the fight through the kitchen window. When the knife wielder had shown up, she'd wanted so badly to rush out to Rowdy's defense. With a cast-iron skillet in hand, she'd waffled, undecided if she'd help or hinder him with her presence—and the bastard had cut him.

She drew in a shuddering breath.

"Avery? Come on, honey. Ignore Logan and tell me you're okay."

"I'm okay." She freed her hand and reached across him to straighten the coat over his shoulders. Since Reese had ripped away his shirt, he was bare chested except for the dish towels patching up his wound and Logan's jacket, which he'd tried to refuse.

His body... Well, even so badly wounded, he made her want to melt. Her hand just naturally gravitated to his chest, smoothed over his downy, dark blond chest hair. She wanted to cuddle into him, put her cheek to his chest and feel his warmth, breathe in his vitality.

She wanted to reassure herself that he was truly okay.

But if she showed too much concern, if Rowdy realized how much she actually cared, would he push her away? So many times she'd seen him hook up with a woman and then the next day he'd give her his friendly but distant smile, the smile that said *we're done*.

She couldn't bear the idea of getting that smile from him. But neither could she keep the words contained. Leaning against his shoulder, Avery whispered, "God, Rowdy, you scared me half to death."

"Sorry." He looked out the window at the dark night. "You shouldn't have been watching."

And if she hadn't been, if Cannon hadn't shown up or if that knife had stabbed him as intended, he could have died in the back of the bar with no one knowing. Those two evil cretins might have dragged his body away and...

Breath catching, hands holding his rock-solid biceps, Avery turned her face into him. He was here now, alive and well if a little bloodied. How many more fights would she have to witness?

And why did he want to fight so much anyway? She should introduce him to the tried-and-true method of conversation.

Rowdy slipped an arm around her. "Relax, babe." And then with morbid humor, "You won't get rid of me that easily."

Logan glanced at them in the rearview mirror. "He really is fine, you know. I don't want to stoke his already healthy ego, but he has a few good moves."

This time Rowdy snorted, probably at the way Logan underplayed his ability.

"I know." Avery couldn't help but wonder what type of life had given him those skills. She recalled how he'd reacted to seeing Marcus—and her blasted heart cracked in two. She tucked her face in more, not wanting him to see her.

With a gentle touch, Rowdy smoothed his fingertips over her temple. "Where I grew up, you lost more than your lunch money if you couldn't hold your own. Fighting isn't a big deal for me, so don't sweat it, okay?"

Not a big deal, and yet he'd looked so different after seeing the boy, devastated in a way no man should ever be.

She desperately needed to know why.

Even without a shirt, Rowdy felt wonderfully warm. She got as close as she could to steal some of his heat. "When Darrell mentioned that he had his son with him, I understood."

"I know you did, and I appreciate it."

He appreciated it? She straightened up and frowned. "What does that mean?"

"You handled it well. Did the right thing by calling Logan and getting Marcus inside."

Dubious, Avery said, "Well, it didn't take a genius to pick up the clues."

"It's called situational awareness, and not everyone has it." He shifted. "Not everyone would have reacted, either."

Avery couldn't believe that. "Only a true monster would ignore something so blatant."

He laughed with grim sarcasm. "If you say so." And then, going serious again: "Give Ella a call and see what's happening with the kid, will you?"

Logan replied before Avery could. "The social worker I called will keep me informed. I know him. He's a good guy who really cares."

Avery could tell that Rowdy didn't like it, but he accepted that this was out of his control. The rest of the twenty-minute trip was made in painful silence.

Just as Logan pulled up to the emergency room doors, his phone beeped with an incoming message. He put the car in Park and read the text.

We sent a unit by Darrell's place. No other kids.

Rowdy had suggested that they check, only to have Logan tell him it was routine to do so. Knowing he

had a younger sister—a sister Logan had married—
gave Avery more insight into how Rowdy thought about
things, and why.

"They found the mom," Logan added. "She was
coked out of her head, unresponsive. Possible OD. They
took her to the hospital."

Rowdy shoved his door open and stalked from the
car. Avery slid out of the seat behind him. Given the
blood on his body, he drew immediate attention but
didn't appear to care.

Knowing he hurt in ways far worse than from a knife
wound, she wished she could console him. "Rowdy?"

He paused, his back to her.

"Wait for me, please." She caught up, stepping in
front of him to once again arrange the jacket over his
wide shoulders. She had to stretch up to reach, and
Rowdy held her waist, patiently letting her fuss.

Logan turned his car over to the valet parking and
joined them. "They'll have questions for me on how
this happened, so try to look more like a victim and
less like a pissed-off marauder, will you?"

If anything, that only darkened Rowdy's countenance
more. He exuded menace, sending others to walk a wide
path around him.

He entered the emergency room on his own steam,
but Avery wouldn't let him go through this alone. Not
any of it.

If he wanted her to back off, he'd have to flat out tell
her. Until then, she planned to stick by his side whether
he appreciated her concern or not.

Unfortunately, Cannon proved correct. Rowdy filled
out his insurance information, Logan explained the situation for a report and an hour later, after only a cursory

check—presumably to ensure he wouldn't die—they were still waiting.

When Logan took out his phone, Rowdy watched him. "Checking on the kid?"

"Calling your sister."

Rowdy went still. "Does she know—?"

Logan shook his head. "When I got the call, she was already asleep. She woke long enough to know I was rushing out, but she didn't know it was for you. She assumed it was routine police business."

"Good." Rowdy stood, removed the jacket and folded it before handing it to Logan. It would have to be dry-cleaned, but Logan didn't seem to mind. "Don't tell her."

His eyes widened. "For that, she would kill us both."

"Yeah, probably." Rowdy ran a hand over his face, flinched at the pain that caused in his back and carefully dropped his arm again. "So how about you go home to her and handle things so that she doesn't come charging down here? Think you can manage that?"

After scrutinizing Rowdy, Logan pushed up from his seat. "I'll do my best, but I'm not making any promises."

His best must have been good enough because even though Pepper called twice to talk with Rowdy, she hadn't shown up in person. Avery was a little disappointed. She wanted to meet the woman who could make Logan and Rowdy quail.

During the phone conversations, feeling very much like an interloper, Avery had listened in. How Rowdy spoke to his sister filled her with a touch of envy.

Rowdy was the same and yet somehow gentler, his tone filled with unmistakable affection. At the end of the second conversation, Rowdy again insisted that he didn't need Pepper to come to the hospital. "You have a husband to tend to." Whatever Pepper replied had Rowdy groaning. "Forget it, I don't need details."

Avery bit back her grin, easily imagining what had been said.

After a few more words, Rowdy ended the call with a gruff, "Love you, too, kiddo."

Emotion got a stranglehold on Avery's throat. She was very, very grateful that Rowdy had someone special in his life.

He deserved that and so much more.

With the call complete, he put his phone in his pocket and again prowled the small space of the room. Like a caged lion, he drew the wary attention of every other hapless patient waiting to be seen. He went to a window and looked out at the parking lot, bright with security lamps.

He had to be exhausted and in pain, and she knew he was worried about Marcus. Avery needed to do something to help.

Coming up behind him, she examined his broad back. With the binding in place, the bleeding had stopped, but all round it, bruising started to show.

When she lightly touched her fingers to him, he stiffened.

Not knowing if it was pain and a rejection to being coddled that made him so tense, she moved to his side. "Do you want a drink?" He didn't answer. "Or maybe I can find you a snack from a vending machine."

His light brown gaze cut to her. "I'd rather you weren't here at all."

She flinched. That hurt worse than she'd expected. With no idea what to say, she stared up at him, helpless, hurting for him.

"Damn it." Rowdy put his hand to her head, smoothed it over her hair. "Don't look like that. I didn't mean... I hate it that you're stuck here with me. I'd ask you to head on home, except that as late as it is, I don't want you going to your place alone."

Praying he'd understand, Avery said, "I feel the same about you."

He gave her a crooked, mean smile. "There's a world of difference, babe."

"You're hurt whether you want to admit it or not." Ready to insist if necessary, Avery said, "You're going to need some help."

"Yeah? What kind of help are we talking about?" His hand drifted from her hair to the side of her face. His thumb brushed her bottom lip. "You gonna help me out of my clothes? Maybe shower with me? Tuck me into bed?"

Even now, he was on the make. She shook her head and did her best not to react. "Listen up, Rowdy. You. Are. Wounded."

"It's not that big of a deal." His heated gaze zeroed in on her breasts. "I sure as hell wouldn't let it slow me down."

His look was so carnal, she had to fight the urge to cover herself. "Well, it'd slow me down!"

"Shhh, relax." The mean smile turned knowing and indulgent. "You're drawing attention."

Horrified by that possibility, she closed her eyes to count to ten.

His warm breath teased her ear. "Say the word, Avery, and we can go as slow as you like."

Oh, God, he sounded serious. Did nothing get to him? She met his gaze, and decided that no, not much did.

She was saved from replying when a nurse appeared, ready to show him to a room.

It surprised her when Rowdy snagged her hand and tugged her along with him. The next few minutes were excruciating as two nurses gave her the stink eye while oohing and aahing over him.

Whatever happened to professionalism?

"Looks like you're in overall excellent health," one nurse cooed.

Avery glared at her.

Rowdy gave his charming, devil's smile. "Thanks."

Of all the… Avery laced her hands together. "Maybe if you check his back instead of his chest, you'll find the injury."

Rowdy's smile expanded into a grin, and he used Avery's hand to pull her close.

Both nurses wanted to know what had happened, which Avery supposed made sense, but they mixed in totally inappropriate comments, too.

"So this happened at your bar? What's the name?"

"And where is it?"

Coy bitch, Avery thought. "Does that really matter?"

The nurse didn't take the hint. She teased Rowdy, saying, "What does the other guy look like?"

"Were you fighting over a woman?" the other asked. "How sweet."

Sweet? "Fighting is never a good idea!"

Rowdy patted her hand. "Sorry, she's had a rough night."

At the breaking point, Avery opened her mouth to blast everyone in the room, but all she got out was "I—" before Rowdy kissed her.

With both nurses watching.

It wasn't a wimpy little kiss. Nope. It was a hot, damp, tongue and teasing show of possession. Whew. Her insides went liquid and her anger melted away.

Rowdy finally let her up for air, kissing her lips once more, her nose and then her forehead.

Avery wavered on her feet. Stupidly, as if that explained his behavior, she said, "I'm, ah, the bartender."

Rowdy, blast him, grinned. "Yes, you are."

Amused, the nurses finished cleaning him up and asking their questions, then left when the doctor finally came in.

Avery needed to sit, but Rowdy still held her hand. On the off chance he actually needed her, she locked her knees, did some deep breathing to send oxygen to her muddled brain and reminded herself, over and over again, that regardless of how Rowdy acted, he was injured and needed to keep the lust in check.

His…and her own.

CHAPTER SEVEN

THE FEMALE DOCTOR, probably in her early forties, model thin and very attractive, wasn't amused that Rowdy kept Avery so close. Not as support, Avery soon realized, but so that he could play kissy face and act outrageous in a dozen other ways.

Was it a defense mechanism? Was he in more pain than he let on?

The doctor pulled on rubber gloves and took a seat behind him. For the longest time she was silent, until finally she murmured, "You've been in a lot of fights?"

Rowdy toyed with Avery's hair, twining one long tress around his finger. "A few."

Somehow, being injured didn't detract from Rowdy's devastating good looks, or his ability to seduce. His body... Well, she'd seen plenty of men shirtless, but none of them looked like him. His chest, his shoulders, those incredible abs...

Fortunately, the doctor didn't seem to notice or care. She, at least, was all business. After accessing the wound, she studied his broad back with a frown. "Some of these scars are pretty old."

Scars? Avery started to move around so she could see for herself.

Rowdy kept her from doing so. "Old, and unimportant." He glanced back at the doctor. "How soon can I get out of here?"

The doctor wasn't put off by his brusque question. "You'll need quite a few stitches. With luck, I won't leave you with another scar."

"Doesn't matter."

"To me," the doctor said, "it does."

In short order, he got a tetanus shot and something to numb the area.

While the doctor put in the stitches, Avery watched Rowdy's face.

"If you're waiting for me to faint," he told her, "you can relax. I don't feel a thing." He tried to draw her in for another kiss.

She tried to avoid it, but he didn't make it easy.

While glaring at Avery as if it were her fault, the doctor said, "This would be a whole lot easier if you'd sit still."

Freeing herself, Avery said in her sternest voice, *"Behave."*

And wonder of wonders, he did.

As the doctor finished up, she went over his instructions as she wrote them. "I don't want you to shower for at least twenty-four hours. When you do shower, make it quick so that you don't soak your stitches. You can remove the bandage and have someone—" here she stared at Avery again "—reapply the antibiotic ointment."

Rowdy gave Avery a wolfish smile.

The doctor pretended not to see it. "Keep it wrapped for three days, and then, if it's comfortable for you, you can leave the bandages off." She looked up. "I don't suppose you have a desk job?"

"He owns his own bar," Avery told her, more than

willing to brag on him. "He works every part of it. Lots of physical activity."

She sighed. "Well, I'd tell you to take it easy for at least a week, but somehow I don't think you'll listen." She came to stand in front of them, put her hands on her hips and said with strict insistence, "Three days."

"Three days of what?" Rowdy asked.

"Three days of you not overdoing it. No running, no heavy lifting." She tipped her head forward in an "are you listening to me" pose. "*Nothing* that will put stress on your injury. Understand?"

Rowdy didn't answer, so Avery did. "I'll see that he's more careful."

"Yes, well, I have a feeling he'll try to talk you around." The doctor raised a brow. "Don't let him."

Good grief, did she mean sex? Avery went hot. "I have no say over *that!*"

With a huff, Rowdy pulled her closer. "You have the most say."

The unspoken words *at least for right now* rang in her head.

The doctor saved Avery from having to reply. "You're going to be uncomfortable. I'm giving you a script for pain meds, but they might make you sleepy. No driving, no drinking and no operating heavy machinery when you take them."

"Not a problem."

"If you can get by with aspirin during the day, I'd recommend saving the stronger stuff for when you go to bed." She turned to Avery. "You'll be helping to care for him?"

Rowdy watched her, saying nothing, so Avery gave

a quick nod. "Yes." *And I'll do my best not to take advantage of his weakened condition.*

"The dressing needs to be changed every day until Friday, and more ointment applied. In about fourteen days, the stitches can come out. Either return here or go to your physician." She frowned at Rowdy. "Do not try taking them out yourself."

Deadpan, Rowdy said, "I'd have a little trouble reaching."

The doctor turned back to Avery again. "Let me know if you see any redness or swelling around the sutures."

"Thank you." Avery took her hand in sincere appreciation. "I'll see to it."

"Good luck with that." After one last glance at Rowdy, the doctor smiled. "As she said, behave."

One of nurses stepped back into the room and handed Rowdy a clean T-shirt. "I wish we had a coat to loan you, but this is the best I could do."

"Appreciate it."

The nursed started to help him pull it on, but Avery insinuated herself between them. "I can do it."

Rowdy smiled, and the disgruntled nurse retreated. When she was gone, Avery gently pulled the shirt over his head. He stuffed his arms through the sleeves without her assistance.

Knowing he was anxious to find out about Marcus, she said, "I'll call for a cab."

As they left the hospital, he was so silent, so withdrawn, she didn't know how to handle him. Not that anyone could ever fully handle Rowdy Yates, but boy, she wanted to try.

"Should we stop on the way to get your prescription filled?"

"I'll take care of it tomorrow." He opened the cab door for her, but surprised her by telling the cabbie his address, instead of hers.

She'd been almost certain that he'd insist on seeing her home first. Heart thumping a slow, anxious beat, Avery watched him settle in the seat beside her, this time far more comfortably now that he'd been tended to.

"You don't mind, do you?" He put an arm around her.

His constitution amazed her. "That we're going to your apartment first? Of course not. In fact, if it wouldn't put you in panic mode, I'd like to stay and make sure you're settled."

"Great." He stared out the window.

No signs of panic at all. Was he just too worried? What could she say to help? That Marcus would be okay? She wasn't sure. She knew nothing about the process of protecting a child from his own parents.

But she had a feeling that Rowdy had far too much knowledge of exactly that.

HE'D WAITED ENDLESSLY in the cold dark night, but Avery and the blond ruffian hadn't yet left the bar. Where the hell were they? Little by little he'd thought to learn Avery's schedule, but this he hadn't expected.

He was just about to give up when a cab slowed at the curb in front of him. The headlights hit his windshield, momentarily blinding him. Sinking lower in the driver's seat of his car, heart thumping in excitement, he waited. Sure enough, that was Avery and her swain that exited the cab.

Despite the dead cold of the night, lover boy didn't

wear a coat. A macho show to impress Avery? Idiot. If an abundance of cash and social influence hadn't done the trick, nothing would. Then again, maybe he'd looked at this wrong. Maybe she went for the brutish type.

But if so, she wouldn't have run off, right?

Whatever the girl wanted, it no longer mattered. The decision to return or stay gone would no longer be hers to make. He was done playing nice.

THEY'D JUST GOTTEN into Rowdy's apartment when his cell phone rang. He figured it'd be Pepper again, and he was all set to tease her about turning into a mother hen. But when he looked at the number, he saw it was Logan instead, and dread consumed him.

"Where is he?" he asked by way of answering the phone.

"If you mean Marcus, then I maybe have some good news."

Nausea burned his throat. So often "good news" from the system meant the kid got fucked over again. "Tell me." He urged Avery down the landing steps and over to the couch, indicating that she should take a seat.

"Well, after pulling a few strings, he's with Reese and Alice."

Luckily, the couch was right behind Rowdy because he dropped onto it. "With Reese?" He hadn't expected that. His thoughts reeled but his tension ebbed. "But… why?" *And how?*

"If she survives, the mother is still going to be in the hospital for a while. The dad was not only involved in an assault on you, but we also found a substantial amount of drugs in his truck, along with a small arsenal of un-registered weapons."

"No shit?"

"The truck door was open," Logan said with a shrug. "One of the unis spotted an assault rifle and more right there in plain sight. Guess they figured on gutting you and taking off."

"Didn't go quite as they planned then, did it?" *Take that, you miserable fucks.* "So how did Reese end up with Marcus?"

"In extreme situations, we—the police—can take a child into protective custody overnight on an emergency basis. After you left for the hospital, Reese called Alice to tell her what was going on. She came to the bar to help out, and…"

Rowdy could guess the rest. "She and Marcus hit it off." God bless Alice; no one could ever resist her and her gentle but curious way.

Maybe wounded souls recognized each other. Heaven knew, he and Alice had bonded right from the get-go.

"She got him to talk to her," Logan said. "Not much, but it was more of a connection than with anyone else. When the social worker started to take him away, he…"

Rowdy held his breath during Logan's five-second, emotional pause.

"…Reese said it was the damnedest thing. In that short time, Marcus had already gotten an attachment to her. He kicked up such a fuss that Alice was on her knees holding him and telling everyone else to back off."

Sounded like Alice. Eyes burning, throat going scratchy, Rowdy avoided Avery's astute gaze. "I'd put my money on Alice."

"Pretty much always, you know?"

"Yeah." Rowdy found his first smile. And once he

had it, the need to touch Avery, to connect with her, nearly overwhelmed him. He put an arm around her and hauled her into his side. "What else?"

"After Reese closed up the bar, he and Alice took Marcus home. Reese told me to tell you not to worry too much. He's sleeping on the couch to make sure the kid doesn't try to take off, and Cash is sticking close to him."

Cash, their crazy-ass rescue dog, had seen his fair share of abuse before living the cushy life with Alice and Reese.

For the moment, it was the best Rowdy could have hoped for. "The kid knows what happened to his dad?"

"That he and one of his thugs attacked you? That we arrested him? No. I don't think it was uncommon for that bastard to take off."

But it would be uncommon for a social worker to show up. Marcus probably had a clue, but Rowdy was grateful that it hadn't been spelled out to him. "Thanks."

"One of these days," Logan said, "you're going to believe that a few bad cops don't represent the whole of the profession."

He ignored that to say, "What happens now?"

"The social worker is getting hold of the family court judge. If that goes well, the judge might be able to place Marcus with Reese until we get everything else sorted out."

Breathing became more difficult. "Reese is up for that?"

"Yeah, you know Reese. He's muscle-bound, but at heart he's just a big softie."

Yeah, that was one truth Rowdy could swear to. Until recently, he wouldn't have believed they existed, but now… Reese and Logan both were proving to be really good men.

Next they'd have him believing in Santa Claus.

Logan didn't seem to think that much of Reese taking on a street rat. "There'll be an emergency custody hearing. Unless we find a suitable family member—"

Rowdy's heart stalled. "No." Other family would have to know what went on, and the fact that it continued meant they didn't care enough to put a stop to it.

And that, as far as Rowdy was concerned, made them unsuitable as guardians.

"Reese could have temporary custody."

How long that would last, Rowdy didn't know, but he wouldn't tip his hand by asking too many questions. Because when it was all said and done, Marcus wasn't going back there. He wouldn't let it happen, no matter what the court said.

As the numbness wore off, his back began to ache and his temples throbbed. "Can I see him tomorrow?"

"Sure. Alice would love that. Reese is taking the day off, so he'll be around, too."

Rowdy knew he owed Logan and Reese more than he could ever repay. But he'd try all the same.

Usually a debt would have eaten at him, but this time, it didn't. This time, weird as it seemed…it sort of lightened his burden.

Smiling as if she felt his relief, Avery leaned into him. Her silky hair teased over his skin. The side of her breast pressed against his ribs.

If he'd known being cut would get her to touch him this much, he'd have figured out a way to get sliced sooner. Maybe she thought he was too hurt to take advantage of her affection.

Even at the worst of times, Rowdy couldn't keep his hands out of her gorgeous red hair. He tunneled his fingers in close to her scalp and kissed her temple.

"Yeah, so, Logan…" What could he say? How did you thank a man for doing what you couldn't? "I… Damn, man…"

"Get some sleep," Logan told him. "We'll talk more tomorrow. But for tonight, know that your bar is fine and Marcus is safe." He disconnected the call.

Hand shaking, Rowdy put the phone on the coffee table and slowly turned to Avery.

"Marcus is okay?"

It felt like her beautiful blue eyes looked into his soul. "He's with Reese." She'd met both Reese and Logan when they came to help with the renovations to the bar. But she couldn't possibly know the lengths they'd go to to serve and protect.

Hell, until recently, Rowdy himself hadn't realized it. Before this, even with the evidence in front of him, he'd told himself that most people had ulterior motives. They were users. They cared only about their own comforts.

Now… Well, now he had to believe that some men had amazing ethics and a deep sense of responsibility.

"What will happen?" Avery asked.

Rowdy shook his head, but said, "I'll make sure he stays safe."

Her expression softened. "Rowdy—"

Driven by hunger and desperation, Rowdy drew her in for a kiss.

With a light laugh, she dodged him. "Not again. You need your rest—"

I need you. He didn't say it aloud, and he didn't let her retreat. "I'm not tired."

"Well, I am." She put her hand to the side of his face. "What do you think? It's awfully late. Would you mind if I stayed the rest of the night with you?"

Vivid sexual images sent his muscles contracting. Hell, he'd figured on having to persuade her. With every new breath, his back hurt more, and still, with her statement, his hunger stirred.

Avery went on in a rush. "To sleep, I mean."

Well, hell. He drew her closer, his gaze on her mouth. "We could sleep after."

"That's not what I'm talking about." Her face warmed. "I want to be here in case you need anything."

This time he couldn't keep the words contained. "I need you."

As if he hadn't spoken, she continued. "I promise not to become clingy. I won't drop in uninvited and I won't make any assumptions."

She should, Rowdy thought, *because God knew she'd probably be right.* He kissed her forehead, the bridge of her nose, that soft, sweet mouth. "You can stay," he whispered. "On one condition."

Her eyes narrowed in teasing threat. "I mean it, Rowdy. Sleep and only sleep."

He could handle that—with a fair trade-off. "All right. But you sleep with me. In my bed."

Her eyes widened again. "You," she said, sounding like a schoolteacher, "are not up for it."

"There's where you're wrong." Just hearing her talk about it had him throbbing.

Her gaze dropped to his lap, and she scuttled off the couch so fast that his fingers got snagged in her hair. "Rowdy Yates, you're… We can't possibly…"

"We could, but yeah, it'd be tricky." Besides, when

he finally got her under him, he didn't want to be handicapped by a zipper of fresh stitches with her still reeling from a night of upset.

Avery continued to stare at his lap.

"That's not helping, honey." Pushing to his feet, he readjusted in an effort to get more comfortable. "It's not a snake and it doesn't bite."

More color rushed into her face until she looked sunburned.

Enjoying her mix of innocence and sex appeal, Rowdy touched her chin and brought her gaze up to his. "What do you say, honey? Ready to crash for the night?"

"Well." She chewed her bottom lip and worked hard to keep her attention off the solid erection straining his jeans. "I could sleep on the couch..."

"I'll feel better if you stick close." He always enjoyed snuggling up with a warm female body. Granted, it usually only happened with sex, but tonight, with Avery, he'd make an exception.

She twisted her mouth, gave him a skeptical look. "You promise you only mean for sleep?"

"Unless you get frisky and go for more." He leaned down and nuzzled her ear. "I'm in a weakened state. You could totally take advantage of me."

She laughed—then slapped a hand over her mouth.

"What's funny?" Taking her shoulders, he eased her against him. She was a tiny little thing, and still they fit perfectly. "I have a feeling I'm missing an inside joke here."

Sighing, she leaned into him, her hands on his chest. "I probably shouldn't tell you."

"Tell me anyway." Hell, now he had to know.

Tipping her head back, she gifted him with a big smile. "At the hospital, I had that very thought." Her curious fingertips touched over his collarbone. "That I could molest you in your weakened condition."

God, he would love for her to try. "Maybe tomorrow you can give it a shot." In the meantime, he prompted her, saying, "Wanna help me get undressed?"

Her eyes flared.

Keeping his amusement under wraps, Rowdy said, "Reaching my shoes, peeling off my socks…" He shifted his shoulder and gave an exaggerated wince. "Pushing down my jeans. I'm not sure I can manage all that."

"Oh." She levered back and looked down the length of his body.

Yeah, the boner was still there. But then, with every pore of his being, he was aware of having Avery Mullins alone in his apartment. Talking about her taking off his jeans kept him primed.

She swallowed. "Of course." And then, big eyes looking up at him, "Should we go by your bed?"

"I was going to wash up first."

"Do you…ah, need help with that?"

Like he couldn't brush his teeth on his own? Rowdy didn't like playing weak, even if the aches and pains were starting to really settle in. Sooner or later, Avery would understand his strength. "I got it covered."

Relief took some of the starch from her shoulders.

"Why don't you go turn down the bed?"

"Okay." She walked with him across the room. "Do you have something I can sleep in?"

My arms. But maybe it was better not to tell her that yet. "What's wrong with your birthday suit?" He wouldn't get any sleep, but he'd sacrifice sleep for a nude female body any day.

Avery looked scandalized. "I can't sleep that way."

"Why not?"

"I just wouldn't." She paused by some of his exercise equipment, eyeing it with curiosity. "I've never slept naked, and I'm not going to start tonight."

Never? So his little bartender was modest? He'd get her over that, but obviously not tonight. Going to a dresser, Rowdy dug out a plain white T-shirt. If she wore only her panties under it, it'd be the next best thing to naked. "Will this work?"

She waffled. "Don't you have something darker?"

"You won't let me have any fun." He found a black T-shirt and offered it to her. "Better?"

She held it up in front of her, saw it'd fall to her knees, and nodded. "Yes, thank you." She turned to the weights on the floor, then indicated the chin-up bar and heavy bag hung from the rafters. "This is your stuff?"

"Yeah." He needed those aspirin to kick in, the sooner the better. "When I can't sleep and there isn't a willing woman around to help me blow off some energy, I work out."

Putting the T-shirt on his bed, she bent to lift one weight—and got it only about six inches off the floor. "Does it help?"

Not as much as fucking. "Sometimes, sure."

She gave up on the weight and strode over to the heavy bag. With a slight push, she got it swaying. "You have trouble sleeping?"

"Doesn't everyone?"

"Sometimes I guess."

For most of his life, he'd been an insomniac. As a

kid, he'd stayed awake listening for trouble—meaning his folks. Later, after they'd died, he'd been vigilant for Pepper.

The idea of Avery not sleeping bothered him. "What keeps you awake?"

"Too much caffeine, scary movies and worrying about stuff. Same as most people." Smiling, she sat on the side of his bed. "You only have a full-size bed."

"So?" If he'd known she was staying over, he'd have moved in a twin mattress real quick.

"I don't want to interrupt your sleep tonight."

He loved interruptions because usually if he fell into a sound sleep, nightmares plagued him.

That is, if you could call memories nightmares.

"Like I said, I'm an insomniac so don't worry about it." He went to the bathroom door. "You'll have about two minutes to change in private if you want."

Seated on the side of his bed, her knees together, her fiery hair trailing over her shoulders, she looked like living, breathing temptation. "Okay, thanks."

Rowdy closed the door behind him, and only then allowed himself to scowl in discomfort. Every movement made his stitches pull, but he also felt other aches and pains. His knuckles were bruised, and one knee was stiff as if maybe swollen. Probably from landing on the damned gravel.

He brushed his teeth, washed his face, then gave quick thought to shaving. If Avery was saying yes instead of no, maybe he would. But since she insisted on sleep only, he decided it wasn't worth the effort.

He stepped out, and there she stood beside the turned-down bed, her hair freshly brushed, her clothes gone in place of his soft cotton T-shirt. He'd known it would swim on her, but he hadn't counted on the enticing way it draped over her every curve, or how the wide neck exposed one shoulder.

Or how possessive he felt seeing her in it.

He could almost hate that shirt for being the only thing between him and the woman who was fast becoming an obsession.

Avery nervously waited for him to say something, but every thought he had was sure to send her running. Very slowly, knowing full well she could see his feelings on his face, he eased closer.

"Rowdy?"

She had beautiful legs, slim but shapely, silky and smooth. Her toes curled as he continued to stare at her. She crossed her forearms over her middle, shifting her stance and inadvertently pulling the material tighter over the swells of her breasts.

He'd had women coming under him and not felt as hot as he did seeing the shape of Avery's body under black cotton.

"You're making me feel naked."

Close enough now to kiss her, he bent his head and nuzzled the fragrant skin of her neck, that supersexy red hair. "One touch, okay?"

"I… What?" Even as she spoke her confusion, she tipped her head, giving him access to continue.

He put his hands at her waist, loving the feel of her beneath the giving cotton. "Just one touch, babe," he murmured. "Tell me it's okay." His fingers opened and closed, relishing the narrowness of her waist, the slight flare at the top of her hips. His mouth brushed her ear. "Just one. Then we can turn in."

She drew in a shuddering breath—and nodded.

To make the most of it, Rowdy caressed both hands over her hips and down to her full, supple ass. A groan caught in his throat. He took a moment to enjoy how his large hands completely covered each cheek, then used his double-handed hold on her to lift her up to her tiptoes, bringing her in close, pelvis to pelvis.

While lust singed him, she gasped in worry and her hands grabbed for his shoulders. "Rowdy, your back."

All he could feel at the moment was the throbbing in his cock. He'd never wanted a woman so much. Sex was great, always, but touching Avery like this was better, so good that it felt like a drug.

He lifted her higher so he could kiss the tender flesh where the neckline of the T-shirt exposed her shoulder.

"Rowdy, *please*." She tucked her face into his shoulder, her voice rough with concern. "You're going to hurt yourself."

It wasn't easy, but Rowdy got himself under control. He wanted Avery's need as sharp as his own, not clouded by worry.

Carefully, he lowered her feet back to the floor. "You have an amazing ass," he said with feeling.

Dropping her forehead to his sternum, she gave a husky laugh. Her long hair hid her face from him. He lifted it back over her shoulders.

Damn, but he loved her hair. One of these days it'd be spread out over his pillow while he sank into her.

He shuddered with the thought.

"You're okay?" Avery let her fingers hover over the waistband of his jeans.

"Better than okay," he promised her, and kissed the top of her head.

Without looking at him, she whispered, "Should I help you undress now?"

He choked back a groan. "Might be better if you give me a minute."

"Okay." She pressed back. "I need to wash up anyway."

"Make yourself at home." The words left his mouth, and he froze. Jesus, he couldn't believe he'd just said that, or that he really wanted her to be at ease.

Her mouth twitched. "You look like that hurt more than the knife wound."

Emotional shit always hurt worse, and Avery made him feel way too much.

Rowdy accepted that it would be a torturous night. "Use anything you need."

"You're sure?" Proving she had a wickedly teasing nature, she said, "You're already so beat-up, I don't want to push you over the edge by getting too comfortable."

"I'm not beat-up, smart-ass. The bastard just got in one lucky cut." He kissed her to prove he was fine, then turned her and gave her a light swat on that spectacular ass. "Now stop harassing me and go get ready."

Ignoring her snicker, Rowdy watched her go, fascinated by the way her body moved under his T-shirt. *Who knew a damned tent of a shirt could be so erotic?* The second Avery closed the bathroom door, self-preservation kicked in. He made quick work of double-checking the locks on the front door before turning out all the lights except for the one on the nightstand.

Sinking down to sit on the edge of the bed, in more pain than he wanted to admit to, Rowdy worked off his shoes and socks. Even if having Avery so close wouldn't keep him awake and on the edge of lust, the deepening pain would make sleep impossible.

When he heard the water shut off in the bathroom, he stood and opened the snap on his jeans, then eased the zipper down over his boner.

Avery emerged. Damp tendrils of hair clung to her forehead and flushed cheeks.

Looking dewy and fresh and so sexy that he burned with need, she padded barefoot across the room to him. "What are you doing?" Her breath smelled minty, and he detected the smell of his soap on her skin. "You'll hurt yourself."

"By unzipping my jeans? Get real." One day soon, he'd make sure she understood his strength. "Did you use my toothbrush?"

Brushing his hands away, she said, "Corner of a washcloth."

Rowdy stared at the crooked part in her hair. "I wouldn't have minded." Would she?

"Maybe in the morning, then. Thanks."

Apparently not. And why the hell did that seem so intimate?

"So." She stared at the waistband of his jeans. "Let's get you undressed."

Ah, hell, if only the rest of his body felt as energetic as his dick. "This might be a bad idea..."

She glanced up at him, her face clean of makeup, the blue of her eyes looking deeper in the low light, her lashes leaving shadows on her smooth cheeks. "I'll be careful, Rowdy, I promise."

That wasn't what worried him.

"Relax." With that said, she hooked both hands in his waistband and tugged down his jeans—which brought her face so close that he imagined he could feel her breath through his boxers.

Pretending she didn't see his erection, she went to a knee and finished dragging the denim down to his ankles. "Step out."

What the hell. If she could take it, so could he. He put a hand on the top of her head and did as told.

Avery folded the jeans. "You can sit down on the side of the bed so I can get your shirt off."

Better if she'd just get *him* off. It wouldn't take much. Seeing her on her knees had almost done it.

Wearing only the snug boxers and a borrowed T-shirt, Rowdy sat.

After putting his jeans on the dresser, Avery climbed onto the bed behind him. He *felt* her there, so close and so utterly still.

Without warning, her fingers gently tunneled into his hair. "Is your sister as blond as you?"

The mesmerizing way she touched him wasn't carnal, and maybe that's why it affected him so strongly. It felt like…affection.

He wasn't used to it.

He knotted his hands in the blankets. "Pepper's hair is lighter, and a hell of a lot longer."

"Is it as thick as yours? As wavy?"

He could feel her breath on the back of his neck. "Hell, I don't know." He twisted to look at her over his shoulder. "What are you doing?"

When she shrugged, the neckline of the shirt slid down. Not far enough for him to see her breast but close enough that his heart almost punched out of his chest.

He did not react this way to women, damn it.

Avery smoothed down his hair and said on a sigh,

"You're pretty irresistible, that's all." Leaning forward, she got hold of the hem of the shirt. "I'm going to be really careful. Let me lift up the shirt and then we can work each arm out, okay?"

It took an excruciating amount of time for Avery to do what he could have accomplished in five seconds. Never in his life would he have allowed a woman to "handle him," but it was kind of nice the way Avery did it. Once freed, she tossed the shirt to the dresser to join the jeans.

A moment later, she breathed, "Oh, Rowdy."

He imagined a lot of bruising had formed around the cut. "It's okay, honey."

Her fingertips moved lightly over his skin. "No, it's not." In a butterfly touch, she brushed her lips to one spot, then another.

Rowdy felt each small kiss in his dick. In a gravelly rumble, he promised, "Before long, it'll be healed up and forgotten."

Silence dragged out as she touched him again, on his shoulder, lower on his back. "Like the rest of these?"

Tension wound through his spine, making him stiff all over.

Her tone far too sad, Avery said, "Now I know what the doctor meant."

Shit. *Scars.* Moving away from her hands and that damn unnerving empathy, Rowdy stood and turned so all she saw was his chest.

And his boner beneath the boxers. He could handle her seeing that, but he couldn't handle her seeing any vulnerability.

"You ready to turn in?" He pulled the blankets back

farther and eased down to his side. He hated that he had to move so slowly, but even a wiggle of his toe was felt in his back.

"Yes." Still on her knees, she drew in a deep breath. "I'm ready." In a unique but innocent sort of torture, she stretched beyond him, her body over his as she turned out the lamp. She settled back in front of him, resting on one elbow.

Moonlight shone through the high windows, leaving her body outlined in a mellow glow, turning the fall of her hair into a muted fire.

Could a woman be more physically appealing?

"What would be most comfortable for you?" Before he could answer, Avery turned, giving him her back, then scooted closer. "Will this work?"

Hell, yeah. That worked just fine. He put an arm around her and snuggled her in, his hand open on her belly, his hips nestled up against her ass. "Perfect."

"Rowdy." He heard her smile when she chastised him. "You won't be able to sleep with me this close."

"Told you I'm an insomniac, so I'm used to not sleeping. But for once I won't mind being awake."

She hesitated before saying, "Okay, then," and wiggled to get more comfortable.

Excruciating.

Laying a hand over his, she let out a long yawn and whispered, "Good night, Rowdy."

It would be a long night, but just as well that he wouldn't sleep. He didn't want to waste a single second of having her like this, with him, in his apartment, in his bed and in his arms.

Maybe it was the turmoil of the day, the dredging

up of old hurts and twisted memories, but damn it, he even considered having her in his life…for more than a one-night stand.

WHEN THE LIGHT went out, he decided to give up his vigil for the night. The big windows should have afforded a decent view, and despite himself, he'd anticipated playing voyeur. But the bed wasn't positioned correctly, so while he could occasionally see a body move past, he hadn't seen enough to make it worth the danger in the area.

He felt cheated, damn it.

Maybe once he had Avery back where she belonged, he'd think about the whole voyeur fetish again. For all his trouble, he deserved that—and more.

CHAPTER EIGHT

AVERY FELT THE drowsiness pull at her, but she didn't quite tumble into slumber. Without even realizing it, she stroked her fingertips over the back of Rowdy's hand that rested on her stomach. Fingers opened, he covered her from hip bone to hip bone.

Such a large man, so solid and strong, and so amazing.

What he'd done today, the compassion he'd felt for Marcus, the outrage he'd shown against abuse...

She closed her eyes, seeing again those awful scars on his back. A small burn, round like a cigarette. A square cut, like that from a belt buckle.

Outrage blurred her vision, made her eyes glisten and tried to close her throat. If she could, she'd find his parents and destroy them. Unfortunately, they'd escaped any real retribution by dying a quick death in a car wreck.

Angst squeezed her heart until she had to fight the urge to turn to Rowdy, to hold him close and cry for him since he would never cry for himself.

Little by little, she better understood him and how he ticked. Sex, as he'd said, was quick and easy comfort.

But, God, she wanted to be more than that to him. She wanted to somehow make his life better. Not that Rowdy couldn't manage that on his own. Single-handedly, he'd protected his sister, built a safe life for them both and once his sister's future was secured, he'd taken over a profligate business and made it not only reputable, but profitable and popular, as well.

She thought of his inventive solution to tone down Ella's over-the-top sensual wardrobe, how he always lent a hand to Jones, the cook.

How he made his desire for her plain without ever trying to force the issue. He was only at his pushiest when trying to protect her. Even as his breathing evened into sleep, he kept her close.

Slowly, she turned to her back. Rowdy's hand just naturally slid to her hip. He made a small sound, shifted a little and sank back into oblivion.

It appeared exhaustion had finally claimed him. She was so glad. His warm breath and the weight of his muscled arm crossing her body tried to lull her to sleep, too, but her mind continued to churn. With everything that had happened, she'd almost forgotten about the phone call.

Now the possible ramifications of it came crashing back over her. She had reason to worry.

But no way would she burden Rowdy with her problems, not when he'd already spent his life dealing with so much. Maybe she could talk to Logan or Reese without Rowdy knowing.

She turned her head to look at him. So sinfully gorgeous, he took her breath away. Even dead to the world, he didn't look entirely relaxed.

Was Fisher Holloway after her? Again?

She couldn't make any other assumption, not after the way their last confrontation had ended—a circumstance that had sent her, literally, packing. She'd been away from home ever since. At first, she'd missed her mother, her old life, the convenience of financial security.

Now… Well, she still missed her mom sometimes, but she'd resigned herself to how their relationship had changed. She'd gotten used to everything else and she didn't really want to return. Ever.

An hour later, Rowdy made a low sound that was part anger, part agony. Alarmed, Avery touched his shoulder hoping to soothe him. His breathing came faster; he shifted again. Was it his back? Should she wake him for more aspirin?

She had just started to sit up when suddenly he clutched at her, dragging her tight to his chest in a hold filled with desperation.

Making shushing sounds, Avery kissed his throat, his chest and shoulder.

He eased, his grip relaxing as he again faded away.

"I'm here," she whispered, and because she couldn't help herself, she kissed his throat again. His weakness—something he'd hide if he was awake—drew her in. She felt so many things: emotionally protective of the boy he'd once been, devastated that he still suffered nightmares, awed by his strength of character and, against all odds, the man he'd become.

She also felt a little turned on.

What woman wouldn't be? Rowdy wasn't hard now, but they faced each other in bed, as close as two people could be without actual intercourse, so her awareness of him—all of him—rose to a keen level. He'd hugged her up to his lightly furred chest so that with every breath his delicious scent filled her head. One of his thighs now rested between hers, pinning her in place, yet somehow making her feel cherished instead of trapped.

Fisher was the last man to touch her like that, and her reaction hadn't been the same.

But then, that time with Fisher hadn't been by choice.

Physically, Fisher Holloway was attractive enough. Just shy of six feet, thick brown hair, shrewd blue eyes, built like an athlete... The memory of his heavy body, his unyielding strength, sent a shudder through her.

She tucked her face closer to Rowdy's chest.

To those who knew Fisher, he was a thirty-four-year-old CEO of a very successful company. A philanthropist who supported many charities. A financial guru generous with those he employed. Her stepfather respected him; her mother adored him. They ran in the same circles, often attending the same affairs.

Everyone thought he'd make the ideal husband for Avery.

Everyone except Avery herself. Whenever they were alone, Fisher was too condescending: ordering her food, critiquing her wardrobe, disdaining her friends.

Her stepfather said he was invested in her well-being.

Her mother said he was attentive to her needs.

Avery hadn't liked it one bit. During a fund-raiser, when Fisher persisted in pursuing her, she'd made her disinterest clear.

God, he'd been so cunning, setting her up for the greatest fall of her life...

She jumped when Rowdy's hand went to her backside, squeezing for a minute before going limp again. Wow, even in his sleep he stayed revved up. Or was he playing possum?

Avery no sooner had the thought than Rowdy started

a soft snore. She smiled, as much at herself as at the sound he made.

Looked like she'd be the one with insomnia that night. But she didn't mind. It gave her more time to enjoy Rowdy without the risk of him realizing the truth—that she'd already gone head over heels for him.

If he knew she'd started falling in love with him almost from the start, what would he do?

Given his track record with women, she didn't want to find out.

ROWDY WOKE DISORIENTED, his brain sluggish, his limbs utterly lax. Sunlight spilled through the tall wall of windows, making him squint. It took him a second to realize that he'd slept like the dead.

Jesus, he never passed out like that. All kinds of shit could have happened without him knowing it. A little alarmed, he rose up on an elbow. The discomfort in his back would have taken precedence—except that he found Avery right there, her head propped on a fist, her tumbled red hair spilling all over the bed, her blue eyes lazy with interest as she watched him.

She said, all husky and sexual-like, "Good morning."

That particular expression of hers was too damn soft, almost dreamy. "Why are you smiling like that?"

Her gaze went to his mouth, then back up to his eyes. "Because I realized last night I'm a pervert."

Whoa. Rowdy made a show of lifting the sheet and looking down at himself.

"What are you doing?"

"Checking that my boxers are still in place."

Her teasing laugh went over him like a slow lick.

"Did you think I took advantage of you without you waking?"

"I was half hoping." Something was different this morning. While he'd been dead to the world, she'd come to some conclusions. Now if only he could keep that progress going when awake. "Obviously you didn't have your way with me, so what perverted things did you do?"

"I checked out your body."

"You've done that before, babe. I know because I've seen you doing it."

"This time, I didn't hurry or try to be subtle. I just soaked up the breathtaking sight of you."

Breathtaking? He tried not to feel self-conscious with the over-the-top compliment. "Anytime you want a re-peat showing, let me know."

"I also enjoyed hearing you snore."

He snorted. "I don't."

She leaned in. "You do." She kissed his chin. "And it was sexy."

Had he awakened into a new dimension? Was he still dreaming? Whatever it was, he liked it, so he nodded and agreed, "That is a little perverted."

The way she smiled was something he hadn't seen from her before. "I loved watching you sleep." She smoothed his hair off his brow, her touch a little too mothering for comfort. "I'm glad you could."

He frowned. "I never sleep."

"Well, you did last night."

And she planned to take credit for that? Maybe she had reason. He only just now realized that he had one leg between her soft, slender thighs, their pelvises aligned.

He needed to clear out the cobwebs, and fast.

With a hand at her waist to keep her right there, he gave in to suspicion. "You stayed here?" He remembered getting comfortable, being turned on…then nothing after that. "All night?"

"Yes." Her hand went from his hair to the side of his neck, then down over his chest. "Snuggled close."

And he'd missed it. *Damn it.*

"You look cross." Her heavy eyes shied away. "Did I overstay my welcome?"

"No." *I'm glad you're here.* He looked beyond her at the clock. Still early, thank God. "We have a lot to talk about today."

"Marcus."

Rowdy nodded, but he didn't go there just yet. His brain was, for a change, blessedly relaxed. He wanted to keep it that way for a while longer. "And Cannon, your car, that phone call."

Her gaze shot up to his. She withdrew her hand, but said only, "What about Cannon?"

Evasive? Now what was that about? For the moment, Rowdy chose to play along. "Depending on how things went last night, he might be staying on."

"To do what?"

"We'll have to see, won't we?" He deliberately included her in the decision.

As he'd hoped, she relaxed again. "So what are you thinking?"

It was kind of nice, lying in bed in the morning and talking with Avery. It'd be better if she lost the shirt and panties, and if he knew this was a prelude to sex, but even so, he still enjoyed it.

Like a good night's sleep, enjoying morning-after

banter was not the norm. "Among other things, maybe he could give you a break every so often."

"You give me breaks."

Without makeup, her face bathed in harsh sunlight, she still looked so damned pretty that he had to fight the urge to reach for her. "I want to spend some time with you when we both aren't on the clock."

"Oh." Her tentative smile could melt a man. "I'd like that, too."

No woman had a right to be so appealing first thing in the morning. Even her tangled hair looked sexy as hell. "When you're working, Cannon could help out in other ways."

"You know I don't want a barback."

She'd just have to get over that. "Yesterday, seeing you manhandled by that—"

"He didn't hurt me," she rushed to say.

Rowdy lifted her wrist, looking at a small bruise that had been left behind. He kissed the mark, then kept her hand close. "Thank God Ella had the good sense to come and get me." Even if he hadn't been personally interested in her, as his employee, Rowdy was accountable for her safety. "I'll feel better knowing a bouncer is nearby, someone I trust to defend you in case I'm not close enough to protect you myself."

"I don't want to be another of your many responsibilities."

She already felt like the most important one. "I'm the boss, so I get to make the rules." To soften that, he added, "Look at it this way. If Cannon works out, he can do the heavy lifting, fetch stuff when you need it, even answer the phone so you don't have to."

At the mention of the phone, her gaze darted away again. "I guess that would be nice."

Ah, so it was the phone call that made her jumpy. Rowdy wasn't dense; he studied her averted face, made note of her new tension and decided to ease into things. "Yesterday, you said you drove to work."

"Yes."

"Where was your car?"

"In the side lot." She tipped her head. "Don't you want some aspirin? Maybe some coffee, too?"

"In a minute." If she hoped to distract him, she'd do better by taking off the T-shirt. "So what do you drive?"

Her nose wrinkled. "We really need to talk about this?"

"Is there a reason we shouldn't?"

"I guess not." Then half under her breath, she mumbled, "Infiniti."

"Yeah?" Nice car. Rowdy watched her. "What kind?"

Lower still, she said, "G37 convertible." She tacked on, "It's two years old."

He had to muffle a laugh. "That old, huh?" To him that'd still be a new car. She'd told him she came from money. Now Rowdy wanted to know why it embarrassed her. "What color?"

Dropping to her back, she sighed. "Cherry red."

"Sounds sweet."

"Yeah." She turned her head to face him. "I haven't driven it in a while, but I, um, decided you were right, that walking home from the bus stop might not be… Well, it was dumb, I guess."

And somehow he just knew this all tied in together. "You can show it to me later before we start work. And speaking of work—I meant to ask you about that phone call you got last night." He said it casually while taking in every nuance of her expression. "Just a customer?"

If she said yes, he'd know she was lying. And then what? He wanted her to trust him—and he wanted to be able to trust in return.

He literally saw her gird herself. "It was no one."

"No one important, you mean?"

"I mean I answered, but there wasn't anyone there." Keeping the sheet tucked in around her bare legs, she sat up. "How is your back? Do you need help into the bathroom?"

No way would he let her start babying him. He believed her about the call, but she had a suspicion about who it might've been. He wanted to know it all.

Rowdy reached for her—and a knock sounded on his door.

They both went still.

"Company?" she whispered.

"Hell, I don't know." Very few people knew he lived here. "A few of the women in the building have been coming by to borrow stuff. Could be one of them."

Avery's shoulders bunched up. "Seriously?"

With an effort, he sat up, too. Jesus, the skin of his back pulled and burned and his muscles tried to cramp. He rubbed his bristly jaw and thought how nice a hot shower would feel—especially if he could get Avery to join him.

The knock sounded again.

"I thought you said no other women had been here?"

"They haven't." He watched her leave the bed and mourned the lost moment. "I don't let them past the door."

As she shoved her legs into her jeans, she said with suggested menace, "Want me to get it for you?"

If she wanted to scare off his neighbors, well, hey, it'd give her something to do besides pamper him. "Sure, thanks. Just tell whoever it is to get lost."

"What if it's something important?" She lifted the hem of the big T-shirt long enough to fasten the snap on her jeans.

That small peek of her belly made him reconsider the idea of getting pampered. Maybe he could say he needed help in the shower, which, judging how he felt right now, wouldn't be a stretch. "If it's Reese or Logan, let him in." One of them could have word on Marcus.

"And if it's one of your pushy neighbors?"

He grinned at her challenge. "Tell her whatever you want."

"Fine. I will." Barefoot, the T-shirt swallowing her small frame, Avery marched across the floor and up to the landing. She opened the locks and pulled the door just wide enough to say, "Hello."

Rowdy sat on the side of the bed and gingerly flexed his shoulders. Yeah, he needed something, but he didn't want any mind-blurring pain meds like what the doc had prescribed. Now that he had Avery hanging around, he had to stay on his toes.

He didn't hear the voice of the visitor, but he assumed it was a woman when Avery said, "Yes, he lives here, but he's not up to visiting."

Pushing to his feet, Rowdy tried to stay quiet until Avery got rid of the unwanted guest. He pulled the sheet around his waist and finger combed his hair away from his face.

Avery said, "I'm his bartender, that's who I am."

He smiled at her bossy tone. Cute. On another woman he might not have thought so, but on Avery, he liked this take-charge persona.

Hell, he liked everything about her.

Barring the door, Avery nodded and replied to something he couldn't hear. "As a matter of fact, I *do* speak for him. He specifically told me to—"

She ended on a gasp when the door swung open hard and Pepper came shoving her way through.

Oh, shit.

"Rowdy!"

Avery had the good sense to get out of his sister's way when she forged down the steps and into the living area.

Rowdy took one look at her face and started forward, the aching in his back forgotten. "What's the matter? What's wrong?"

Long blond hair hanging free, her eyes red, Pepper spotted him and strode forward. "You were hurt, that's what!" She opened her arms.

He braced for her impact, but Avery said, *"His back."*

Catching herself, Pepper drew up short.

Instead of slamming into him headlong, she ducked around behind him, then gasped so loud he felt it on the back of his neck.

"Oh, my God." Her hands muffled the appalled words.

"It's not that bad."

She stopped him from turning. "Rowdy?" Her fingertips touched his shoulder near a very old scar, and almost stopped his heart.

Locking eyes with Avery, he jerked the sheet up and over his shoulders so Pepper couldn't see a thing. For most of their lives, he'd managed to insulate Pepper from the worst of his parents' anger. She didn't know half of what they'd done—and he very much wanted it to stay at that way.

AVERY'S LIPS PARTED as if she suddenly understood. She shot forward. "I'm so sorry. I didn't realize you were his sister."

Ignoring her, Pepper tugged at the sheet. "I stayed away as long as I could, but God, Rowdy, it wasn't easy."

"Stop that." Shrugging the sheet into place, Rowdy stepped away and turned to tower over her. "It's fine, kiddo. Quit fussing."

Avery gave an exaggerated roll of her eyes, no doubt for Pepper's benefit. "He really does rebel against any coddling at all." She leaned in as if confiding a secret. "He even refused to stop last night to get his prescribed meds. We came straight back here."

Pepper looked more than a little devastated, and definitely confused. "Who are you, again?"

In stepped Logan. "I already told you—she's the bartender." He lifted a big bag of pastries in one hand, a cup holder with four large coffees in the other and used his foot to nudge the door shut. "We stopped for breakfast, but Pepper refused to wait with me while I parked." His gaze slid over to Avery. "Sleep well?"

"Shut up, Logan." Rowdy wanted a shower, food and Avery—not necessarily in that order. He did not want a social call. But never would he do anything to hurt his sister; not on purpose, anyway.

Hands on her hips, Pepper scrutinized Avery. "I've never seen her at the bar."

"You," Rowdy said, "haven't been in during hours of operation."

"You don't want me there!"

"Pepper." Logan strode the rest of the way into the room. "The bar is great, but it's not a place for you to go alone. If you want, we'll both go visit soon."

"I was there when all the work was being done."

"So was I," Avery said. "I pitched in where I could, but we must have missed each other."

"Maybe," Pepper conceded, her tone filled with suspicion.

Rowdy held the sheet with one hand and rubbed the back of his neck with the other. The movement pulled at his back, reminding him just how wretched yesterday had been. "Why don't you guys go grab a seat at the table? We just woke up, so give us a minute."

Pepper opened her mouth, but Logan stepped in front of her. "Take your time." He nudged Pepper along toward the kitchen area, saying sotto voce, "Give the guy a break, honey."

Yeah, more and more each day Rowdy appreciated his new brother-in-law.

"Come on." He snagged Avery's hand and tugged her with him right into the bathroom.

Scandalized, she gasped, "What are you doing?"

"This." He closed the door, backed her into it and kissed her before she could protest. And damn, she tasted good, a hell of a sight better than coffee or pastries.

With a little persuasion, her mouth opened under his. When he prodded gently with his tongue, she reciprocated, and things went steamy hot in a heartbeat.

She curled her hands over his shoulders, pressed closer and let him have his way—for about thirty seconds.

Easing away, she licked her lips. "Mmm. Thank you."

"You're welcome."

Lashes lifting, she stared up at him. "Your sister and brother-in-law are *really* close by."

"Believe me, I know." He nuzzled her neck. "Want to shower with me anyway?"

"Absolutely not." She sucked in a big, fortifying breath, then sidled out of his hold and went to his medicine cabinet to get out the aspirin. "Take these." Her hand trembled as she held the pills out to him.

He tossed them back and then bent to the sink to drink straight from the faucet.

"Now step out and give me two minutes. After that I'll take off the bandages so you can grab a quick shower, *quick* being the operative word."

Insane, but he even liked seeing her this way, trembling with need but still refusing him. "Afraid I'll leave you alone with Pepper and Logan?"

"Not at all. They both seem really nice." She smoothed a hand over his chest, down to his ribs and down farther to his abs. After a soft groan, she dropped her hand. "I'm afraid you'll go against doctor's orders and linger too long."

He let the sheet drop. "Tell you what, honey. I'll shower at the speed of light if you'll promise me something."

She didn't even try to keep her attention on his face. "What's that?"

"Soon as I get doctor's clearance, you'll shower with me, and we'll both linger."

She shocked the hell out of him when she cupped a hand under his testicles, caressed him once, then trailed the backs of her fingers up the length of his instant boner.

While he stood there stunned silent and on fire, she turned the doorknob and gave a tug.

Rowdy moved forward. He tried to figure out what to say, but nothing witty came to mind.

"I need two minutes, remember?"

Ah, hell. He hoped his sister and Logan were in the damn kitchen because he sported major wood.

As he started out, Avery handed him the sheet, smiled up at him and whispered, "I promise."

Rowdy found himself staring at a closed door, a lop-sided grin on his face. She'd as good as said they'd be having sex, and soon. Diabolical. And a serious turn-on.

Might as well use the two minutes to get together some clothes—and work on calming down the old John Henry. He'd just returned to the bathroom door with clean boxers and jeans when Avery stepped out.

She made sure they were alone. "Since you said it was okay, I did use your toothbrush. Thank you."

Her whisper amused him. He put his forehead to hers. "I don't care if they hear us."

"I do." She gave him a quick kiss, then led him in, turned him and carefully removed the bandages from his back. She took forever doing it, saying repeatedly, "I'm sorry if I'm hurting you."

And he repeatedly assured her, "You're not."

When she finished, she brushed her cool fingertips over his skin. He heard her swallow, and her barely audible whisper when she said, "You could have been killed."

"Not a chance. Not by those two yahoos."

"Being cocky does not make you invincible." She came around to the front of him, tears in her eyes.

"Don't do that, babe. You've held it together this long. If you start now, it'll push Pepper right over the edge and she'll be out on her damned white horse, trying to avenge me."

As he'd hoped, she smiled and wiped at her eyes. "No crying, I promise. It's awkward enough knowing what they're thinking without me going typically female."

He snorted. "Trust me, you don't have a clue what either of them are thinking, so don't worry about it." He lifted her chin and kissed her. "Ten minutes tops. Now go make nice with my sister. If she growls at you, understand that she's worried and out of sorts."

Nodding agreement, Avery said, "And she loves you very much."

"That, too." The mention of Pepper's love reminded him. "I'd prefer that you not say anything to her about..." How should he mention something that he didn't want to discuss with Avery, either?

The tears welled in her eyes again, but she nodded with grave sincerity. "Your old scars, I know. You've protected her this long, so of course I won't say a word." She smoothed her hair and straightened the dark T-shirt she still wore. "How do I look?"

She looked like *his,* like she belonged with him. Not just today, but maybe... Rowdy shook his head, disturbed that he kept thinking about forever-type commitments. He was honest enough with himself to know he was out of his element. Way the hell out.

He wanted to lighten the mood with a joke, maybe say, *You look totally fuckable,* because, hey, she really did.

But he couldn't be that mocking. Not to Avery.

"You look like a fantasy, honey." *My fantasy.* He finally admitted the truth, saying, "I'm glad you're here."

Before he got any sappier, Rowdy closed the door. Avery Mullins was the whole package.

And for the first time in his life, he was starting to want it all.

CHAPTER NINE

"So." As IF she expected her to sprout horns at any second, Pepper kept a sharp eye on Avery. "He kept you?"

Avery choked on her coffee.

Logan rolled his eyes. "She's not a stray dog, Pepper. I told you—she works for him."

"She works here, in Rowdy's new apartment, in Rowdy's shirt? Overnight?"

Avery's smile started to feel strained. "It was late when we got back from the hospital."

Pepper narrowed her eyes. "You say you're the bartender?"

"Yes." After dabbing her mouth with a napkin, Avery decided to level with Rowdy's sister. "Believe me, I'm as amazed as you are that I'm still here. Rowdy said I'm the first woman to see the place." She waved a hand, as nonchalant as she could manage. "Something about hordes of women hounding him for unrivaled sex if they knew where to find him."

Logan took a turn at choking.

Pepper wasn't amused.

"It's probably not far from the truth." Avery took another, deeper drink of her coffee. She needed the caffeine kick to survive Pepper's suspicious nature. What did she think? That Avery would somehow work her wiles on Rowdy? Fat chance. She was pretty sure she didn't have wiles. "He does draw attention from the ladies. I think he fills every available minute with sex."

Logan looked around, likely wishing Rowdy would hurry it up.

Pepper sat back in her seat. "So if you know that, if you really understand my brother that well—"

Good grief, even his sister knew it to be true!

"—then should I assume that you also—"

"Make no assumptions. That's always the safest bet." If Pepper was even a smidge as protective of Rowdy as he was of her, then Avery knew she'd want to chase away the users. "The cut on his back, while not life-threatening or anything, did require some stitches." Like a million or so. "Rowdy will deny it, just because he's that way, but sex is out of the question for right now."

Logan began to whistle.

Both women ignored him. "And the bandages need to be changed each day." Avery gave a credible shrug. "Rowdy can't very well reach his own back, now can he?"

"So you're just here playing Florence Nightingale?"

Wrinkling her nose, Avery leaned in to whisper, "I'm here because I care about him, but if you tell him that, he'll probably boot me to the curb. I'm sure I don't have to tell you that he's an incredible boss, but an even more incredible man."

"Hmm." One brow going high, Pepper said, "You're more honest than I expected."

"I can't lie to your brother. I figured fudging the truth with you wouldn't be any easier."

Logan laughed. "Be forewarned—they're more alike than you can imagine."

"You're saying she's incredible?"

"Well…" Caught, Logan took the easy route and agreed. "Yeah. Very much so."

Avery smiled. "What Rowdy did for Marcus…" It astonished her still, how Rowdy hadn't hesitated to insinuate himself into a bad situation to try to make Marcus's life a little easier. "I've never seen a man so determined to help someone else. It's enough that Rowdy is so incredibly good-looking, and so rock solid."

Logan made a rude sound. When Pepper glared at him, he took a big bite of a doughnut.

"But he's also a really, really good guy. He likes to hang in the gray areas, and he just loves to fling around his bad-boy rep for all the world to see. But for anyone who actually knows him, he's golden through and through."

From behind them, Rowdy said, "Jesus, are you writing my eulogy? Did I die and not notice?"

Pepper jumped up. "What took you so long? Are you sure you're okay?"

"I'm fine." His gaze cut to Avery. "She makes an adequate nurse."

Avery noticed that he wore a loose flannel shirt. He needed the ointment and bandages reapplied, but he wouldn't want it mentioned in front of Pepper.

"Sit," she told him. "Logan brought coffee and doughnuts. We saved you a cup."

Both Logan and Pepper stared at her with wide eyes.

Rowdy sat. "Thanks." He tasted the coffee and sighed. "Perfect. Just what I needed." He leaned forward in his seat, but Logan said nothing about it and Pepper was too busy pulling a chair up alongside him to notice.

"Tell me everything," his sister demanded. "Who is the guy? *Where* is the guy?"

Rowdy took great satisfaction in saying, "Logan has him and his buddy in lockup—out of your reach."

"Traitor," Logan mumbled. And then to Pepper, "They're not going anywhere. And, no, you can't talk to either of them, so don't get any harebrained ideas about defending your brother. He can handle his own defense."

"He's right, Pepper." Rowdy rested both forearms on the tabletop. "I need you to stay out of it."

Surely they weren't serious? Avery looked at Pepper and realized they were. What did they think she could do?

Pepper clued her in by asking, "Do they have cohorts who might be out for revenge?"

Oh, no. Avery blanched over the possibility. "I hadn't even thought of that." Of course they probably did. Those type of bullies hung in packs like wild animals. "What if more men show up?"

Rowdy dismissed any threat. "Don't worry about it."

Logan agreed. "We've got it covered."

"How?" It was bad enough that someone was after her. Avery wasn't sure she could take it if Rowdy got hurt again.

"I can put the word out on the street, get some names, some addresses," Rowdy said. "The fact that I have a cop for a brother-in-law ought to be good for something."

Pepper said, "He's good for all kinds of things."

"Thank you, sweetheart." Logan's grin got him poked by Pepper's pointy elbow.

"One of the *many things* I'm good at is questioning

perps." Logan picked up another doughnut. "We'll find out what we need to know."

Pepper scowled. "Don't you dare make a deal with that son of a—"

"Pepper." Logan pulled her out of her chair and into his lap. "That wouldn't be up to me, but I don't think they're high-level enough to warrant it anyway."

"Tell me about Marcus," Rowdy said, deftly changing the subject.

"You already know the social worker came to the bar last night. He saw how taken Marcus was with Alice right off. For now, they have temporary custody. There'll be an emergency court hearing in family court within seventy-two hours. Marcus will get a guardian ad litem. That's like a kid's lawyer, a legal voice to act in Marcus's best interest."

Avery watched Rowdy. Sadly, she could read his thoughts all too clearly: he didn't trust that anyone would act in the boy's best interest because experience had taught him differently.

Logan went on. "I see no reason why the social worker and guardian ad litem wouldn't recommend the continued placement with Reese and Alice. They usually go with any strong, but safe, attachment that makes the kid feel more secure." He went quiet, turning his coffee cup, introspective. He hugged his wife closer. "It's possible Marcus might have information. He's probably seen things… The court will want him in a safe place, and what's safer than with a good cop?"

Avery assumed Logan knew about Pepper and Rowdy's upbringing. And like her, the knowing probably cut him deep.

"Trust doesn't come easy to abused kids." Logan met

Rowdy's gaze. "But he trusts Alice. If you visit with him today, you'll see what I mean."

"How's this going to work long-term?" Rowdy shifted. Avery knew he was as uncomfortable with the idea of Marcus's future as he was with his many stitches. "What if the dad gets out of jail? You guys screw up all the time."

"Not this time. But even if he did, now that we know about the abuse, the judge will find that continued removal is necessary for Marcus's protection. In order to get the court back on his side, good old dad would have to work a case plan with social services. That means maintaining housing, getting and staying legitimately employed, and he'd have to complete a substance abuse assessment with counseling, then pass the subsequent drug screens."

"It'll never happen."

"For most, that's true. For dicks like Darrell? He'll fail the drug screens if he bothers to show up for them, and no way will he go to counseling—which guarantees Marcus won't return home."

Rowdy looked cautiously hopeful.

"With things as they stand—the dad in jail and the mother's recovery uncertain—the judge can okay the placement, but Reese and Alice will have to do foster-care classes." He answered Rowdy's unasked question. "They're already setting it up. After six months they'll be able to petition for adoption."

"Adoption?" Rowdy straightened with astonishment. "They'd do that?"

Logan made a gruff sound. "I'd like to see someone try to take that kid from Alice." He turned his coffee cup. "Reese isn't a slouch. He has decent savings. But if the legal end gets costly, well, Pepper and I talked about it and I have that damned trust fund I'm not really using, so we know it'd go to good use."

Such generosity touched Avery, but Rowdy...he looked sucker punched. Voice faint, he said, "They'll actually get to keep him."

Avery loved how he said that, showing he considered Marcus a wonderful gift, not a burden.

"It's a rough road ahead," Logan said. "There aren't any magic shortcuts."

And finally, Avery saw Rowdy's charming smile. "I'll go over this morning and see if I can help get things started."

IT HADN'T BEEN easy talking Avery into going back to her place while he visited Marcus. She'd badly wanted to come along, but when he made it sound like a hardship to wait for her to shower and change, she'd relented.

Truthfully, he missed her already. But being here, knowing what Marcus thought and how he felt, left Rowdy raw. He didn't want Avery to see him like this, his emotions exposed.

Alice... Well, he had a feeling Alice already knew him inside and out. From day one, he hadn't been able to hide a single thing from her.

As she formally introduced Marcus to Rowdy, Alice kept an arm around the kid. He wore a pugnacious expression of dislike for Rowdy, while almost pushing Alice off balance as he tried to get closer to her. Cash sat on the other side of the boy, whining.

Kneeling down, Rowdy said, "C'mere boy." And Cash launched at him, licking his face, trying to crowd into his lap. Laughing, Rowdy dropped to his butt to accommodate the dog.

"Will he hurt your back?" Alice fretted.

"He's fine." When he got Cash to calm down, Rowdy stroked his neck and scratched his long black ears. "You like dogs, Marcus?"

The boy's bottom lip quivered, then firmed. "Guess so."

So much belligerence. "Ever had a pet before?"

He shook his head.

"I never have, either. My parents didn't allow it, and after they were gone…" He shook his head. "I was never really settled enough to have a pet."

"He's settled now, though," Alice said.

"Whenever I come around, Cash gets so excited that half the time he pees on my shoes."

Marcus looked horrified by that idea, but Alice just laughed. "Now, Rowdy, you know he hasn't done that in…a month."

True, the dog was learning and rarely had accidents anymore. "Seeing me gets him extra wound up for some reason." Maybe Cash's adoration would soften Marcus's attitude toward him. "But I don't mind too much, do I, buddy?"

Speaking to the dog like that really got him going, and Cash went berserk all over again. He almost knocked Rowdy over.

Marcus stepped behind Alice's legs.

Rowdy understood. Adults could be unpredictable, seeming open and friendly one moment, obscenely violent the next. He got it.

Laughing, he asked Marcus, "Has he peed on you yet?"

Marcus shook his head.

"Just you wait. I can tell he likes you a lot. Did Alice tell you how Reese got the dog?"

Alice smoothed the boy's hair. "A few times now," she said.

"Reese is like that," Rowdy agreed. "My brother-in-law, Logan, too. They're cops. You know that, right?"

Staring at his feet, Marcus mumbled, "Yeah."

That one word held so much suspicion; it felt like a rhino sat on Rowdy's chest. "They're good guys, Marcus. Good friends."

"The best," Alice agreed.

Marcus didn't look convinced.

"Reese saved Cash, ya know?" He tickled under the dog's chin. "And Alice, well, she likes to save everyone, me included."

Marcus looked up at her.

Alice laughed. "That's not true, Rowdy, and you know it. You saved yourself long before I ever met you."

Marcus's small face pinched with curiosity.

Sitting there on the floor, a dog sprawled over his legs, Alice smiling, Marcus terrified, Rowdy wasn't sure how to proceed.

Maybe seeing the kid wasn't such a great idea. What the hell could he say?

The truth? He doubted anyone had ever been square with the kid. Sure, Marcus was only eight or so, but he'd already seen more in his short life than most ever had to suffer.

Remembering his own youth, the uncertainty from not knowing, Rowdy tried to think of a way to reassure him.

Maybe the truth would do what platitudes couldn't.

He met Marcus's gaze. "I was a lot like you, except that I have a sister. I did my best to make sure my parents never hurt her."

Time ticked by in silence. Other than Alice's hand stroking through the boy's hair, no one moved.

"Did they anyway?"

That small voice filled Rowdy with blinding hope. "They made her feel bad, hurt her feelings and stuff like that, which is sometimes almost as bad."

"Yeah."

"But they didn't touch her because I protected her. I'm pretty good at that, at protecting people." He couldn't look at Alice again, not with her gaze suddenly so tender and compassionate. His throat got tight, his voice scratchy. "You don't know me well enough yet to believe me, but I promise that I won't let anyone hurt you, either."

Suddenly Marcus inched out around Alice. She wiped her eyes and let him go.

Rowdy whispered, "I'm probably not supposed to discuss stuff like that with you."

Alice said, "Baloney." She sniffled loudly. "I trust you completely, Rowdy, especially in this. I'm sure if you want to talk to Marcus, it's something worth hearing."

Marcus looked hungry for him to continue, and Rowdy didn't want to disappoint him. "I didn't trust people much—until I met Reese and Alice and Logan. Now I have friends when I never thought I would."

Talking to Marcus wasn't bad, but he felt awkward as hell with Alice looking on like a proud parent.

He glanced at her. "Think you could scrounge up some cookies and drinks for Marcus and me?"

"Of course." She touched Marcus's shoulder. "Why don't you sit with Rowdy and Cash while I do that?"

Rowdy patted the floor beside him and offered a bribe. "I brought you something." He reached behind him for the bag he'd carried in. "Cash first, just to keep him busy."

Marcus inched closer.

Offering the dog a new chew fresh from the pet store got him off Rowdy's lap. Cash took his prize and loped over to the sunny spot in front of the patio doors.

When Rowdy dug in the bag again, Marcus breathed harder. He withdrew a small car. "I hope you like green. What do you think?"

Marcus didn't move.

"It's for you." Rowdy sat it on the floor a few feet in front of him. "A car isn't much good without track, though, so I got a length of that, too."

The plastic track was meant to hook into additional pieces. Eventually, they could create a whole highway.

Bit by bit, Rowdy thought.

When Marcus kept his distance, Rowdy put the car at one end of the track and gave it a push. It slid over and off the other end. He looked at Marcus. "Your turn."

Marcus swallowed hard, and then came and sat down cross-legged. Tentatively he lifted the car and looked at it.

"What's your favorite color?" Rowdy asked.

"I don't know."

"Why don't you think about it? Next time I visit I'll bring another car, whatever color you like."

Marcus slid the car back to him. "When's next time?"

Good question, Rowdy thought. "How about tomorrow? Same time?" He returned the car along the track.

"I like purple." Alice stepped back into the room with the snacks on a tray. She didn't suggest they come to the table. Instead she seated herself near them so that together, they formed a semicircle. "Tomorrow we're going school-clothes shopping. Won't that be fun?"

Rowdy winced, already sympathizing with the kid. "If you say so."

Marcus grinned at him—and damned, but it almost broke his heart. The kid had a chipped front tooth, a bruise on his chin and his hair hadn't been trimmed in forever. But he was an adorable little guy.

Rowdy had to take a minute, draw a deep breath before he could ask, "So how old are you, Marcus?"

"Almost nine."

"Yeah? When's your birthday?"

Marcus shrugged. "Soon."

Fuck. If the kid didn't know, then that meant his parents hadn't done much to celebrate. No surprise there.

Alice touched Rowdy's arm. "You know Reese and I bought a house?"

"Yeah, I heard about that."

"We move in soon. Marcus will have his own room, close to ours, and a nice backyard to play in. But since we'll all be moving together, we're getting all the paperwork together to get him registered for school there."

So she'd find out when he was born—and maybe they could throw a party or something. "I'm not much of a shopper. What about you, Marcus?"

"I dunno."

"It'll be fun," Alice said. "We'll get lunch while we're out, and maybe Marcus can get a haircut if he wants."

"Yeah, dude." Rowdy reached over and ruffled the kid's hair. "I can barely see your eyes."

Marcus went very still as Rowdy touched him, almost frozen, but Rowdy pretended not to notice. "You going to get him some new kicks, too, Alice? Because I think he'd looked good in some boots like mine."

Rowdy lifted his big foot to show his lace-up black steel-toed boots that had seen better days a year ago.

Alice snickered and put her hand on Marcus's head when he inched closer to her.

"Well, shoot," Rowdy said. "Looks like I need some new boots, too."

"Tell me your size and I'll pick them up when I get Marcus's." Her gaze drilled into his, letting him know she saw it as a ploy to make the whole thing easier for Marcus.

"Sure, thanks. Size eleven." He'd have to pay her back later for that. No way was he letting Alice and Reese buy him shoes. He slid the car back across the track to Marcus and then grabbed up a cookie. "So if you guys are shopping tomorrow, when's a good time for me to come by?"

"We won't go until after your visit, so you tell me."

Rowdy set a time with them. While he finished his juice—which was way too sweet for him—and tossed back two cookies, he saw Marcus hide a cookie in his pocket.

The emotional turmoil the kid generated had Rowdy ready to crawl out of his own skin.

Marcus talked a little more, played with the car and finally it was time for Rowdy to head to work. "So what's it to be? A purple car for Alice and for Marcus—what color?"

Marcus thought about it for a long time before raising his pale blue eyes to Rowdy's gaze. "I like green."

And just like that, Rowdy felt like he'd conquered something monumental. His damned eyes burned and his tongue felt thick. "Well, since you already have green, how about I grab you a red one next?"

Hopeful, Marcus nodded. "Okay."

Cash bounded over to see him off. Thank God the dog offered a distraction and a way to get his shit together. Rowdy took his time with Cash because, he realized, Cash was important to him, too. Then he went to one knee in front of Marcus and offered his hand.

"Marcus. It was good visiting. I look forward to seeing you tomorrow."

Clinging to Alice's leg, his face averted, Marcus reached out and took Rowdy's hand.

All in all, great strides.

That rhino on his chest did a little stomping, but as he went out the door, he thought about seeing Avery next, and damned if he didn't find a smile of anticipation.

CHAPTER TEN

EVEN BEING A few years old, Avery's sporty little convertible was too valuable to be left in the parking lot. Rowdy rubbed the back of his neck, unsure what to do about it. He didn't like the idea of her driving home alone any more than he'd liked the idea of her walking a block from the bus stop.

The security lights overhead would keep the area well lit. But with bright lights came heavy shadows, and even as he walked the lot, he felt an ominous stare. With plenty of daylight remaining, he looked around but saw that no one was noticeably watching him. That meant someone was trying to be covert.

Idiot.

He let his gaze wander, taking in minute details, studying everything, everywhere—and there. Parked on the side street, more hidden than not, he spotted the same damn BMW that had tailed him. That new, slick, silver four-door hybrid stood out even more noticeably than Avery's little cherry-red ride.

Ready for a showdown, Rowdy took a step in that direction and the car peeled away.

You better run, you bastard.

"Trouble?"

Rowdy turned to find Cannon behind him. "Damn, but you're sneaky." Twice now, Cannon had come upon him without his noticing. It unnerved him and pissed him off. "Any reason you're skulking around?"

"Just showing up for work." Cannon grinned. "You were busy giving that car the death stare or you'd have heard me."

Rowdy noticed that Cannon didn't ask him why he'd been watching the car. "You've seen it before?"

"Haven't been the recipient of that stare yet, thank God, but the car was here last night after you left for the hospital, basically doing the same thing." Cannon shrugged. "Hanging around and looking suspicious. The windows are darkened, so you can't easily see inside. I got the license plate number if you need it."

Son of a... "Already got it myself." Hands on his hips, cold wind cutting through his clothes, Rowdy studied his new hire. "Any reason why you noted it?"

"Sort of a habit to pick up on those things." Cannon remained utterly immune to Rowdy's death stare. "You know what I mean."

"Yeah, I do." He started for the bar, and Cannon followed. "So how'd it go last night?"

"No problem." He grinned. "Your buddy Reese is handy behind the bar."

"You met Alice?"

Cannon nodded. "The kid took to her."

"So I heard." Rowdy opened the back door and waited for Cannon to enter first. "Alice has a way about her...."

"Hard to miss." Pulling off his hat, Cannon kept pace with Rowdy straight to his office. "If there's anything I can do to help with the boy, let me know."

"Appreciate that." So far, Rowdy wasn't sure what to do. He understood Marcus, but he feared making a misstep, doing something that would somehow sadden Marcus more. Though they shared a similar history, not everyone felt the same about things, especially such weighty issues as abuse and neglect.

"You have a nice place here," Cannon said.

"It's better than it was." Rifling through a desk drawer, Rowdy found an employment form. "Any hours you can't work?"

"No."

"Got an aversion to mopping floors or doing dishes?"

"Love it."

"You'll be bounced around, doing whatever odd job needs doing."

"Keeps it interesting."

They both knew Cannon would be wasted as a fill-in. "Think you can handle being a bouncer?"

He didn't miss a beat. "Long as you're asking me to keep the peace and not suggesting I randomly bust heads."

"Someone wanted to use you as muscle?"

Cannon stared him in the eyes. "Several have tried to insist."

By his own admission, Cannon came from a rough area filled with rougher criminals. You either joined in, or you got the hell out.

Rowdy had a feeling that Cannon hadn't done either. "Will I find anything in a background check?"

"Clean as a whistle."

Relaxing a hip on his desk, Rowdy asked, "Now, why does that surprise me?"

"Maybe because I live in the slums, I understand the way thugs think and you don't intimidate me." He gave a slight smile. "And by the way, it's because I understand how thugs think that you don't intimidate me."

"I'm a thug?"

"Nope. And see, I can tell the difference even if you'd rather no one could."

"Here's a tip—save the psychobabble if you want to stay on here." Rowdy handed him the paperwork. "I can pay you cash for last night, but fill out the forms and get them back to me before you start today."

Cannon looked them over. "Got a pen?"

Twenty minutes later, after showing Cannon around and giving him a rundown on what to expect—though Cannon had a handle on it already—Rowdy located Avery at the bar.

For such a small woman who'd been up all night, she had an abundance of energy, as if all her hundred and ten pounds packed unleashed power. She never complained about the workload, but now that he'd hired Cannon, she'd have help with that.

And he'd be able to get her alone more often.

They had half an hour before they opened, so he went to her, took her hand and dragged her off to his office.

"Rowdy! I have to finish setting up."

"You're finished."

Only partially under her breath, and with only a little annoyance, she said, "You're causing a scene."

"If you mean Ella smiling like a sap and Jones elbowing her, so what? They already know I have a thing for you." A big thing. A thing that was so damned unfamiliar he didn't quite know how to deal with it.

"A sexual thing," Avery said. "Yes, I'm sure everyone has picked up on it."

"A *lust* thing, since we haven't yet had sex." He got

her into the office and shut the door behind her. "But I'm counting down the minutes now that you've promised we will."

She surprised him again by leaning into him, her nose against his neck. "You smell like the outdoors. All crisp and fresh and sexy."

Damn, he hadn't expected that reaction from her. Had she missed him as much as he'd missed her? And since when did he miss women anyway?

To block the disquieting thoughts, Rowdy caught a handful of her hair and directed her face up to his so he could take her mouth in a grinding, hungry kiss. He wanted to draw her into him, use her to ease the edgy angst that had begun creeping up on him as soon as he left Alice's apartment—as he'd walked away from Marcus.

The signs were all there; it was going to be one of those nights, a night when he needed the release of sex to bury the ugliness.

But Avery still wanted him to wait. *Shit.* He lifted his mouth from hers and instead hugged her tight.

Picking up on his mood, she asked, "How is your back?"

"Forget my back." If she forgot about it, maybe he could convince her to—

"Can I see?"

"Nothing to see." He set her away from him, separating himself from her and that damned mothering instinct that was both jarring and annoyingly nice. "I picked up the pain pills after I finished my visit with Marcus. If I need one tonight, I'll take it." But he'd rather have Avery near again. She was more of a drug than a pill ever could be.

Avery touched her mouth, now swollen from his kiss. "How'd it go with Marcus?"

He watched the movement of her fingers over her lips and should have felt regret, but instead he wanted to taste her again, deeper this time, longer and hotter and… "He's fine."

"How can that be?" she asked too gently. "His world has been turned upside down."

"His world was never right in the first place, not with his parents, not with…" He trailed off, almost hating himself over the telling outburst. Through his teeth, he said, "Forget I said that."

"I'd rather you talk to me."

He gave her a sharp look. Kissing her again seemed like a better idea than unloading his emotional crap. "I'd rather change the subject."

"But this is important—"

No, it was depressing and infuriating. "I told you, it's fine."

She made a huffing sound. "Just tell me to butt out if that's what you want!" Bristling with attitude, she stalked toward him. "But don't give me that 'fine' business when we both know it's a lie."

Rowdy pulled back. "What's got you fired up?"

"Your back is not *fine*. Marcus is not *fine*." Grabbing a handful of his shirt, she went on tiptoes and still only reached his shoulder. "This whole dicked-up situation is not *fine*."

"Okay." Damn, he'd never seen her blow like that before. "Take it easy."

"Know this, Rowdy Yates. Talking to me, sharing with me, won't make me misunderstand."

Every time she got pissed at him, she used his whole

name. Made him feel like a kid being scolded. "Misunderstand what? You're not making any sense."

The hand she had fisted in his shirt thumped his chest once. "You. I won't misunderstand you or what you want. I won't misunderstand your interest, or…or take simple conversation as a proposal of marriage."

"Marriage!" Jesus, way to stop his heart, tossing a word like that out there. No other woman had dared—

"Don't swallow your tongue, Rowdy. You can have a relationship that isn't too serious but also isn't just sexual, you know."

"It can't be *just sexual* when we aren't even having sex, damn it!"

Cannon tapped at the door. "Room isn't as soundproof as you might've hoped. Should I come back later with the papers?"

Fuck and fuck again. "Yes!"

Cannon laughed. "All righty, then."

Avery, all but huffing in ire, still had her small hand twisted in his shirt. He covered it with his own. "Ease off, will you?"

Horror crossed her features. "Oh, my God, did I hurt you?"

"No." Why did she have to consider him so weak? "You can't hurt me. But I don't want to be mauled by your temper, either."

She threw up her hands. "Fine. Don't tell me anything. But I'm still coming over tonight to change your bandages."

"Glad to hear it. And from what Cannon said, everyone else probably heard it, too." He caught her by her apron strings when she started to storm away.

She tugged, almost fell and he hauled her back, lifted

her off her feet and plopped her up on his desk. Before she could slide back off, he stepped between her thighs, blocking her.

She went still.

Taking advantage of her silence, Rowdy suggested smoothly, "Let's start over."

A pulse tripped in her throat. She gave a cautious nod of agreement.

"Hello." Only by sheer will did he keep his body from reacting to the suggestive alignment of their pelvises.

After one slow breath, she smiled. "Hi."

It'd be so incredibly easy to lean her back on the desk, to cover her. He toyed with one long lock of hair. "You're touchy today."

"Not enough sleep."

If he got her jeans off her, he could take her this way and it wouldn't cause even a twinge in his back. "Because you stayed awake like a... What'd you call it? A pervert?" He liked how her face warmed. "Watching me sleep, right?"

"Yes, but it was worth it."

"Personally, I don't see the appeal. But I am more rested than usual."

Ducking her head, she fiddled with his now-wrinkled shirt. "I'm glad."

The crooked part in her heavy hair drew him. He skimmed his mouth there, inhaling the sweetness of her shampoo, of *her*. "I'm sorry I lost my temper."

"Me, too."

"It's...difficult." What an understatement. Talking about his past sent sharp claws of anger after his insides, shredding his heart, his guts.

Avery's curious fingers moved over his shirt, teasing his chest, then up to his collarbone, over to his shoulder. "I know."

Rowdy *had* to kiss her. He nudged her face up with small pecks along her temple, her jaw. He meant to take her mouth, to get some tongue action going, to lose himself in her taste.

Instead he heard himself say, "Marcus is so damned small."

As if she didn't realize how those words were torn from him, she nodded and carefully put her arms around his neck. "He's a skinny little guy, but Alice will have him caught up in no time."

Morbid reality settled over him, and he hid his face in Avery's hair. "I saw him slip a cookie into his pocket."

"Oh, Rowdy." Proving she did understand, she said quietly, "Saving it for later."

"Worried there won't be more when he wants it."

Sadness brought her closer. "I am so glad that you interceded." Her small, soft hands cupped his jaw. "Alice and Reese will be very good for him. But, Rowdy, I think it's important that you're there, too. You identify with him and the things he does—the things he'll do." She kissed him lightly, and her breath touched his lips when she whispered, "How he feels."

No, he didn't want to start delving into his own twisted past. No good would come from revisiting that black void. It was too much.

He put his hands on Avery's lush little ass, his mouth over her soft lips and he got her as close as he could, his tongue licking deep, her breasts and pelvis crushed to his body.

The hungry little sound she made spurred him on.

She opened to him, kissed him back, stroked over his chest—and somehow, in some unfair way, she gentled him so that soon he was only lightly kissing her, caressing her.

The tenderness of it overwhelmed him, and ramped up his lust to a fever pitch. "I want to be inside you, Avery."

On a vibrating moan, she said, "I want that, too." Another kiss. "So much."

He squeezed his eyes shut. "Then—"

"Shhh." She stroked his jaw. "You have to let your back heal."

"Forget that. There are positions that'll work."

"Like this?" With her legs open around his hips, she looked down at his erection straining his jeans. "I've already thought about it, you know."

"Good, because I'm having a hell of a time thinking of anything else."

"But what if I forget and wrap my legs around you? I'd die if I hurt you or made your injury worse."

It'd be pure torture, more for him than her, but Rowdy said, "Let me show you, okay?"

"Show me?" Scandalized, she looked around his office. "Here?"

"Not sex, honey. Not yet." He wanted her ready, without reservations. "Just a demonstration. Okay?"

She bit her bottom lip, then nodded. "Okay."

He took her shoulders and carefully lowered her back to the desk. Once she rested there, her gorgeous hair spread out everywhere, he caught her knees and, watching her, pressed them back.

Avery gasped. "Rowdy…"

His gaze locked with hers, he nudged in against her.

"Just like this, babe." Oh, God, he could almost feel it, how hot and slick it'd be to press inside her. "No pain or problems. Just me sinking in and us both coming apart."

Her face flushed, but her heavy gaze stayed focused on his. He watched the rise and fall of her breasts as he continued to slowly rock against her.

He'd meant it to be only a short example, but then her breath caught, and he watched her hands curl, felt the muscles in her thighs tense. "Damn."

She parted her lips to breathe more deeply. Her dark eyes glittered; her cheeks warmed.

Half disbelieving the telltale signs of her rising excitement, Rowdy studied her every reaction. No way was she...

"Rowdy."

Yeah, maybe she was. His heart started hammering and his cock swelled more. She arched her back a little. He should have taken her shirt off her so he could see her breasts.

Next time he'd make that a top priority.

Readjusting, he hooked his arms through her knees and leaned down to kiss her. The new position freed up his hands so he could cup each breast.

Liking that, she moaned brokenly.

Her nipples were tight little points, pressing up through the material of her bra and T-shirt.

"Jesus, I wish you were naked." Still thrusting rhythmically against the apex of her jean-covered thighs, he took her mouth, cuddled her breasts and when she gasped, stiffened, she took him right to the edge.

Even caught up in the moment, he made sure to muffle her sudden cries, to hold her steady so that she couldn't buck too much.

Arching her neck, her hands fisted tight in his hair, she keened under his kiss.

It was so fucking awesome that he gave up and did the unthinkable.

He joined her.

Fully dressed, on a hard desk, in the bar...*but with Avery*.

It felt too damned perfect.

With his brain now depleted of dark thoughts, his muscles gone utterly lax, all his worries and pain just faded away. As the sizzle ebbed, he became more aware of Avery's soft body cushioning his, the muskiness of her natural fragrance, how her fingers now stroked lazily through his hair.

It took Rowdy a few more minutes before he really got his brain to function again, and then he wanted to kick his own ass.

Way to go, Romeo.

His first time with her...and he hadn't even gotten her top off. Worse, there was a barroom full of people nearby—and her work shift was due to start in... Rowdy glanced at the clock. Hell. Three minutes ago.

Dreading how she might look at him, he levered up to his forearms.

Avery kept her eyes closed.

For some reason, that amused him. "Coward."

"Hush." Her brows knit together as if in concentration. "I'm still recuperating."

Damn, but he...what? Wanted her. That's all. He wanted her, and until he had her his brain would keep getting muddled about things. "You see?" He kissed her parted lips. "Entirely possible."

"Be quiet so I can find my brain cells." She frowned more. "And my legs. I think they've gone missing."

He stroked both hands along her soft, wide-open thighs. "Feeling weak, huh?"

"Boneless, if you want the truth." She put a hand over her mouth and yawned. "I think I could sleep here, just like this."

"With me crushing you?"

"Mmm." She moved enough to wind her arms around his neck. "You're a warm, heavy blanket, and you smell so good."

He'd just made the biggest sexual faux pas of his life, and yet Rowdy realized he was smiling. "Tell you what, babe." He touched her cheek and knew if he lived to be a hundred, the picture of her across his desk, replete and so damned sexy, would be emblazoned on his brain forever. "I'll have Cannon start behind the bar. Take as much time as you need."

She got one eye open. "You are not replacing me with Cannon."

No one could replace her— *Damn it.* There he went again with those intrusive, alarming thoughts. Drawing her arms down to her sides, he levered up and off her.

Avery didn't move. She had both eyes closed again.

"I told you, he'll give you breaks."

"And fill in when I'm otherwise occupied doing debauched things in the boss's office?"

"I like the way you think." Walking around behind his desk to the locker, Rowdy drew out a change of jeans and shorts.

Avery twisted around, looked at his face, then at the clothes in his hands. "No way."

He was just disturbed enough to say, "You already

know me, hon. Do you think I'm ever unprepared?"
He kept the change of clothes mostly for spills, which
happened often at bars. But no reason to share that detail with her.

Let her think what she wanted. Maybe it'd help him
to keep his head on straight if she got pissed again.

She sat up in a rush, pushed the mass of her di-
sheveled hair from her face and watched him until he'd
kicked off his shoes and opened his zipper.

Abruptly she turned. "Well, I'm recovered."

His gaze cut to her again. As he stripped down to
his bare ass, he asked, "Did you expect to cuddle on
the desk?"

"Nope." She scooted to sit on the edge, her legs hanging over, her hands braced beside her hips, her spine
rigid. "With you, speaking strictly of sex, I have no expectations other than that you be good—and you were."

Huh. Now, why did that insult him? Did she think
him incapable of anything more?

Stop being an ass.

Rowdy zipped up the fresh jeans and sat to pull his
boots back on. "If you count that as good, I can blow
you away with the real deal."

"Bragging?" She glanced over her shoulder, saw he
was decent again and hopped off the desk.

Her legs wobbled, making him smile. "Just forewarn-
ing you."

"Well, let me forewarn you, too." She lifted her chin.
"I did some preparing of my own."

"Yeah, how's that? Got an extra pair of panties
tucked away in your purse?"

"No!" She drew a calming breath, laced her fingers
together, rocked back on her heels and finally said, "But

I did set an appointment to see my doctor so I could get started on the pill."

Rowdy froze in the process of tying his boots. "When?"

She lifted one shoulder. "The other day, when I came in early to get my phone… That's why I needed it."

So she'd wanted him all along and just hadn't bothered to tell him? Sneaky. But also satisfying.

"After walking in on you, well, I'd rethought things, but… I do know my own limitations, and you, Rowdy, are too much temptation to resist. So…" She shrugged. "I have an appointment next week."

Was that one reason she wanted to wait? To ensure, on her own terms, that they didn't have any mistakes? "Responsible, intelligent women are so sexy."

"Based on your past relationships, no one would know you felt that way about it."

"Don't confuse yourself, honey. I already told you I don't do relationships." Except for now, with Avery. He shook his head as something else occurred to him. "Why weren't you already on the pill?"

"I wasn't doing anything with anyone, so why bother?" She pulled her hair over her shoulder and tried finger combing it. "I also packed a toothbrush and pajamas in my car. In case, you know, after I change your bandages, well…" She stopped fidgeting and gave him a direct frown. "I still want to follow doctor's orders and wait a few more days."

"You know that's not necessary." He pushed up from the chair. "I thought I just proved that."

She didn't meet his gaze and she didn't acknowledge what he said. "Now that I have my car, I can help you get settled and still have a way home—"

"No."

"No?" Her gaze shot up to his. "You'd rather I not come again?"

"I definitely want you to come." The way he said it left no misunderstandings as to what he meant. "Again."

"Rowdy."

He appreciated the picture she made, somewhat timid, a whole lot tempting and still chiding him. "You know you want it, too."

"I do." She sighed. "But we need to wait, so it's just as well that you don't want me to stay over."

"But I do want that. In fact, I insist." Keeping her around all night gave him the twofold pleasure of knowing she was safe while he got to enjoy her sweet little body.

Rocking again, she looked at the office door, then back at the small closet that held a toilet and sink. "I'm glad you have a bathroom in here."

"Need to do your own refreshing?" He wished they had more time and privacy. He'd love to feel her all hot and wet.

And damn it, he sort of wanted to cuddle.

Her nose wrinkled. "I think so, yes."

When he finally got her naked in his bed, he'd tend to her himself. But for now, he didn't want to embarrass her more than he already had. "Take your time." He stopped in front of her, took her shoulders and kissed the tip of her nose. "No reason for us to walk out together, looking like we've just done the nasty."

"Cannon knows."

"Forget Cannon." Now that he knew she considered Cannon good-looking, it irked him even to hear her say his name. Rowdy kissed her again, this time on her mouth, only briefly. She stared up at him, her tumbled hair framing her face, her uncertainty showing even though she tried to hide it. "You are so incredibly beautiful."

The compliment earned him a sweet smile.

Knowing he was losing it, Rowdy brushed his knuckles over her cheek and made a fast getaway, closing the door quietly behind him.

His mood was improved, his lust temporarily slaked, but his damned heart bounced around in his chest in a strange sort of warning…that also felt like a triumphant yell.

What the fuck had Avery Mullins done to him?

CHAPTER ELEVEN

AVERY DROPPED INTO Rowdy's chair and stared at the ceiling, appalled, stunned.

Wow, just…wow. Who knew such a thing was even possible?

Rowdy, damn him, took it in stride as if he got fully dressed women off across his desk with little effort every other day.

For all she knew, maybe he did.

Putting both hands over her eyes, she groaned. And smiled.

He was so remarkable in every way.

And boy, she wanted more. A lot more.

The trick would be to take all she could get without him ever knowing how she really felt. She had too much pride to get dumped, so when it ended—and she knew it would—she wanted Rowdy to believe it was by mutual decision.

Somehow she'd find a way to convince him of that.

He was used to calling the shots, so he probably expected her to hang out in his office for a while. She refused to be one more woman who fell into line for him, so she pushed out of his chair and, ignoring her exhaustion and still-shaky limbs, went into his tiny bathroom and refreshed herself.

Within ten minutes she was back out front. On her

way to the bar, she picked up a heavy crate of liquor from the back room to bring with her.

Cannon saw her, excused himself from the bar and hustled over to retrieve it from her. "Where do you want it?"

"Behind the bar near the ice chest." She went along with him. "So you're working the bar right now?"

He nodded. "Only until you're ready."

"Then what are you doing?"

"Whatever needs to be done."

So if she took over now, he'd have to...what? Wash dishes? Clean tables?

Cannon flashed her a grin. "Don't worry about it. It's all the same to me."

Avery noticed again what a good-looking man he was. The bar lamps put blue highlights in his shiny black hair, highlights that matched the pale blue of his dreamy eyes. And those thick lashes, the warm way he smiled, that small dimple...

His grin widened.

Such a wicked grin it was, too. Avery shook her head and collected her flagging wits. "I'd prefer to bartend."

"Then have at it." He turned to go, but Ella had approached. He nodded at her, saying, "Ma'am."

Which made Ella twitter and blush.

Wow. Avery had to do a double take over that. "Never thought I'd see the day."

"Excuse me?" Cannon said.

"Nothing." Avery smiled at Ella. "Everything okay?"

Ella slid an order slip over to her without looking away from Cannon. "Just stopping by to greet our new coworker."

"Thanks." Without missing a beat, Cannon took the slip and filled the drinks. "We met last night, right?"

"We did, very briefly," Ella said. "But with all the confusion I didn't get to welcome you proper."

"Appreciate it."

She wound a finger in her brown hair and flirted shamelessly. "So you're staying on?"

"Looks like." He loaded her tray and then glanced back at Avery. "Rowdy told me to take my direction from you, so what's it to be? Anything you want me to do to help out here, or should I check with Jones?"

Ella stared at him adoringly.

So Rowdy had put her in charge? After what had just taken place in his office, she would feel self-conscious about that, except that neither Ella nor Cannon seemed to think anything of it.

She took in the crowded floor, growing more so by the minute, and said, "Looks like we have a crush all of a sudden."

"Friendly football rivalry," Cannon said. "The guys at the bar are the winners, and the ones sulking in the booths by the far wall are—"

"Not happy," Ella supplied. She winked. "But I'm working on cheering them up."

Cannon lifted a brow. "I bet you'll have them down-right giddy in no time."

It was nice that Cannon fit right in. She'd have to remember to tell Rowdy what a good choice he'd made. "Why don't you help Ella get the orders going, and then see if Jones needs a hand? Maybe bounce back and forth."

"Sounds good." He grabbed an order pad and pen from behind the bar and started out to the floor.

The second he stepped away, Ella pretended to collapse back in a heap, making Avery laugh.

"Dear Lord," Ella said, "that young man is potent."

"He is easy on the eyes," Avery agreed.

"That apron looks better on him than it ever will on me. Now, if he *only* wore the apron..." Her gaze tracked him as he went across the floor. "I could really appreciate it when he walks away."

Laughing, Avery swatted at her. "Behave yourself."

"Ha! Look who's talking about behaving." While Avery tried to fight off a blush, Ella winked. "Rowdy's a morsel, no doubt about it. But you just might have a tiger by the tail with that one. Know when to turn him loose, okay?"

Dreading the answer, Avery asked, "How much did you hear?"

"Hear?" Ella's brows arched up. "I *saw* Rowdy drag you off, honey, and it was plain to everyone what he wanted."

She swallowed hard, and squeaked, "What?"

"You." Ella squeezed her hand. "I think it's nice that he couldn't wait to get you alone to steal a kiss."

Steal a kiss? Is that all Ella thought had happened? As her spine turned into a noodle, Avery said, "He's... impetuous."

"I'd say he's outrageous and downright sinful." She lifted her loaded tray. "Every woman here envies you. Enjoy it while it lasts."

While it lasts. Ugh. Such a depressing thought—one that wouldn't leave her even as the hours passed and she stayed busy filling nonstop drink orders.

The football players said, "Keep 'em coming," and

they meant it. Avery barely had time to draw breath, much less rest.

Out on the floor, a drinking game almost got out of hand. Rowdy sent two men home, thankfully with their designated driver. He cranked up the jukebox and a few couples chose to dance. Toward the back, laughter and the clanking of pool balls rounded out the din.

All in all, it was an upbeat night.

Just when she thought she'd drop, Rowdy came over with Cannon. "Take your break. Cannon can fill in."

"Perfect timing." More than ready, she pulled off her apron and wiped off her hands. After the chaos of yesterday, the sleepless night and the crush of customers today, she was so tired that she felt like she could curl up in a corner and doze off.

Not caring what anyone thought, Rowdy took her hand. "We'll be in the break room for about fifteen minutes if anything comes up."

Already zipping through drink orders, Cannon said, "Take your time."

Once they had some privacy, Rowdy asked, "Coffee or a Coke?"

"Coffee. And maybe a Danish." She went to her locker to get her purse but Rowdy waved her off to a chair.

"I've got it." He dropped coins into the vending machine to collect her drink and snack, then set everything in front of her before taking the chair to her right and turning it around. He straddled the seat.

Around a jaw-breaking yawn, she mumbled, "Thank you."

"Do you need something more to eat?"

She shook her head. "Jones gave me soup and a sandwich for my dinner break."

"You know, you could run over to my place to grab real food if you wanted."

Another yawn snuck in on her, hiding her surprise at the offer. "No, this is good." She didn't want to start overstepping herself, or take advantage of the nearness of his apartment. "Thanks anyway."

He used his baby finger to tuck her hair back. "You need a nap."

She most definitely did. "Unlike you, I'm mortal and require sleep." She added an extra sugar packet to her coffee. "But I have a feeling that if I took a nap, it'd turn into a full eight hours."

Half smiling, Rowdy touched the top of her cheek. "You have dark circles under your eyes."

"Great. Good to know." Around a bite of Danish, she added, "You'll just have to put up with it because I don't feel like fussing with makeup right now."

"You're still sexy as hell."

She shook her head. "Your idea of sexy is warped."

He hesitated, his expression too serious, before he said, "You know, if you need to cut out early tonight, we'll manage."

She burned her lip on the hot coffee, then almost dropped the cup.

She hadn't had enough sleep, they'd been busier than usual and now Rowdy wanted to ditch her?

Grabbing up napkins, he asked, "You okay?"

That little tease in the office had only whet her appetite and made her want more, but had it satisfied him enough that he wanted a reason to avoid her? Well, too bad. She wasn't ready to end things yet. She narrowed her eyes at him.

Rowdy sat back in his chair. "What did I do?"

She worked her jaw a moment before saying, "If you'd rather I not be at your place tonight, just say so. You don't need to trump up concern over a few yawns."

Now his jaw tightened. "I wasn't suggesting you not come over."

"So you thought I'd go home, sleep then get up in the middle of the night and come over when you got off work?" How in the world did he think that would be restful?

"I figured you could go right on next door to my place and catch a few hours' sleep before I get in."

Was that a joke? No, he definitely looked serious, and a little put out that she'd misunderstood. Her chat with Ella had left her brooding over Rowdy's habit of one-night stands, so no way had she expected him to want her in his apartment when he wasn't even there.

Suspicion got an ugly hold on her mood. "So you're going from a 'no women allowed' policy at your apartment to me being there without you?"

"I trust you not to snoop too much."

He looked like he meant it, and that just leveled her. "I will never understand you."

"What's to understand? I'm horny, and you look dead on your feet. Doesn't bode well for my evening."

She almost choked on her coffee. So he wasn't appeased. *Thank God.* She hated to admit the level of her own relief, so she mustered up some censure instead. "We've been over this already. The doctor ordered three days of inactivity before we…" What? Take the big step? To Rowdy, it wasn't a big step at all.

He caught her hand. "Before we shed our clothes and reenact what we already did in the office?"

She didn't know what to say to that. "It would be different and you know it."

"Yeah." His voice went rough and deep. "I'd be inside you."

Avery's heart tripped.

"And you'd be all nice and wet." He lifted her knuckles to his mouth, pressed a damp kiss there. "Squeezing me tight—"

"Rowdy," she pleaded. If he didn't stop, she'd be begging him for an encore and to hell with what the doctor ordered.

For the longest time, he searched her face. "I scare you a little?"

He scared her a lot, but probably not for the reasons he thought. "I've been celibate for over a year." *And you make me feel every minute of the wait.* She bit off another big bite of her pastry.

Watching her, Rowdy's eyes darkened with anticipation. "That's an awfully long time to deny yourself."

Painfully long—though she hadn't realized it until Rowdy came along.

He bent a little to meet her averted gaze. "Wanna tell me why?"

She shrugged. *Out of necessity, and because you weren't there to tempt me.* "Sex wasn't a priority."

"And now it is?"

Sex in general, no. But sex with Rowdy? She got hot flashes imagining it. "You know I want you, Rowdy." She wasn't that different from other women. "A lot." And she'd have him. "But I won't risk prolonging your recovery, and that's that."

"Okay, then." Rowdy unfolded his big body from the chair and stood over her. "Plan on sleeping tonight."

She lifted her coffee cup in salute. "Just try to keep me awake."

"I mean *only* sleeping."

Avery couldn't believe her ears. "That's a major turnaround."

Deadpan, he said, "Yeah, but unfortunately, I'm not that into comatose women."

Well, she wasn't *that* tired…but she'd go with any good excuse to give Rowdy the time he needed to recover from the knife attack. "If you're sure…"

He smirked, letting her know he recognized her ploy. "When we happen—and we will—I want you to feel everything, Avery. Not be numbed by exhaustion."

Wow. She sort of felt it right now.

Ella peeked into the break room, looked from one to the other of them and grinned. "Sorry to interrupt, kids, but Avery has a call."

"Who is it?" Rowdy asked.

"Some guy." She winked at Avery. "I didn't ask for a name."

"Next time," Rowdy told her, "ask." He pulled back Avery's chair. "You can take it in my office if you want."

Ella choked on her laugh, gave a quick wave and left.

"That's okay." Avery finished off her pastry and, carrying her coffee cup, started from the room. "I was about done anyway. And no, I don't need to leave early, but I thank you for the offer."

"You're sure?"

As they walked into a boisterous crowd, she said, "Positive." She'd carry her own weight and that was that. "You're slammed tonight."

"I'm glad I hired Cannon when I did." Rowdy kept

a hand at the small of her back as they maneuvered through the crowd.

She was thrilled for the success of the bar, but she wished Rowdy had a little more downtime. She'd taken each of her breaks and an hour for dinner, but Rowdy had barely slowed down at all.

They stepped around a cluster of people and both drew to a halt at what they saw.

Instead of the football players lining the bar, women of all ages and appeal sat perched on the bar stools, crowded in between, leaning on and over the bar—all ogling Cannon.

Avery barked a very unladylike laugh, then slapped a hand over her mouth.

Rolling his eyes, Rowdy said, "He's going to cause a riot."

"Told you he was a hottie." She turned her face up to his. "Between the two of you drawing in ladies, the men won't have room!"

"And then Ella might quit on me." He gave her a quick kiss. "Take your call, and then tell Cannon to work the floor with Ella. That ought to help disperse the bar crush."

At the mention of the phone call, Avery quickly lost her humor. Still, she gave Rowdy a salute and hurried along. *It's just a customer,* she told herself. *Not a big deal.*

Lifting the receiver, she said in her cheeriest voice, "Getting Rowdy Bar and Grill. How may I help you?"

The silence made her feel ill.

"Hello?" She waited, but no reply. From across the room where she'd left him, Rowdy watched her, his attention palpable.

Hoping he wouldn't question her, she shrugged and started to put the phone back in the cradle.

Through the receiver, a loud crack—maybe gunfire—made her jump so hard that she almost dropped the phone. She stared at it in horror.

Was that a warning? Or had someone just been shot?

Laughter came over the line.

Masculine laughter.

In a rush, she slammed down the phone—and belatedly remembered that Rowdy stood there taking in the whole thing.

What to do, what to do. Forcing all panic from her expression, she glanced at Rowdy and tried for a cavalier laugh. He wasn't amused. The determination in his gaze told her that he knew something was wrong.

Just how wrong it might be… That's what Avery wanted to know.

Her heart continued to pound too hard and fast as she took over and sent Cannon to work the floor. As Rowdy had predicted, the women followed, and men quickly claimed their empty seats.

For the remainder of the night she was so frazzled that she spilled drinks, bruised her hip on the ice case and accidentally dumped a bag of pretzels all over the floor.

Over and over again, she heard that awful gunshot.

They had two more hours until closing, and she couldn't wait to call it a day. Knowing she'd go home with Rowdy, that she wouldn't have to spend the night alone, was the only thing helping her to hold it together.

Despite the exhaustion, the thought of sleeping with him again had her toes curling inside her shoes. Snuggled up safe against Rowdy, breathing in the essence of his skin and hair, feeling his warmth… It was almost enough to revive her.

She was mopping up the bar with a rag when she saw a woman come up to Rowdy. It seemed like her eyes just naturally knew where to find him and sought him out every few minutes.

Over and over again women came on to him. He'd laugh, tease, chat. But he didn't get overly familiar with any of them.

This time, however, was different.

Rowdy greeted this lady with a hug.

Avery forgot what she was doing. The whiskey-soaked rag hung limp in her hand. The bubbly little brunette took care not to hurt his back, even cupped a hand to his face and spoke intimately with him.

Ice ran through her veins, followed by a tidal wave of heat. Without realizing it, Avery squeezed the rag, and the whiskey she'd just mopped up all squished out again. The guy sitting in front of her said, "Hey!"

Irked, Avery mumbled, "Sorry," and again cleaned the spill. She tried turning away. She really did. But she couldn't keep herself from looking back once more.

Rowdy smiled, teased, even tucked the woman's hair behind her ear in that same tender way that Avery had stupidly felt was special for her.

Special. Ha! The only thing *special* was that she hadn't yet slept with him. Once she did, Rowdy would move on. She knew that, and maybe, just maybe, that accounted for part of her insistence that they wait.

She glared so hard that Rowdy suddenly glanced up, and his gaze clashed with hers.

She thrust up her chin and turned away. Then had to

peek back. Rowdy now had his arm around the woman's shoulders, but he wasn't smiling anymore.

It didn't matter. Avery had already accepted that she had no hold on him. Of course he'd flirt. It was in his nature, a vital part of who he was as a man. And with the way women gravitated to him—

Her murderous thoughts stalled when Rowdy started leading the woman toward her.

He wanted to introduce them? No, no, no. That was too much to ask.

But what could she do? She glanced around in a near panic. Abandon the bar? Show that it bothered her?

The hell she would.

If he wanted her to meet his admirers, then she'd pretend it didn't bother her at all.

Before he'd quite reached them, Avery pasted on a stiff smile that made her cheeks ache.

Rowdy dragged the woman right up to her. "Avery, this is a friend of mine."

The woman smiled happily. "Hello."

A friend, huh? Avery barely suppressed a sarcastic snort. And just what the hell did Rowdy's "friend" have to be so happy about?

Doing her best to play along, Avery said, "Nice to meet you," and then, even though she couldn't see the bar through tunnel vision, she tried to get back to work.

"Avery." Without lowering his voice one iota, Rowdy stated, "I'm not sleeping with her."

Gasping, Avery spun back around. "Rowdy!"

The woman gave him a sappy, indulgent look of warm affection. "Of course he's not." She flapped a hand. "He's tempting enough, but we worked that stuff out early on. I needed to know his expectations and he—"

Rowdy interrupted her, saying, "That's enough."

She leaned into him, but spoke to Avery. "I bet Rowdy has you confounded, doesn't he?" She tipped her head back to smile up at him. "You do that to every woman."

They were so damned cozy together that Avery's molars ground together. "I know exactly what he does to *every* woman."

Rowdy pulled his friend closer. "How can you know, Avery, when you and I haven't yet—"

Avery threw the whiskey-soaked rag at him.

It almost hit the woman, who squealed and ducked back.

It *did* hit Rowdy, splatting right in the center of his solid chest, and then slowly dropping to the floor with a sodden plop.

He stared at her with incredulity.

Avery stared back, disbelieving that she'd done such a thing, but also sort of tickled with Rowdy's look of shock. She'd seen many expressions from him, most of them intimidating, but never this hilarious blank surprise.

A nervous giggle escaped her.

Rowdy's eyes narrowed.

All around them, the racket from boisterous drinkers seemed to fade. With a hand covering her mouth, Avery took a cautious step backward.

That only hardened Rowdy's expression and tensed his broad shoulders.

Grinning, his *friend*—Avery couldn't think of her that way without a mental sneer—grabbed napkins off the bar and patted Rowdy's chest. "Oh, that was too funny. Glad it missed me, though!"

Avery said, "I wasn't aiming for you."

Ms. Touchy-Feely chuckled. "I'm sure Rowdy had it coming." She leaned forward to whisper, sotto voce, "He's the quintessential badass, you know."

Rowdy's gaze never left Avery. "I'm the one who was just attacked."

"He's a rascal, too," she said while using the napkins to soak up some of the mess off his shirt—and in the process putting her hands all over his chest.

Avery tried not to care, but damn it, she did. Too much.

"He takes great personal pleasure in being disreputable and, well, rowdy." The annoying woman leaned into him again and said with sugary sweetness, "But he's also *so* lovable."

"That's enough, Alice."

A dousing of ice water couldn't have been more jarring. Avery felt her heart hit her feet. Oh, crud. So this was Alice?

Alice smiled knowingly. "Rowdy can take a punch— or a soggy rag, as the case may be—but beware if you try to compliment him. That's when he gets surly."

Avery wished for a dark hole to crawl into. She'd made a colossal fool of herself in front of the paragon who had connected so strongly with Marcus. She winced. "I'm sorry."

"Don't be," Alice said. "I understand. Rowdy is so special that he can have that disorienting effect on people."

Proving he couldn't take a compliment, Rowdy said, "I am *not*—"

Alice didn't give him an opportunity to interrupt her

praise. "I think he likes to cultivate the whole bad-boy image. But at heart, he's a really good guy."

Rowdy stepped in front of Alice. "She really is just a friend."

Alice leaned around him. "More than a friend," she protested. "But we have never—" she looked around and bobbed her eyebrows *"—gotten busy."*

Because Alice appeared to want a reply, Avery said, "Okay."

"I have my own hunky guy," Alice bragged. "He's a police detective."

Suddenly Reese loomed behind them. "If you want to hang on to someone, honey, my arm is available."

Rowdy slowly closed his eyes—then pried Alice loose.

She immediately turned to Reese. "And here he is!" Hugging up to Reese—who truly was a hunk—Alice said, "Reese, have you met Rowdy's special lady?"

Special lady? Avery sputtered, "I'm just the bartender."

Saying nothing, Rowdy crossed his arms and looked put out by it all.

"Yes, we've met," Reese said to Alice. "Remember when I helped Rowdy work on the bar? Avery was here sometimes, pitching in where she could. Last night she rode with Logan to take Rowdy to the hospital. That's why she wasn't here when you came to see Marcus."

Alice took that as confirmation. "There, you see? She's very special, just as I said."

OH, HOW HE would have loved to see Avery's face when he fired the gun. Though he'd never wanted her to hear him for fear she'd recognize his voice, he couldn't stifle the laugh as he'd imagined her shock, her probable fear.

Fear was good; it'd make her more amicable to his plans.

If she didn't feel safe at the bar, in the company of hoodlums, then getting her back where she belonged would be oh-so-much easier.

Already he'd wasted too much energy on this little endeavor. Time to bring the brat back home, where she belonged.

Once there, he'd see to it that she never ventured off again.

CHAPTER TWELVE

ROWDY WASN'T MOVED by Alice's statement. Avery *was* special. Did Alice think that was news to him? Not being obtuse, he'd already come to that realization all on his own. He didn't know what to do about it, or what it meant to him, but he'd known enough women to see that Avery was very unique.

Not knowing what else to say, he asked, "Where is Marcus?"

Alice's smile fell. "He's at home, in bed. Pepper and Logan are with him."

Rowdy liked how she stressed the word *home*. It gave him a warm feeling inside, especially since he'd never really had a home of his own. "Everything okay?"

With his thick arm around Alice's shoulders, Reese said, "She needed to get out, and she won't leave Marcus when he's awake, so we waited for him to go to sleep."

"He sleeps through the night?" Following Reese's lead, Rowdy went to Avery and put his arm around her. She stiffened up from head to toe, but she didn't move away.

Probably because she didn't want to cause a scene.

Course, that hadn't stopped her from zinging the dirty bar cloth at him.

Reese lifted a brow over Rowdy's possessive hold,

but didn't comment on it. "We worried about that, but Marcus pretty much just conks out."

"Maybe he finally feels safe," Avery offered.

Cold alcohol kept Rowdy's shirt sticking to his chest. He'd find a creative way to get even...but not tonight.

Tonight he intended only for Avery to sleep.

"Could be." He knew well how difficult it was to catch any real rest when you couldn't let down your guard. For him it had become a lifetime habit.

Except when he'd slept with Avery.

"Kids are resilient," Alice said softly. "He'll be okay."

Reese gave her a squeeze. "We'll see to it."

Customers came to the bar, so Avery excused herself to pour drinks. Alice put a hand on Rowdy, whispered, "Nice catch," and then went around and found a seat so she could talk more with Avery.

Now that he and Reese were alone, Rowdy asked, "What's going on?" He knew it took more than Alice needing a break to have the two of them out so late.

Reese ran a hand over his tired face. "The kid's mother passed away."

If Reese wanted him to feel sorry about that, he'd be disappointed. "One less obstacle."

"Yeah, I know." Reese looked over to his wife. "I've never seen Alice so torn. It's not in her nature to wish anyone ill, but she was relieved. The shit that kid lived through..."

"I know." Rowdy's guts burned every time he thought about it. "What's that have to do with this late-night visit?"

Reese found a wall to lean on. He looked emotionally spent. "We got the call that she'd died." He flexed his big fists. "Alice insisted on going to the hospital to see her."

Rowdy stepped behind the bar to fill a glass with ice and cola. He handed it to Reese. "Morbid streak?"

"That's not funny." He downed half the drink. "Alice wanted to tell her that she'd take care of Marcus. I guess...just in case the mom had some latent maternal streak, you know?"

"At least dead people don't argue."

"Yeah." Reese finished off the cola, then held the cool glass to his forehead. "She's something else, you know?"

Yeah, he did know. "Alice is too caring for her own good."

"Marcus might argue that point with you." Reese lowered his arm and pinned Rowdy with his steady gaze. "Alice says the same about you, too."

Rowdy didn't want to talk about Alice's warped perception of his character. "What's happening with the dad?"

"Basically, he's screwed. The weapons we found in the truck were stolen and used in other felonies. He had enough drugs for intent to distribute. And given his history, well, let's just say he won't be going anywhere anytime soon."

"They were arraigned?"

"Yeah." Reese handed over his empty glass. "Thanks."

"More?" Rowdy offered. "Maybe something stronger?"

He shook his head while eyeing the crowd, mostly making sure no one got too close to his wife.

Reese was big enough that a few people backed away from the bar rather than chance it. "You're scaring off my customers."

He didn't care. "There won't be any bail for the bozos, which means they'll be locked up until the completion of their trial."

"How long will that take?"

"Couple of months, maybe longer, to get before the grand jury where they'll be formally charged. Could take a year or two before it actually goes to trial."

"Good. Let them rot." Rowdy didn't care what happened to them, as long as they weren't turned free.

"There's enough evidence against them that Lieutenant Peterson is thinking of offering them up to the feds. If that happens, they'll try to make a deal."

No way. If it came down to it, Rowdy would handle the bastards himself—

Reese straightened and stepped closer to Rowdy. "Get that look out of your eyes right now."

"I don't know what you're talking about."

"The hell you don't." Reese glanced toward the bar, then lowered his voice even more. "Everything is on track. When we first took them in, they told us to go fuck ourselves."

"Can I echo that sentiment?"

"If you do, I'll tell Alice."

Rowdy clenched his jaw until his temples throbbed.

"Get a grip, Rowdy, and let me tell you how this is going to go down."

"Spit it out then, damn it."

For some insane reason, that amused Reese. "Right about now, the seriousness of the situation is starting to sink in on old Darrell and his buddy. With so much evidence against them, only idiots would go to trial."

"They *are* idiots."

"Yeah, sure. But as career criminals, they know

they'll get put away for good if they go that route. By saying we'll offer them up to the feds, we'll get them to take a plea deal, which would simplify things and they'll still get fifteen to twenty years."

It wasn't long enough, but then, Rowdy wasn't sure a lifetime would be long enough to satisfy him.

Reese clapped him on the shoulder. "Lighten up, man. They won't ever again get near you or the kid, and that's what matters the most, right?"

The ringing of the phone drew Rowdy's attention. He turned to see Avery stare at it for three seconds before wiping her hands and cautiously lifting the receiver.

The relaxing of her spine and the relief on her face told him it was only a customer. *This* time.

Reese said, "What's that about?"

"What?"

He nodded toward Avery. "She treated that phone like a venomous snake, and you watched her as if waiting for a clue."

Sometimes detectives were a pain in the ass. "Something's going on with her, but I don't know what."

"Ex-boyfriend, maybe?"

"Maybe." Rowdy didn't want to break Avery's trust, so he didn't explain that she'd been flying solo for over a year. More likely, the caller was someone she'd met recently, someone who didn't have the sense to take no for an answer. But just in case, Rowdy told Reese, "We were followed the other day."

"By who?"

"If I knew that, why would I tell you about it?"

Aggrieved, Reese said, "Because I'm the law and you aren't?"

That had never stopped Rowdy before. "I saw the car

just hanging around, too." While telling Reese about the incident, he picked up a bar napkin and a pen and jotted down the plate. "Think you could run these for me?"

Reese took the napkin, looked at it and put it in his pocket. "Sure, but in the meantime, watch your back."

"I always do." And for the foreseeable future, he'd be watching Avery's back, as well.

TWENTY MINUTES BEFORE CLOSING, Avery saw her step-father walk in, and it was such an incongruous sight that it almost knocked her over. *How the hell had he found her?*

Rowdy had just given the last call, and the crowd had thinned out.

Avery searched the room, but she didn't see Fisher anywhere, thank God. Usually, wherever Meyer Sinclair went, Fisher was sniveling close behind. They were friends, but more importantly, they were business partners. Meyer had the stability of history and accumulated resources, and Fisher had fresh success and a very bright future.

She just knew Meyer would want her to come home, and blast it all, she didn't want to.

Exhaustion couldn't compete with resentment. When she'd most needed her family to believe her, to support her, they'd sided with Fisher instead.

Why in the world was Meyer Sinclair here now, especially at nearly two in the morning? He looked the same as he had the last time she'd seen him more than a year ago. Wearing a long black wool coat over tailored slacks and a designer sweater, he smoothed his wind-blown, thinning, brown hair. The cold had left his fair cheeks ruddy. He removed his glasses to clean them.

Avery stood there, watching him, unsure what to do.

After he replaced his glasses, he searched the bar. At first his gaze went right past her, but then shot back. As if he couldn't take it in, he looked at her, around her, and disapproval showed in every line of his posture. Brows drawn, he started toward her.

No one remained at the bar, thank God, so Avery started out to meet him. If she could keep him near the door, then maybe she could more easily be rid of him. Not that she had anything against Meyer. She didn't. In fact, she mostly liked him, definitely respected him and knew he adored her mother, which was a plus.

But like everyone else, he'd believed Fisher's lies, and that meant she wanted to keep him as far away from Rowdy as she possibly—

Rowdy intercepted him. "Can I help you?"

Oh, shoot, shoot, shoot.

Meyer barely gave him notice. "No, thank you." He made to step forward—and found himself running into Rowdy again.

Avery hastened her step and reached them a breathless five seconds later. Still hoping to send Meyer packing, she wrapped her arms around Rowdy's biceps and hugged him like a giddy, infatuated girl. "Rowdy, this is my stepfather." She leaned into him, smiling as if she weren't still offended over being called a liar. "Meyer, meet Rowdy Yates."

It was almost ridiculous how big Rowdy looked when compared to Meyer's shorter stature and lack of physical presence.

She had no idea what her mother saw in the man, other than his obvious wealth and complete adulation.

Meyer dismissed Rowdy, saying, "If you'll excuse us…"

No, you don't. Avery clung to Rowdy, but he didn't even make a pretense of budging.

She gave Meyer a smug smile. Her stepfather had clout wherever he went, and most recognized it by his attitude alone—unless, apparently, he ventured into the wrong part of town, or, more specifically, into Rowdy's domain.

With any luck, Meyer would see them as a couple and he'd be dissuaded from nagging at her to return to her old life. Of course, she needed Rowdy to play along. In an effort to convince him, she stopped squeezing his arm and instead slipped an arm around his waist, low enough that she wouldn't hurt his back, which sort of put her hand over his muscled tush.

Brows drawn, his expression flinty, Rowdy glanced down at her…but he didn't call her bluff. Instead, he reciprocated, his arm around her, his hand on her hip.

Avery was so surprised by that, she faltered. "Meyer." Her laugh was a little too loud, and way false. "I'm surprised to see you here."

He took in their familiar embrace and bristled with discomfort. "Is there someplace private we can talk?"

"I don't know. Are you here alone?"

"You didn't think I'd bring your mother here, did you?"

No, it wasn't her mother she was worried about. But she didn't want to say Fisher's name. Rowdy already looked like a dog waiting for a bone to chew on. She wanted him as camouflage, but she didn't want him compelled to defend her.

And wasn't that nice? Because she knew without a

doubt, unlike her mother and stepfather and all her so-called friends from her past life, if she told Rowdy what happened, he'd believe her one hundred percent. She sighed at how wonderful that made her feel.

Taking her silence as more stubbornness—the accusation he often leveled at her—Meyer puckered up in displeasure. "Yes," he bit out, "I'm quite alone."

"Then sure, we can talk." Yet when she started away from Rowdy, he held on.

Yes, she definitely had a tiger by the tail.

"Rowdy," she coaxed, "do you mind if we use your office?"

"Good idea." He lifted a hand and beckoned Cannon over. "Finish up here, will you?"

"Sure thing." Cannon didn't ask any questions. He just got to work.

"Come on." Rowdy led the way toward the back office while Avery tried to think of a way to keep him from knowing too much.

Her staid stepfather trailed along.

Rowdy said as they walked, "We were just closing up for the night. A few more minutes and only employees will be here." He opened his office door. "Can I get you anything to drink? I think there's coffee left in the break room."

"That's not necessary. I won't be long." Again Meyer took in his surroundings. It was clear by his sanctimonious expression that he found everything lacking.

That set Avery off again. She had thought to talk to her stepfather privately, to ensure Rowdy didn't get drawn into her problems. But she'd be damned before she let Meyer slight him in any way.

Giving him her brightest smile, she said, "Thank you, Rowdy."

Taking the bait, her stepfather cocked a brow. "Yes, thank you."

Rowdy gestured to a chair. "Grab a seat." Keeping Avery at his side, he leaned a hip on the desk.

So many times she'd imagined reuniting with her family, but never, not once, had she pictured it taking place in the bar. With everything that had happened, she couldn't help but feel defensive.

"Why are you here, Meyer?"

Meyer considered the chair, but chose to stand behind it instead, his hands resting loosely on the chair back. "You should come home."

"No. Anything else?"

"I see you're still being stubborn."

"Not at all. I've made a new life for myself. There's nothing back there for me."

"What about your mother?"

Guilt only made her more defensive. "I've called Mother. We've talked." Or more like debated, with her mother insisting she should forgive Fisher for any imagined slights. God, it made her furious all over again.

Meyer frowned, not in anger but with concern. "I suppose she hasn't told you?"

The way he said that slammed the brakes on her agitation. "Told me what?"

"She didn't want to worry you, but I felt you should know."

Alarm straightened her spine. "Know *what?*"

"Sonya has breast cancer."

Fear socked Avery like a physical blow.

"The prognosis is good," Meyer hurried to say. "She

had a surgery to remove a small lump and now she's going through follow-up treatment. They found it early, so the doctor expects her to make a full recovery."

"She's never said a word." No matter Avery's efforts, the conversations invariably led to her mother asking her to return, and Avery always refusing.

"We only found out recently." He readjusted his glasses, saying, "Perhaps if you were at home where you belong—"

Oh, God. The way Rowdy stroked her back helped to remind her that she was a different person now. She would not let Meyer bully her, not even for this. "You really want to go into that now?"

Meyer held up a hand. "No. I'm not here to debate the past. My sole mission is to invite you back home for a visit, if nothing else. I think it would give your mother comfort to see you before her next treatment."

"When is it?"

"Tuesday."

Avery put a hand to her head. "That's only a few days away."

"The treatments leave her weak, sick. She's starting to lose her hair." The corner of Meyer's mouth lifted. "But you know your mother. She's turned it into a challenge and is already spearheading a fund-raiser to get underprivileged women tested."

Yes, that sounded like her mom.

Rowdy was silent, but he stayed with her, strong, unwavering. If she wanted the time off, he'd give it to her in a heartbeat. A million questions bombarded her brain. "What type of treatments?"

"Chemo and radiation. She's concerned about finding an appropriate wig when necessary, but I've told her she'll be adorable, regardless."

Avery had always considered Meyer's most redeeming quality to be his undying love for her mother. "I'm so very glad she has you, Meyer."

"She needs you, as well." Like a broken record, he again played his favorite refrain. "You should move back home."

Home, with Fisher? She shook her head. "I'm only a half hour away. I can visit as often as she needs me."

Meyer paced away from the chair.

Rowdy looked at her, his gaze inquiring, but with her stepfather right there, she couldn't possibly explain.

Meyer jerked around to face her. "Enough, Avery! It's time to stop being a selfish girl!"

The sudden verbal attack made Avery flinch.

"Careful," Rowdy said in warning.

Meyer didn't pay heed. "We should be having this conversation in private! *You* should be having it with your *mother!*"

Rowdy straightened from the desk, and Avery knew she had to do something, and fast. "I work until late at night."

"Every damn day?" Meyer asked.

"Every day except Sunday."

"It's absurd!" He slashed a hand through the air. "The only reason you would work in a place like this is to spite us."

"You're wrong." She cared nothing about spite. "I *like* this place." Avery took a step ahead of Rowdy. She hated to make the admission in front of him, and at least this way she didn't have to see his reaction. "I enjoy earning my own money now."

Meyer ran a hand over the back of his neck. He gestured at Rowdy. "In the same way that you enjoy *him?*"

That was a slight she couldn't ignore. She shot forward, saying, "Yes, I enjoy him!"

"Then bring him along."

Uh-oh. Her thoughts scrambled. She needed a tactical retreat—

Rowdy asked, "When?"

Oh, no, no, no. She glared at Meyer. "You can't drag him into our family squabbles."

"If he's your boyfriend, then I'm sure your mother would enjoy meeting him."

Rowdy actually choked, then choked some more.

Going stiff, Avery refused to look back at him. She didn't know if it was the term *boyfriend*—a description far too lackluster for a man like Rowdy—or the idea that they might be a couple that had him wheezing for air.

"Back off, Meyer." She understood his ploy. Her mother would do a comparison to Fisher, and while Avery knew Fisher could never measure up, her stepfather thought Rowdy would be lacking.

Bastard.

"Why don't you want to bring him?" Meyer asked.

The choking stopped, and instead she felt Rowdy's gaze boring into the back of her head.

Screw it. She'd just have to pray that Fisher wasn't around, and if he was, well... She glanced back at Rowdy. Fisher wasn't an idiot. He wouldn't openly provoke a man like Rowdy Yates, a man who could easily take him apart despite all his bravado and bullying. She'd be safe with Rowdy along, and Rowdy would be safe—if she handled this correctly.

"I'd love to bring him. Thank you."

"Does tomorrow morning work for you?"

Wow, so soon. Meyer left her little time to sort things out in her mind, little time to find a good explanation for wanting to bring Rowdy along.

With no choice, she turned to face him.

Something…volcanic showed in Rowdy's light brown eyes. "It works for me if it works for Avery."

Wow, he said that like a challenge. Did he believe Meyer's nonsense, that she was somehow ashamed of him? She turned back to Meyer. "Is eleven too early?"

"That'd be fine."

Rowdy pushed away from the desk, and more than ever, he looked big, hard and imposing. "I need to know something first."

Avery all but cringed. She didn't want Rowdy to start digging into her past, asking questions about the situation that had sent her running. She didn't want to be exposed for a coward, and she didn't want to take advantage of Rowdy's natural tendency to protect.

Those worries were put to rest when Rowdy voiced a whole new set of concerns. "Why didn't you just call?"

"I didn't have a number, for one thing." Meyer cut his gaze over her. "When she ran off, she also switched phones."

"Not to avoid you or Mom." She again glanced at Rowdy. "I was part of their family phone plan then, but changed to get my own basic plan with calling only."

"She's called her mother, but never me," Meyer said. "And since Sonya didn't want to bother Avery with this, I couldn't very well ask for contact information."

Rowdy crossed his arms over his chest. "So how did you find her here?"

Oh, my God, Avery hadn't even thought of that. Rising anger had her facing off with her stepfather. "It was you on the bar phone?"

"What?" Meyer looked between them. "What are you talking about?"

"Did you give me breather phone calls? *Did you shoot a damn gun just to scare me?* Avery didn't get far from Rowdy before he drew her back. She was too suspicious to think before speaking, and she asked with accusation, "Have you been watching me?"

Meyer drew up in affront. "Don't be absurd."

Far more relaxed that she was, Rowdy asked, "What type of car do you have?"

"I don't see why that matters, but I drive a BMW."

Avery didn't know why it mattered, either, but she appreciated Rowdy's line of questioning. "So how'd you find me?"

"Oh, please, do you honestly believe your mother would let you leave without knowing where you were? She immediately requested that I hire a private service to track you down."

"No shit?" Rowdy eyed him up and down. "That sounds costly."

"Very."

Avery's temples started to pound. "Would the private service have called me?"

"I have no idea how they discovered your whereabouts, but I can ask if it's important."

Was it? It seemed like a mighty big coincidence for her to get weird calls, and then out of the blue, her stepfather showed up. But she honestly couldn't see Meyer, or a reputable service, making the weird calls she'd received.

Meyer adjusted his glasses. "Look, all I know is that the people I hired contacted me with this address some months ago. I knew it was a bar, but the name changed or something—"

"That happened when I bought it," Rowdy told him.

"It's now named after you?"

Rowdy shrugged. "The name of the place was Avery's idea."

"Yes, well, I was dubious about actually finding her here, so I came myself to have it verified."

"And here I am," Avery confirmed. "Mission accomplished."

Fed up and not bothering to hide his irritation, Meyer said, "It's late and I have a thirty-minute drive to get back home. Why don't we finish this conversation tomorrow after you've reunited with your mother?"

And hopefully there'd be an opportunity for her to get Meyer alone and talk to him without Rowdy listening in. "All right."

Meyer gave Rowdy a curt glance. "Tomorrow, then." He headed for the door. "I'll see myself out."

The second Meyer was out of sight, Rowdy pinned her with his darkest look.

She started to explain—how, she didn't know—but Rowdy shook his head. "Let's lock up here. We can talk at my place."

And maybe, Avery thought, by then she'd be able to figure out what to tell him.

An hour later, as they prepared for bed, Avery had the fleeting hope that Rowdy had decided not to question her after all.

She was sorely mistaken.

ROWDY HAD WAITED for the inquisition, choosing instead to concentrate on getting Avery ready for bed. He didn't know what was going on, but he could see her fatigue, so he chose to prioritize.

Why had she shanghaied him into visiting her parents with her?

All she had to do was tell her stepfather that he wasn't her boyfriend—what a stupid term. But instead, she'd acted like she was in love with him.

For Meyer's benefit? Or did she actually care that much for him? He wasn't sure.

No one had ever taken him home to meet the folks. Hell, the women he usually screwed cared only about a repeat performance. With Avery, everything was ass backward.

Normally he'd have bowed out if anyone had dared to suggest he tag along for a family reunion. But again, Avery wasn't every other woman. If she wanted him there, she had to have a reason.

Apparently, whatever the reason might be, she didn't intend to tell him.

He'd given her plenty of time to bring things up herself. Instead, as she'd eaten a bowl of cold cereal in his kitchen, she'd watched him as if expecting him to jump on her.

He'd done enough interrogations to be a little smoother than that.

With Avery, he planned to use kid gloves.

She'd already washed up in his bathroom and brushed her teeth. Her pajamas were not designed to fire lust, but they did all the same. Especially when she knelt on the bed behind him to change his bandages.

"This already looks better," she said.

Rowdy felt her delicate fingertips graze his skin. "The stitches itch like a mother."

"I'm sorry." She blew softly on his skin after reapplying the ointment. "Does that help?"

It gave him a boner, which was no help at all. "Finish up so we can get some sleep."

She must've taken that to mean they wouldn't talk, because she moved fast, reapplying the gauze and tape, then scrambling around and crawling under the covers. She had them up to her chin, her red hair spread out on the pillowcase, her blue eyes hopeful when Rowdy turned to face her.

Damn, she looked so…endearing.

And just when in the fuck did he think of women in his bed that way? He didn't.

Standing, Rowdy stripped off his jeans.

Avery made a sound, but he wouldn't look at her again until he had his head on straight. "I'll be done in five minutes," he said on his way into the john. He brushed his teeth and tried to stop thinking about Avery in such melodramatic ways. He was a man who stayed grounded in reality, and the reality was that he wanted her. Period.

Anything else… Well, he wouldn't think about it. He'd shove it from his brain so that he could concentrate on more important things.

Like whatever secret Avery was trying so hard to hide from him.

CHAPTER THIRTEEN

ROWDY TURNED OUT the lights, pulled back the covers and stretched out along Avery's side. With one arm he scooped her in close and slid the other under her head.

She was stiff as a board, her hands still clutching the covers to keep them covering everything but her face. Silly woman.

Nuzzling her ear, he said, "Relax."

"Did you take a pain pill?"

"I don't need one. It feels better today."

Even in the darkness, he knew she looked up at him. "Rowdy Yates, you do not need to be noble with—"

He put his mouth over hers, stifling that absurd suggestion. Noble? Not likely. Nobility was not part of his DNA.

She didn't loosen up, but Rowdy wouldn't let it deter him. He continued to kiss her, brushing his mouth over hers until her breathing quickened. Taking advantage of her parted lips, he skimmed his tongue over her bottom lip, and heard the catch in her breath. He kept it light, nibbling, teasing—until finally he licked in, slow, deep, taking the kiss from subtle to full-blown possession. He moved over her so that his chest pinned her down and, God Almighty, that felt incredible.

Her hands snaked out from under the covers to tangle in his hair and pull him closer.

Out of self-preservation, he lifted his head. "That's better."

"Better than what?" she asked breathlessly.

He trailed his fingers through her silky hair, kissed her once more. "You cowering away from me."

He started to kiss her yet again, but she planted her hands on his chest and shoved.

Grinning, Rowdy moved to his side. "No more kissing, huh?"

"I was not cowering!"

"Could've fooled me."

She rose up, nose to nose with him. "I'm *tired*, remember? One of us didn't get any sleep last night."

"Damn, honey, stop growling like that." No way could Rowdy take the amusement out of his tone. He was grinning too much for that. "You sound ferocious."

"Screw you, Rowdy Yates!"

"Eventually." He caught her before she could shove her way out of the bed, then had to carefully wrestle with her to get her pinned down again without hurting her. "For a weary woman, you have a lot of fight left in you."

She bucked hard, almost taking him by surprise. He laughed and put a leg over her. "Does this animosity have anything to do with you trying to avoid our talk?"

She went still, then more frantic.

He held her and kissed her forehead. "Settle down."

"All right," she huffed, while still straining under him. "But only because I don't want to hurt your back."

"Only thinking of me, huh? Good, because I'm tired, too, and if we're heading out to see your folks in the morning, we both need some rest."

She turned her face away from his.

Rowdy nuzzled her neck. "What's going on, Avery?"

"I haven't been home in a year."

The same length of time she'd been denying herself? Huh. "Personal reasons?" He was unsure with the whole family dynamic. All he really understood about families was that most were fucked, and few understood real loyalty—the type of loyalty he had with Pepper.

"Very personal," she whispered.

He cupped her head, brushed his thumbs over her cheeks and tried to wade through the unfamiliar territory. "You dislike your stepfather?"

"Where'd you get that idea?"

Let's see…because she'd accused him of something, like maybe stalking her via telephone? "You didn't seem that happy to see him."

"It took me by surprise, that's all." Her fingers toyed with his chest hair, making him a little insane. "And I figured if he was here, something must be wrong."

Something like…she'd been found? "You were right, I guess, if what he said about your mother is true."

"It is. He would never make up something like that. He loves her too much."

So he sounded like a great guy. "Then why did you ask him if he'd been calling?"

"I don't even know." She pressed her head back into the pillow and groaned. "It was stupid. I should have realized that Meyer Sinclair would never do anything that undignified."

"Breather phone calls?" He hoped they were still talking about the same thing.

"Yes. He would never lower himself to anything that ridiculous. It's not his style."

"Then the million-dollar question is, who do you

think is making the calls? And, no, don't start retreating again." He held her face, kissed her hard and fast. "I pay attention, Avery. I remember the first call where the guy asked for you. Then I saw you today on the phone, and I heard what you said to your stepfather. Someone's been bugging you, right?"

She nodded. "It's only happened those few times." And then in a rush, "It could have been a prank. You know, someone who saw my name while he was at the bar drinking and he decided to make a pest of himself."

"Maybe." But the fact that she thought it was more made him think it, too. "Do you know anyone who'd want to pester you?"

It took her too long to say, "Not really."

"Avery."

"Don't *Avery* me. No, I don't know anyone who would be dumb enough to play juvenile prank phone games. It's just that… I don't know. It made me nervous." She added with blame, "Probably because you've got me seeing the boogeyman everywhere I look now!"

"How is this my fault?"

"You're the one who insists my place isn't safe."

Damn, she was good at turning things around on him. "It's no place for a woman to live, and that's a fact, not a suggestion."

"Rowdy?"

The way she said his name made it impossible for him to ignore the feel of her small, giving body under his. "Hmm?"

She slowly laced her arms around his neck. "You remember what the doctor said, right?"

Some bullshit about him waiting for sex. "Yeah, she said for you to take care of me."

Avery laughed, and even that, the husky sound of her humor, made him nearly frenzied with powerful lust.

"She said three days, and you know it. But you're making it so hard—"

"That's my line to you, babe." He nudged his erection against her hip.

She did this funny little half laugh, half groan. "Tomorrow will be the day, right?"

Meaning she'd hold him to his promise to give her tonight to sleep. That plan had seemed better hours ago than it did now.

His turn to groan, and he didn't bother holding back.

"Rowdy, stop misbehaving. You know it's for the best."

He did, but still he said, "The best would be stripping those cute pajama bottoms off you and—"

Her fingers touched his mouth. "Tomorrow, I promise, I won't wear pajamas." She ended that with a yawn, reminding him that she hadn't had much rest in the past twenty-four hours, and it was his fault.

"Go to sleep, honey." He moved to the side of her, settling himself carefully so that he didn't put too much pressure on his back, which, despite what he'd told her, was still tender. He drew her up against his body, and after a kiss to her neck, said, "Tomorrow is Saturday, you know."

"So?"

"So Sunday the bar is closed. I'll have you tomorrow when we close up the bar—and all day after."

She shivered. "Honest to God, Rowdy, I can hardly wait, myself."

He was still smiling when he felt her body wilt into sleep. Without meaning to, his arm tightened around her and he put his nose in her hair, breathing in her now-familiar scent.

It was so damn odd, especially considering he still had wood, but he liked this a lot. Holding her. Just… being with her. There was a certain comfort to having his little bartender so close.

He didn't yet know who might have called her, or why she'd seemed so defensive with her stepfather. But he'd figure it out. And in the meantime, she'd be with him, safe from harm.

He had nothing to worry about.

Nothing—except the overwhelming possessiveness he felt toward her. Rowdy rested his chin on the top of her head, closed his eyes and, holding her close to his heart, allowed himself to sleep.

ROWDY WAS FAR too enigmatic during the drive to her stepfather's house. Avery had seen him in many moods, but he'd never been this closed off from her. She'd tried to engage him in casual conversation, only to have him give short, succinct answers that didn't encourage a reply.

"Are you okay?"

He glanced at her. "Why wouldn't I be?"

"I don't know. You're so quiet." Avery admired his strong profile. They'd slept in—an aberration for both of them—and had to rush to get out of the apartment in time. Rowdy had taken a quick shower but wasn't freshly shaved. He looked ruggedly gorgeous with the whiskers on his lean jaw, his dark blond hair finger combed. "Is your back bothering you?"

"No."

"It can't be comfortable sitting in the car that way."

She'd offered to drive, but not only had he refused to use her car, he'd kept the keys to his own well out of her reach. Men. "I wish you had let me drive."

"I wasn't sure if we might get followed again, and since I know how to lose a tail, I figured it'd be better if I drove."

Oh. So it had nothing to do with the man-woman thing? "You could have told me."

"I just did."

Exasperation threatened her mellow, well-rested mood. "So were we followed?"

"Haven't seen me doing any fancy driving, now, have you?"

She supposed that was the best answer she'd get with him in this mood. "I think it's going to storm."

He leaned forward to look up at the storm clouds overhead. "Probably." With a glance her way, he asked, "You have a warmer coat than that?"

They'd each dressed casually, Rowdy in jeans and a black T-shirt that showed off every amazing muscle in his torso, she in jeans and a beige pullover sweater. He'd brought along a flannel shirt; she wore her lightweight jacket.

"I have a regular winter coat, I just hadn't figured on needing it yet." For October, it was unseasonably cold with storms rolling in.

"How's the heat in your apartment? Warm enough?"

Seeing the train of his thoughts, Avery leaned toward him and put a hand on his solid biceps. As always, his obvious strength gave her shivers. "You don't have to worry about me, Rowdy. I can take care of myself." His skin was so warm, taut over bulging muscle.

Tonight, after work, they would have sex. It was

going to be a very long day, starting with her family reunion.

Under her hand, his arm flexed. "I wasn't *worrying.*"

"Showing concern, then. It's not necessary. I promise I have enough sense to feed and dress myself, and to stay out of the elements."

He gave her an inscrutable frown. "Almost there."

She remembered Alice saying that Rowdy could take a punch, but wasn't good at accepting compliments. Apparently any and all human emotions seemed like weaknesses to him and ranked right up there with compliments.

She knew why, and it tugged at her heartstrings. Scooting closer, she hugged herself up to his arm and put her head on his shoulder. "Thank you for asking."

He shifted, put a hand on her thigh and said, "If you do need anything, let me know, okay?"

No, she wouldn't do that to him. His parents had mistreated him. His sister had needed his protection. Society had abandoned him. And women wanted to use him for sex.

At least in this one small way, she could be different. Instead of Rowdy taking care of her, she wanted to take care of him—for as long as he'd let her. "Thank you for coming with me today. I'm sorry that you got put on the spot."

His hand caressed her leg. "Not a problem, honey. But before we get there, do you want to tell me why?"

"Why what?"

"Why you wanted me along."

"Meyer suggested it."

"And you could have told him I'm not anyone's *boyfriend.*"

True, but she couldn't very well tell Rowdy she'd wanted to defend him. If he didn't like a compliment, he definitely didn't want her defense.

"Good company?" she offered as her excuse. Given the look he gave her, he didn't buy that. "It's true. Don't get alarmed, Rowdy, but I enjoy being with you. And no, that doesn't mean I'll always expect you to—"

"You're worried about seeing your mom again?"

So he didn't want to hear her reassurances, either? Fine. She wouldn't keep telling him; she'd just show him. "No. I mean, it feels a little awkward. I've been away for so long and I didn't leave under the best circumstances."

"The circumstances being?"

She'd had time to think about this, about how to explain without going into too much detail. "We had a disagreement. Remember, I told you that my folks wanted me to settle down? Well, so did my stepfather. He thought he could hook me up with the perfect guy. Only I didn't think he was so perfect." That was all true enough, though it didn't come close to covering it all. It didn't tell him how pushy Meyer had been about it, or how abusive Fisher had acted.

It didn't tell him that no one had believed her, that they'd all believed Fisher's lies.

"My mother wants to pamper me, and Meyer wants to make her happy, so…they really felt like I should follow some pattern."

"The pattern being marriage and home and hearth and all that?"

"Pretty much. They saw marriage to the right guy as a lock on a secure future, which for them also equates to happiness." She slipped her fingers under the sleeve of the T-shirt so she could feel his rock-solid shoulder. She loved touching him, loved the smell of his skin, his incredible warmth. "I wanted to see more of the world."

"By working in a dive on the wrong side of the tracks?"

She protested that. "It's not a dive anymore!" Hadn't been, not since Rowdy took over.

"Still in a shit part of town." As he turned a corner, he grumbled under his breath, "Your stepfather sure as hell noticed."

She shrugged. "I like my job." And she loved… *No. She wouldn't even think about that.* "You're a terrific boss, and Ella and Jones feel sort of like family now."

"And Cannon?"

"I have a feeling he'll fit right in." She looked down the street of impressive homes on large lots and a pang of sentiment curled around her heart. "There, at the end. The gray stone two-story."

"Jesus." Rowdy slowed the car. "Are you fucking kidding me?"

She hadn't quite expected that reaction. "What?"

"It's a damned castle."

She looked at the Tudor-style house again. She supposed the stone turrets and expansive arches did bring to mind a castle, only this house had all the modern conveniences and then some. "I told you Meyer was well-to-do." But honestly, she didn't think about it. She'd come from that background, so to her, it was just a nice house. Again, the differences in their lives filled her with remorse for what Rowdy had never known. "It's not a big deal."

He pulled up to the curb, then just sat there, staring at the house.

"You can pull into the driveway."

"No, I don't think I can. Not in this trap."

"Rowdy." For her, a car was a car was a car. Sure, what he drove had seen better days, but it got him where he wanted to go and that's what counted. "It doesn't matter."

"It leaks oil. And there's not so much as a dry leaf on that damned driveway."

"Oh." Trying for some errant cheer, Avery said, "So we'll have a nice brisk walk up to the house." She slipped on her jacket. "Let's go." Now that they'd arrived, she was anxious to see her mother.

Face set in stone, Rowdy put the old Ford in Park and turned off the engine. He pocketed the keys and opened the door to step out. As he stood there looking toward the grounds of Meyer's home, a gust of wind played with his hair and plastered the black T-shirt to his back.

Beneath the soft cotton, Avery could make out the outline of his bandages. Leaning toward the driver's side, she asked, "Your back is still okay?"

With an effort he pulled his gaze from the house. "What? Yeah, it's fine. Don't worry about it."

He sounded cross. She'd have to remember to stop fussing so much.

Shrugging into his flannel, Rowdy said, "Why do I have the sudden suspicion we might be underdressed?"

"They're not that hoity-toity, I promise." Stepping out, she pulled her jacket close around her. "Wow, that wind is cold."

Rowdy moved around the car to her and put his arm over her shoulders. He took in the expanse of the home with brooding displeasure. "Might as well get this over with."

Was he really dreading it so much? Because it meant nothing to her, she hadn't even considered how it might make him feel to have wealth thrown in his face. His reaction showed her insensitivity.

She wasn't better than other women, not if she ended up making him uncomfortable, forcing him into unfamiliar situations.

Drawing him to a stop, she looked up at him. "We don't have to go in."

One eyebrow lifted. "You want to hang outside in this cold?"

"No, I mean we can just turn around and go back." With a hand gripping each side of his open flannel, she leaned into him. His hands automatically went to her waist. "Meyer will understand if I say I need to reschedule. I can come back later, tomorrow maybe—"

"I don't think so." Rowdy bent to nip her bottom lip, then slowly soothed it with his warm tongue. "Tomorrow you will be naked, open and under me."

Her stomach took an excited tumble over those suggestive and descriptive words. "That sounds perfect, but I could come—"

"Several times." He closed his mouth over hers, his tongue just barely teasing her lips, slipping inside to touch her tongue, then retreating again. "Guaranteed."

She had difficulty thinking when he did things like that. "Come *here,* in the morning, or early evening, and we could still spend the majority of the day together."

"You're not listening, babe. Tomorrow, all day, you're mine." He slid a hand down her back to her behind. "It's going to take every available hour for me to get my fill."

Would it really be that simple for him? Once they had

sex, however many times in one day, would he *have his fill* and be done with her?

Probably, yes, and the reality of it saddened her, but she wouldn't saddle him with her effusive emotions. He'd been honest with her all along; she knew their relationship would be very short-lived, and she knew what he wanted from her—sex.

Somehow, when things ended, as she knew they would, she'd just find a way to deal with it. "All right, then. If you're sure you want to stay, we may as well go on in instead of giving the neighbors a show."

His narrowed gaze abruptly scanned the area, and he smirked. "The houses are all so far apart, I seriously doubt anyone can see us." He did release her, though, taking her hand instead and starting them up the drive.

Smiling, Avery let him tug her along. She liked the way his large hand engulfed hers, how his long, strong legs covered so much ground so easily.

The way his worn jeans hugged that sexy backside of his.

The man was totally put together, and tonight she'd get to explore him—naked—head to toe. Regardless of what he said, she'd show care for his back. But there were all sorts of creative positions they could use.

She wanted to try them all.

At the top of the driveway, surrounded by manicured landscaping, Rowdy stopped and stared at the silver BMW parked there. Avery went cold from the inside out. She knew that damned car and—

"Well, hello, you two."

Eyes flaring, she twisted to face the front entryway…and there stood Fisher Holloway. Residual fear tried to emerge, but she fought it back. Today, now, she had nothing to fear.

She had Rowdy Yates with her.

That meant she had the upper hand.

She'd spent a very long time gaining her independence, building up walls against the hurt and putting the past behind her.

No way in hell would she let her uncertainty show. Not to this man.

She narrowed her eyes, and with venomous sarcasm said, "Fisher. What a surprise to see you here."

ROWDY NO LONGER had the urge to leave. Hell, no. He wanted to stay, and he wanted to get answers.

Like for starters, why was the very car that had been following them parked front and center in her stepfather's driveway? Had Meyer lied? Had he been tailing them? And if so, why?

When Rowdy turned to see who had welcomed them, he gave thanks to Mother Nature for the physical gift of his height and bulk. The clown smiling at Avery like a long-lost lover wasn't a slouch. In fact, he looked like a damned linebacker and stood right at six feet.

But Rowdy was bigger and taller, and that gave him the advantage of smiling down on the other man.

No jeans for this bozo. No, he wore creased charcoal slacks and leather shoes and some designer-style polo. Rowdy spotted a chunky gold ring on his hand and a gold chain around his neck.

He fought to keep his lip from curling.

Avery scooted closer, and that one small telltale gesture, more than anything else, sharpened his senses.

The other dude stopped smiling at Avery long enough to come down the walkway and extend his hand.

"Hello. You must be Avery's...*friend* who Meyer told us about."

Rowdy took the hand, amused when the man tried to tighten his grip. "Rowdy Yates. Avery works for me." He squeezed back, and Fisher's smile slipped.

"Fisher Holloway," he said around a near grimace. "I'm a close family friend and a business associate."

Rowdy let him off the hook, releasing his hand and nodding toward the silver BMW. "Is that your car?"

Fisher shoved his hands in his pockets. "One of them, yes. She's about ready for a trade-in, though. Why, you looking for a new ride?"

"No, and I couldn't afford that anyway. It's nice."

Fisher bent his knees and laughed. "And what? You can't afford nice?"

"Not that kind of nice, no."

Avery suddenly shoved herself in front of him. The move was so absurd—her stance so obviously protective—that it left Rowdy chagrined.

"That's not what he meant, Fisher, and you know it."

Such a snarling tone from Avery. On his behalf? Had he misunderstood her nervousness?

"No offense intended, honey." Fisher smiled at Rowdy in a knowing, man-to-man way. "I was just jesting."

Locking his jaw, Rowdy took Avery's upper arms, lifted her and physically set her to his side. "It was accurate all the same. I can't afford a car like that." Where the hell did this guy get off calling Avery "honey"? Did they have a past?

Was it even *in* the past?

Still riled, Avery said, "Rowdy owns his own business and he's putting all his assets into that."

Assets? What assets? If he sold everything he owned, he still wouldn't be able to afford that car.

"A bar, right?" Fisher shared a smug smile. "Meyer said it was really…quaint."

"Then he was trying to be polite." Rowdy took Avery's hand in a bid to control her absurdly defensive tendencies. "I'm sure you've never been there, have you, Fisher?"

"Afraid I haven't had the pleasure."

Bullshit. He'd scoped out the place, so why lie about it? "You sure? Could've sworn I saw that exact car just recently."

Avery didn't hear the accusation, but Fisher got it loud and clear. "I doubt mine is the only silver BMW on the road."

No, but it was the only one with those exact plates. Rowdy shrugged. "A car like that stands out in my neighborhood."

"Hmm. In my neighborhood, it's not that different from every other car."

Score one for the dirtbag. Rowdy let it go before Avery did catch on. The last thing he wanted to do was ruin her reunion with her mom. "Should we go in? I know Avery is anxious to see her mother."

"And vice versa," Fisher said. He gestured for them to precede him. "I told Meyer I would bring you both in. They have a light lunch set up in the sunroom."

What the hell was a sunroom? As Rowdy stepped past Fisher, his skin prickled with warning. He didn't like having the guy at his back. His instincts were rarely wrong, but this time, he knew the uneasiness could have been from…

Jealousy.

Dark, ugly, *mean* jealousy.

From the second Fisher had smiled at Avery with warm familiarity, Rowdy had wanted to mangle him.

Either Fisher didn't realize his peril, or he was confident enough to discount it, because he moved to Avery's other side and, walking too close to her, said in intimate undertones, "It's good to see you again, Ave."

Ave? What kind of nickname was that?

Avery's hand tightened on Rowdy's and her voice went a little shrill. "Why are you even here, Fisher?"

"Meyer invited me. And of course I agreed. I've missed you."

What, was he invisible? Rowdy didn't mind being ignored, but not so Fisher could attempt to move in.

"Is that how you tell it?" Avery asked.

"When it comes to you, Ave, I always tell the truth."

She growled something incoherent.

Rowdy had no idea what all those nuanced comments meant, but they were being slung around so freely, he felt bludgeoned by them. For certain, Avery and Fisher had a history.

Did that history include sex?

Or worse, *love?*

Maybe that's why Fisher had been hanging around, covertly checking up on her. In his shoes, Rowdy might have done the same. If she left this area to go slumming in his, only a moron wouldn't have been concerned. And Fisher might be a dirtbag, but he probably wasn't stupid. He'd understand the trouble that would come Avery's way.

Trouble like... Rowdy Yates.

"While you're here," Fisher murmured, "I'd love for us to have a chance to talk. Privately."

Fuck that.

Rowdy was ready to speak up when Avery said, "No."

Good. So she wasn't keen on a private chat, either. Suited Rowdy just fine.

Before stepping through the open front doors, he brought Avery around in front of him, which effectively put Fisher at his back again. If he had to bodily keep them separated, he would.

The role of jealous *boyfriend* was about as comfortable as a cactus seat, but he didn't give a damn.

"I've been a close confidant to Meyer and Sonya," Fisher said. "I've comforted them while you were away."

Avery trembled. With anger? Upset?

As they stepped into a massive foyer, Rowdy looked around and badly wanted to leave—with Avery thrown over his shoulder, if necessary.

CHAPTER FOURTEEN

It LOOKED LIKE wealth had thrown up costly shit everywhere.

"Nice place." Rowdy tried to cover his awe, but what the hell? The entry alone was big enough to be a hotel.

"The sunroom is this way," Avery said. Gripping Rowdy's hand, she charged through the house at a fast-paced trot, showing no regard for the museum-like pieces inside.

Fleeing Fisher or anxious to see her mom?

Being around Avery in this setting left his perception blown, making it difficult to sort out overriding emotions, but he voted for the first.

Since her mother had remarried, he knew Avery hadn't grown up here. But was this home much different from what she was used to? She sure seemed to take it in stride, going right past a sweeping staircase, columns and chandeliers, marble and cut glass and... all kinds of fancy crap.

Finally they entered an octagonal room at the back of the house. Walls of sparkling windows rose up to meet the twelve-foot vaulted ceiling. The view of a parklike backyard filled with massive trees drew his gaze to a fancy pool that looked like part of nature.

Rowdy was so enthralled with what he saw that he

almost missed the petite woman who quickly rose from her seat.

His gaze locked on Avery's mother.

Something a little sick and a lot needy twisted inside him when the woman rushed over and grabbed Avery up tight. She was petite like Avery, feminine in a clingy sweater dress and low-heeled shoes. Her features were like Avery's, but instead of the rich red hair of her daughter, the mother had very fair hair half-hidden by a silk scarf. She was probably kicking sixty, but still looked soft and elegant and trim.

Easy to see where Avery got her good looks and that killer little body.

Rowdy felt like a lummox just standing there, an interloper without the right to smile as Meyer and Fisher both did.

Stepping back, he tried to remove himself a little from the personal scene.

Tears hung from the mother's lashes, but she cupped Avery's face and laughed. "I have missed you so much."

Avery pressed in close for another hug. Arms entwined, heads together, both rocking gently side to side.

It was something to see. Really nice.

How a mother and her child should be, not that he had any firsthand knowledge on that.

Rowdy shoved his hands into his back pockets and willed himself to look away.

He couldn't do it.

The women didn't just embrace, they squeezed. Tight. So much sentiment filled the air he almost choked on it. He couldn't swallow, could barely breathe.

Then suddenly Avery was free and back at his side, leaning on his shoulder in that familiar way, hugging one of his arms. Smiling, her own eyes red, she sniffled and said, "Rowdy, this is my mother, Sonya. Mom, this is Rowdy, my boss."

Sonya's smile faded. "I'm not sure that's the proper *hold* for a mere boss, dear."

Rowdy felt like a damned spectacle. He looked past Sonya to where Meyer and Fisher stood aligned, ripe with animosity, bunched up with caution.

Then Sonya extended her tiny, delicate hand. "Rowdy, thank you for bringing my daughter home."

And it was a home, Rowdy realized. A home of love and protectiveness and all the wonderful things that home should mean. All the things Avery deserved.

Why had she left?

And what the hell was *he* doing here?

Sonya's hand was so small. He held it gently. "She brought herself, ma'am. I'm only along for the ride."

"Will you join us for lunch?" She indicated a table set with more dishes than he'd ever seen.

"Thank you." He saw fruit, tiny sandwiches, pickles and some type of fancy chips on the table.

Fisher pulled out a chair. "Ave, here's your seat."

She gave him a dirty look and stayed glued to Rowdy's side. With an arm around her, he ushered her forward and pulled out a chair, but Sonya said, "Thank you, Rowdy," and seated herself.

She patted the chair next to her. "Please. I'd love to talk with you more." She twisted around. "And, Avery, I want you on my other side. We have so much catching up to do."

Well, hell. He'd just been outmaneuvered by Sonya, Rowdy realized as he watched Fisher take the seat beside Avery, leaving him caught between Sonya and Meyer.

Talk about uncomfortable... He tugged at his ear but said nothing as he took his seat.

The minimal food—light lunch—was served, and then Sonya and Avery started a quiet, private conversation. From what Rowdy could hear, they were at odds about something. Not an outright argument, but definitely some displeasure.

A second later, Sonya said, "Please don't wait for us," and she and Avery left the table.

Rowdy watched them step away to a set of windows on the other side of the room, where they both gestured and whispered and occasionally embraced again.

"So, Rowdy." Fisher cut a goddamned strawberry like he would a steak.

He defiantly bit one of the little sandwiches in half. "What?"

"Did Ave tell you why she's been away?"

As if on cue, Meyer said, "Excuse me." And he, too, left the table.

Alone with Fisher. Interesting. Rowdy had the distinct feeling he'd been set up in a big way.

"She didn't go into details," Rowdy told him.

"What did she tell you about me?"

"She didn't." Choke on that, you pompous ass. "In fact, she's never mentioned you at all." Which made Rowdy damned curious, given Fisher appeared to be a very accepted part of the family.

Fisher looked across the room at Avery, his gaze filled with tenderness. "We had a falling-out. When I wanted her to marry me and settle down, she said I was too controlling."

Rowdy glanced at Avery. Her face stricken with worry, she held one of her mother's hands and with the other she straightened the scarf. Her mother seemed to reassure her.

He remembered her talking about regrets, saying her folks had wanted her to marry. Obviously they approved of Fisher as the chosen one or he wouldn't be here right now.

Rowdy said, "Win some, lose some, Fish." See, he could do shortened names, too.

"I still love her," Fisher said, all pretense at good manners long gone. "I want her back."

Furious as it made him, Rowdy didn't know if Fisher would have any luck with that or not. But he did know one thing. "It won't be happening today, so I suggest you step back."

Feigning amusement, Fisher gave a smarmy grin. "You think you have a chance, is that it?"

A chance to get his fill, yes. Beyond that? He was honest enough with himself to know the odds weren't in his favor. That didn't mean Avery would fall for an ass like Fisher. She was far too genuine, too sincere and *real* to fall for a guy in a gold chain.

"I know she came here with me, and she's leaving with me. For now, that's enough." What a lie. It wasn't even close to enough.

"I don't know about that. As I told Avery, I've remained close with the family. I've consoled them in their grief over her behavior, her…abandonment. But she's here now, and if her mother asks her to stay…" He left the words to hang in the air, the possibilities unspoken.

Shit. Rowdy hadn't even thought of that. He glanced

at Avery again and saw that both women were now smiling. They could be wrapping up that little chat real soon, so he might as well get it said. "I recognize the license plate, Fish. You've been hanging around, spying on her."

For only a moment, Fisher looked surprised before he shrugged. "Watching over her, actually."

Rowdy didn't debate that possibility, because damn it, it made sense.

"Ave is not cut out for the seedy side of life. She's rebellious right now, proving...something to her folks." Fisher forked another strawberry with far too much precision. "When her father died, it devastated her. And then Sonya remarried, adding more changes to their lives, and Avery hasn't been the same since."

"How so?"

Fisher grinned. "Moving out. Working in a low-class bar." He pointed the forked strawberry at Rowdy. "Bringing you home to flaunt her rebellion under their noses."

Was that why Avery had wanted him along? He sure as hell couldn't think of any other reason.

"I'm sorry," Sonya said as she rejoined them at the table. Both Rowdy and Fisher stood, but it was Meyer who returned in time to hold her chair.

To Rowdy, Sonya said, "I've been away from Avery for some time and we had some catching up to do. I hope you'll forgive the rudeness."

Rowdy looked past her to Avery, who was far too solemn. "I understand." It damn near killed him, but Rowdy said, "If you need the day off, Avery, we can work it out."

"No." She cut her tiny sandwich into two tinier pieces. "No, it's fine. Mom and I already worked that out, and I promised to come back soon to visit again."

"But if you change your mind…" Sonya offered tentatively.

"Sorry, Mom, but I can't. I'll visit often, but Rowdy needs me there during work hours. Since he's taken over the bar, the crowd has quadrupled."

Meyer asked, "What time does the bar open today?"

Rowdy had a mouthful, damn it. He swallowed down the food and used the snow-white linen napkin on his mouth. "We open at three-thirty. The kitchen closes at eleven, last call is at one and we close up the bar at two. That's six days a week, but we're closed on Sunday."

Fisher sat back in his seat. "I understand the establishment used to be a hot spot to barter drugs and traffic women."

"Yeah?" Rowdy wasn't sure how much Avery wanted her mother and stepfather to know. "Where'd you hear that?"

"Relax, Rowdy," Meyer said. "No one is trying to accuse you."

Tag team, huh? He tipped his head and stared at Fisher long enough to let the worm know what he thought of him. "I'm plenty relaxed."

Sonya touched his forearm. "You're sitting like a nun in church."

He couldn't rest back in his seat, not with his stitches, and he knew just enough not to prop his elbows on the table.

"Rowdy is always relaxed and confident and comfortable." Avery leaned forward to see around her mother. "He was injured in a fight so he can't rest back," she said with a glare at Fisher. "And no one would have any reason to accuse Rowdy of anything."

Grinning, Fisher held up his hands. "Isn't that what we just said?"

"Injured how?" Sonya wanted to know.

Looked like he wouldn't be eating anything more. Rowdy pushed back his plate. "It's nothing."

"He got cut with a big knife."

Shit. Rowdy wondered what Sonya would think if he stuffed one of the fancy cloth napkins in Avery's mouth.

Hand to her throat, Sonya stared at him. "A knife fight?"

"It wasn't that dramatic, and it wasn't that much of a fight."

"Did this happen at the bar?" Meyer demanded to know.

Rowdy shook his head. "It happened outside the bar—"

"Only because Rowdy took it outside," Avery said. "And even after he got cut, he still kicked their butts."

"Good Lord," Sonya said.

"He was defending a little boy!"

"You let kids in the bar?" Fisher asked.

Bombarded by their accusing stares and Avery's enthusiastic retelling of things, Rowdy felt his strain amplify. "No." If Avery wanted to air it all, then by God, he'd do some airing. "As you said, the bar had previously been used for trading drugs, and yeah, there was a link to human trafficking that got shut down."

Sonya looked ready to faint.

With relish, Avery said, "It was pretty bad there before Rowdy cleaned it up."

Her mother jerked around. "You worked there when that was going on?"

She shrugged. "I was a waitress, yeah."

Egging them on? Rowdy had no idea what Avery was up to, but he didn't like it. "I bought the place, Avery stayed on and for the most part we kicked out the—" *assholes* "—criminal element."

"But guys showed up wanting to finish a deal they'd made with the previous owner," Avery explained. "One of the buffoons brought his son along."

Sonya and Meyer shared a horrified glance. Fisher barely kept his satisfaction to himself.

"Thanks to Rowdy," Avery said with glee, "the man is in jail now, and the little boy is staying with one of Rowdy's friends, who just happens to be a detective."

Sonya swallowed audibly. "You mentioned a knife fight?"

Rowdy opened his mouth—but Avery beat him to the punch.

"The guy Rowdy pulverized had a cohort. That guy pulled a knife. Even after he cut Rowdy, though, Rowdy still took him apart."

Great. Way to be discreet, Avery. Rowdy scratched his chin, waiting for the inevitable questions.

Fisher got things started. "So do you do a lot of street fighting?"

"I avoid it when I can." Not entirely true, since he sometimes took great relish in pounding on the right people. "Sometimes I can't."

"Because of where you live and work?"

He shrugged. "Probably."

Avery gasped. "That's not true. It's because he defends people when necessary." Here she glared at Fisher. "Often when no one else will step up to do it."

Sonya shifted uncomfortably; Fisher narrowed his eyes. Meyer made a sound of disgust.

"And when those occasions arise, you're…equipped to handle it?" Meyer wanted to know.

"I can hold my own."

"He's incredible," Avery countered. "Very fast and strong. I was amazed at how good he is."

Meyer threw down his napkin. "You were *there*?"

"Watching through a window, yes, since Rowdy insisted that I stay inside."

"Thank God for small favors," Fisher muttered.

"Oh, Avery," her mother whispered. "I don't want you to go back there."

Great, Rowdy thought. If Avery kept it up, they'd tie her down before letting her leave with him.

"It was a little scary," Avery admitted, "especially when the guy sliced up Rowdy's back."

Sliced up? It was one damn cut. Rowdy picked up his tea. "I don't think you need to embellish things, honey."

"I'm not! You know you handled them both with ease. Those thugs didn't stand a chance."

"Well." Fisher taunted Avery with a narrow stare. "Apparently he wasn't fast enough to avoid that knife, now was he?"

Going pale, Avery started to argue, but wasn't given a chance.

"And what if he'd been killed?" Meyer demanded. "What would have stopped those goons from coming in after you?"

Sonya gasped at the possibility.

Avery waved off their concern. "Meyer, really, give me some credit. I had the door locked. Besides, I'd already called the cops. They got there just as Rowdy wrapped things up."

Rowdy could feel Fisher, Meyer and Sonya staring

at him with the same type of horror reserved for a train wreck. Hell, he could even hear their thoughts.

They were wondering what someone like him was doing with someone like Avery. They were blaming him for Avery's new bloodthirsty tendencies.

They wanted him away from her, pronto. And to be honest, he couldn't blame them one bit. Put Pepper in a similar scenario and he'd feel the same.

No way did Avery miss it. She was too astute for that.

So she…what? Wanted them to know what he was capable of? But why?

To rub it in, as Fisher had said? To show them just how far she'd gone in her rebellion? He hated that thought, but nothing else fit.

As if she hadn't already done enough, Avery added, "I've seen Rowdy fight a couple of times now. He can be lethal."

Fine, if that's what she wanted, then he'd share it all. Rowdy forgot about his back as he relaxed in the chair. "Learning to defend myself came with the upbringing."

"What does that mean?" Meyer wanted to know.

"My sister and I were raised in a rusted trailer on the riverbank. At five, I was fighting off hungry rats, and I guess I never stopped." Avoiding Avery's gaze, he lifted his tea in a toast. "If you don't learn to fight, you get your ass beat on a regular basis. So yeah, I can handle one idiot with a knife."

Everything, everyone, fell silent.

Screw them all, Rowdy decided. He reached across the table to snag up another of the puny sandwiches, tossed it in his mouth and pushed back his chair. "Time for us to hit the road." Standing there, feeling all their eyes on him, he tipped up his tea glass and finished it off, too.

And without waiting for Avery, he started out of the room. He heard Fisher snicker and thought about going back to beat the shit out of him, but he had never taken his bad temper out on anyone who didn't deserve it.

Fisher might be annoying, but that didn't earn him a coat of bruises.

Right now, Rowdy was the only one who deserved to have his ass kicked. He'd been a blind idiot, a complete fool.

As Meyer and Sonya tried to convince Avery to stay, he heard the rise of voices. *Let her,* Rowdy thought.

But he knew deep down he wasn't going anywhere without her.

Furious, mostly at himself, Rowdy stopped outside the sunroom and, hands on his hips, waited.

A second later Avery came hustling out with Fisher at her side. She shook off the other man, spotted Rowdy and slowed with…relief.

Bull. He wouldn't let her draw him in again.

"Sorry," she told him brightly, as if their visit hadn't gone completely off the rails. "I had to say my goodbyes."

Sonya and Meyer were right behind her, still spewing arguments for her to stay. When they saw Rowdy, they clammed up.

Good breeding could be a hindrance, huh? Rowdy almost laughed.

"If you want to take a minute to make plans for another visit," Rowdy offered, "I can wait outside."

"No, that's—"

Fisher interrupted her. "Meyer and I can wait with him, Ave. Take your time."

"No!" She started forward. "I—"

"Yeah, *Ave,*" Rowdy mimicked, stopping her in mid-step. "Take your time. Can't claim to be a gentleman, but I'm not crude enough to leave you behind." His own bad disposition took him out the door and as far as the driveway. Having Fisher at his back didn't feel any more reassuring now than it had earlier, but this time Rowdy hoped the creep would do something, anything, deserving a beat down.

Instead, his hands in his pockets, his tone nonthreatening, Fisher said, "Sorry, man. I know it couldn't have been easy for you to come here."

"Yeah?" Arms crossed over his chest, Rowdy leaned back on the fender of the bastard's car. "Why's that?"

Meyer shook his head. "Now you see that Avery is… well, she's confused about some things. But she needs to return home. Her mother needs her here."

"Got nothing to do with me."

Fisher shared a look with Meyer. "You could fire her."

The hell he would. Rowdy showed his teeth in mock humor. "I'll let her know you suggested it, Fish."

Fisher sighed. "If you want to make this more difficult, I can't stop you. But for her sake, I hope you reconsider."

For her sake. Yeah, for Avery, Rowdy would do just about anything.

Sucked that he was only just now realizing it.

She stuck her head out the door, saw him and again her blue eyes went soft with relief. She and her mother came out.

Sonya looked distressed, but Avery said, "I'll be back soon, Mom. I promise. If you need me, I'm only a phone call away."

"I don't want to be a burden."

Avery smiled. "You could never be that."

Sonya shivered in the cold breeze, so Meyer went to her, his arm around her shoulders.

"Go on in," Avery told them, holding her own jacket close around her. "It's too cold out here."

Rowdy wanted to snuggle her closer, too, to share his warmth, but he didn't. He ignored Fisher and said to Avery's parents, "Thank you for the lunch."

Meyer replied, "Drive carefully."

Indecision held Sonya for a second before she stepped forward. "Thank you, Rowdy. I hope we see you again."

Not likely. He got one side of his mouth to smile, nodded and turned to go. Avery hustled to keep up with him.

Full of confidence, Fisher called out, "We'll see you again soon, Ave."

Mouth pinched tight, she ignored him and stared straight ahead. For Rowdy it was a little harder. He wanted to level the smug bastard.

At the end of the driveway, Avery stepped closer, her shoulder bumping his arm. Rowdy moved away from her on the pretense of circling the car.

She stopped and stared at him a moment before going on to open her own door.

If she thought he was a gentleman, then it was past time for Avery Mullins to accept the truth. She'd laid it out for her folks, and he'd be happy to drive it home for her.

He was a street rat, through and through. Immoral when it suited him, driven by his own rules and to hell with what society thought. He and his little bartender had nothing but sexual chemistry in common.

Much as he might wish it otherwise, Rowdy knew that could never be enough.

AVERY TOOK THE silence for as long as she could, but she grew more stressed with each minute that passed. Finally she felt as if she'd jump out of her own skin if she didn't say something.

"My mom says she's in overall good spirits. They got all the cancer and her prognosis is good. She's recovering quickly."

Nothing.

"Cancer is always serious, of course. But Mom assured me that she'll be fine, that much of the treatment is just precautionary. She said Meyer exaggerated things."

"He wanted you home, where you belong."

But she didn't belong there. Not anymore. She needed Rowdy to understand that. "Mom apologized for Fisher being there. I guess Meyer invited him, and he showed up last minute."

It crushed her that even now her mother didn't see what a creep Fisher was. She claimed he had been so helpful to them, that Fisher was every bit as heartbroken by her long absence.

If her mother hadn't been ailing, Avery would have walked out again.

"She wanted me to take some of my old clothes with me. She disapproves of my jeans, but I've really enjoyed being so comfortable."

Rowdy's face tightened, but he didn't reply.

"I think she's accepting that I made my own way. Especially now that we've sort of reconciled. I told her I'd come back more to visit." When Fisher wasn't around—

that was one stipulation she'd given, and her mother had agreed. "She'll call to talk, to keep me updated on what's happening."

No reaction at all.

"She said she'd really like to get to know you better, too."

Other than Rowdy's eyes narrowing more, he didn't acknowledge her in any way.

Avery knew he'd disapproved of her bragging. He couldn't possibly understand why she'd done it, and Avery couldn't tell him.

Better than most, she knew how deceptive Fisher could be. Despite appearances, he wasn't a principled man, and he didn't fight fair. As long as Fisher believed that Rowdy was a complete and total badass—which wasn't a stretch—then he just might leave Rowdy alone.

But if Rowdy knew the truth, no way would he let Fisher off that easy. He thought himself invincible, and in some circumstances, it might be true. In a fair fight, one-on-one, face-to-face, Rowdy would destroy Fisher.

Unfortunately, Fisher wasn't a dummy, but he was the worst kind of coward. If he ever attacked Rowdy, it wouldn't be in any honorable way where Rowdy would have a chance to defend himself.

If only she'd known Fisher was going to be there... Damn Meyer for his meddling.

As Rowdy continued to ignore her, her heart grew heavy in her chest. "Rowdy?"

"What is it, *Ave?*"

She winced at the bite in his tone. "Please don't call me that. It's some ridiculous thing that Fisher picked up. I don't like it."

He turned down a road toward the bar.

They only had a few more minutes. "I'm sorry if that was uncomfortable for you."

He laughed without humor. "Funny, but Fisher said the same thing to me."

"Fisher is an ass." What else had he said to Rowdy? Her heart punched hard at the possibilities.

"Hate to point out the obvious, honey, but he shared your sentiments."

"No. Fisher and I share nothing." She reached out to touch him, but without moving, Rowdy somehow made it clear that he didn't want her to. Crestfallen, she withdrew her hand. "I meant that with Fisher being so hostile... I didn't know he'd be there."

"He wasn't hostile at all," Rowdy denied. "He cares for you."

She wanted to scream, *No, he doesn't.* Instead she tried a deep breath. "We were never together. Fisher likes to remember it otherwise." *Fisher likes to lie.* "But I never cared for him that way." *Not how I care for you.* "I guess you could tell that Meyer and my mom wish things were different. They like him and approve of him—"

Rowdy gave another grim laugh.

"Stop that!"

He didn't even glance her way. "Stop what?"

He'd frozen her out and it hurt. So damn much. "Stop being so condescending, so...cold."

Rowdy pulled onto the street for his apartment. "You used me, Ave."

God, how she hated that butchering of her name. But she couldn't deny what he said. She had used him.

To show Fisher that she wasn't without resources of her own.

She wasn't alone, vulnerable.

To show him that Rowdy was not a slouch, and wouldn't be an easy target. He wasn't a person who would turn tail and flee the danger.

And that's what scared her so badly. Fisher didn't lose. If he couldn't run Rowdy off the easy way, he just might get rid of him for good.

Rowdy pulled into the bar, then around to where her car was parked.

She stared at him, confused. "What are you doing? We don't open for two more hours."

"I figured you'd want to run home to shower or change or whatever."

"But—" She wanted to talk to him, to reach him. To repair whatever damage had been done...

"I need to go see Marcus." He reached past her and pushed the passenger door open, a blatant order to get out. "Have to hurry it up if I'm going to get back in time."

Wow, talk about rejection. Hurt had a death grip on her heart right now. "Rowdy, if you'd let me explain..."

His gaze met hers, and the volcanic emotion there stunned her. "Go ahead, babe. Lie to me. Tell me you didn't use me."

Words wouldn't come. She shook her head, feeling so damned helpless. "I don't lie." More than anything, she needed Rowdy to believe that—because no one else had, not even her mother.

Rowdy smirked. "Shoving me under their noses really taught Mommy and Stepdaddy something, didn't it? Too bad you didn't clue me in beforehand. I could have unearthed some of my best stories. Like the time I stuffed a human trafficker in my trunk, took him to an abandoned warehouse and taught him the error of his ways with my fists."

Her lungs compressed, leaving her breathless.

"Or the time I dared a mob boss to shoot me so that Logan could sneak up behind him and get the upper hand."

She covered her mouth, unable to bear the thought of it. "Stop it," she whispered.

"Why? You wanted your folks to hear the nitty-gritty. I have some real shit stories we could have passed around the table over fancy finger food. Course, that might not have given you enough time to talk to your mother about her cancer." He put an arm along the back of the seat and toyed with her hair. "Did you manage to squeeze in any concern, honey? Or were you too busy sticking it to them?"

Chased by heartache, hurt and anger, Avery launched out of the car. It crushed her to know he had such a low opinion of her, making her hands shake as she fumbled in her purse for the keys to her own car, then fumbled some more trying to get the damn door unlocked using the clicker. Tears burned her eyes and blurred her vision.

Once inside, she fired up the engine, then, unable to stop herself, she glanced back at Rowdy. He sat in his car, the engine idling, his cell phone to his ear.

And she knew. He was calling someone to keep an eye on her, to ensure she got home safely.

She deflated with that realization. He was hurting, too; that's why he'd been so cruel.

But that didn't make it any easier. Somehow she'd have to make him understand her motives without telling him too much. Regardless of the malicious way he'd just used to get her out of his car, she didn't have a single doubt what Rowdy would do if he knew the truth about Fisher. Right now he was a disgruntled, wounded bear, but deep down, he was still a protector. He'd been born to it, and for every day of his entire life he'd been fulfilling that duty.

She could have been a stranger on the street, and still she knew he would react on her behalf. It was in his nature, the biggest part of his psyche. God love the man, he was a hero, no matter how nasty he acted right now.

Avery kept staring at him until he'd finished the call and tucked the phone away. He put his car in gear and, with sudden determination, she smiled at him.

That threw him. He paused, his gaze narrowing on her.

She wiped her eyes, lifted her chin and pushed back her hair. Then just to let him know he hadn't chased her off for good, she saluted him.

His expression turned to stone. Avery didn't wait to see what he'd do. She drove out of the lot, her thoughts rioting. She'd go to her apartment all right. But she wouldn't give up on Rowdy.

She wouldn't let him forget that he'd promised her tonight, and all day tomorrow. Whatever it took, damn him, he would make good on that promise.

Before he left her for good, he'd give her that memory, one that would last her for the rest of her life.

CHAPTER FIFTEEN

THINGS HADN'T GONE quite as he'd planned. No one had played their part correctly, most especially not Avery. She was different now, more outspoken, more confident and independent.

Being on her own for a year hadn't weakened her. No, it had given her inner strength.

He grinned. That wouldn't last, though. Next time he got everyone together—everyone but Sonya, because really, when it came to his plans, she'd been more a hindrance than a help—he'd make sure all the pieces fell into place. And then Avery wouldn't be so high-and-mighty.

He could hardly wait.

ROWDY AGAIN SAT on the floor, spending precious minutes greeting the dog while Marcus stood back, watching in apprehension. Alice, bless her, went straight for the kitchen and more cookies and juice. Maybe this would be their routine, makeshift picnics in the apartment with him working hard to put Marcus at ease.

"I got that red car," Rowdy said as he produced the small vehicle and another length of track. "What do you say we hook them up?"

Hanging back, Marcus glanced toward the kitchen where Alice hummed while getting their snack. When he looked back at Rowdy, he chewed his lip, then asked, "Are you mad?"

Damn. Had the kid picked up on his mood? He thought he'd covered up pretty good, but he knew all about survival, how you had to learn to judge those things, even at a very young age.

Rowdy had already decided that he would never lie to Marcus, no matter what. So he said, "At you, no."

Rubbing a forearm under his nose, Marcus shifted nervously.

Rowdy found himself expounding, trying to put the kid at ease. "It's nothing, really. Just a disagreement with a…friend." God, Avery was so much more than that. Or at least, he'd thought so. Now he just didn't know.

"Who made ya mad?" Marcus asked.

It struck him that Marcus feared his bad mood would spill over onto him. Probably in the past, with his asshole parents, he'd caught the brunt of everything bad that happened.

His mood soured more, but Rowdy finally got Cash to settle down. He stroked the dog's back. "You know, Marcus, mostly I'm disappointed, I guess." He cupped Cash's furry face, rubbed his long ears. Dumb as it sounded, he said, "I got my feelings hurt about something, and I'm gloomy about it. But I think playing cars will make me feel better. So do you want to?"

Alice walked in with a tray. The big faker didn't fool him one bit. She'd heard everything, even though she pretended she hadn't.

"Let's eat!" She sat yoga-style on the floor, perpendicular to Rowdy so that Marcus could sit across from him, then set out cups of juice and cookies on napkins. "The cookies are fresh from this morning. Marcus helped me make them."

"No kidding?" Rowdy took a big bite and groaned. "Man, that's good."

Now, with Alice close, Marcus inched over and seated himself. His bony knee hit the cup of juice and it spilled, sending a puddle spreading out.

Marcus froze, his face going pale, his eyes wide.

Alice said, "Oops!" and scooted so the juice wouldn't soak into her slacks. "Good thing I brought napkins."

Rowdy leaned forward. "Marcus?"

Mouth pinched, shoulders hunched, the boy looked down at the floor.

Rowdy wanted to pull him into his lap, to cuddle him as he'd cuddled Cash, to swear to him that nothing bad would ever again happen to him, because he wouldn't let it. But he knew better than to try that. "It's just juice, buddy. I'm forever spilling something, and it's not a big deal. It wipes up."

"Already done," Alice said, making a point of not really looking at either of them. "No harm done." She stood. "I'll refill your glass, honey."

Marcus still didn't look up. Rowdy heard him swallow.

Fuck it. "You know what I'd like to do, Marcus? I'd like to hug you and tell you not to worry about it. But I know you need time to believe that it's fine. It hurts my heart, man, really bad. Right here…" He put a hand over his chest. "To know you're worried about it, so please don't be."

In a small voice, Marcus said, "You can keep the car."

God, he would slay dragons for this kid if he could.

But all he could do was sit here with a cheap-ass toy and reassurances that didn't mean shit. "I want you to have it. I want us to be friends and to play together, and I don't want either one of us to worry about anything bad happening." Rowdy held out the car. "Please, will you take it?"

Looking miserably confused, Marcus accepted the car, more because he was afraid not to, Rowdy thought, than because of any trust.

Jesus, this entire day had been a bitch. He rubbed the back of his neck and forced a smile. "Thank you." Very, very gently he reached out to cup a hand over Marcus's head. He said again, "Thank you, Marcus. I appreciate it."

Again, the kid held perfectly still until Rowdy removed his hand.

Alice came in with more juice and a roll of paper towels. "I brought these out in case we have any more accidents. Heaven knows I'm as likely as you are, Marcus, to bump something over." She sat down and leaned near to him. "When Cash was getting house-trained, I had to carry paper towels with me everywhere. I don't think there's a single spot in this apartment that hasn't been sprinkled." She grinned as if it amused her to have a dog leaking everywhere.

Marcus watched her with fascination—much as Rowdy had often done.

They ate all the cookies and drank all the juice. Marcus finally loosened up enough that they connected the tracks. Rowdy gave Alice a purple car—a little convertible with a hood that opened. Marcus had his red and green cars. Rowdy had a white truck.

They played for a half an hour until Alice said, "I

hate to break up this fun party, but Rowdy needs to be getting to work."

Rowdy groaned. "I wish I could stay and eat more delicious cookies. You're both good cooks."

Marcus grinned, and it so stunned Rowdy that he nearly lost it. Damn, but his eyes burned. "I had fun, Marcus."

"Me, too."

"So what color car should I get next?"

Given the way Marcus hesitated, how he chewed his lip and rubbed that forearm under his nose again, he didn't trust the offer.

"Any color you want," Rowdy promised. "How about a black sports car? Or maybe a purple convertible like Alice's."

"My car is very sweet," Alice said, and she took it on another spin along the two lengths of track.

Finally, peeking up at Rowdy with gut-wrenching hope, Marcus said, "Your white truck is neat."

Optimism sent his blood pumping. "Awesome, little dude. We have the same great taste!" Rowdy lifted the truck. "I'll pick up another one for you, but until then, how about you hold on to mine for me?" To ensure Marcus couldn't refuse, Rowdy set it on the floor and rolled it toward Marcus, then came to his feet.

As usual, he took a minute to say goodbye to Cash, then, cautiously, he went to Marcus. "I'll be back, okay?"

Marcus looked at his feet, but he nodded.

Rowdy knelt down. "I had fun. Thank you."

"You're not mad anymore?"

"I was never that mad, remember? But even if something did happen to make me mad, even if it made me furious, it wouldn't make me mean. Not like you're thinking. Never to you. Okay?"

"So you're not mad anymore?"

Aware of Alice standing there, Rowdy laughed at himself. He ruffled Marcus's hair, and he didn't even care that Marcus went typically still. "No, I'm not mad anymore." He stretched back to his full height.

Putting her arms around his neck, Alice went on tiptoe to hug him. She said low, "Please don't do anything dumb, Rowdy."

What the hell? He caught her shoulders to pry her away. "No, I won't."

"Baloney." She turned him loose, then put a hand on Marcus's shoulder. "Something happened between you and Avery, but she's a very nice woman." She said in an aside to Marcus, "Avery is his girlfriend."

Boyfriend, girlfriend, where did people get off using those namby-pamby terms for good old sizzling lust?

"And," she said to Rowdy again, "whether you admit it to yourself or not, you care about her. I see it. I know it. So I say again, please don't do anything dumb. I don't want you to have regrets."

"Yes, dear." He kissed her forehead, and then, without really giving it much thought, bent and put a kiss to the top of Marcus's head, too. With Cash thumping his tail, he laughed and kissed him, too—and that made Marcus chuckle.

Eventually, Rowdy thought, Marcus would recover. But if that was true, why hadn't he?

AVERY WASN'T SURPRISED when Rowdy started the workday by ignoring her. As her boss, she figured eventually he'd have to talk to her, and then she'd have an opportunity to break the ice.

But as the day wore on, he managed to avoid her altogether. He delegated many of his usual responsibilities, including filling in for her, to Cannon. Not even once did he approach her himself.

To make things worse, he flirted. Boldly.

When one blonde came to talk to him, standing far too close, Rowdy stared at her boobs until she was giggling.

When later a brunette asked him to dance, he actually took a few minutes to hold her on the dance floor, swaying in time to a slow song, pelvises aligned.

That had every other lady lined up for a turn. But Rowdy laughed it off and got back to work.

The jerk.

Avery was stewing, both furious and jealous, when a familiar redhead came in.

The memory of Rowdy in his office with that woman, what she'd witnessed them doing, sucked all the air out of her lungs until she couldn't breathe.

A customer said, "Another beer, honey," but Avery ignored him.

The woman went up to Rowdy, hugging him from behind, slipping one hand into the neckline of his shirt, the other far too close to the fly of his jeans. He looked startled, wincing in discomfort at how tightly she grabbed him.

But when he turned and saw it was her, he didn't excuse himself.

He looked up and met Avery's gaze.

It felt like an eternity that they stared at each other

until finally Rowdy pulled his gaze away to address the woman.

"Hey, another beer."

Almost by rote, Avery filled the chilled glass, but as Rowdy smiled at the woman, she couldn't seem to do anything but stare.

The jealousy was so red-hot, Avery couldn't even breathe.

Cannon nudged her. "Hey, you okay?"

"I'll kill him."

"*Him* being Rowdy, I take it? I mean, that's the guy you're killing with that laser-like glare, right?"

She gave one sharp nod.

"Tell you what. Why don't you take a break?" Cannon pried her hand off the beer mug and handed it over to the disgruntled customer. "I'll take care of things here."

"No."

Cannon gave an exaggerated sigh and a pitying shake of his head. "You're only showing him how much it bothers you. While I don't know you well, I sort of took you for the type with a lot of pride."

Yes, where was her pride? She needed to find it and fast. It took a lot of inner struggling, but Avery finally got her gaze off Rowdy and the other woman. She put a hand to her forehead and concentrated on collecting her wild emotions.

"Hey." Cannon tipped up her chin. "I think Rowdy's fighting his own demons tonight. Don't take any of that shit too seriously, okay?"

"So you don't want me to kill him?"

His fingers still under her chin, Cannon grinned. "I get the feeling he's already suffering, you know?"

Yes, she did know. But if he went off with that woman…

Out of nowhere, Rowdy shoved between them. "Avery, take your break. Cannon, you can go help Jones finish up in the kitchen."

More amused than ever, Cannon said, "Sure thing, boss." And off he went.

Rowdy didn't look at her, but his presence was so big that all he had to do was get near to make her aware of him in every pore. She wanted to ask him if his back was okay. She wanted to hug him, and she wanted to smack him.

Avery searched the room and found the redhead seated at a table. So she was still out there…waiting on Rowdy?

Over her dead body.

"Go on," he said.

Instead of leaving for her break, she glared at Rowdy. "What is she doing here?"

"It's a free country, Ave. She can go wherever she wants."

Ave again. Lowering her voice, she demanded, "Are you taking her to your office?"

"Why? You want to watch again?"

That low blow actually took her back a step. Lips parted, breathing shallow, she wondered how quickly she could get out of there.

Except, this time, she didn't want to run. This wasn't like with Fisher. This hurt so much more.

Rowdy glanced at her, then cursed low. "No."

She didn't understand.

He reached around her for a glass. When she didn't move, he paused, a muscle ticking in his jaw. Time stretched out while he stared into her eyes. He leaned in, his voice like broken glass. "No, I'm not taking her to my office. I don't want to fuck her. I don't even want to touch her."

He sounded furious…at himself.

Tension ebbed away, leaving her wilted. "Okay." The wild thumping of her heart calmed. The invisible fist squeezing her throat eased up. She almost said *thank you,* but that'd be too absurd.

She touched his arm, stroking over his thick wrist once, then she darted away. They needed to talk, but she had to regroup first. If she tried it now, she'd end up making declarations that Rowdy didn't want to hear, and that would make matters worse.

She was in the break room swilling coffee when the storm started. Rain came down in earnest, sending sheets of rain against the windows. The lights flickered and thunder rattled the floor beneath her feet.

Wow. She finished up her break and went back to the floor. Some of the guests stood near the windows looking out. Overall, the storm chased people away—including the redhead, blonde and brunette! With the low crowd, the rest of the night was easy, but as dismal and tumultuous as her thoughts.

The lights flickered a few more times but stayed on. Rowdy had flashlights near the bar, and of course emergency lights were installed. Still, Avery was very glad to call it a night.

When the last customer was gone and Rowdy had locked up, she knew she had to confront him. It was now or never.

Coat on, nervousness chewing her up inside, Avery found him in his office. Ridiculously formal, she tapped on the door before stepping in.

Because he stood off to the side, she didn't realize that Cannon was there, too, until she entered.

Rowdy glanced at her as he pulled on his own jacket. "Do me a favor, Cannon, and see her out to her car, okay?"

Avery froze.

Looking uneasy, Cannon pulled on his knit hat and shrugged. "Sure, I can do that."

Get a backbone, Avery. She stepped forward. "Rowdy..."

He tossed the keys to Cannon. "Lock up on your way out."

Avery couldn't believe it when he went right past her and out the back door. She stood there, staring at the door, willing Rowdy to change his mind, to come back in and apologize. To say they needed to talk.

Even to argue with her.

He didn't.

Slowly, she turned to Cannon.

He looked down at the floor, then up at the ceiling. He cleared his throat. Twice. "You ready to go, honey?"

A refreshing surge of anger boiled through her. For such a long time now, Rowdy had chased her hot and heavy. He claimed to want her. Bad. But now, over a big misunderstanding, he intended to just blow her off?

Hell, no.

She did not easily get in bed with men. After Fisher, well, she wasn't sure if she'd ever again trust a man enough to want him. But she wanted Rowdy, and by God, she would have him.

Tonight—as he had promised.

"I'm ready all right. You can bet I'm ready. More than ready." She went to the back door, slammed it and closed all the locks. "Let's go."

Cannon rubbed his mouth. "Are we talking about the same thing?"

"No, we're not." She grabbed his arm and dragged him to the front of the bar with her. "Come on. If I wait, I might lose my nerve, but I want to do this."

"This?"

She nodded. "I've been celibate too damn long. I *need* to do this."

"Uh, Avery…" He bumped into a chair, stepped around it and tried to free his arm.

She held on. With what she had planned, she needed to steal some of his strength. "I have to go out through the front."

"Maybe we should talk a little."

"Not now."

"You know, Rowdy won't be happy about this. I mean, I just got hired on and he doesn't strike me as the type to share, so…"

Realizing what he thought, Avery cast him a look. "Get real, Cannon. You know I'm hung up on Rowdy."

He wasn't at all discomforted by the conversation. "I figured, yeah. But generally speaking, if a woman starts locking doors and leading me off, it's to—"

"Not this time." She wanted Rowdy Yates. Period. And one way or another, she'd have him.

Cannon grinned. "Know what? I'm equally bummed and relieved."

If that was his idea of flirting, he'd wasted it on her. "You wouldn't do that."

"I'd be tempted…" When she frowned up at him, his smile warmed. "But no, I wouldn't."

She shook her head and unlocked the front door. The rain pounded down, washing over the street, bending the few straggly trees that disrupted the brick and concrete landscape.

Cannon stepped just outside the door. "I don't suppose you have an umbrella?"

"No." She stared at Rowdy's apartment and saw the lights come on. If she stared hard enough, she could see a few shadows moving past his big front windows.

"Want me to bring your car up here to you, then?" Even from where he stood under the overhang, he got soaked. Wind blew in from every angle.

"I don't need my car."

"No?"

"I'm going to Rowdy's apartment."

"But not by car?"

"It's across the street." She pointed. "Right there." So close...but given how Rowdy had all but looked through her, it felt very far away.

Cannon followed her gaze and nodded. "Ah. Makes sense, I guess."

"What does that mean?"

As he locked up, securing the bar, he said, "I've seen him go in the building. I thought maybe...never mind."

"That he had a woman there? Given his proclivity for sleeping around, it's a logical assumption." Accepting the keys from him, Avery dropped them in her pocket, then turned up her collar. A useless effort that she knew wouldn't do her a bit of good.

Cannon eyed her, then started to take off his coat. "Why don't you put this over your head so—"

She held up a hand to forestall him. "I won't melt." As she said it, the rain lightened up a little, providing a small break in the storm.

"Now or never."

Taking her arm and standing close, Cannon said, "You might want to keep in mind that Rowdy was fighting himself more than you today."

"You think?"

"I'd bet on it."

Avery stared at him in amazement. "Wow, so you not only know everything about running a bar, but you're a trained fighter and a relationship expert, too?"

He gave her a philosophical look. "I'm a guy, so I know how guys think. That's as expert as it gets."

"Are you in a serious relationship?"

He did a double take over that question. "As you just said, I have a full plate. No real time for a relationship."

But Avery would bet he didn't skimp on female company. Men. In so many ways, they were all alike. Luckily, when it came to being considerate, hardworking and protective, Cannon and Rowdy had a lot of similarities.

"Thank you, Cannon, for everything." She marched out from under the covering of the overhang.

Cannon kept pace with her.

"You can go on home." Her feet splashed through puddles in the road.

"I'll make sure you get in first."

Yup, very protective. The area looked so damned dark, she could only be grateful for his vigilance. "All right, thanks."

Though the rain had slowed, they were both drenched in the short time it took them to reach the front door to the building. Avery drew a deep breath, opened the door and turned to Cannon. "Now, if only Rowdy lets me in…" The wind whipped up again, throwing her jacket open.

He glanced down at her chest, then away. "He'll let

you in. Trust me." He took the door from her to keep
the wind from ripping it away. "Go on, then."

Avery glanced down at her chest, too. Oops. The rain
had penetrated her jacket and her shirt. It clung to her
skin, outlining...everything. Added to that, her jeans
were soaked to midthigh, her hair sodden.

Slowly she smiled. Being drenched just might work
to her advantage. "Wish me luck, okay?"

"I think Rowdy's the one that needs it, but sure, good
luck to you." He flicked the end of her nose. "Go easy
on him."

With a little more confidence, Avery turned and trot-
ted up the steps. Her heart beat wildly—with worry,
with hope, but mostly with anticipation.

Tonight she would have Rowdy Yates. At the moment, nothing else mattered.

BRISTLING WITH IRRITATION, Rowdy peeled off his damp
clothes and changed into dry jeans. He couldn't look at
the bed. When he did, he saw Avery there, that beautiful red hair of hers spread out around her face, the way
she smiled and how she teased, her delicate aroma and
how comforting it had been to hold her while they slept.

No matter that his mind had decided he wouldn't
touch her, his body still craved sexual satisfaction.

But only with Avery. Right now, no other woman
would do.

Hell, he'd had so many offers tonight, one of them
from two women looking for a three way, that he could
easily have spent the night working off tension the good
old-fashioned way.

Instead, he planned to read. Since buying the bar,
he'd studied up on small enterprise solutions. He didn't

have much in the way of an education, but he had enough street smarts to know it required knowledge as well as hard work to make a business survive.

And above all else, he was a survivor.

Barefoot, he went into the kitchen and opened a beer, then found the book on the shelf. Whenever he did a lot of reading, he needed glasses. Nothing prescription, just readers he'd bought at the drugstore. Carrying the beer, the book and the reading glasses, he went to his couch and dropped down.

Leaning back didn't hurt that much, not with the thick bandages in place. They needed to be changed, but he couldn't do it himself. Tomorrow he'd get Pepper to take the wrappings off, and he'd leave them off.

He took a big drink of the beer, opened his book and...thought of Avery. No matter how he tried, he couldn't keep her out of his head.

Or his heart.

He'd left her with Cannon.

Demons chased around his brain, making him imagine all sorts of scenarios guaranteed to keep him awake through the long night.

Closing his eyes, he leaned his head back and willed himself not to care.

Impossible.

When the knock sounded on his door, he lifted his head, a scowl already in place. The last thing he wanted to deal with was another pushy woman. The neighbors were nice enough, but they watched for him to come in, and then they found a reason to pester him.

He wasn't in the mood to be gracious tonight.

Shoving the glasses to the top of his head and setting his book aside, Rowdy left the couch, went up the few short steps and opened the door.

Like a sucker punch to the gut, the sight of Avery standing there, soaked to the skin, shivering, that stubborn chin of hers lifted, sucked his breath away.

"Can I come in?"

His gaze tracked over her, from the long sodden ropes of her hair, to her open jacket and the way her shirt clung to her breasts, to her dripping jeans. Already a puddle had formed around her.

He braced himself against her impact. "You should have gone home."

She lifted her chin another inch. "You promised me sex."

Jesus, he hadn't expected that, hadn't thought she'd be this brazen, this bold and…sexy. He breathed a little harder, and felt his dick stir.

Avery stepped in. "I'm here to collect."

What the hell did she think? That she could manipulate him with sex? Backing up from her, he said, "No." Then he turned his back and went down the steps, putting some distance between himself and temptation.

Going to his couch, he sat down and, pretending he wasn't coiled tight and on the verge of asking her to stay, he put his glasses back on and picked up his book.

As the seconds passed, he pretended to read and Avery held silent. He wouldn't look at her again.

"I'm freezing, Rowdy."

He heard the chattering of her teeth, and he clenched his muscles to fight the compelling need to comfort her. He glanced at her over the glasses but said nothing.

"My jeans are completely soaked."

He didn't mean to, but he said, "Take them off." Then

his heart started jumping, and he breathed deeper, waiting to see what she'd do.

It felt like a lifetime that they stared at each other before Avery turned, closed the door and locked it.

CHAPTER SIXTEEN

WITH A FULL-FLEDGED boner straining his jeans, Rowdy watched her strip off her insubstantial jacket. She needed a coat, damn it. Something warmer, weatherproof... *It wasn't his concern.*

Avery hung it over the rail at the landing, then bent to remove her shoes and socks. She placed them beneath the jacket. Barefoot, her bottom lip caught in her teeth, she straightened and turned toward him.

Rowdy couldn't help it. Lured by an unspoken promise, enthralled by possibilities, he sat forward. When her small, trembling hands went to the waistband of her jeans, he sucked in his breath and held it.

She opened the snap, pulled down the zipper and worked to get the wet denim down her slender legs. She stepped out and straightened, wearing no more than a clinging T-shirt and tiny beige panties.

Rowdy set the glasses aside, but he didn't leave the couch.

Holding the jeans in front of her, she asked, "Could I use your dryer?"

He wanted to see her walking across the room, wanted to see her ass in that little bit of material she called underwear. He worked his jaw, then muttered, "Help yourself."

She held the railing on the steps, walking carefully,

shaking all over. Icy rivulets of rainwater dripped down her narrow back, tracking over the curve of her ass and soaking into her panties; her small bare feet made no sound on the cold floor. In the kitchen, she opened the stack dryer and bent to put the jeans inside.

Biting off a groan, Rowdy stiffened—all over. Apparently he could be manipulated with sex after all.

"Rowdy?"

He stood, but stayed by the couch, a safe distance from her dangerous appeal.

She pulled the shirt away from her body. "This is wet, too."

There went the last piece of his imagined control. Grinding lust roughened his voice when he whispered, "Take it off."

After the briefest hesitation, Avery nodded, caught the hem and peeled it up and over her head.

He'd fucked his way through a miserable upbringing, using sex to counter the ravages of poverty and abuse. He used it still to rid his mind of plaguing memories. But now, with Avery, the need that consumed him had nothing to do with any of that—and everything to do with her.

She half turned toward him, her eyes big with both uncertainty and resolve, her slender body bare except for a bra and panties that left little to the imagination.

His jeans felt too restrictive, and without looking away from her, he readjusted himself.

When he made no move toward her, she drew in a shuddering breath, blinked back tears and turned to put the shirt in the dryer with her jeans. Arms around herself, shoulders hunched and knees together, she gave him a defiant stare.

Yeah, he was a goner.

Only Avery could muster up that particular attitude while standing naked and vulnerable, cold and wet.

More than a little predatory, Rowdy stalked toward her, taut from head to toe. He stopped right in front of her, close enough to breathe in the scent of her wet skin and hair, mixed with the sweeter perfume of her excitement.

Her hair hung over her shoulders, partially hiding her breasts from him. With an exaggerated lack of haste, his movements methodical, he used both hands to move her hair back so he could see her nipples.

Her bra was as wet as the T-shirt had been, made of the same material as her miniscule panties. She shivered, her skin prickling and her nipples drawn tight.

With the back of one knuckle, he teased over her right breast.

Her breath caught. "Rowdy?"

"It's wet." He dropped his hand, his gaze clashing with hers. Very softly, he ordered, "Take it off."

When she reached behind herself for the clasp, he cupped both breasts, teasing her stiffened nipples with his thumbs. She paused.

"Go on," Rowdy told her.

Fumbling, breathing faster, she tried to hurry, and finally the bra loosened. He stripped it down her arms and tossed it into the dryer, then went back to toying with her nipples.

"I… I need to change your bandages, too, while I'm here."

"Maybe later." He liked that catch in her voice, how sensitive her nipples were and how quickly she reacted to his touch. He touched the waistband of her panties. "Let's see if I can get these wet, too."

She put hands against his chest. "Rowdy, wait."

Fuck. Stepping back again, he crossed his arms and tried to prepare himself for whatever she had to say. He'd known, of course, that she hadn't just come for sex. Avery wasn't made that way. She had enough pride for three men and enough backbone to stand up to bad temper.

But he'd hoped that maybe, just maybe, she'd come because she...cared.

Hardening his heart, he waited without comment.

Shivering again, Avery stared up at him, her blue eyes pleading. "I... I need to tell you two things."

He was as ready as he could be. Eyeing her breasts, he said, "You have my attention."

She shook her head. "No, not yet." Her tongue licked over her bottom lip, and she stroked his chest suggestively. "After."

He straightened. Maybe he'd underestimated her intent after all. Stepping closer, he slid his hand over her waist. Her skin was chilled, damp, and he wanted to warm her. He wanted to protect her. Make love to her.

Cherish her.

But he couldn't. Not yet.

Eyes narrowed, he asked, "You want sex?"

"God, Rowdy, you know I do." She tried to burrow closer. "But I have a few conditions."

His lust didn't cool, but his heart turned to ice. "I don't think so, babe. You don't get *conditions*." He looked her over, so petite but shapely, so fucking sexy. He made himself say the words: "It's all or nothing."

She nodded, but said, "It's just that I..." Her voice trailed off.

"You just what? Want to manipulate me?" Never would he let that happen, not even for Avery. "You have an agenda, honey? Is that it?"

Sadness weighed down her shoulders, but that damned determination remained in spades. "I want to *protect* you."

What a laugh. "From who? You?" So far, she'd been by far the biggest danger he'd ever faced.

"No." She licked her lips again, leaving them damp, sharpening his urge to feel that soft mouth on his, on his body. "You don't know everything about me."

"No kidding." The way she'd used him had blind-sided him because he'd thought her above that type of shit. He'd thought her genuine and caring and honest.

"I... I'll tell you, but you have to promise me you won't change your mind."

More demands? "About what?"

"Wanting me, this." She gestured helplessly. "Having sex."

And there was the biggest joke of all. "I'm not about to turn down easy sex." He couldn't. He needed her too much. "If you stay," he said by way of an answer, "you'll definitely be under me."

She slowly inhaled, then said the unexpected. "I left my old life behind because someone...someone tried to hurt me."

Ice ran through his blood. In a voice so faint he barely heard it himself, he whispered, "How?"

She rushed through the explanation, her hands open on his chest, sort of clinging. "I was almost raped."

He took that one on the chin, staggered by the rage that exploded. He would easily kill anyone who dared—

"*Almost,* Rowdy. It didn't happen." She petted him, soothing, ripe with concern. "But I *had* to leave. No one...no one really believed me when I told them."

Leveled, Rowdy searched her face and knew without a single doubt that she was telling him the truth. Everything he'd just been thinking faded behind the red mist of rage. "I believe you." Avery might've thrown him for a few loops, but she wouldn't make up something like that.

She wilted against him, tears of gratitude hanging on her lashes. "Thank you."

He rubbed her upper arms. "Give me a name."

"I don't want you involved." He opened his mouth, but she said, "No, Rowdy! I mean it. It's not your problem."

"Like hell."

She went on as if he hadn't spoken. "But that's why I wanted you there with me when I went back home. That's why I bragged about your ability."

Stunned, he said, "Your folks didn't believe you? That's who you meant?" Son of a bitch. And here he'd been thinking they were such nice people. It didn't matter if he told Pepper he'd been attacked by an alien. She would believe him and back him up, no questions asked. *That* was family.

And here he'd been sort of envying Avery....

She touched his collarbone, then his shoulder. "They know him. He's a reputable man, by all appearances a very good person. They thought I was exaggerating. And he had a story all ready about how we'd argued, how I'd overreacted."

Hearing the hurt she still carried amplified his fury. Through his teeth, his muscles knotting, Rowdy asked, "Fisher?"

Those damn tears swam in her eyes again. "I don't want you to do anything, Rowdy. That's what I'm trying to tell you."

"You'll see him again." Her mother's medical condition dictated that she'd be around the bastard because he had a feeling Fisher would take every opportunity to close in on her.

"Yes, but now I know to be more careful. Now I know to avoid being alone with him."

Using his thumb, he brushed a tear from her cheek. "He's a threat, honey, and threats are best dealt with head-on."

"I don't want to be another burden!"

Crazy Avery. It wouldn't hurt her to show some faith. "Trust me, babe, dealing with Fisher won't be a hardship." He already looked forward to it.

"He's not what you think. He's not a dumb thug like Darrell. He has power and resources and—"

"He's scum, and I've met every kind there is." He thought that would reassure her, but she threw her arms around his neck, her trim little body up flush against his. Her skin was still chilly. He needed to get her wrapped up and warm. "Avery…"

She tucked her face in by his chest. "The other thing I wanted to tell you?"

There was more? He sighed while stroking her back. "Let's hear it."

Her breath came faster. The seconds ticked by while Rowdy resisted the urge to palm her behind, to kiss her.

Very slowly, Avery disengaged. She kept her hands

on his shoulders but tipped her face back so she could see him. She looked devastated, worried and full of remorse, and that worried him.

He'd kill Fisher, he decided. He'd rip him apart. He'd—

Avery put her small hand to his jaw. "I love you."

To be on the safe side, Cannon hung around for a few minutes. If Rowdy proved to be more bullheaded than he imagined, he didn't want Avery out in the storm alone.

He was already soaked, so what did a little more rain matter?

After twenty minutes, though, he decided it was safe to leave. He realized he was grinning, but what the hell? It was kind of funny to see a guy like Rowdy Yates struggling over an itty-bitty thing like Avery Mullins. As a couple, they amused him a lot.

They also made him grateful that he wasn't caught in that damned emotional trap.

Women were all well and good. Hell, he adored women. Respected them, too. But he had a lot of plans that had nothing to do with getting involved in a relationship.

He spent his mornings working out and training. Before getting hired on at the bar, he'd used the rest of his free time playing vigilante, clearing out some of the scum from his neighborhood. It really pissed him off that so many areas had gone downhill, run by lowlifes and losers who wanted to blame everyone but themselves for not stepping up.

After meeting Rowdy and taking his measure, he'd decided a bar would be a good place to get the lowdown on criminal activity. So far, he was right.

What he hadn't expected was Rowdy's own little mystery, with strangers hanging around, Avery getting upsetting phone calls and a whole wealth of drama to go along with the cryptic happenings.

He'd help where he could, of course. With any luck, Rowdy would settle things with Avery tonight. But even if he did, Cannon still planned to stick around, to stay alert and to be available—if needed.

AVERY HELD HER breath as Rowdy stood there, staring at her in stark surprise. *Please, please, please don't tell me to leave.*

Eyes darkening, he stared at her so long and hard that she thought about running.

She held her breath, so hopeful it hurt.

And then he scooped her up and his mouth was on hers as he strode to the bed. Avery held on, thrilled that he wasn't sending her away but fearful of him hurting his back.

As he lowered her to the bed, coming down on top of her, she freed her mouth to say, "Rowdy—"

Ruthlessly he kissed her again, his hands holding her head, his tongue exploring her mouth as he kneed her legs apart.

Giving up, she kissed him back and carefully wound her legs around his thighs.

His mouth left hers to put a hot, openmouthed kiss to her throat, her shoulder. He bit her lightly, making her tingle all over, then licked the spot, there and lower, down to her nipple.

When he sucked her in, she arched her back on a wave of red-hot pleasure.

He groaned, switched to the other breast and teased,

licking her, tugging gently with his teeth, suckling softly.

She squirmed under the carnal onslaught. "Rowdy, take off your jeans."

Without answering, he slid farther down, leaving a damp trail of kisses along her ribs, over her belly, her hip bone. He nuzzled against her, breathing deeply, groaning again.

Avery lay there, letting him do as he pleased, loving it all.

Loving him.

He sat up and hooked his hands in her panties, dragging them down and off. His chest labored as he lightly touched his fingers to her sex. "So pretty." He looked up at her breasts, reached a hand there to cuddle her while still touching between her legs.

It was so intimate, so personal, she turned her face away. But that wouldn't do, not when she so enjoyed looking at Rowdy. He was waiting for her to look at him, and as soon as she did, he parted her, his fingers exploring.

"Already wet and hot." He pushed two fingers into her, his gaze hard, going darker with her gasp. "Nice and tight, too."

The pleasure coiled, and she tipped her head back, arching again.

On his knees beside her, Rowdy touched her breasts even while fingering her, and all the while, he watched her in absorbed fascination.

"I want you to come for me, Avery, like this." He brought his thumb up to her clitoris, touching her with a tantalizing rhythm. "Once I get inside you, I'm not going to last."

What he said and how he said it turned her on as much as what he did to her.

She got her eyes open and stared at him. "Please kiss me."

He looked at his hand between her legs. "Here?"

Oh, God. She swallowed and held her arms out to him. "Rowdy."

Half smiling, he leaned down and lightly brushed his mouth over hers. "Tell you what," he said, then sealed his mouth over hers in a hot, tongue-twining kiss that left her breathless. When he lifted his head again, he murmured against her mouth, "There's that kiss."

Muscles already quivering in a rising climax, Avery stared at him, suspended in anticipation of what he'd do.

He touched his mouth to her throat. "And this kiss."

Next his hot breath teased her breast right before he drew on her nipple in a soft leisurely suckle that ended with a lick. "And that one."

He worked his way downward again, and with each kiss the pleasure sharpened until she was gasping.

"And now…here," Rowdy whispered, lightly kissing her where she was most sensitive, priming her before he closed his mouth around her and drove her wild with the rough stroke of his tongue.

There was no holding back, no conscious thought of guarding his injured back. All she could do was cry out as the climax swelled inside her. Flattening one hand on her abdomen to keep her still, Rowdy pushed her, moving his fingers in her, his tongue on her.

She fisted the sheets to anchor herself until finally the orgasm began to fade.

Rowdy groaned, holding her close a moment before rushing to his feet and shedding his jeans.

Breathing hard, her heart drumming furiously, Avery watched him through a fog of satisfaction, how he hurriedly rolled on a condom in record time.

He stepped back to the bed, hooked his arms under her legs and pulled her to the edge of the mattress. "Sorry," he murmured, his face set with some dark emotion. He positioned himself, then used her wetness to glide against her.

With all her nerve endings still tingling, the sensation was too acute and she tried to pull back. Impossible with the way Rowdy held her.

Watching her intently, he leaned in and slowly thrust in. She groaned and drew tight around him.

"So good," Rowdy murmured, straining against her as he buried himself and then went still with an obvious effort.

"Rowdy," Avery whispered, loving him so much. She touched his shoulders, down over his chest hair. He was rock solid all over, now more so with his arousal. She loved the contrast of his solid muscles and soft chest hair. "You don't need to wait," she promised him. "I'm ready, and I want this. I want *you*."

His jaw locked, shoulders tensed and gaze burning... *"Fuck."* He broke, driving into her hard and fast, keeping her legs high, pressing them out and back until he was going so deep Avery felt another climax building.

She continued to watch his face, seeing everything he felt, which made her feel it, as well. He pressed closer to kiss her, and that was incredibly hot, too. This time when she came, it took her by surprise. Instead of building, it hit her like a tsunami, racking her body and emptying her mind of all thought but the pleasure.

Having Rowdy inside her, filling her up and rocking

her with that slick friction, made it almost too intense to bear. He put his forehead to hers and growled as he joined her with his own powerful release.

Avery held on to him as his big body slowly relaxed over her. He kissed her oh-so-gently this time, carefully untangling her legs from his arms, easing them down. But he didn't relax. Already he explored her again, stroking, fondling.

A little amazed, Avery said, "Rowdy?"

"I need about twenty minutes." He lifted his head to look at her. His gaze went over her hair and though he didn't smile, she saw something in his eyes, something lighter than the usual emotion there.

"Twenty minutes?"

"Yeah. To recoup." He blew out a breath and moved to the side of her, staying up on an elbow so he could look her over in more detail. "This little body of yours is even sexier than I'd imagined."

She had no idea what to say, but she was starting to feel… Well, not so much flattered. Maybe…less inhibited?

Rowdy was just so bold, so raw about his sexuality. The appreciative way he studied her let her know he liked what he saw.

He put his hand on her stomach, his thumb dipping in her navel. As if he talked about the weather, he said, "I want to roll you over and take you from behind so I can get a better look at that sweet ass."

Her mouth opened, but nothing came out.

"That'd be fine for my back, so don't worry about it, okay? In fact, I can't even feel my back right now. So why don't you forget about it, too?"

"I…"

"I want you just to feel, Avery." He drifted his hand down between her legs. "I like this, by the way."

She lifted her brows. "This?"

He smiled. "A true redhead." Leaning over, he kissed her breast. "And these soft pink nipples...all put together you make such a hot package."

Never had she been complimented on anything so ridiculous. She didn't know what to say, but tried a lame, "Thank you."

He smiled lazily. "You're welcome."

She didn't want to bring up Fisher, but she had no idea if his change in mood meant he forgave her. She tried a roundabout question. "May I spend the night?"

"Since I'll be fucking you for hours, yeah. You should stay."

She scowled at how he worded things, but that made Rowdy laugh.

"Oh, no, you don't, lady. Don't get all prim on me now." He cupped a hand over her jaw, amused and not bothering to hide it. "You damn near stopped my heart, skinning down to those see-through panties and sashaying across the room like it was nothing."

"I don't sashay." She'd been so nervous—and so cold—it had taken considerable concentration just to get one foot in front of the other.

"All this," he said, running his fingers over her still-damp hair, "playing peekaboo with the good parts." He gave a low growl of appreciation. "You are the sexiest little package I've ever laid eyes on."

"The things you say." He sounded like he meant it, which left her warm with pleasure. No one had ever showered her with outrageous compliments, especially not on anything so private.

She'd dated, of course, but men did not beat her door down in pursuit. In comparison to how the women flocked to Rowdy, she was in the minor league.

"It's true," he said. "You have a sinful little body made for fun."

"You're the only man I know who ever thought so."

Only after the teasing words were out did Avery realize it was the wrong thing to say, because it reminded him of Fisher and the secret she'd shared.

As if it had never gone, Rowdy's regular, hard-edged demeanor fell back into place. Shadows filled his eyes and anger tightened his muscles.

He didn't move away from her, didn't stop stroking her so gently, but everything…changed.

"I guess that brings us back to Fisher, doesn't it?"

She shook her head, but Rowdy sat up. "Shower first, I guess." He removed the condom as if he didn't have one very fascinated lady watching. "I'll find you another shirt to wear while you turn on the dryer."

Grateful for the reprieve, brief as it might be, Avery sat up and pushed her hair away from her face. "Could I just go ahead and wash everything?"

"Do whatever you want." He looked her over again, then shook his head. "Make yourself at home." Going to the dresser he found a T-shirt—this time white—and tossed it to her.

As she tugged it on, he asked, "Hungry?"

Now that he mentioned it… "A little."

His attention lingered on her legs. "Can you wait for an hour?"

She had planned to be sleeping in an hour, but she shrugged. "I guess. Why?"

He caught her hand and pulled her forward. "Because

I've changed my mind. Fisher can wait." His hands went to her backside, palming her under the T-shirt. "Right now, this is more important."

"What—"

Lifting her up, he kissed away her protest.

The man definitely knew how to use his mouth— in many ways.

He seemed to take a lot of pleasure in her hair, too, tangling his hands in it, bringing it over her shoulders to rest over her breasts. He stripped the T-shirt right back off her.

Avery thought he'd rush her, and after coming twice, she wasn't sure she could keep up. But if that's what Rowdy wanted and needed, she was more than happy to accommodate him.

What a joke.

By the time he bent her over the bed and slowly entered her, she was wild for him, demanding that he hurry.

Holding her hips, he said, "Rise up on your arms, honey."

She struggled to her forearms.

"Nice." He stroked her waist. "Arch your back a little—that's it." He groaned, nuzzling against her nape, giving her a hickey or two.

He said near her ear, "I like it this way," in a voice dark with arousal. "I can get to you easier."

She found out exactly what he meant when he slipped one hand between her legs, the other up to a breast.

The way his fingers toyed with her, she was on the edge of release in minutes. *"Rowdy..."*

"Not yet, babe."

She moaned and pressed back into him. He tightened, so she did it again, rocking against him, clenching her muscles.

"Avery," he growled in warning.

"Soon as I can get you on your back," she promised, "it's going to be my turn—"

"Damn it." He went still for a second, trying to prolong things.

Needing him now, Avery encouraged him, squeezing around him, moving.

He straightened, clasped her waist and gave in with a harsh groan.

This release was just as incredible, going on longer, easing away more slowly. She relished every second, languid from expending so much energy, numb from head to toe. She collapsed to the bed with a moan, Rowdy sprawled over her.

If he'd left the decision to her, she'd have dozed off just like that, warmed by his natural heat, cocooned by his big body. But he stayed with her for only five minutes before groaning and manfully pulling away.

"I need that shower more now than ever."

Avery made a sound of agreement, but didn't bother opening her eyes or moving.

She sensed Rowdy walking away, heard the shower start, and then he was back, scooping her up again. He kissed her forehead tenderly and said, "I'll wash you if you can stay on your feet."

The smile came sleepily. "No." She put her nose in his neck and sighed. "I'll take off your bandages and wash your back."

"Appreciate it."

"But we have to make it quick," she admonished.

"No problem. I figure we need to eat and then catch a nap before I can have you again anyway."

Her groan ended on a laugh. The man was insatiable. How much luckier could a woman get?

CHAPTER SEVENTEEN

ROWDY DID HIS best to act like business as usual, but she'd left him poleaxed with her disclosures. It was starting to make sense now, how jumpy she'd been the night she missed the bus, the weird phone calls she kept getting.

Fisher's car trailing them.

She believed it wasn't Meyer, but prank phone calls, while a sick and effective way to torment her, were a little lame for the rapey type. Rowdy wanted to know everything, but he could wait until she finished her peanut butter and jelly sandwich.

He enjoyed the sight of her at his table in nothing more than a T-shirt. He wore only his boxers. It was… cozy.

If she'd be hanging around—and she would—he needed to pick up some real groceries. As a bachelor who, until very recently, had moved around a lot, he'd never gotten into the habit of stocking up on food. Little by little he'd accumulated a few things, but he'd get a list from Avery and…do what? Fucking play house?

Disgusted with himself, Rowdy bit into his own sandwich.

Avery eyed him. "Are you sure you don't want me to put the bandages back on?"

He shook his head. "Feels better without them." He

sat back in the chair to prove it to her. "I might need one more night before I can have you bouncing on me, but sleeping on my back won't be a problem."

She threw her napkin at him.

Rowdy grinned. "I can picture it now." He cocked a brow at her breasts. "And the picture inspires me."

Pausing, she looked at his chest, down to his abs, and smiled. "Sort of inspires me, too."

Oh, dirty pool. Not joking, he said, "Keep it up and we'll be back in bed before you finish your milk."

"No way." She pointed her sandwich at him. "I need sleep, Rowdy, and so do you. You'll just have to rein it in until morning."

"We'll see."

Brows pinching down, she took a deep breath to deny him, and Rowdy said, "So all that boasting you did about me being a badass, that was meant as a deterrent to good old Fish, huh? You used me to warn him off?"

She deflated with guilt and looked away. "Can I be totally honest with you, Rowdy?"

"That's how I'd prefer it." What did she think? That he wanted her to lie?

"Well, *I'd* prefer that you not go after Fisher."

"We'll talk about it." She could give him her reasons why he shouldn't, and he'd explain why he was. Easy enough.

She wasn't convinced, but she gave in anyway. "You are a very capable man and you know it. I had hoped that Fisher would realize it wouldn't be easy to get to me again. That maybe he'd think I wasn't worth the trouble."

He knew Fisher's type. Men like that didn't want to lose—ever. And Fish himself had spelled out his continued interest. "You figure it's him dicking around on the phone?"

"That's the only thing that makes sense." She pulled the crust off the last piece of her sandwich. "In one of the calls, I think he fired a gun."

Rowdy lost his teasing mood. "A gun?"

"That's what it sounded like. At first there was no one, then the gunshot." She fidgeted. "After that...a man laughed. I can't say that it necessarily sounded like Fisher, but it was muffled and I was shaken."

Hell, if she'd told him that earlier, he'd have annihilated Fisher on the spot, piece of cake with a cherry on top. When he'd met Fisher at her homecoming, he'd wanted to stomp the bastard anyway.

Now he had good reason.

"He was the one following us that night." Rowdy finished off his milk, giving her time to take that in.

Eyes rounding, Avery stared at him. "But...you're saying he already knew where I was?"

"Guess so. I recognized the car and license plate when we got to Meyer's."

"That's why you asked about it."

He shrugged. "Fisher didn't deny it. He said he was making sure you were safe."

"He's the reason I'm not safe!"

Pushing the last of his food aside, Rowdy leaned his forearms on the table and gave her his no-nonsense stare. "I need to hear all of it, babe. No more secrets and no more holding back. What exactly happened between you two?"

She withdrew, emotionally and physically.

Done playing, Rowdy left his seat, scooped her up and headed for the bed.

"Rowdy!"

He did like holding her. "Hmm?" No way should he have been horny again, but she pushed all his buttons, even when disgruntled. He needed to take it easy or she'd leave him just to rest.

"You cannot keep toting me around like a—"

He dropped her onto the bed, then crawled in beside her and situated them both so that they reclined, he on his back, she tucked into his side.

Avery fussed at him, shoving and swatting to free herself, but not really giving it her all.

"This would be more fun," he said, tugging at the T-shirt, "if you were naked again."

She gave up.

He kissed her forehead. "Comfortable?"

Sighing, she snuggled closer and nodded. "Yeah." Her hand on his bare chest, she asked, "It's okay on your back?"

It was his dick he was worried about. If the damn thing didn't stay down, how could they finish talking? "All good. Now, about Fisher?"

She tucked her face against him. "Mom and Meyer wanted me to marry him. They were pushing big-time, but I never felt that way about Fisher."

"You two dated?"

"A few times. Mostly company events. That sort of thing."

"Ever sleep with him?"

She shuddered. "No."

Satisfaction rushed through him. "So what did you do with him?"

"A few kisses only, and that was more than enough."

"No need for details." The last thing he wanted to

hear about was Fisher touching her in any way sexual, even a simple kiss.

"There isn't anything intimate worth telling anyway. I didn't like him. He's not the sterling example Meyer and Mom see him as, or the caring philanthropist everyone else thinks him to be. He does what's expected of him to keep his good name, to get a write-off, or to build a connection to another company, not because he actually cares. To me he was condescending and bossy and critical."

"Critical how?"

"No matter what I wore or what I said, he didn't think it was good enough."

What an ass. Rowdy teased his fingertips down her arm, her waist, her hip. "I like you best when you're wearing nothing, but you look awful cute in your jeans, too."

He felt her smile, then a kiss to his ribs. "Thank you."

"And your hair..." He stroked his fingers through it. "Gotta say, it's a turn-on."

"Fisher tried to insist I get it cut and styled. He even set up an appointment with his salon."

"Fisher has a salon?"

"A very expensive and exclusive place where he goes to get his hair cut. He had me scheduled for the works because he said I looked like a wild child."

Rowdy had to lift up and stare at her. "You're shitting me?"

She blinked up at him. "Uh...no."

"God, he's an idiot." He rested back again. "You're always classy. Nothing wild about you." He gave her a brief hug. "Except maybe in bed, and Fisher knows nothing about that."

"No, he doesn't."

"So you told him to hit the road, and what happened?"

"Well, I tried to be a little kinder than that. I told him that we didn't suit, so I didn't want to take up more of his valuable time and that it'd be better if we just parted ways as friends, and only friends. He pressed me, saying my parents disagreed and that once I got settled down, I'd find my way."

"Your way to *what?*"

"To being a good wife to him." Her hand fisted on his abdomen. "He wouldn't let it go. For weeks, he kept dogging me everywhere I went, showing up at events and acting like we were a couple."

Hiding his growing turmoil, Rowdy waited, saying nothing, just encouraging her with casual strokes down her arm, over her silky hair, her cheek.

"We were at a park fund-raiser." She swallowed hard. "I tried to dodge him, but he wouldn't leave me alone. He was obnoxious, being deliberately rude. He embarrassed me. So I was going to leave. I thought I had slipped away from his eagle eye by going out the back door of the pavilion. I figured if I could just make it to my car, I'd leave and then I'd stay away, regardless of Meyer's business and the stuff Mom expected me to attend."

Rowdy knew only too well how hard it was to outrun your problems. "He found you?"

She nodded. "I have no idea how he knew I'd left, but he was furious, saying I'd walked out on him. It didn't matter that I wasn't there *with* him anyway, that we'd arrived separately with no arrangements to hook up. In his mind we were a couple and I was just supposed to go along with that." Curling in closer, her voice strained, she said, "He grabbed me. He'd been…rough before, deliberately hurting me, but not like this."

"Hurting?"

For the longest time she didn't reply, then she crawled up to his chest. "When you picked me up and carried me in here, you didn't hurt me. Not at all. I knew if I said for you to stop, you would."

"I'm glad you realize that."

"We were sort of playing, and I enjoyed it." She kissed his chin. "But every time Fisher would touch me, he'd… I don't know. Squeeze my arms too tightly, push me too hard." Her breath became more shallow, her words tight. "Everything with him was on the verge of being pain. It was almost like he enjoyed seeing red marks left behind. He'd hold my wrist so tight that I'd wince, then he'd look at it and… I don't know. There was something in his eyes." She swallowed, looked away and whispered, "Like maybe it turned him on."

God, how Rowdy wished he had Fisher close at hand right now. "It was worse that night?"

With a trembling hand, she pushed her hair away. "He grabbed my upper arm and…and literally dragged me into the natatorium. I was so scared. I screamed for him to let me go but he wouldn't."

It wasn't easy to ask questions when all he really wanted to do was hunt up Fisher and teach him the error of his ways. "A natatorium?" He'd never heard of such a thing.

"It's a building that houses a pool. That time of night, with the fund-raiser at the pavilion, it should have been locked. But somehow he had it opened." She touched Rowdy's jaw. "That's the thing about Fisher, you know?

He's so well received in the community, so trusted, a supporter of so many causes, that he has unbelievable access…and trust."

"You're not alone now." Rowdy wanted her to understand that. He hadn't liked Fisher on sight, and now he had a good reason to chew on that dislike. "I trust *you*, not him."

Her eyes grew wet. "That means so much." Firming her lips, she stoically fought off tears. "No one else believed me, but I know Fisher intended to rape me. He deliberately ripped my dress and the way he kissed me—" She had to fight for another breath. "It hurt. I tried to turn away from him, but there wasn't anything I could do."

"Shhh." He stroked her, kissed her and wished he could kill Fisher with his bare hands.

"I had his fingerprints on my arm for a week." She looked at him. "And for more than a month, I could barely sleep."

He knew all about having reality plague your dreams. Rowdy hid his rage and continued to soothe her. "How did you get away?"

She shook her head, as if remembering and sorting it out in her mind. "He'd backed me up to a wall and was trying to…to paw me. I wouldn't hold still, so he just grabbed the front of my dress and tore it away."

Yeah, Fisher was a dead man.

"When he tried to pull me down to the floor, I pushed away from the wall and we both stumbled. Fisher tripped over the material of my dress and fell backward. There was some pool equipment there and… I don't know…he just sort of floundered and his feet came out from under him and I heard a big splash."

Using his fingertips, Rowdy trailed up and down her arm. "You ran?"

Avery nodded. "It was dark and I couldn't see that well, but I knew he fell in awkwardly. I heard the thud before the splash, but it wasn't until later that I found out he'd hit his head on the way in. He ended up with a black eye and a busted nose and several stitches."

"He deserved a hell of a lot more."

She didn't disagree. "Before I could even get home to tell Mom, Fisher had called them on his way to the hospital. He'd made up this elaborate lie about me accusing him of cheating and being furious."

"Bullshit. You were furious at me and all I got was a soppy bar cloth to the chest."

She gave a watery, tearful laugh and bent to kiss him. "I'm sorry about that."

"You've long been forgiven." He was glad to lighten her mood—but the teasing did nothing to alleviate the storm gathering inside him. He despised abuse at any time. But against a woman? Against Avery? That was almost too personal to bear. "I guess your folks believed you'd caused the problem?"

"They claimed I'd misunderstood and overreacted. He told them that he was upset at how badly I'd treated him, and my dress got ripped as an accident when I refused to talk to him. He said he was reaching for me and I shoved away—and of course, that's how he fell in the pool and got hurt. But, Rowdy, I swear, I know what he was going to do. He was so…ugly. So mean and out of control."

"Shhh. I believe you." She shivered, so Rowdy pulled her down and wrapped his arms around her. "That's when you left home?"

"Only a few days later. Fisher had already spread his lies far and wide. I was furious that my friends and family all thought me a nutcase who'd had a jealous fit and attacked poor Fisher. I was humiliated and hurt and I just wanted away from it all."

"Do you ever think you'll return?"

She said immediately, "No." Coming up to see him again, she added, "No, permanently. I meant it when I said I like my life now. I'm...free."

"And poor."

"And *free*." She kissed him softly. "I have everything I need."

Was he one of those things she needed? She'd said she loved him, but that could have been desperation, a way to find a safe haven. A way to get protection.

He was more than happy to oblige her. And maybe, even after he resolved the issue with Fish, she'd feel the same. "Stay with me."

Around a yawn, she said, "Okay."

It was an enormous step for Rowdy. Gigantic. Mind-boggling. But it was what he wanted. He tucked her hair back, then cupped her face in his hands. "Not just tonight, Avery." Brushing his thumbs over her downy cheeks, he said again, "Stay with me where it's safe."

Surprise parted her lips and widened her eyes. She searched his face. "You won't go after Fisher?"

Of course he would, but he said only, "We'll figure it out in the morning. You need to sleep now. You have those dark circles under your eyes again."

Her smile twitched and she mumbled, "Jerk." Then reached past him to turn out the light. After a few seconds, she said, "I'll stay. Thank you."

Rowdy kept her close. He had a lot to think about. His feelings for this one particular woman. His life.

What he would do to Fisher to keep him away from Avery.

But now that his back felt better, the grinding lust was somewhat sated and Avery was here with him, soft and safe and smelling so damn sweet, he could sleep.

Again.

She was like a drug, the very best kind. She'd turned his world upside down, but for the first time in forever, things were starting to feel right.

AVERY WOKE WITH the sun pouring through the tall windows. The storm had passed. She squinted against the light, stretched and bumped into Rowdy.

He stirred, turning to his side away from her.

Very slowly, she sat up to look at his broad back. The stitches still looked painful and angry, but the redness was almost gone. He healed remarkably fast.

That thought took her attention to his other, older scars. God, she loved him. It was such an awful thing, wishing she could take away hurts a decade old. The urge to touch him, to kiss his marred shoulder, burned in her heart.

She didn't want to disturb him, so she tried to sneak out of the bed.

Alert, Rowdy twisted toward her, his hair rumpled, his jaw dark with beard shadow. "Avery."

Her smile quirked. "Still me."

His gaze dipped to her breasts under the T-shirt, and he finished turning to his back, reached for her and hauled her in close. "Where are you going?"

"Bathroom."

"Ah." He kissed her neck, his bristly cheeks tickling. "Hurry back, then."

As she crawled out, he fondled her behind. Unbelievable. He wasn't even wide-awake yet.

She rushed through brushing her teeth, and even combed her hair. She had whisker burn in interesting places. Muscles that she seldom used ached a little. Deep inside herself, she still tingled.

"Hurry it up, babe."

She turned from the sink and found Rowdy standing there in the doorway, his boxers tented, his slumberous gaze appreciative.

"It's all yours." As she stepped out, he looked her over.

"You don't need to primp, you know. I'm already as interested as a guy can get."

"Your eyes aren't even fully open yet."

"I see you just fine—and I always like what I see." He gave her tush a pat and walked into the john.

Smiling, Avery headed to the kitchen to start the coffee. His apartment was chilly, the floor especially cold, so once the coffee machine was set, she went to his closet and found a flannel shirt to borrow, then sat on the side of the bed and pulled on thick socks.

She was back in the kitchen preparing two mugs when Rowdy emerged. He came right to her, hugged her from behind with his hands on her stomach, and kissed her neck. His face was damp, his breath minty, his hands big and warm and bold.

"I like waking with you, Avery, seeing you in this cute getup in my kitchen." He lightly bit her earlobe. "This could be the start to a new favorite fantasy."

"A woman ridiculously dressed fixing your morning coffee for you?" She tsked. "Surely you can do better than that."

"Yeah." Pinning her against the counter, he lifted his large hands to cover her breasts. "I can do better."

A solid erection pressed her backside. His thumbs found her nipples and, casual as you please, he started a slow, easy, red-hot seduction.

She needed to talk to him, and if she didn't put a halt to things now, they'd never get to it. "Rowdy?"

"Hmm?" He opened his mouth on her neck.

She already had two hickeys and shivered as he gave her a third. Reaching back, she put her hands over his thighs. "I need a few minutes."

"Take all the time you want." One hand left her breast and coasted down her belly to nestle between her legs, gently exploring her through her panties. "I'm in no hurry."

The way he touched her... "I need coffee, too."

"In that case, let's make it quick." He rearranged her hands, planting them on the countertop, then sliding her panties down to her knees. "Later you can get me on my back, as you promised."

Yeah, she definitely would. But for now... "How quick is quick?"

"Think I can make you come in under ten minutes?"

"*Make* me come?" She looked over her shoulder in time to see him roll on a condom. Had he carried it with him from the bathroom? So much confidence.

So well deserved.

"Yeah." He had his boxers pushed down just enough to free himself and now he stepped up to her again, lightly nudging her legs farther apart. "Open them as wide as you can."

The panties restricted her, and somehow that made it feel even naughtier than sex in the kitchen against the counter.

With one hand Rowdy pulled the T-shirt up above her breasts and with the other, he touched between her legs, teasing, preparing her, making her squirm.

"I like this," he said. "Having you bent over, and the smell of fresh coffee in the air. Two of my favorite things."

He was so outrageous, and so skilled. Already wet, hot, Avery pressed back to him. "The coffee will get cold at this rate."

He laughed, and slowly worked two fingers into her. "Better?"

"I want you, Rowdy." *Only you. Always.* "Please."

"And here I thought this scene couldn't get any hotter." He toyed with her nipple, lightly tugging. "I like hearing you ask me so pretty."

As her eyes sank shut, she put her head back to his shoulder and murmured, "I swear to you, I will get even."

"Damn, little bartender." For a moment he went still, his breathing deeper, then he removed his fingers and nudged his erection against her until he could fully sink in, growling in accusation, "Way to push me past my control."

Since that had been her intent, Avery held in her moan of triumph and suggested, "Now why don't you push me past my control?"

He pressed deeper. "Consider it done."

True to his word, Rowdy had her crying out with a powerful orgasm in under ten minutes. To protect her from his strong thrusts, he put his arm around her, creating a barrier between her body and the sharp-edged counter.

Soon after her pleasure ebbed, Rowdy tightened around her, growled deeply and gave in to his own release.

A few more minutes passed with both of them gasping, still slumped in front of the coffeemaker.

Laughing a little, Rowdy hugged her. "I'm awake now, just so you know."

Avery barely acknowledged him. She honestly felt like she could doze back off just like this—as long as her legs held out.

Moving away from her, Rowdy rearranged himself, then pulled up her panties. He eased her away from the counter and directed her to a chair. "I'll get the coffee."

Slumped in her seat, Avery watched him all but whistle as he put sugar in her cup and then got out the creamer. "You're insatiable."

"You're the one who was flaunting her wares here in the kitchen."

"Ankle socks, Rowdy. And a flannel shirt." She put a hand in her hair. "And even though I combed it, my hair is still a ratty mess. I need to wash it and blow it out and—"

"I think you're turning me on again." Smiling, he set the coffee in front of her and joined her at the table. "Do you realize it's almost eleven? We slept late."

Avery tasted her coffee, approved and after another drink she took a long stretch. "We're allowed. It's our day off."

He watched her every move. "I figured I'd visit Marcus then hit the grocery store. Maybe load up on whatever you like."

Stalling, she slowly dropped her arms and stared at him. "So you were serious about me staying?"

"I don't say things I don't mean."

She wanted to ask if he cared about her at all. Her, specifically. She'd told him she loved him, and without replying, he'd taken her to bed.

At least he hadn't sent her packing.

Yet. She realized, of course, she'd eventually have to find another job. She couldn't bear the thought of seeing Rowdy with anyone else, but if she stayed at the bar, how could she avoid it? When he moved on from her, he wasn't going to become a monk. No, he'd go back to his old ways, basking in the attention of every woman who saw him.

And then what would she do?

She loved him, so very, very much.

She could not pretend she didn't.

From under the table, Rowdy nudged her with his foot. "What are you brooding about?"

God, he was perceptive.

"Worrying about Fisher?" He curled a lip. "Because you don't need to. I can—"

"Will you be with any other women?" The second she said it, she wanted to slap a hand over her mouth. She'd blurted it out without any lead-in. Bam. There it was.

Of course, that needed some clarification. "While you're with me, I mean. Are we…" She couldn't think of an appropriate word for Rowdy's outlook on things. "Exclusive. Right now I mean. That is, I'm not asking for a long-term commitment or anything like that. But if I'm staying here…"

Given the way Rowdy watched her, she gave up and closed her mouth.

Seeming mostly unaffected by the suddenness of it, Rowdy answered with his own question, saying simply, "Between work and you, when would I have time?"

So he planned to keep her with him 24/7? That suited Avery just fine.

"Speaking of time." He deftly changed the subject—for his benefit or hers? "How long will it take you to get ready?"

"For what?" If he meant more sex, she'd have to call it quits, at least for a little while.

"I told you. We need to go visit Marcus today. You okay with that?"

Belatedly, Avery realized that he wanted her to go along. Marcus was staying with Alice and Reese. She couldn't imagine they wanted her as an uninvited visitor. Much as she loved the idea, she said, "I shouldn't intrude."

Setting his cup aside, Rowdy frowned at her. "You don't want me to murder Fisher, either, so as long as that bastard is out there, you go where I go."

Avery, too, set aside her cup, preparing for a confrontation. "Is that supposed to be an order? Because you should know right now, I don't take well to orders."

He grinned at her ferocious tone. "A request, honey—and very necessary for my peace of mind."

"That's better." She sat back in the seat. "You think Alice will be okay with that?"

"She'll love the company, but to be sure, I'll call her and let her know."

He and Alice seemed to have a very special relationship, so naturally Avery wanted to get to know her better. "Do you plan to visit Marcus every day?"

"I was thinking about that." He turned his cup, re-arranging it as he stared off at nothing in particular. "I can't just drop in on Alice every day. She's getting Marcus set up for school in the neighborhood where they're moving next week. That means he won't be home until I'm at work, and on weekends, I imagine they'll have stuff they want to do as a family."

"I got the feeling that they consider you family, too."

Rowdy ignored that. "I need to let the little dude know that I want to be around, but it can't be every day. But I don't want him to think I bailed if he doesn't see me for a while."

"You want him to trust you." Avery knew all about that particular desire. "That might take some time, though."

Rowdy snorted. "It'll take an eternity. But we'll get there."

Did he say that because he'd never learned to fully trust? Avery feared it might be so.

Well, she wanted his trust. One way or another, for as long as this lasted, she wanted Rowdy to know he could confide anything to her.

"You're brooding again," he pointed out.

"No, it's just…" Avery took in the mellow satisfaction in his golden-brown eyes, his rumpled blond hair and that to-die-for muscular body. Scars and all, Rowdy Yates was more man than any man she'd ever known, or even imagined. But he wasn't superhuman. He didn't have to carry his burdens alone. Not when she definitely wanted to share them with him. "Can I ask you something?"

"Sure." He sipped at his coffee. "Doesn't mean I'll answer, but you can give it a shot."

Of all the— "If you're not going to answer, why would I bother asking?"

He plunked his cup back down. "This is about Fisher, isn't it?"

Avery let out a breath. He didn't sound happy. And yes, she needed to talk to him about that, but first… "I told you what happened with Fisher and me. After everyone more or less called me a liar, I had decided I'd never again tell anyone. But I trust you, Rowdy."

"I'm glad you do."

Because he figured he could handle anything and everyone and never break under the pressure of responsibility. But he didn't have to do that anymore. Not with her. "I'd really like it if you'd trust me a little, too."

"You think I don't?"

"To a degree, maybe." He wouldn't let her in his home if he didn't. But she needed more than that. Hoping to find the right words, she gave herself a little time by drinking her coffee. She couldn't very well say *I want more* because she had no idea what Rowdy wanted. Except more sex. He'd been pretty plain about that. "Will you…will you maybe trust me with something private?"

"How private are we talking?" He lifted a brow. "You're not going to grill me about past hookups, are you?"

"God, no!" That was the last thing she wanted to hear about. Her face heated just recalling what she'd walked in on in his office. "Ass."

He grinned. "Then stop tiptoeing around and spit it out."

"All right, fine." She bit her lips, girded herself for his reaction and asked, "Will you tell me about those other scars? Not the scars from adult fighting but...the scars I assume came from your parents."

That sudden stony expression on his face didn't bode well.

Avery sat forward, pressing him. "Will you trust me, Rowdy, the same way I've trusted you? Will you trust me enough to share your past?"

CHAPTER EIGHTEEN

ROWDY LEFT THE table and stalked to the bedroom. He heard Avery's feet padding behind him in a rush, and a second later her body impacted with his, her arms coming around his waist, her face on his back beside the stitches.

"Rowdy, please don't run from me."

He snorted. He didn't run from anyone, sure as hell not a woman who weighed a buck ten soaking wet. Catching her hands, he started to pry her loose, but she clung like a vine, squeezing tighter.

Her head barely reached his shoulder, she was as delicate as dandelion fluff in the wind and yet she held on to him like she'd never let go. *Damn, it felt good.*

Rather than risk hurting her, Rowdy covered her hands with his own. "It's not a good story, honey. Nothing you need to hear." *It doesn't matter*—but damn it, he knew it did. He'd just never had anyone to tell.

"You're wrong." Keeping hold of him, she sidled around to the front, then stared up at him. "If it had happened to me, would you want to know?"

Denying even the possibility of her being hurt like that, he shook his head. "Don't say that, honey." He cupped her face. "It's not the same thing."

"No, it's very different." She breathed faster. "Because I *love* you."

Jesus, she'd just said it again. Eyes flared and heart pounding, Rowdy struggled with what to do. He sort of…panicked. Turning away, a hand to his neck, he fought the claws of tension sinking in.

Avery didn't move. He fucking felt her stillness behind him.

He didn't want to make her feel bad, ever, but either way he went with this, it was going to happen. Keeping his back to her, he said, "Last chance, babe. We can dress and get out of here."

She said nothing.

"Or I can unload a few lousy stories on you." He turned to face her. "Your call."

A shuddering breath lifted her chest. She went to the side of the bed, sat and waited.

Shit.

He couldn't sit. He couldn't do that. Pacing to keep up with his frenetic thoughts, he tried to figure out where to start. "I've never talked about it with anyone." But Avery wasn't just anyone, and he knew it, whether he ever admitted it to her or not.

"You can talk to me about anything. I promise."

She wanted him to. She'd feel rejected if he didn't. Without looking at her, he said, "I was about twelve when I got the burn."

"It's from a cigarette?"

Her gentle voice washed over him. "Yeah." Moving back and forth in front of her, Rowdy tried to sum it up without too much fanfare. "They wanted to go out." His muscles knotted, ached. "They wanted to take Pepper. I said no."

"You stood up to them even when you were that young?"

When it came to Pepper, yeah. He'd fought tooth and nail. The memories made his chest squeeze tight so that breathing became more difficult. Not memories of pain, because any real physical hurt had passed long before the fucking, insolvable weight of impossibility. He'd thought to have a lifetime of fighting them.

Luckily, that hadn't happened.

"I did what I could. I was a big kid, and Dad was drunk, so I blocked the doorway. I dunno, I think I had a bat or something." It was so damned stupid. So… Jesus, impossible.

"You would have hit him?"

"Would have. Did. More than once." He'd fought back, and he'd fought for Pepper. "Didn't usually do me much good. While I was yelling, telling them to leave her, she was crying and struggling to get loose." And finally she had. "Pepper got out the door past me. She knew to go to the river. That's where we'd hang out 'til the folks were out of sight. But I was so focused on her getting away, I didn't see my mom reach past Dad. She was a regular chimney, always smoking…"

Avery covered her mouth, her hand shaking. "She burned you on purpose."

"She was pissed. Said I always caused such a fuss." He'd lurched away and run after Pepper, but he hadn't told her. Hell, he didn't want to tell Avery, either. He'd hidden the burn with his shirt and given thanks that the folks had left without any more trouble.

"Will you please sit with me?"

She looked so fragile, so upset, Rowdy found himself beside her before he remembered that he needed to move, needed to walk off the gnawing bite of the memory.

He tipped up her chin and tried teasing her. "Don't you dare cry." A quick kiss to her soft mouth felt so good that he went back for another. "It didn't even hurt that much. We swam in the river and the water was cold…. It healed up pretty quick."

She crawled right up into his lap and tucked her face into his neck. "They stayed gone most of the night?"

"All night and half the next day." Putting his chin to the top of her head, he rubbed up and down her narrow back. "It was always easier without them hanging around anyway. I remember Pepper slept in my room that night, curled up at the foot of my bed, which was sort of funny since we were both tall even then. I blocked the door, just in case the folks did come back, and we camped out like it was a treat." He shook his head, even found a grin. "Pepper was always great about that, making shit out to be an adventure instead of…"

"So ugly."

And eternal. "Yeah."

Her arms reached around him, and she touched another scar. "This is from a belt buckle?"

He shrugged. "I was tussling with Dad when I was about ten. Young. I barely remember what he was mad about, but I almost never took it without giving back some grief. He'd said he was done with me not listening. I don't think he meant for the buckle to hit me, but he was hammered and could barely stay on his feet when he started swinging."

"I wish he was here now so I could take a belt to him."

Putting his face in her hair, Rowdy breathed deeply. God, he loved how she smelled, how she felt and how she could make him feel. "It wasn't the only time, but it's one of the few times that caught me that bad. Mom snapped at him, saying he'd have children's services up her ass again if he didn't stop. So he did."

Avery put a hand to his jaw. "She didn't defend you?"

"She could barely defend herself."

"Was it always that way, Rowdy? Were they never good parents?"

Damn it, he didn't want her to get so upset. "It wasn't always that bad. I mean, they were never cut out to parent, that's for sure. But they'd go weeks without getting slammed. Times like that, they'd mostly ignore us." He thought back while touching Avery, coasting a hand down her spine, back up and into her hair. "I sort of remember Mom making pancakes when I was real young, before Pepper was born. She wasn't maternal, but she was kind occasionally."

"Your dad?"

"He had a few jobs here and there. Not enough to matter. When he was around, I mostly just stayed out of his way."

"You're right." Lifting her face, Avery touched him gently, his brow, his jaw. Her small smile was the sweetest, most tender thing he'd ever seen. "That is a pretty awful story. And it amazes me all the more how you turned out to be so wonderful."

Wonderful. That's what she thought? "Did you listen when I told Fish and Meyer just how off the rails I am?"

"I heard you talk about doing the right thing, even when the right thing is a very hard call."

Laughing, Rowdy scrubbed a hand over his face. "Yeah, well, I won't argue that beating on a human trafficker is right. The low-life scum had it coming and I enjoyed it."

"And you got needed info," she insisted.

Maybe because she didn't want to acknowledge his lack of morals, the base pleasure he got in doling out justice, she needed that clarification. "I did, yeah."

"You are the most wonderful human being I know, Rowdy. There isn't anything you can tell me that would ever change my mind."

What if he told her to go? What if he said that he didn't know jack shit about playing house or…or loving one woman enough to commit to her?

Would her opinion change then?

As if she'd read his thoughts, Avery shook her head. "Thank you for trusting me, Rowdy. And for letting me stay with you for a while." Her hand drifted down to his shoulder, then to the front of his chest. "But know this. You don't owe me anything. You don't have to take on my problems." She cut him off, speaking over him when he started to protest. "I appreciate that you're willing, and I know you're certainly able to help. If I need you to do anything, I promise I will let you know. But please don't pursue this. Please don't make me feel like a burden."

"You're not." To emphasize the trade-off, he cupped her ass. "Didn't I just prove how handy it is to have you around?" He kissed the side of her neck. "You don't even make me work hard for it anymore."

Swatting him, Avery leaned away. "So I'm a convenience, huh?"

"The sexiest kind."

Instead of looking insulted, she grinned. "I rather like the perks myself."

"Tease." Glad to move past the blackness of his youth, he started to lower her to the bed when his phone beeped with a message. Groaning, he said, "What now?" He stretched out an arm to the nightstand to snag his phone and read the message. He groaned again.

"What is it? Is anything wrong?"

"My sister will be here in about ten minutes. She wants to visit Marcus with me today."

"Oh, okay. Well, I guess I can—"

"Go along with us." He wanted Pepper to get to know Avery better. With any luck, his sister would like her, but he'd never before had a woman hanging around, so who knew how that'd go? 'Course, he'd had to get used to Logan, so it was only fair—

Whoa. Pepper had married Logan, and he was nowhere near thinking anything that crazy.

Avery leaned up and kissed him. "I should shower and get dressed before she shows up. And you need to let Alice know she has a group of visitors coming, not just you. It's the polite thing to do." She stroked down his chest, lightly cupped his testicles, then slid away from the bed and headed for his bathroom.

Huh. Watching her go, his body still rioting with need—not all of it physical—Rowdy had to rethink things. He knew nothing about being a significant other.

But he should probably start learning. It'd have to be a hell of a lot easier than ever letting her go.

IT SURPRISED AVERY how friendly Pepper was this time. She had a dynamic, carefree personality that overtook a room as soon as she entered.

First thing upon arrival, she'd insisted on seeing Rowdy's back. He'd given her a flash peek by lifting his shirt just enough. Far from squeamish, Pepper had approved Rowdy's recovery, all while hugging him and luridly cursing the men he'd fought. "Next time," Pepper had told him, "be more careful."

Next time. Avery was still reeling over that. Pepper and Rowdy were both awesome survivors who viewed life through their own uniquely shaded rose-colored glasses. She admired them both very much.

They'd ridden to Alice's separately from Pepper, since Pepper's plans for the rest of the day varied from theirs. But as soon as they arrived in the parking lot, Pepper started chatting with Avery as if they'd known each other for a while—or would. It seemed that in such a short time, everything had changed.

The sun shone down on them, countering the brisk October breezes.

"So," Pepper asked, without an ounce of subtlety. "Are you two shacking up?"

Rowdy said, "Butt out, kiddo."

"I know she stayed the night again." To Avery, Pepper said, "It's unheard of. My brother, seeing the same lady twice?" She tsked. "There's some strange juju going on or something."

Rowdy shook his head. "You don't know as much as you think you do, brat."

"I know you've never been able to stay still long enough to actually know a woman." As they started in, she walked around to Avery's side. "One time, when we were on the run—Rowdy's told you all about that, right?—anyway, I had to go collect his stuff from a cheap hotel room." With great drama, Pepper said, "He'd left a bimbo in the bed! I had to oust her, and let me tell you, she wasn't anxious to go."

"Pepper."

Avery listened with fascination.

Pepper ignored her brother. "Back when we worked at the club, Rowdy didn't date the customers, and that left behind a string of broken hearts." She sized Avery up with a long look. "Never known him to camp out with a lady before."

Rowdy reached around and caught his sister's wrist, then dragged her over to his side, separating her from Avery. "That's enough from you," he said.

Too late, Avery thought. Already bolstered by Pepper's insight, she couldn't keep from snuggling with Rowdy, holding his hand and leaning on his shoulder as they went up the walkway to the apartment entry doors. Rowdy curled his big hand around hers, and it was all she could do to contain her happiness.

He had opened up to her, telling her things he'd never told anyone else.

Surely that had to mean something.

She had no illusions about building the perfect life with him. He'd been through so much, and though he'd play it off as nothing, his life had been hell. Instead of using that as an excuse to become a creep himself, he'd gone the opposite direction and was a true hero, a remarkable, caring man.

That took so much strength of character, and a core of morality few possessed.

Loving him, even without any form of commitment, was the easiest, most natural thing she'd ever done.

Her long blond hair stirred by a cool breeze, Pepper leaned around Rowdy to see Avery. "Keep smiling and sighing like that and I'll think you two are ready to elope."

Avery stumbled over her own feet, horrified that Pepper would make Rowdy uncomfortable.

But Rowdy only gave Pepper a playful shove, making her stumble away two steps. "Married life has pickled your brain," he told his sister with good humor.

Pepper laughed, coming back to bump shoulders with him. "Married life is *orgasmic*."

He groaned theatrically as he opened the doors to let the ladies enter. "A little nauseating, too, at least from my end, having to hear about it from you!"

They had such a relaxed camaraderie with each other, Avery almost sighed again.

Reese was at work, but Alice greeted them all as if they'd been formally invited. Cash was beyond euphoric to see all the visitors.

"Don't worry," Alice told them. "Marcus and I already took him out, so he should be empty. No piddling on your shoes."

"Well," Pepper said to the dog while rubbing his long ears and kissing the top of his head, "if you do have to go, aim for Rowdy's feet. They're bigger than mine."

It was sort of funny for Avery. Alice and Pepper were so different in every way, but they appeared to be fast friends.

While Rowdy took his turn greeting Cash, Pepper went to Marcus, treating him as she would any other kid. Marcus stared at her in awe, but Avery could understand that reaction.

Tall, stunning and bold, Pepper had the same dominating presence as her brother. Put them together in a room, and it was a wonder anyone else could find oxygen enough to breathe.

"So, squirt," Pepper said, "it's good to see you. You looking forward to the new house?"

Marcus slid a quick, uncertain glance at Rowdy. "I guess."

After giving the dog one final pat, Rowdy brought Avery forward. Cash followed, still wiggling from head to tail in excitement. "You remember Avery?"

Hoping her visit wouldn't dredge up bad memories of that night at the bar, Avery said, "Hi, Marcus. It's good to see you again."

Marcus went shy, looking down and nodding.

She stepped closer. "I haven't seen pictures of the new house. Have you?"

He nodded again. "We went to see it."

"Really? What's it like?"

"Big." He peeked at Rowdy again. "It has a yard."

"A nice big backyard." Rowdy crouched down to give Cash more attention, which also put him on a better level with Marcus. "I was thinking Marcus could help us build a swing set and stuff. Maybe a tire swing from that tall oak tree."

"Oh, that'd be wonderful," Alice said. "Great idea."

Cash barked as if he agreed. "You're going to like that yard, aren't you, bud? Lots of room to run, and you'll have a lot of spots to choose from when you do your business."

Pepper jumped in. "Back when we were kids, Rowdy hung this old rotted tire from a tree on the riverbank. We'd swing out and drop into the river. It was wild and super fun, until this one time that the branch broke."

Rowdy groaned. "I landed on my butt in the mud instead of in the water. I swear, even though the mud was squishy it still rattled my teeth."

"You should have seen him," Pepper said around a wide grin. "The mud splattered everywhere. In his hair and face. He even found a crawdad in his pocket. Hilarious!"

Smiling at them, Marcus asked, "What's a crawdad?"

"You don't know? Oh, wow, Marcus. It's like a tiny lobster with little pinchers. Really cute."

"Said no woman ever, anywhere, except Pepper."

She ignored Rowdy. "We used to catch them just to play with for a few minutes, then we'd let them go. They run off backward."

Avery had never heard such a thing. She had to admit, she was a little intrigued herself.

"Come summer," Pepper said, "we'll have to take a trip to the river. Or we could use Dash's lake house. Dash is my husband's brother, now my brother-in-law, and a good guy. He won't mind."

Rowdy snickered. "As I recall, Dash kept that place as a hideaway."

"Maybe, but now he lets us use it whenever we want. Actually, Logan is thinking of getting his own summer house. Wouldn't that be awesome? We could spend a weekend there, all of us together."

Since she looked at Avery while saying it, Avery felt included, and it warmed her.

"The guys could go fishing while I take Marcus, Alice and Avery for a walk on the shore. I could show them how to catch crawdads, or rock bass. Or we could all swim or take out a rowboat."

Smiling at Pepper's enthusiasm, Alice said, "I take it you miss the water."

"It's so fun." Pepper hugged her arms around herself, glowing with the memory. "The hot sun and the cold water. You'd have a great time, Marcus. Guaranteed."

Marcus looked at Alice, who nodded. "We would

love that. And maybe even before summer, we could do a picnic at the river. There are a lot of nice spots." She put a hand on Marcus's shoulder. "And a big playground. We'll be moving next week and then Marcus will start school again, but as long as it doesn't get too cold, we'll still have the weekends for playing around."

Marcus kept silent, and Avery worried. She could tell Rowdy noticed, because he stood again, saying to Pepper, "Why don't you let Alice show you some pictures of the new house? Marcus and I are going to play cars—that is, if Marcus has his cars handy."

Marcus pulled two little metal cars from his pockets.

Avery started to follow Pepper, but Rowdy caught her hand and pulled her down to the floor with him. "I didn't get a chance to pick up more cars, but I will," he told Marcus. "I think Avery will need one or two."

Marcus waffled a moment before sitting down. Cash went to lie beside him. Marcus idly stroked the dog.

"Something on your mind, Marcus?" Rowdy draped his wrists over his knees and just waited. "You can talk to me, you know."

He screwed up his mouth, gave Rowdy a measuring look and asked, "You still gonna visit after we move?"

"Heck, yeah. Can't wait to see the new place once you're all settled in. I think Reese and Alice are planning to get a lot of new furniture to fill it up. I'll probably help them when they move. Lots of boxes to be carried and stuff to set up."

"I'll help, too," Avery offered. "That is, if no one minds."

Rowdy kept his gaze on Marcus. "What do you say, Marcus? The more the merrier?"

He shrugged. "Will I help?"

"You bet. You look plenty strong enough to me to carry some boxes. And we'll need someone to keep an eye on Cash while we're going in and out."

Marcus put a car on the floor and rolled it a bit while he thought about things. "Okay." He'd already set up some track, so he pulled that over and then, surprising Avery, he offered her one of his cars. "You can play with this one."

Oh, wow. Emotion burned the backs of her eyes, leaving them damp. She put a hand to her heart, deeply touched. "Thank you, Marcus."

Rowdy nudged her, probably wanting her to get it together. And so she tried.

While Pepper sat in a stuffed chair and started going through photos, Alice brought over a snack of cookies and juice.

"The regular," Rowdy told her, and thanked Alice.

He handed a cookie to Avery, then one to Marcus. "No matter what, Marcus, we're buds now, right?"

Marcus bit into his cookie. "All right."

"Things sometimes change. A different house, a different school."

He nodded. "Mom is…gone."

Avery froze, horrified by that small voice.

But Rowdy nodded. "I know, and I'm sorry."

Marcus rubbed under his nose. "I don't think I'll see Darrell anymore."

"You okay with that?"

"Yeah." He rolled the car again, turning it along the track. "I'm kind of glad."

Avery knew Alice and Pepper were both listening in but pretending not to. She swallowed hard, wishing she had a magical way to make the hurt go away.

Rowdy reached over and clasped Marcus's bony knee. "We'll always be friends."

Marcus said nothing.

"There'll be days when I make it out to visit, and some that I won't. But I'll always be around if you need me. I promise."

Without looking up from the photos, Pepper said, "He's a man of his word, Marcus. As his sister, I should know."

Again, Marcus looked at her in awe.

Rowdy leaned forward in a conspiratorial way. "Pepper's loud and nosy, but she's okay. You'll like her."

"I certainly do," Avery said.

Marcus looked at them all, then, as if the storm had passed, he grabbed up another cookie.

Rowdy relaxed back, his gaze dark, searching. He reached over and took Avery's hand, giving her a squeeze.

For her sake, or for his? Either way worked for Avery.

CHAPTER NINETEEN

A FEW HOURS LATER, as they unloaded several bags of groceries and the new Crock-Pot Avery had chosen, Rowdy thought how domestic it felt.

He'd always been a neat freak, maybe in contrast to the filth he'd grown up in—though that theory didn't apply to Pepper. Before moving in with Logan, she'd been a real clutter bug. Maybe that had more to do with her being unhappy than anything else. Now that she'd married, she and Logan kept their place up real nice.

On top of groceries, Avery had chosen some new shampoo and lotion, a potted plant and a sun catcher for one of the big windows.

Watching her move around his place—move *in* his place—had a profound effect on him. It felt like forever since he'd had her.

She went to the sink and began preparing stew for the Crock-Pot. As she cut up the beef, she said, "With you right next door, we could maybe grab a real lunch."

Rowdy caught her hips and stepped in close, breathing her in, absorbing her nearness. "You don't like Jones's cooking?"

"Ha! You got a great catch when you hired him. But the menu gets tiresome."

"Maybe if we scoot over here for lunch, we could

also grab a quickie." He kissed her neck, her shoulder. "Help me make it through the night."

"Like you ever need help. Your energy level amazes me." She dropped the beef in the pot, seasoned it and plugged in the Crock-Pot. After washing her hands, she turned in his arms. "Do you cook?"

"Do I look like I'm starving?"

"No." Her hands went up and over his shoulders. "But you could be eating fast food every day, or living off cold cuts."

"I know how to cook simple stuff. Steaks, chops, breakfast, sometimes chili when I just mix up stuff from a can with ground beef."

"A man of many talents."

"Speaking of talents…" He touched her chin. "You were good with Marcus today."

"He breaks my heart." Probably drawing nonsense comparisons, she hugged him. "I'm so glad he has you."

"I'm glad he has Alice and Reese." Those two had fallen into the perfect partnership. The love was there, so obvious that even a cynic like him couldn't miss it. Reese was exactly what Alice needed, and vice versa. Much like his sister and Logan.

And now they had Marcus, such a terrific little guy who'd probably never expected, or even dared hope for, a family like them. Surely it would make a difference.

Rowdy didn't want Marcus to be like him. He wanted much more for him than that.

If he could help from the periphery, then he'd be happy to. While he wasn't the influence Marcus needed, he would sure as hell be the backup if it ever became necessary.

The faint thought of Avery with a kid danced through

his mind, disturbing him, making him edgy in ways he didn't recognize because it had nothing to do with lust or anger or any of the other powerful emotions that usually dominated him.

Rowdy slipped his hands down her back to her ass, snuggling her in, rocking her a little. He wanted her, but he also enjoyed this, just holding her, talking. Getting to know her better each and every day, though he already felt like he'd known her a lifetime.

"I'd like to take you to Dash's lake house. I can see you under the hot summer sun, lying out in a bikini—"

Laughing, she leaned back in his arms. "Sorry, but I'm more a one-piece kind of woman."

Modest, sexy, smart and sweet. She was the kind of woman who'd gotten a toehold on his heart when most would deny he had one. "Then maybe I could talk you into leaving the one-piece behind and we could run with nature."

"Skinny-dipping?"

She looked so scandalized that Rowdy smiled. "There's no one around to see."

"There'd be you!" She laughed and slipped away from him, but caught his hand, tugging him along.

"Where are we going?"

"To bed." She looked over her shoulder at him. "I have some payback to give, remember? No time like the present."

It took little from Avery, a look, a promise, and he was straining his jeans.

For him, sex had always been a way to cope, to get by, to fill the time with pure, mind-numbing physical release. But now, with Avery, sex was so much more.

It had nothing to do with forgetting the past or dealing with the present.

It was about enjoyment—of each and every moment.

LYING IN BED, Avery half sprawled over his chest, their legs entwined, was about as nice as it got. His body was still damp, relaxed, as he stroked his fingers through her hair. He could feel each slow, heavy beat of her heart until it almost felt like his started to match it, their hearts aligned.

Idly, she pressed her soft mouth to his ribs in a warm kiss, then rubbed her small nose against him. On a sigh, she whispered, "I could just stay like this…" Her voice trailed off, but in his head, he heard the rest.

Forever.

Apparently, Avery didn't want to say it out loud any more than he did.

He lifted her small hand, rubbing his thumb over calluses that a woman like her shouldn't have. That thought led to another. "What will you do about your mother?"

She drew her slim thigh over his. "I'll call her later today. I want to find out a good time to visit again." Wrapping her fingers around his, she pulled herself up higher atop him. "Okay?"

It was hard to think with her shifting around on him. "That you talk to your mom? Yeah, sure."

Teasing lights entered her eyes. "You are a complete stud, Rowdy. My entire body is still tingling. But you're not so good that my brain has been pickled."

He had no idea what she was talking about, so he just raised a brow and waited.

"I'm not going to ask permission to run my personal life." She kissed his chest to soften that rebuke. "I was asking if this position is okay for you. I don't want to add my weight if your back is starting to—"

"Tell you what, honey." Ready to do his own teasing, Rowdy hauled her up atop him, arranging her so that she draped him like a blanket. "You don't ask me about my back anymore, and I won't do this." His hand smacked her backside, making her jump.

"Ow!" Half giggling, half protesting, she tried to reach back to rub the spot, but Rowdy held her hands locked together behind her.

"Rowdy!"

With his other hand, he cupped her now-warm cheek. "Mmm?" He kissed her stubborn chin, the corner of her mouth. He grinned, but he was also fast getting turned on again. It was insane how she kept him so fired up. "Want me to kiss it and make it all better?"

"Give me another hour and…maybe."

Before he got too distracted with need, Rowdy brought her hands up to his shoulders and wrapped his arms around her. "At the risk of offending your independent spirit, can I get a promise that you won't go back to see your mother without me?"

"You're worried about Fisher or Meyer being there?"

"I don't like to take chances." *Especially not with someone I care about.* "If you want time alone with your mom, I'll go along but stay out of the way. I can even sit in the car if that helps. But I want to be nearby." *Just in case you need me.*

Cupping his face, Avery repeatedly kissed him as a way to punctuate outrageous compliments. "You are the most amazing—" Kiss. "—giving—" Kiss. "—wonderful—"

"You looking for another spank, woman?"

She snickered. "With you wounded, I can't fight back."

In one fast move, Rowdy turned to pin her under him. "Promise me you won't go back there alone."

The laughter faded. Very solemn, she nodded. "I promise."

When she looked at him like that, with so much admiration, it made him feel desperate. He wanted to be inside her again, losing himself and clearing his mind of conflict.

"Rowdy?" She drew him down and hugged him tight, staying like that for half a minute before finally, her voice full with emotion, she whispered, "Thank you for caring."

It was the oddest damn thing, having Avery's gratitude.

And, if he believed her, her love.

For the first time that he could ever remember, the future looked pretty damned bright.

A MELLOW MOOD stayed with Rowdy as he and Avery headed for the bar late Monday morning. She'd spent Sunday wringing him out, emotionally and physically. He knew every inch of her body, but she'd been no less determined to explore every inch of his, as well.

They'd talked about everything—except for a future together. He just didn't know what to say about that. Around her he felt like a new person. A person he barely knew.

For the longest time he'd believed that once he had her, things would get back to normal. He'd get her out of his system and be able to focus again.

But instead, he kept thinking of the ways he hadn't yet had her.

He wanted to teach her to play cards.

She wanted to take him to the zoo.

He wanted to swim with her.

She wanted to curl on the couch together to watch a scary movie.

They talked endlessly…and didn't run out of things to say.

How the hell was a guy supposed to understand that shit?

He'd just unlocked the door into the bar when her cell phone rang. Rowdy waited until he realized it was her mom. Avery had called Sonya yesterday, but the woman kept a very busy schedule.

If she was ailing during her treatment, she hid it well.

When he saw Avery smile, Rowdy smiled, too. She and her mother were close, and for some reason, that made him feel really good. Obviously her mother wasn't perfect, but given his own experience with parents, imperfections didn't matter as long as there was caring and support.

He was about to follow her into the bar when Reese pulled up, so he waited for him.

Reese parked at the curb and joined him. "I was hoping to catch you here. Nothing's wrong, but I wanted to talk a minute if you have the time."

"I always get here a few hours early. I'd rather have everything set up before customers arrive than have to rush." Rowdy led the way through the bar. "Want a drink?"

"I'm good. I'd rather look around while we talk."

Few men towered over Rowdy, but Reese was so damn big that he threw a shadow over everyone else. "Help yourself."

Reese gravitated to the back room and the billiard tables. He rolled the cue ball, letting it clack against the rest, sending them to scatter and drop into pockets. "The place looks better every time I see it."

"Those have been here awhile now." Maybe, Rowdy thought, he could teach Avery to play. "The younger crowd likes it more than the regulars."

"The night I filled in for you, you had so much business I couldn't leave the bar long enough to look around."

"We've been fortunate." Wondering why Reese had come to visit, Rowdy folded his arms and leaned back on the wall, ready to wait him out.

"And you run a good business." Reese checked out the jukebox. "Alice wants to come back some night, too. Maybe after we get settled in the new house."

"Alice doesn't belong here."

Reese turned to face him. "And Avery does?"

There went his mellow mood. "If you've got something to say, Reese, say it."

"All right." Reese propped a hip on the side of a pool table. "You're remembering the dive it was. It's better now. Nicer. If you weren't so close to it, you'd probably see that yourself."

"Did you come here to nettle me or to schmooze?"

"Neither, actually." He picked up a chalk cube and shook it in his hand. "Here's the thing. You're good with Marcus."

Rowdy straightened away from the wall. "What's happening?"

"Nothing."

"Bullshit."

Grumbling, Reese set aside the chalk and stood.

"Alice and I would like to name you as one of Marcus's guardians. You know, for emergencies and stuff. If something should happen—"

Alarm sent a rush of heat down his spine. "What would happen?"

"Hell, Rowdy, I don't know. Your own parents died in a car wreck, right?"

"They were drunks."

"Well, I'm a cop. I know how fragile life can be. I'm not expecting anything to happen, but if it did—"

Panic throbbed in his temples. "You have Logan and Pepper."

"Yes, we do. And they'd be great. But Marcus..." Reese pinched the bridge of his nose, then dropped his hand to pin Rowdy with his stare. "The kid admires you a lot. In rapid order you've become a hero, a pseudouncle and a friend to him. I want him, and the courts, to know that you are in fact his family in every way that matters. That includes putting you in a will."

Anger started to edge out other more disturbing sensations. "What the fuck, Reese? Are you on your period?"

Reese scowled.

"What's with all the morbid shit?"

"Reality is not morbid, damn it."

For Rowdy it always had been. Until Avery. And now...

"I love Alice," Reese said, his voice raised. "And I'm determined to make things right for Marcus. That means I'm going to do everything in my power to see it so—including binding you to them."

"You're not making sense."

Annoyance growing, Reese loomed closer. "I don't

want you getting some harebrained idea about packing up and leaving again. You have roots here. You'll have more roots if you know you're partially responsible for Marcus. Is that too much to ask?"

Rowdy went tense from his ears to the soles of his feet. He wanted to stay and be settled and plan…things.

Carrying a crate, Cannon went past the entry to the billiard room. If he listened, Rowdy could hear Jones rattling pots and pans in the kitchen. Ella would be showing up soon.

And Avery… She'd be behind the bar by now, setting up her station and for some insane reason, happy to do it.

He shook his head at Reese. "No."

"No what, damn it?"

"It's not too much." Hell, he had a life here now. A good life. He thought of Avery again and almost smiled. "I'm honored that you'd think of me."

"Well." Reese seemed surprised by the sudden turnaround, but didn't question it. "Good. You'll have some papers to sign."

"No problem." He leveled a look on Reese. "But be careful so it's never necessary for me to do more than be around, taking part. Got it?"

"That's the plan." He reached in his pocket for a piece of paper. "In other news, I got a name to go with those plates." He flipped open the paper and looked at it. "Fisher Holloway. Know him?"

"Yeah, sorry. It's old news." He'd totally forgotten that Reese was checking on things for him. "I know who the bastard is and I'm taking care of it." Rowdy started out of the room.

Reese caught his arm. "No."

Looking at that hand on his arm, Rowdy raised his brows. "'Fraid so." He freed himself from Reese's hold and walked away.

"Damn it, Rowdy." Reese kept pace with him. "You can't always do things your way. There are laws."

Rowdy laughed. What did Reese expect him to do? Murder and mayhem?

Fuming, Reese asked, "Who is it?"

"Avery's ex." Though that wasn't accurate since, according to Avery, they'd never really been together. "Don't worry about it."

"You involved me," Reese insisted. "I'm here. If she's having problems with some bozo, tell me. I can—"

"Not happening." Rowdy got out the whiteboard to write up the day's specials.

"Fine. Have it your way." Reese pulled out his phone. "I'll call Pepper. And Logan."

Rowdy frowned at him.

"Might as well tell Alice, too."

Of all the idiotic…

"I assume Avery knows what you have planned?"

Temper sparked, Rowdy set the board aside. "I don't know what the fuck you think you're doing, but—"

"Rowdy?" Her gaze going back and forth between them, Avery approached. "Is everything okay?"

"It's fine."

Reese snorted.

Avery smiled at him. "I couldn't help but overhear you guys bickering."

That annoyed the hell out of Rowdy. "We weren't bickering."

"Actually," Reese said, "I was trying to convince Rowdy not to be so pigheaded."

"Good luck with that." Avery laughed at his expression. "I'm just teasing. I'm sure you'll be entirely circumspect and cautious in all you do."

"Avery," he warned.

Grinning, she took his hand. "My mother is busy for the entire week, but she said she'd love for us to visit next Sunday. Does that work for you?"

"Whatever you want, honey."

"Okay, I'll let her know." She went on tiptoe to kiss him. "Thank you."

After she went back to the bar, Reese dropped back against the wall and stared.

"What's your problem now?" Rowdy asked.

"I'm in shock." He blinked twice. "Did you actually say you were heading home with her to meet her mother?"

"Already met her." Rowdy began lowering chairs off the tables. "She's nice enough. Jury is still out on her stepdad."

"You're kidding me." Reese pitched in with the chairs. "And the ex? Did you meet him, too?"

"Grade-A prick." The next chair landed a little harder than he meant for it to. "Her folks like him, though."

Reese shrugged that off. "I'll take your judgment over theirs any day."

Rowdy hated to admit how much that meant to him. "He says he followed us out of concern for Avery. You know, just checking up on her to make sure she was okay."

"Right." Being facetious, Reese said, "I'm sure he had only altruistic motives."

Without thinking about it, Rowdy shared another

concern. "It's been a rough time for her. She's struggling with some things."

Reese clapped him on the shoulder. "I think you're doing a little struggling of your own."

Ready to flatten him, Rowdy said, "Go bug someone else, will you?"

Grinning, Reese pointed at him. "Don't do anything with her ex. If he bothers her again, let me know. If you murder him, you'll be the one in jail and Avery will be alone. Then how will she feel?"

Yeah, maybe something to think about. "You made your point."

"Several points actually." He waved to Avery. "Let me know if you need anything."

"The same." Rowdy walked with Reese to the door.

As long as Fisher left Avery alone, he wouldn't have to deal with him.

But if the bastard ever thought about hurting her again, all bets were off.

CANNON ENJOYED WALKING. It was good exercise, gave him an excuse to look around the area and check on things and it freed his mind.

Even on an overcast day, he could fill his lungs with fresh air, watch a bird fly by and hear the buzz of the neighborhood.

Hands in his pockets, his stocking hat pulled down over his ears, he checked out every building, those closed up and those still trying to get by.

At a small, family-run pawnshop, Cannon watched an elderly man sweep leaves away from the front door. Cannon knew everyone, at least well enough to wave and exchange a greeting, so he was already aware of the owner's eighteen-year-old granddaughter, Yvette.

She spotted him and immediately started to flirt. Though barely legal, she was old enough to know how to look at a guy to get the biggest reaction.

Although amused, Cannon kept his nod reserved, polite, but nothing more. Yvette was at the age where she liked attention a little too much, always flirting with danger. Being stacked and really cute, she could find that danger whenever she wanted, but she wouldn't find it with him.

At the corner, gangly youths hung out, probably because of the girl. They hadn't yet caused any real trouble, but they were at risk of getting recruited by the real thugs. If he got his gym opened soon, that might help. He'd need another six months or so. Possibly longer, depending on how his next fight went.

When the boys noticed him, they called out. Grinning, Cannon lifted a hand—and his gaze got caught by a luxury sedan coasting slowly toward the bar. Not the silver hybrid this time, but a new model Audi.

Like money on wheels.

Even as the hairs on the back of his neck prickled, tinted windows kept him from seeing inside.

The boys noticed the car and made a big fuss about it. Cannon didn't want them to draw attention, so with a final wave he jogged the rest of the way to the bar. They wouldn't open for another forty-five minutes. Why would a slick ride like that be hanging around?

Instead of going to the front entrance, Cannon went down one building more, then cut through the alley and around to the back door. He was always cautious, and he didn't want to let the driver of the car know he'd been noticed.

He tapped once, and then waited until Jones let him in through the kitchen.

Pulling off his hat, Cannon asked, "Where's Rowdy?"

Always busy, Jones went back to his stove and the massive pot of soup he had cooking. "Last I saw him he was in his office going over some invoices."

"Thanks." He skirted past Jones, anxious to reach Rowdy before the Audi took off again.

Rowdy was just stepping out when Cannon reached him. "We have trouble. C'mon."

Without asking questions, Rowdy followed.

"New car," Cannon explained. "An Audi. Probably seventy-five thou."

"Here?" Rowdy asked with a load of suspicion.

"Hanging around, yeah. Watching the bar." Cannon glanced at him. "Did you scare off the silver BMW?"

"Maybe." Rowdy's face tightened. "I confronted the bastard."

"So you know who that was?"

Full of bad intentions, Rowdy snarled, "I know."

"Wish I'd been there to see that." Cannon sensed there was more to the story, but it wasn't in his nature to pry. "So now there's a new car. Hell of a coincidence, ya know?"

"Or an outright taunt."

"Could be," Cannon agreed as they neared the front window. "If someone wanted to be sly, that is not the sedan to drive."

Scowling in indecision, Rowdy stood back—out of view from anyone on the street. "Which way out front?"

"I walked up South Street, which brought me up

behind it." Because he knew something was going on, Cannon asked, "What do you want me to do?"

"Stay here with Avery while I check it out."

"Sure."

Rowdy had just turned to go toward the back when Avery came out from behind the bar. "Rowdy!"

Her tone stopped them both.

Holding the bar phone, her face pale, she said, "The police just called."

Cannon watched Rowdy switch priorities in a heartbeat. It was one of the things he respected most about him—how quickly he adapted to changing situations. That bespoke experience and the calm detachment needed to deal with crisis situations.

Admirable traits, as far as Cannon was concerned, traits that would come in handy while working in this neighborhood.

Rowdy reached Avery in only a few long strides. "Logan or Reese?"

"Not them, no."

"Then who?"

She shook her head. "I don't think I got a name."

Going hot around the collar, Rowdy asked, "What did they want?"

Brows pinched with disbelief, Avery shook her head. "I'm not sure I buy it, but they said my apartment was broken into."

When Rowdy took the phone from her, Avery said, "They already hung up, but, Rowdy, they wanted me to meet them there as soon as possible."

Wow. Knowing a setup when he heard it, Cannon whistled.

Like a prizefighter, Rowdy bunched up. His killing

mood showed as clearly in his physical stance as it did in the black glare he sent toward the Audi waiting on the street outside.

Someone was messing with Avery, and if Rowdy had his way, they'd soon be paying the price for that error.

Cannon wasn't a betting man, but if he was, he'd put all his money on Rowdy.

CHAPTER TWENTY

SINCE SHE'D WITNESSED Rowdy in defense mode before, Avery recognized the signs. All hell was about to break loose.

"Fuck that," Rowdy said. "It's a setup."

"That's what I was thinking, too." Rowdy looked so furious that she hooked her hand in the waistband of his jeans, determined to keep him from leaving. "Could we call Logan or Reese to have it verified?"

Cannon stepped up. "No need. I'm on it." He had his phone to his ear, and a second later, he spoke to someone. "Can you check on the lady's place? See if there are any cops hanging around or if it looks like it's been broken into? Thanks." He disconnected the call. "I'll know in under ten minutes."

"In the meantime," Rowdy said, "stay here with Avery."

Avery grabbed for him with her other hand, too. "Where are you going?" Even Rowdy wouldn't be impulsive enough to charge into a trap.

"Just outside." He shared a male-inspired glance with Cannon. "I'll be right back."

"Oh, no, you don't." If he insisted on defending her, then she could damn well insist on knowing the details. "I have a right to know."

"I just need to check out something. I won't be long."

As he started off she kept pace with him, still holding on to his belt. "Call Reese or Logan," she insisted again.

"Why don't you do that for me?"

So she'd have something to do other than follow him? She shot his words back at him—sort of—saying "Screw that."

"I've got this, boss," Cannon said. "Why don't you stay here with Avery and I'll—"

"No." Rowdy caught her wrists and lifted her hands away. "There's a car out front. An Audi. Does Fisher own one?"

That's why he wanted to leave? To confront someone? She shook her head. "I don't know."

"He owns the BMW. Can he afford both?"

Very aware of Cannon standing there, hearing everything, Avery nodded. "Yes." She tried to collect herself. "But he also said he was trading in the BMW, remember?"

"I remember." Stern, Rowdy lifted her chin. "I'm going to see if it's him hanging around, that's all."

"Baloney! What if it is him? Then what? You'll confront him and—" She looked at Cannon, wishing for a little help. "He's dangerous."

"I know, babe. I'll be careful." He said to Cannon, "Keep her in here."

Avery took exception to that. "I don't need a damned babysitter. And just so you know, I'm calling Logan right now!"

Rowdy either didn't believe her or he didn't care. He went down the hall to the back door and Avery started to shake in indecision. What should she do next?

Cannon helped her decide when he asked, "You'll stay put?"

By way of answer, she gave him a shove. "Go. I'll be fine."

With a salute, he took off after Rowdy. Meager backup, Avery thought, but it was something.

Running back up to the front of the bar, she dug her cell phone out of her purse, fumbled through her contacts and found Logan's number. While the phone rang, she went through the bar to the front window. She could see the car sitting across the street but hadn't yet spotted Rowdy or Cannon.

Logan answered with an official sounding, "Riske here."

"Logan, it's Avery." The words came out more rushed than she'd intended.

With new awareness, Logan asked, "What's wrong?"

Of course as a police detective, he picked up on her worry. "Rowdy went outside to confront a guy in a car, but it could be a trap of some kind because police called to say my apartment was broken into, but I'm not sure I believe that and it's too many things happening at one time." She sucked in a breath. "I think Rowdy might be in danger."

That convoluted explanation could have muddled even the sharpest mind, but Logan said only, "Are you inside? Safe?"

"Yes. I'm in the bar."

"Make sure the doors are locked and stay put. I'm not that far away." He hung up, leaving Avery standing there with only her rising worry.

Ella touched her shoulder, and she nearly jumped out of her skin.

Giving her a funny look, Ella patted her. "What's going on, sugar? You okay?"

Avery wanted to shout. Just that morning everything had felt so promising, so fresh and safe and...wonderful. She turned back to the window. How could she explain to Ella something she didn't quite understand herself?

Jones joined them, too. "What's going on?"

Knowing she had to tell them something, Avery pointed out the window. "See that car?"

Ella leaned in close. "Ohhh. Fancy."

Jones cocked a brow. "What's a car like that doing hanging around here?" He made a wrong conclusion. "Rowdy ain't selling the place, is he?"

"No, nothing like that." Where was Rowdy?

"Then what?" Ella asked. "You're shaking."

Avery clasped her hands together to calm the nervous movement. "It could belong to..." *A man who wanted to rape me.* No, she couldn't say that. "There's a guy who wanted to marry me, but..." *I ran away from my entire life to dodge him.* She searched for Rowdy but didn't yet see him. "The thing is—"

"There's Rowdy," Ella said.

Her stomach dropped. Wide-eyed, Avery watched as he came up behind the car on the passenger side where he'd be less noticeable. There was no hesitation in his stride as he approached. He didn't hunker down or sneak.

Hand to her heart, Avery waited.

Ella snuggled closer.

Jones wrung his hands on his dishcloth.

They stood there together, collective breath held. Was Cannon close? If something happened, what would she—

Rowdy stepped around to the driver's side, his head

dipped down to see in the darkened window, his hand reaching out for the handle—

The car suddenly pulled away from the curb with screeching tires. Lurching back, Rowdy barely missed being run over. He stood there watching, fists propped on his hips, as the car disappeared around a corner.

Avery wanted to wilt. For now, at least, Rowdy was safe.

Jones pulled out a chair and said, "Here, now, sit down."

"Thank you, but I'm fine."

"You don't look fine," Ella said, and she took the chair. "So what was that all about?"

"A guy I used to know," Avery summarized. "He's not a nice person."

"He's been bothering you?" Jones asked.

"I'm not sure. Maybe." She stayed glued to the window until Rowdy headed back in. Rather than have him walk around back, she went to the front door and unlocked it. She wanted to throw herself against him, to hold him tight. And she wanted to smack him for scaring her like that, for taking unnecessary chances.

Since Cannon had come out of the alley and joined Rowdy, Avery didn't do either one. Somehow she would convince Rowdy that she wasn't a damsel in distress. He didn't have to take risks for her.

As soon as Rowdy got close enough to hear, she said, "Logan is on his way."

"Thanks." He came in past her and closed the door, then took Ella's order pad from her and jotted down a number.

"License plate?" Avery guessed.

"Yeah." He folded it.

Cannon's cell rang. Everyone waited as he answered it.

Nodding, he gave his thanks and tucked the phone away again. "Her apartment looks as tight as ever. No signs of cops or a break-in."

Ella and Jones stood there confounded, waiting for an explanation. Avery had no idea what to tell them. She didn't want the world to know her private past, but now that the past had invaded her present, these people could be in danger.

Rowdy didn't suffer the same indecision. "Listen up. We've had a creep hanging around, making prank phone calls and giving veiled threats that may or may not be real. If you see anyone or anything that makes you uneasy, no matter what, I want to know about it. Got it?"

Jones tugged his graying ponytail. "I don't see much from the kitchen, but sure. I'll let you know."

Rowdy turned to Ella. "You, too, hon. Any customers who seem out of place, you need to tell me."

Ella patted Avery's arm. "Of course, sugar." She gave Avery a pitying look. "Thing is, guys ask after her all the time."

"They do?" That was news to Avery. Sure, guys talked to her. She was a bartender—it came with the job. But she'd rarely noticed any real interest.

"You don't see it," Ella said. "You're too busy watching Rowdy."

Oh, good grief. Heat rushed into her cheeks, especially when Cannon coughed and Jones grinned.

"But she draws attention," Ella continued. "And since no one knows the status…" She shrugged.

Rowdy gathered steam. "What are you talking about? What status?"

"Between the two of you." Ella hugged Avery. "You

two flirt around about it and all, but Avery has that 'hands off' attitude and you've got the bachelor stamp permanently branded on your head, so the great mystery of whether she's available or not keeps guys guessing."

"Great mystery?" Avery choked.

"Does make things interesting," Cannon agreed, then held up both hands when Rowdy turned on him. "Not to me. I know the situation."

Oh, God, Avery thought. There was a situation?

Rowdy stood there fuming for no apparent reason before saying, his voice icy calm, "Here on out, if anyone asks, she's taken." And with that, he stalked off to the bar.

Cannon watched him go. "I do enjoy working here. There's never a dull moment."

Jones beamed at Avery as if she'd accomplished some difficult task. Ella shrugged.

To add to the confusion, Logan arrived.

After greeting him as if nothing out of the ordinary had happened, Rowdy sent Ella and Jones back to work.

He tried to do the same with Avery. "We'll be open in another twenty minutes."

Not about to be cut out, Avery didn't budge. "I have everything ready."

Doing the opposite, Cannon excused himself. "I'll get to work, but if you need me for anything, just let me know."

"Keep an eye out," Rowdy told him.

"For her admirers," Cannon asked with a straight face, "or for threats?"

Without taking the bait, Rowdy said, "Both." He turned to Logan. "Thanks for coming."

In nothing more than his shirtsleeves, his tie loosened and his expression weary, Logan looked around. "Guess I missed all the excitement."

"There wasn't much." Rowdy led the way to his office, and then took a few minutes to explain what had happened.

"You shouldn't have approached the car. If this guy is crazy enough to keep pushing the issue, he's crazy enough to be a threat."

Avery agreed with him there. "Is there anything you can do?"

"I can check the plates." Logan called it in while pacing the room. "We should hear back soon. Takes less than a minute to run them."

He looked so tense and tired that Avery regretted involving him. "Would you like some coffee while we wait?"

He went to a chair and dropped into it. "That'd be great, thanks."

"No problem." She gave Rowdy a meaningful frown to let him know that she did not want him taking advantage of her absence.

His return look told her he'd make no promises. Blasted stubborn man. "Logan? This concerns me more than anyone."

Confused, Logan looked between them. "Okay."

"Don't let Rowdy make plans without me." Instead of waiting for his agreement, she hurried to the break room to fetch three cups of coffee. In her haste she almost spilled one, but made it back just as Logan got news.

As he disconnected the call, he said, "The plates don't belong to the car." He accepted the coffee with gratitude. "Whoever was hanging around didn't want to be identified."

Rowdy seemed to take that in stride, as if he'd expected it. "Old plates?"

"Yup. Probably stolen."

That made it all seem so elaborate. Not just a random drive-by to snoop, to maybe follow her home, but a deliberate, covert plan to draw her out. She felt a little sick, and a lot afraid. "My apartment?"

"I sent a squad car over to check on things." Logan sipped his coffee. "No one in our department called you."

"You look beat," Rowdy said.

"Busy day, that's all." He shot a glance at Avery. "I was in this neck of the woods anyway."

"I guess we shouldn't ask?"

"Not yet." He drank more coffee—and his cell rang.

Avery went to stand by Rowdy while Logan took the call.

Had someone wanted to get her alone? Was Fisher foolish enough to try to grab her right outside the bar? Or had he planned to tail her back to her apartment, where he'd have more opportunity to make his move?

Memories rushed back in on her, how Fisher had grabbed her that night, how ugly he'd been in his anger, his abuse. She remembered the awful choking fear when she'd realized his intent.

No doubt to reassure her, Rowdy put an arm around her, his hand at her waist.

What if she had left and Rowdy had gone alone?

Fisher might have been hoping for that. He was so good at lying, at covering his tracks, that he might have come up with a way to rid himself of Rowdy while blaming others.

She wouldn't put anything past him.

Near her ear, Rowdy said, "You're okay, and you're going to stay that way." His mouth brushed her temple. "I'm not about to let anyone hurt you."

That scared her most of all. How far would Rowdy go to ensure her safety?

"Sorry," Logan said. "The officers looked around but nothing seemed disturbed. The place is still locked up and quiet."

Same report they'd gotten from Cannon's friends. Frustrated, Avery rubbed her brow. "What now?"

"Unless you have more to tell me about this past relationship of yours, there's not much we can do." Logan waited, brows raised, but neither Avery nor Rowdy had anything else to offer.

A year had passed since Fisher had attacked her. They had no real proof that it was him coming back around now, but Avery couldn't fend off the memories, or the fear.

What would it take to discourage Fisher? Could she just avoid him until he gave up? And what about Rowdy? He wasn't a man to sit back while threats existed.

She needed a way to protect him, to keep him from putting himself in harm's way.

"I wish there was more I could do." Logan finished off his coffee and crushed the paper cup. "But hanging around a bar isn't a crime."

"Fictitious plates are," Rowdy pointed out.

"Sure, but how do we unravel that mess without throwing some serious resources behind it? Without good reason, the lieutenant would never go for it."

Rowdy crossed his arms. "If it is Fisher—"

"I can have a talk with him." Logan's smile was mean with anticipation. "Not a problem."

Avery had no idea what the right move might be, but she hated being the source of so much trouble. "If we just stay away from him…"

"He has Meyer's approval, honey." Rowdy rubbed her shoulder. "What if he's there every time you try to visit with your mother? Maybe even with her blessing."

"I'll talk to Mom and make her understand."

"Yeah, you can try that," Rowdy agreed. "But in the meantime, I'm going to talk to Fisher about the car."

The way he watched her, it was like he willed her to trust him. And she did. Avery knew, despite his rep, Rowdy didn't go around mangling innocent people or doling out lethal retribution if there was another way.

Unlike Fisher, he wasn't a bully.

He definitely wasn't a murderer.

Rowdy Yates was a defender, and more honorable than any man she knew. "Okay."

"Hold up," Logan said. "How and where do you plan to talk to him?"

"That depends on his schedule," Rowdy said. "And I'm hoping Avery can help me with that."

Avery's stomach bottomed out. "I haven't seen him in a year!" She detested the note of desperation in her tone. "You know that, Rowdy."

"I do, but some things never change. Fish strikes me as a man of habit."

A man of habit? He was a certifiable cretin! "I don't want you anywhere near him."

As if she hadn't said that, Rowdy continued, "You can find out for me if he has a routine. He obviously hits up the gym on a regular basis."

Logan nodded. "You could meet him in a public place."

"Exactly. If he's as worried about appearances as Avery says, he won't want to cause a scene."

She shook her head, but neither man appeared to notice. "Why don't you just call him?"

"I want to look him in the eyes when I ask about the car."

Her heart pounded so hard it almost stole her breath. "He *lies*."

"He won't be able to lie to me." He brushed a knuckle over her cheek. "Either way, he'll know we're on to him."

"That could cause him to back off," Logan agreed. "Or it could push him over the edge and make him do something stupid."

Knowing Rowdy had made up his mind, Avery clutched his hand. "I'm going with you."

He gave a short laugh. "No, you're not."

How dare he dismiss her like that? Slowly, she straightened away from him. "If it's safe, *public* like you said, then what difference does it make if I'm there?"

"I don't want you near him."

"Ha!" She put a finger to his chest. "I don't want *you* near him, either."

Behind them, Logan cleared his throat.

Countenance darkening, Rowdy pushed away from the desk. "I'm not you, babe."

"There's a news flash," she said with a healthy dose of sarcasm. "But here's another—this is my problem, not yours."

"I'm making it mine."

"You want to help, Rowdy? Great. I'm grateful."

He looked like she'd slapped him. *"I don't want your fucking gratitude."*

No, he just wanted to put himself at risk, always, for everyone. But she was determined that at least with her, things would be different. "Tough! You have it anyway."

Logan said, "Maybe I should—"

Avery twisted a hand in the front of Rowdy's T-shirt. "I told you I love you. Do you have any idea what that means?"

A long whistle sounded from Logan.

Rowdy puffed up like an enraged bull. "It sure as hell doesn't mean you get to dictate to me."

That almost made her laugh. "Like I would even try? I'm not stupid." She went on tiptoes. "It means that I would be destroyed if anything happened to you, especially when you were acting on my behalf."

Rowdy breathed a little harder.

"Do you *want* me destroyed?"

"You're pushing it, honey." He closed a hand over her wrist, but didn't pull her fist from his shirt.

"No, of course you don't." Avery softened, but just a little. This was too important to water down. "You want to protect me because that's who you are. And I love you for that and for so many other reasons. But if it's truly not dangerous, then let me go with you. It is my problem, whether you like it or not. I have a right to be there."

With tension arcing between them, they stared at each other, neither willing to relent.

Into the quiet, Logan said, "She's right, you know."

Rowdy's right eye twitched. "Fuck you, Logan."

"It'd probably be a good idea to take her along—as

a witness, as a reminder to keep your cool. And for Fisher to see that she's not cowed by what's happened."

Rowdy said nothing.

"If she's with you, Fisher will be less likely to get out of hand, and you're less likely to threaten him."

"I don't make threats."

No, Avery thought, Rowdy made promises—that he kept. "You could come with me when I visit my mom again." She searched his face, praying that he'd understand. "I can set it up as soon as you need me to. If Fisher is there, we'll both talk to him. And if he's not, we can find out his schedule from my mom or Meyer."

"It's that important to you?"

"*You* are that important to me." She'd confront Fisher once and for all. She'd let him know that she wasn't the same easily intimidated person.

If he came after her again, he'd have a major fight on his hands, one that she'd pursue with every resource left to her.

Rowdy took his time thinking about it, mulling it over until she was ready to clout him.

Finally he nodded. "All right."

His agreement made her smile and left her limp. "Great."

"Set it up, the sooner the better." Half under his breath, he muttered, "I want this over and done with."

"Glad that's settled." After checking his watch, Logan sat forward. "If anything else happens, anything at all, let me know. In the meantime, I'd suggest you take extra precautions."

Rowdy walked to the door. "She's staying with me."

"Tonight?" Logan asked.

"Indefinitely."

Though Logan quickly recovered, Avery saw his surprise. "I know," she said, deadpan. "I'm still shocked, too."

Rowdy didn't find either of them funny. "I'll go to her place to get whatever she needs, but she won't be back there alone."

Logan looked back and forth between them again. "I'm sure that's for the best, at least until we get things figured out." He joined Rowdy by the door. "You need to be careful, too."

"He will be," Avery promised. One way or another, she'd see to it.

With a half smile, Rowdy told Logan, "After we see Fisher, I'll let you know if we find out anything worth repeating."

"Appreciate it."

Avery held out a hand. "Logan, really, thank you so much for coming over."

He ignored her hand and pulled her in for a hug. "Anytime at all, okay?"

They were about to leave the office when Cannon showed up. "Sorry to interrupt, but you said you wanted to know." He tried unsuccessfully to moderate a big grin. "A group of guys just came in—firefighters fresh from their shift. Nothing threatening, I don't think, but they're asking for Avery."

Well, shoot. Avery started out of the room. "I'll get to it."

Rowdy pulled her back, anchored her to his side and together, followed by Cannon and Logan's amusement, they entered the crowded front of the bar.

Rowdy even made a point of lifting her chin and kissing her with more heat than necessary. Flustered,

Avery scolded him, but that just got her another kiss before, far too grim, he got to work.

If he'd wanted to make things clear, well, that sure did it. Her lips continued to tingle, and her heart soared.

Rowdy might not have said the words, but his actions were clear enough—for all to see.

There were no more calls or idling cars hanging around, and the rest of the night went by without incident—until ten o'clock, when a sexy brunette came in and set her sights on Rowdy.

CHAPTER TWENTY-ONE

For a Monday night, they were busier than usual. Rowdy did his best to keep an eye on Avery. Seemed every damned guy in the place found a reason to chat her up.

He'd known she was popular, an integral part of the bar's success. But he hadn't before realized how often she got hit on. He couldn't deny a touch of jealousy. But he also felt pride.

Because Avery didn't reciprocate.

She was friendly and funny and always professional. She served up drinks and laughs and the occasional advice, all without taking any guy too seriously.

Her smiles were kind, not a come-on.

Without trying too hard, mostly just by being herself, she drew attention. The way she tucked a wayward curl behind her ear. How she twisted that supple little body from the ice chest to the tap to the bar top.

She was fanatical about keeping things clean and tidy, and she organized like a librarian.

Better still, when danger came calling, she utilized a wealth of common sense.

All in all, there wasn't a single thing about Avery not to love. From the start, he hadn't stood a chance against her.

He was lost in thought, staring at Avery and trying

to decide what his next move should be, when he saw her glance toward the door.

He followed her gaze—and got caught.

Well, hell, the night needed only this.

Unable to help himself, Rowdy looked over the lady. She wore skintight black jeans with heels and a V-neck sweater that exposed a notable rack.

Reese and Logan might like to deny that their lieutenant was a woman, but no other man seeing her now would make that mistake—and plenty of men were looking.

Why the hell was she here?

Only one other time had Rowdy seen her dressed in anything other than her business suits or uniform, and that was during a sting where she'd been undercover.

A ballbuster of the first order, Lieutenant Peterson liked her stiff, mannish attire. Probably because it kept guys like Reese and Logan in line. It hadn't really worked on him.

Or on Dash, Logan's brother.

Lieutenant Peterson scanned the crowd, and Rowdy had a horrible suspicion she was looking for him.

"Shit." He hadn't figured Peterson as the type of woman who liked to walk on the wild side, but there'd be no other reason for her to show up in his bar dressed like that and looking for him.

One glance at Avery and Rowdy knew this night wouldn't end well unless he took some precautionary measures right now.

Turning his back to the lieutenant, Rowdy strode away to his office. Dropping into the chair behind his desk, he flipped through the contacts on his phone, located the number he wanted and hit the call button.

What was Lieutenant Margaret Peterson doing here this time of night on a Monday? The phone rang five times before Dashiel Riske picked up. "I'm listening."

"Did I wake you?"

"Rowdy?" Around a loud yawn, Dash said, "What's up, man? Everything okay?"

Might as well lay it out there. "I know it might be inconvenient, but you need to come to the bar."

"Yeah? How come?"

"Trust me, you'll thank me."

"Meaning you have naked ladies dancing on the tables or something? Because seriously, I was about to turn in."

Logan might be in denial about Dash's attraction to the lieutenant, but Rowdy had no such qualms. "One lady, and no, she's not naked—though she does look pretty fine in tight jeans and a low-cut sweater."

"I'm listening."

Rowdy was about to explain further when a knock sounded on his open door. "Hang on, Dash." He covered the phone and said, "What is it?"

Ella leaned in. "Avery wants you up front. She says you have a visitor."

Damn it, had Peterson already approached Avery to ask for him? She'd been through enough today without the additional hassle. "Tell her I'll be right there." When he returned to the call, he said to Dash, "You coming or not?"

"You have me curious, so sure. I'll see you in a few."

Luckily Dash wasn't more than fifteen minutes away. That is, if he headed right out. Working at his own construction company, Logan's younger brother rose with the birds. He occasionally hung out at the bar, but only on weekends.

Rowdy found Avery engaged in conversation with Margaret as she poured her a glass of wine. Though her smile looked a little tight, Avery was her usual pleasant self.

The lieutenant had her shapely little ass perched on a bar stool, legs crossed, elbows on the bar. Silver hoops dangled from her ears, reflecting the ambient light. More makeup than usual turned her smoky blue eyes mysterious. As she turned toward him, Rowdy saw a nice display of cleavage. Yeah, Dash would definitely thank him.

Stopping beside her, Rowdy said, "Lieute—"

"Shhh." Leaning toward him, she touched a fingertip to his bottom lip. In a husky whisper, her eyes gazing into his, she said, "Not tonight. Tonight I'm just Margaret."

Oh, hell. "Sure thing." He took the stool next to her. "So, Margaret, you've been drinking already?"

"Not much." Smiling, she let her gaze travel all over him. "How've you been, Rowdy?"

"Getting by." He leaned a forearm on the bar and smiled at Avery. "You met Margaret?"

"I served her."

So during their little chitchat, the lieutenant hadn't introduced herself? "Margaret Peterson, this is Avery Mullins. Avery, Margaret is the—"

"Rowdy." The lieutenant slid off the stool and up against him, her gaze smoldering. "Could we talk privately?"

Rowdy tried leaning back, but Margaret just followed. "Uh…"

Abandoning him, Avery said, "Excuse me" in clipped tones as she moved down the bar away from them.

The lieutenant's thighs were against his, her breasts almost touching his chest. She stared up at him with some silent message that Rowdy didn't want to read.

Her tongue came out to dampen her lips, and she whispered, "Say yes, damn you," with a smile that contradicted the words.

Hurry up, Dash.

"All right." No way in hell would Rowdy take her to his office. He just knew what Avery would think if he did. "Let's go to a booth." Rowdy picked up her wine, then took her arm and started her toward the back near the billiard room.

"Thank you."

There was no real privacy on the floor, not for anything…intimate. But in the booth, with the clatter of pool balls behind them and the jukebox in front of them, they could talk a little more freely without anyone hearing.

Rowdy seated her first, and then slid into the booth across from her. Peterson had her back to the room, but he could see everything—which was the point.

She leaned over the booth toward him, and being male, his gaze just naturally went to her boobs.

"Rowdy?"

"Hmm?" He got his attention up to her face—and saw a wealth of attitude before she masked it. Suspicion prickled.

She stared into his eyes. "I'm hoping you'll agree to do me a big favor."

Hopefully the favor had nothing to do with getting naked or horizontal. "If I can."

"It's...personal."

The way she said that made him uneasy. Damn, but he hated games like this.

Luckily, he saw Dash come through the front door. He must have rushed to make it so quickly.

"Hold that thought. Let me take care of something and I'll be right back." Ella started past, and Rowdy caught her to say, "Her drinks are on the house, okay?"

Ella eyed Margaret, scowled at Rowdy and cocked out a shapely hip. "Sure, honey. Whatever you want."

Great. Now Ella thought he was already stepping out on Avery. A week ago he wouldn't have cared, but in the past week with Avery...yeah, it had started to matter.

A lot.

"She's a friend," Rowdy said, but damn it, he felt like an ass for explaining himself. "Forget it. Just give her whatever she wants until I return."

With any luck, Peterson would play her games with Dash and let him off the hook.

Hoping Margaret wouldn't yet notice Dash—just in case she planned to be stubborn about things—Rowdy made his way across the crowded floor to meet him. One way or another, he would excuse himself from her attentions.

He had something solid going with Avery, and he wouldn't let an uptight, prickly, pain-in-the-ass cop ruin it for him.

PLENTY OF WOMEN noticed Dash when he came in. Rowdy supposed it was the prospect of fresh blood to the week-day crowd. Most of them had never seen Dash before.

After meeting under shitty circumstances—with serious threats against Pepper—he and Dash had hit it off. Dash was only a year older, and they shared a near-identical height of six feet four inches. But where Rowdy saw the worst in most everyone and everything, Dash saw the best.

He was a funny guy, much more so than his brother Logan. Of course, Rowdy's opinion on that might be biased by the fact Logan was a cop and married to Pepper.

Like Logan, Dash was well-off, gifted with financial security from their parents. Rowdy respected the fact that Dash still worked damn hard at his construction company.

The physical labor showed, evidenced by all the female attention Dash got as he stripped off his coat.

And thinking about how the ladies were all drooling over him—Rowdy twisted around to look at Avery.

She was watching him.

Him, not Dash. Not any other man.

That fact filled Rowdy with incredible satisfaction.

Bringing him back to the here and now, Dash clapped him on the shoulder. "You're this busy on a Monday night? Nice." He gazed around. "The setup is different."

"We've made a few changes. Got rid of the poles, put in a billiards room."

"It's looking good. More upstanding."

"That's the point."

Smiling, Dash eyed a tableful of women. "I bet the weekends are insane."

"We do all right. We're not open on Sunday, but I have a new employee who's working out, so that might be changing, too." Cannon could fill in when Rowdy was away. He'd need to hire a few more people, especially someone to help Jones in the kitchen. But he'd figure it out.

"I can see it now," Dash said. "Folks will hit up church first, then plan on Getting Rowdy."

He never should have let Avery name the place. "The rowdiest crowd waits for the weekend. The weekday regulars aren't too bad."

"Obviously I've been away too long." He nodded to two women flirting with him. "Sorry about that. Overload of work lately."

"You have a life." And he wasn't obligated to visit the bar.

"So you haven't missed me, huh?"

Rowdy checked his watch. "I would have figured you'd lose some of your good humor after ten."

Dash grinned at him. "Okay, so let's hear it. What's my surprise?"

"More like a problem. A *woman* problem."

Dash looked first at Avery behind the bar, and then, somehow, despite the crowd, his gaze shot straight to where Lieutenant Margaret Peterson sat.

He didn't look away. "More than one, from the looks of it."

"Yeah, well, she was getting clingy." Rowdy rubbed the back of his neck. He wasn't in the habit of fobbing women off on other men and he felt a little awkward. "I know it's late for you, but do you think you can do me a solid and take her off my hands?"

"Sure," Dash said without hesitation, but then added, "Which one are we talking about?"

What the... Dash would have made a move on Avery? Rowdy thought about flattening him. "Peterson."

While still staring toward the lieutenant, Dash smiled. "Oh, yeah, I can handle that."

As if she felt the way Dash stared at her, Margaret twisted in her seat to search the room.

She zeroed in on Dash.

For an uncomfortably long time, they locked gazes. Rowdy shouldered Dash hard. "Quit eye fucking her already. It's embarrassing."

Suddenly Margaret jerked away, giving them her back. She was always rigid, but never more so than now with the current set of her shoulders and the steel in her spine.

Undisturbed by Rowdy's crude comment, Dash whispered to himself, "Surprise, sweetheart."

Rowdy witnessed Dash's satisfaction with a shake of his head. "Hate to break it to you, but she looks pissed."

"She's fighting herself." Dash slowly inhaled. "And she's losing."

Sure, the lieutenant was a looker, but still a lieutenant. Rowdy didn't quite understand Dash's fascination with her, but to each his own.

Suddenly Margaret stood, snatched up her purse and headed back toward the pool tables. Rowdy expected Dash to go after her.

He didn't.

"Think I'll let her stew a minute or two. She's less guarded and more entertaining when she's riled." Dash started for the bar. "Why don't you get me a drink? It's the least you can do for dragging me out tonight."

Bullshit. With the way the two of them had shot sparks off each other, Rowdy was starting to think Dash owed him for the favor.

At least now he could reassure Avery; she had no reason at all to be jealous of the lieutenant's attention, not with the way she'd reacted to Dash.

They'd just paused by the bar and Rowdy was waiting for Avery to finish serving a customer, when from
behind them, a female customer said, "Hey, sexy," and
they both turned.

A tableful of ladies issued a lusty invite to join them.

Dash looked interested; Rowdy was not.

When he turned back to Avery, she started snicker-
ing and couldn't stop.

Glad she wasn't stewing, Rowdy asked, "What?"

That only ramped up her hilarity until she was laughing outright.

Folding his arms over the bar, Rowdy waited. "Are
you going hysterical on me?"

"You both looked!" She covered her mouth, trying
to muffle her humor. "Both of you!"

Leaving Dash to deal with the ladies, Rowdy circled
the bar. As long as Dash didn't forget about Peterson,
he could do whatever he pleased.

When he got close, Avery fought her humor long
enough to say, "Hey, sexy."

"Smart-ass." He caught her hips and pulled her in
close to kiss her. It was a tickling kiss at first because
of her giggles, but as he kept at it, she mellowed and
heated and soon he had her in a full-blown mating of
the mouths.

Damn, she tasted good.

She eased away, breathing fast. "People are looking."

"Let them." He wanted everyone to know that Avery
wasn't alone, not anymore.

She looked around, saw Dash and grinned again.

"It's not that funny." But he found himself smiling,
too. Before Avery, he couldn't remember ever being so
lighthearted.

She'd changed him, maybe irrevocably.

Probably for the better.

"It's hilarious." Hands on his chest, Avery frowned up at him. "Unless you're planning something unseemly for that poor woman."

Did she miss nothing? "If you mean Lieutenant Margaret Peterson, she is not a poor woman, trust me. She devours guys like Dash. I just threw him to the wolves. It'll be a miracle if he survives."

One brow lifted, Avery gave a pointed look at where Dash talked with four women while they more or less fawned on him. "Yeah, poor guy. He looks like a lamb to the slaughter."

"He's just warming up. Wait and see."

Not a minute later, Dash excused himself from his admirers and started toward the back.

"He's going to her?"

"Yeah." Rowdy pitched in, helping Avery with refills. "She's up to something, but no idea what." He only knew he didn't want to be a part of it.

"She came to see you."

"Maybe." He wasn't entirely convinced of that, either. He and Peterson had come to an understanding of sorts, but there'd been no sparks between them. Before Avery, sure, he wouldn't have kicked the lieutenant out of bed. But she *was* a lieutenant, so he wouldn't have pursued her, either.

Cops in general put him on edge. Female cops with a mean streak...not really his thing.

And now that he'd had Avery he plain wasn't interested in anyone else.

Dash disappeared from sight into the back room

where Peterson had gone, but Rowdy didn't hear any fireworks, so maybe they'd work it out.

"She's very attractive," Avery pointed out.

"In a cold-steel type of way, sure." Avery and the lieutenant were both petite women, but that's where the similarity ended. The lieutenant had short-cropped dark curls and a military posture. Avery's long red hair, even when tied back, could inspire fantasies, and he much preferred her laid-back, easy way.

Just then, Peterson and Dash emerged. Dash tried to lead her back to the booth, but Peterson wasn't cooperating. People glanced their way as Dash grinned at her and Peterson balled up her fists as if she might attack.

"Shit." Rowdy handed over a beer mug he'd just refilled and wiped off his hands. "Looks like I need to run interference." He gave it some quick thought, and made a decision. "Have Cannon give you a break and then join us."

Avery stepped back. "Oh, I don't want to intrude—"

"I need you with me, okay?" What better way to dissuade Peterson than by showing her he had other interests?

Avery looked like he'd doused her in ice water. She stood there staring up at him, lips parted, eyes wide.

What the hell?

Belatedly, she got herself together. "Yes, of course." She smiled brightly. "Go on. I'll be over as soon as I can get Cannon here."

Was she that thrown by him asking a favor? "Thanks, babe."

He reached Dash and the lieutenant in time to hear her say, "I am not doing this with you, Dash."

"Well, Rowdy's out, so it's me or you go home empty-handed."

Ah, hell. Were they bartering sex? Rowdy nudged Peterson toward the booth, saying, "How about we sit down and talk this out?"

She wrapped her arms around one of his and dragged him into the seat with her. Pulling him close, so close Rowdy thought she was going to kiss him, Peterson said, "I'm undercover, you ass."

Huh.

"I need you to shore up my cover." She slid a hand to his chest, stroking him. "And I don't want this other ass—" she looked at Dash so there'd be no misunderstandings "—in my way."

Dash said, "And yet, here I am."

When the lieutenant's thumb brushed over his left nipple, Rowdy nearly jumped out of the booth. Catching her wrist and lifting it away, Rowdy disengaged as much as he could. "Why are you here, in my place, if you're undercover?" The last thing the bar needed was more trouble.

She leaned in again, so close that her boobs were on his arm, her moist breath in his ear. "What do you know about BD videos?"

Bondage and discipline pornos? He rubbed his ear, wishing Avery would hurry it up. "That I don't need or want to see them. Why?"

"Sometimes…" Her mouth firmed. "Sometimes the women aren't as willing as you'd think."

As he made some quick mental connections, ice ran through his veins. "You think someone is forcing them? Women from *my* bar?"

"I think the ones producing the videos might hang out here."

"Why would you think that?"

Her fingers walked up his chest to his chin. "Evidence."

"See what I'm dealing with?" Dash leaned forward, forearms on the booth. "She needs help with her cover. If she just hangs out here looking like that, every dick in the place will be on her."

"You," Peterson said, still teasing her fingers over Rowdy. She turned those big blue eyes on Dash and enunciated clearly, "Not him."

No, and no again. "Sorry, I can't oblige." Rowdy forcibly set her a few inches away. "Earlier today I went out of my way to let all and sundry know that I'm with Avery. If I mix it up with you, they'll think she's fair game again."

Peterson's brows lifted. "And she's not?"

"Definitely not."

"And here I got the impression you weren't the type to settle on one woman. Interesting." Her gaze slid to Dash. "You still won't do."

"You'd have to try me on for size before you make that judgment."

Rowdy half expected Peterson to shoot Dash. He didn't have a single doubt that she was packing. The lieutenant was not a woman who went out and about unarmed.

She surprised him by being reasonable. "I need to be here in the evenings. You work construction. The nights could be late...."

"I'll persevere." Knowing he had her, Dash sat back

and smiled. "I own the company, remember. I can set any hours for myself that I want."

Finally Avery showed up. With her bottom lip caught in her teeth, her gaze tentative, she paused by the booth and dried her hands on her apron.

Dash scooted over to make room for her, and Avery slid into the seat beside him.

Rowdy muttered, "This is fucked up."

"Rowdy," Avery chastised, glancing at Peterson in apology. "Language."

Peterson gave a startled laugh, looked at Rowdy, and then at Avery and laughed again. "Oh, I like her, Rowdy. I really do."

Dash stretched an arm out along the back of the booth. "Me, too."

"She's heard worse," Rowdy said. And if Dash touched Avery, he'd—

"Still," Avery said. She held out her hand. "I'm the bartender."

Peterson looked more than a little delighted. "Very nice to meet you."

Dash leaned down close to Avery's ear, no doubt on the pretense of subterfuge, not that anyone paid any attention to them. "She's Logan's lieutenant," Dash said. "And she's undercover to catch some men who are forcing women into bondage videos."

Avery's eyes widened. "That's why you're here and why you were hitting on Rowdy?"

"Why else?"

"The usual reasons?" Avery reached over the table and took his hand. "That's why most of the women chase after him."

The lieutenant's mouth quirked. "No, not the usual

reasons for me." Still amused, she turned her attention on Dash. "Overall, I don't have time or patience to put up with men."

"But now you need me." Dash held out his arms. "And lucky for you, I'm ready, willing and able."

"I suppose you'd be better than some unknown." Peterson drummed her fingertips on the booth. "I have rules."

"You can tell me all about them when we're alone."

Rowdy looked around, but they still had relative privacy. "You mentioned evidence that involves the bar?"

She glanced at Avery, who looked ready to excuse herself again.

Rowdy laced their fingers together and held on to her. "You can speak in front of Avery. In fact, it's better if she knows. She interacts with the customers more than I do."

Giving it some thought, Peterson tugged at a small curl behind her ear. She must have decided to trust Avery because, voice low, she launched into a quick explanation. "Reese and Logan know about this, but not many others."

Dash said to Avery, "She has major trust issues."

"I don't like to take chances," Peterson corrected.

Rowdy knew the station had once been rife with corruption. To his knowledge, Peterson had cleared house, kicking out everyone on the take. But he didn't blame her for remaining cautious.

She turned her wineglass, her expression tight. "A young lady claims she was forced to take part in a discipline video. She wasn't hurt too badly—physically that is. And they eventually let her go. But you can imagine her humiliation and the fear she suffered."

Avery sat frozen in horror; Dash looked disgusted.

Rowdy thought any man involved needed to spend the rest of his life behind bars—or worse.

"Because she'd been blindfolded during transportation, it took her some time to show us the area where she'd been held. We raided the building where the videos were being shot, but by the time we got there, they'd already cleared out."

Avery covered her mouth. "The woman is okay?"

"Yes." Peterson tightened more. "She's still scared, probably always will be. But other than some bruises, she's not too badly hurt."

"You found a connection to the bar?"

"Cocktail napkins and a matchbook."

And here he'd only recently gotten those in. "That's not much to go on."

"It's all I have right now. But know this, Rowdy. The woman was grabbed right off the street not that far from here. You might want to put up some extra security cameras and be a little more cautious."

He'd planned to do that anyway, here, at his apartment and at Avery's. "I'll get right on it."

"In the meantime, if you see anything at all that looks suspicious—"

"I'll let you know first thing." He had a sudden burning need to get Avery someplace safe—even if it was away from him. She wasn't cut out for this life, being in this area, surrounded by the worst society had to offer—

Avery took his hand. "We'll be extra vigilant." With a squeeze, she reassured him, almost as if she'd known his turbulent thoughts.

Looking at Avery only ramped up his awareness of

her, of the reasons why he shouldn't tie her to him and the sordid, uncertain life he'd built for himself.

He slid out of the seat, drawing Avery out, too. "We need to get back to work." To Peterson, he added, "I won't tell the other employees, but feel free to come to Avery or me for anything you need."

"Thank you." She smiled at Avery. "I suppose we'll be seeing a lot of each other."

Avery leaned into him, her hand around his biceps. "Now that I know you're not actually after Rowdy, I'll enjoy that."

As he and Avery went behind the bar to relieve Cannon, Rowdy checked his watch. "Only a few more hours and I can get you alone."

"I hope you're thinking what I'm thinking," she teased. "Because I need one of those hugs that turns into sex."

Sounded good to him. He planned to fill up every available minute with loving her. And maybe, in the time left to him, it'd be enough.

CHAPTER TWENTY-TWO

"HEY, SEXY."

Rowdy smiled even before he got his eyes open. Avery rested half over his chest, one leg over his lap—just as she'd slept all night. He moved his hand, realized it was curled over her ass and said, "Looking for another swat, huh?"

She kissed his chin, his jaw, the top of his cheekbone and finally his mouth. "The wonder of it is that Dash somehow thought the women were talking to him." The kisses trailed over his throat to his chest. "Because you are by far the sexiest man I have ever known."

He rumbled a groan, enjoying how she rubbed against him. "I can't imagine a better start to my day than having you naked, your mouth on my body."

"My hand doing...this?" She curled her fingers around his erection, squeezing gently.

"Yeah," Rowdy managed to say. "That, too."

"Then you'll love this." He heard the smile in her voice, and the growing lust.

She kissed her way down his body, her mouth so hot and sweet that he stopped thinking and could only feel. She'd wrung him out last night, not only physically but emotionally, too.

When she'd climaxed, twice, she'd told him again that she loved him.

More and more she said it, and more and more he enjoyed hearing it.

He needed to hear it now.

"Tell me again." Tangling a hand in her hair, Rowdy held himself perfectly still as she lightly bit his abdomen and then licked the spot.

"I love you, Rowdy Yates." She brushed her cheek over the head of his dick. "So much."

After last night, he should have been mellow. Instead, she easily put him on the ragged edge.

Never, not once, had Avery asked him how he felt about her. She didn't demand he reciprocate. She didn't insist on a declaration.

She just gave to him. "Again."

"I love you." Her lips touched his shaft in a butterfly kiss, making his every muscle coil tight.

Like an addict needing a fix, Rowdy squeezed his eyes shut and begged, "Again."

Her tongue licked from the base up to the head.... "I love you." She closed her mouth over him.

He groaned loudly, lost, immersed in sensation. His hips lifted off the bed as he strained upward against her.

She took him deeper, her tongue curling around him, her mouth so hot and wet—

"Avery." He loved saying her name. He loved feeling her mouth, having her pleasure him. He loved...her.

Oh, God, he was lost. So fucking lost.

She stayed with him, sucking, licking, and he knew he wouldn't last a second more.

He cupped one hand around her nape, keeping her close, and cupped the other to her cheek, his thumb finding her wet bottom lip. Such a turn-on. So fucking hot.

"Avery," he said again, this time lower, his voice like gravel as he felt his testicles tighten, the hot surge of release.

It was too much.

It would never be enough.

He held her to him and let go, pleasure ripped from him, tension drained away.

He wasn't aware of Avery crawling back up over him, or of her snuggling in close and holding him tight.

But he heard her when she whispered, oh-so-sweetly, "I love you, Rowdy Yates, and I always will."

Still breathing like a bellows, he struggled to get it together, to fight the dampness burning the back of his eyelids. Thank God, Avery asked nothing of him. She just stayed close, curled around him, her hand over his thumping heart.

Time passed and still he didn't move. He wasn't sure he could. He knew Avery hadn't gone back to sleep because she idly stroked him and every so often, almost as if she understood his turmoil, she pressed a gentle kiss to his ribs.

He could have stayed there like that for hours, recovering, wallowing in her love, fighting demons and struggling to make decisions, but the intrusion of his cell phone forced him to move.

Avery rolled to her back and stretched. That stalled him for a minute, seeing her lithe little body drawn tight, her hair all fanned out around her, her small pink nipples and her sex—damp with need.

She relaxed again, smiled at him and said, "The phone?" with such a knowing, seductive note that he felt himself stirring again.

"Yeah." Rowdy twisted and grabbed up the cell

phone to check the caller ID. His sister. Shit. He answered with, "What's up, kiddo?"

"I'll be at your door in five minutes. If you're doing anything I don't want to see, stop and get dressed."

He knew Pepper well enough that he could tell nothing was wrong. "The reason for the visit?"

"Logan is off working and I'm worried and I need a distraction. Alice and Marcus are busy with house stuff today, so you're it."

Avery had already sat up and pulled on a T-shirt, but no way would he leave her unsatisfied. "Can you make it ten minutes?"

"Seriously, Rowdy? It's the butt crack of dawn. I figured I'd be waking you."

"Sorry, no. Give me ten and then we'll greet you."

She sighed dramatically. "I'll stop to buy coffee and doughnuts."

"Perfect, thanks." He disconnected the call and caught Avery before she could leave the bed. "Not so fast."

"That was your sister, right? She's due here soon?"

"I have ten minutes." He drew her down flat to the bed. "And now it's my turn."

Trying to fend him off, she laughed. "You just had your turn."

"And I thank you for that. But as incredible as it was, I enjoy getting you off, too."

She touched his face. "I can wait."

"Maybe." He slid a hand between her thighs, found her hot, creamy, and his heart punched into overtime. "But I can't."

ROWDY WAS IN the shower when his sister knocked on the door. Feeling very self-conscious—*he'd told Pep-*

per to give them time to have sex!—Avery went to the door to let her in. Whenever Pepper was around she felt unaccountably nervous, in large part because she knew how close they were. They shared a love stronger than any she'd ever known, and that made Pepper a very special person to Rowdy.

Which also made her a very special person to Avery.

Dressed in requisite jeans and a T-shirt, with one of Rowdy's flannels to help ward off the morning chill, Avery hurried to the door. She loved his loft apartment, but the floors could be so very cold, and the high ceilings made it difficult to heat. If she ever truly moved in, she'd put down colorful area rugs.

But she and Rowdy weren't there yet. Her place in his life was tentative at best; she would do nothing to rock the boat.

After giving herself a quick pep talk, Avery opened the door and before she could say a word, Pepper swept in. She carried coffee and doughnuts and, as always, she looked beautiful.

"Where's Rowdy?"

So much for hello. "He's taking a quick shower." Avery secured the door again and followed Pepper down to the kitchen. "He won't be long. Doctor's orders. He can only take quick showers until the stitches are removed."

Pepper grinned at her. "Hi."

"Good morning."

Pepper set everything on the table. "You know, I never thought I'd see the day where I had to deal with my brother having a significant other. One-night stand, sure. Groupie, no problem. But a regular?" Pepper shook her head. "Unheard of."

Disapproval, or mere observation? Avery wasn't sure. "I'm sorry."

"Hey, I wasn't complaining." Making herself at home, Pepper got sugar and creamer and put them on the table. "I think it's awesome. Rowdy deserves someone who cares, and he deserves to be happy."

"Amen to that."

Pepper raised a brow. "Meaning you do care?"

Seeing no reason to lie about it, Avery lifted one shoulder. "I love him."

Pepper did a double take before smirking. "Huh." She loaded one of the cups with sugar. "Have you told him that?"

"Many times." Often, regularly, especially during sex—when Rowdy seemed to enjoy hearing it most.

Pepper missed the coffee cup and sugar went all over the table. "You've told him?"

"Yes." Avery pulled out a chair and grabbed her own cup of caffeine. Her hands shook just a little, but then, Rowdy had made her wild in such a short time, she still hadn't quite recovered from the mind-blowing release. "I felt he had a right to know."

Coffee forgotten, Pepper, too, pulled out a chair, her attention rapt. "Wow. And you're still here?"

"Amazing, I know." Grabbing the sugar bowl, Avery doctored her own coffee. "But then, I haven't asked him for anything in return. I know how he feels about settling down." She hesitated, but because Pepper kept staring at her agog, she gave a mental shrug and continued. "I also know some of his past. Your past. I understand why he doesn't trust the idea of love, and why he's...uncertain about settling down."

Pepper continued to stare.

"Some might think that because he's bought a bar and obviously enjoys working it, he's put down roots. But that's a deceptive notion. If he decided to move on again, the bar wouldn't keep him here." She smiled at Pepper. "The fact that *you're* here would be the only reason he might stick around."

"We're super close," Pepper said in an aside, then, "That doesn't bother you? I mean, knowing he might up and take off again?"

"Not enough I guess." She propped her head on a hand. "Rowdy is such an amazing man in so many ways. How could I not love him?"

"Yeah." Shaking herself, Pepper used a hand to clear the sugar off the table and went to dump it in the sink. She said nothing as she washed her hands, came back to finish prepping her coffee and took a big drink.

The shower shut off, letting them both know Rowdy would soon join them.

Avery gave her time. She understood that Pepper might distrust her. The last thing Rowdy ever needed was more hurt.

"What will you do if he tells you to hit the road?"

"I'd go without causing a scene." Avery smiled sadly. "Eventually it'll happen, right? But my heart keeps telling me *maybe not.*" She blew out a breath, shrugged. "So I'm happy to stay and wait and love him and… hope."

Rowdy came out dressed in jeans, still pulling a T-shirt over his head.

Pepper launched from her seat and went to him. "How's your back?"

"I'm ready to get the damn stitches out." He caught her up in a hug before she could get behind him. "No, don't start mothering me. My back is fine and you looking at it won't change anything. Avery checks it enough for ten women."

"Hey!" Avery gave mock protest. "I'm not that bad."

"You're not bad at all." He winked at her. "So, kiddo." Slinging an arm around his sister, he steered her back to the table. "You're at loose ends today?"

"Logan is working on a big case, so I need to be preoccupied." She said to Avery, "Cleaning house and doing laundry just doesn't cut it for me, not when I start worrying. And I *hate* worrying."

"That's what you get for marrying a cop."

Pepper rolled her eyes at Rowdy. "*Cop* is not a dirty word, you know, no matter how you say it."

Their banter never failed to make Avery smile. "I always enjoyed mindless work, but I know what you mean. When I want to be distracted, playing bartender does the trick. I get so busy I don't even have time to think."

"I should learn to do that." Reseating herself at the table, Pepper picked up her coffee. "I could help out at the bar and—"

"No." Rowdy fished a doughnut out of the bag. "Get that thought out of your head right now."

"Why not?"

"I don't want you hanging around a bar, that's why." He pointed the doughnut at her. "And I can guarantee Logan will feel the same."

Mulish indignation straightened her spine. "If it's okay for Avery, why isn't it okay for me?"

Rowdy didn't look at Avery—a very deliberate move, she knew.

"It's not great for her, either," he grumbled.

"Don't go there, Rowdy." Though he wasn't ready to admit it, Avery knew he was starting to care. Not as much as she did, but enough that he saw things differently now. "I love my job and I'm keeping it." *Until you break things off, and then I'll go to mend my broken heart elsewhere.*

He hooked a chair, turning it so he could straddle the seat. "I'm still the boss."

"And you're fair." She wouldn't let him start making her decisions for her. "That means you won't fire me unless I deserve it, and we both know I don't." *Please tell me I'm right, that you wouldn't do that to me.*

"You're a good worker," he agreed. Taking his time, he sipped his coffee, took a bite of doughnut. "But I was thinking you could just work an earlier shift—"

She sat up a little straighter. "I need all the hours I can get." And she wanted to be there with him. "All the hours I'm *used* to getting."

"You're staying with me now." He threw that out as if it made perfect sense, as if they'd somehow committed to each other when they both knew that wasn't the case. "That cuts back on your bills, right?"

But for how long? She wouldn't put him on the spot by asking. "I still have my apartment, still have the bills associated with it."

"So cancel your lease."

Her heart nearly jumped into her throat. What was he suggesting? She searched his face, but she couldn't tell. He could be so damn enigmatic when he chose. "I like my independence, Rowdy. You know that." *But if you tell me you care, that you want me to stay with you, I'd risk it all.*

What he said instead was, "It's not safe for you there."

Her heart sank again. She wanted him to want her, not just feel a need to protect her. "Maybe not right now," she agreed. "But once we deal with Fisher—"

"Once we deal with him, there'd be no reason for you to stay away from your folks."

Hurt stole her breath. "You're telling me to go back home?"

"Wow." Pepper's timely interruption kept Rowdy from answering. His sister bounced her gaze back and forth between them. "What's going on? Who's Fisher?"

Rowdy gave her a very abbreviated explanation. Protecting her privacy, he made Fisher sound more like an annoyance than anything else.

"Sounds like a real dirtbag."

"A wealthy dirtbag," Rowdy agreed.

"The worst kind." Pepper wrinkled her nose. "I agree with Rowdy. Don't go back there alone."

"And speaking of Fisher…" He slid his cell phone across the table to her. "Give your mom a call, see if you can set up that visit. I'd as soon not wait around for him to make another move."

She'd just promised Pepper that she wouldn't cause a scene or kick up a fuss. But the timing was all wrong, coming out of nowhere. Somehow she'd expected to sense when Rowdy started to pull away.

Instead, he'd blindsided her.

Pepper didn't seem to realize that Rowdy was setting up an exit plan, but Avery saw the signs loud and clear. She just didn't know what to do about it—except to give him what he wanted.

She picked up the phone and rose out of her chair. "I'll make the visit for as soon as I can." Quietly, she walked out of the kitchen, going to the couch for a modicum of privacy to talk.

Rowdy could hear Avery on the phone, but not exactly what she said. She sat with her back to them, her head bowed, her shoulders showing defeat.

Pepper kept talking to him. She had a hundred questions about Fisher, and he answered as succinctly as he could without giving away anything important—like how much he loved Avery. How important she'd become to him.

How, in such a short time, she'd impacted his life.

He needed some time away, right now, before he cracked.

Avery rejoined them. "Mom is busy until next weekend. Is that too far away for you?"

Like a stay of execution, he was glad for the additional time with Avery. "That'll be fine." He pushed to his feet. "I'm going to run to the security store to get some stuff." Before either woman could ask, he detailed the measures he'd take. "I want to put up some more security cameras at the bar, but also here at my apartment." He reached out to touch Avery's hair, letting a long corkscrew lock glide through his fingers. "At your apartment, too."

Pepper lifted her brows. "I thought you wanted her to get rid of the place."

He knew he'd confused his sister, but then, he was also confused...by so many things. "I do. But either way, as long as others think she's there, I want to take some precautions so if anyone comes around there snooping, we'll know it."

Avery didn't pull away from him. "I can be ready in ten minutes."

"Why don't you and Pepper hang out and visit? I won't be long." He picked up his keys, put them in his jeans pocket.

Suspicion brought Avery out of her chair. "You promise you're not going after Fisher?"

"I told you we'd confront him together." He didn't look at her as he went to the bedroom to get his shoes. "I don't lie."

Avery said gently, "I know."

At the same time Pepper snorted. "Since when?"

To his sister, he clarified, "I don't lie to you, and I don't lie to Avery. That's what I meant." When necessary, in other situations, he had no problem at all saying whatever he needed to.

Then again, he'd just told Avery that she should stay with him, without explaining that he wanted her to get rid of the apartment, to cut back at work, all because he wanted her safe—away from the inherent danger in his world.

A lie of omission, if not an outright whopper.

The significance of that statement wasn't lost on his sister; he'd just elevated Avery's importance to him in a very big way.

Again Pepper looked back and forth between them. She caught on, understanding that he needed some time alone but didn't want to leave Avery by herself. He and Pepper had always had that special connection, a way of communicating without words.

Faking a bright smile, Pepper said, "I would like to hang out, Avery, if you don't mind."

Avery's smile was too strained. "I'd enjoy that, thank

you. If you don't mind, I'll go take my shower right now, and then we can visit."

Rowdy caught her hand as she headed past him.

She hung back a few seconds before coming in close, wrapping her arms around him.

God, it felt good. Rowdy hugged her close and pressed his mouth to the top of her head. "I won't be gone that long, babe. A few hours, tops."

"I know."

But he sensed her gloom and it bothered him. "If you're fretting, don't." He nudged her face up so he could see her eyes. "All I have planned is to buy security equipment, maybe go by your apartment to get whatever you need, then come back here with you." He looked into her eyes, willing her to understand. "Believe me?"

Her smile touched his soul. "Always."

Hand over her heart, Pepper said with stageworthy drama, "So romantic. I'm ready to swoon."

Rowdy tossed one of the bed pillows at her.

She caught it and hugged it tight. "If you're going to install new equipment at the bar, I can help with that, right?"

"Sure." Keeping Avery close, he asked, "How late will Logan be working?"

"Hard to say. Guess it depends on what he finds." She tossed the pillow back to the bed. "Since he's out being heroic and all, I probably shouldn't complain."

Keeping in mind what Peterson had disclosed, Rowdy understood why Logan might be so busy. Like him, Logan wanted to keep Pepper safe, well away from the cruelty that existed in everyday life.

To help keep Pepper busy, he made an offer—with conditions. "I don't want you leaving the bar alone, but if Logan comes by to get you when he's done, then you can hang out with us as long as you want."

Pepper agreed, then called Logan to fill him in while Rowdy finished getting ready to go.

He was glad Avery would have company, and appreciated the opportunity to go by her apartment to make a few arrangements. If Fisher even drove by, Rowdy would know about it.

He was an expert at setting up surveillance, and he knew how to cover his tracks. Fisher was as good as busted—and then he'd be out of Avery's life once and for all.

CHAPTER TWENTY-THREE

EVEN KNOWING PEPPER waited on her, Avery took her time showering, washing her hair, then applying some makeup. Pepper was so incredibly beautiful that she felt like a dud next to her.

Her plain jeans, flat shoes and sweatshirt couldn't compare with Pepper's take-no-prisoners attractive style. Pepper had one of those figures that no matter what she wore, it looked sexy. Today she had on skinny jeans, high boots, and a black, snug-fitting thermal shirt that not only emphasized her curves, it also made her incredible blond hair even more noticeable. Pepper wore makeup like a pro, but looked just as stunning without it.

When she exited the bathroom, Avery found Pepper on the couch, making herself at home. She'd removed her boots and had her feet propped on the table as she flipped through the pages of a book.

Avery would have asked if she wanted anything, but she saw that Pepper had already switched from coffee to cola.

Taking the chair opposite her, Avery curled up, her feet tucked under her, and waited for Pepper's attention.

"My brother really is pretty amazing."

"Yes."

She held up the book on small-business management. "He's always done stuff like this. Educated himself in whatever way he needed to." Pepper set the book aside, then drifted her fingers over the cover. "Mostly that meant teaching himself to fight, to steal and how to cheat without getting caught."

"Necessary traits, I'm sure."

Pepper grinned with her. "He used those talents to keep us safe, fed and clothed. So yeah, pretty necessary." She turned pensive, looking around the apartment as if only then noticing the unique architecture. "Whenever Rowdy could keep a legit job, he did. But it wasn't easy."

What an understatement. "He did more with what life gave him than any other person I know."

"He's so used to it just being us that he's still adjusting. It was enough that he had to get used to Logan, but then Reese, too, and Alice."

"And now he has Marcus in his life."

"Little by little, he's digging in. Making commitments and getting settled." Pepper sat forward. "The bar, this apartment. Friends." She tipped her head at Avery. "You."

I'm only temporary. But Avery couldn't bring herself to say that out loud. "You do realize he asked me to stay with him mostly so he could protect me?"

Pepper barked a laugh. "Yeah, right." She stood to pace, looking around the apartment. "My brother wants to play protector to just about everyone, but he doesn't go moving in random women to do it."

Avery would have loved to believe that, but she didn't want to delude herself. "I'm not all that random. I'm his bartender."

"Ha! And you think that's what he cares about, protecting his own interests? You must not know him as well as you think."

"No, I didn't mean it like that." Far as she could tell, Rowdy was never motivated by mercenary selfishness. "I meant that because we work together, we were already friends before we got intimate. I'm not *just* a woman he's sleeping with."

"You have other women working at the bar?"

"Sure." Ella was the most regular, but others filled in, too, as part-time waitresses.

"Has he ever slept with any of them?" Pepper didn't give her a chance to answer. "No, he hasn't. Because my brother is smart enough that he wouldn't want to muddy the waters. And screwing a woman he works with, when he knew he only wanted sex, would definitely muddy it up."

Avery hadn't really thought about it like that. "He hit on me even before he bought the bar."

"And soon as he got it, he made you the bartender— which sort of ensured you'd keep hanging around—then *still* came after you, right?"

She nodded.

"I'm guessing he was already hung up on you way back then, otherwise he'd have steered clear of you, or fired you if he couldn't." Pepper shrugged. "So don't underestimate what he wants based only on what he's said or hasn't said."

It occurred to Avery where Pepper's insight might come from. "Is that how it was with you and Logan?"

"It was worse. Logan used me to get to Rowdy. He arrested my brother, put him in danger...." Holding on to the pole, Pepper turned a lazy circle. "I didn't think I'd ever be able to forgive him. But I figured out leaving him would be the hardest thing of all. Especially after he got hurt."

Gently, Avery said, "I'm glad things worked out for you."

"Yeah, they really did." She pushed away from the pole and went to Rowdy's bookcase to peruse the other titles. "Now I want Rowdy to be just as happy as I am."

Could she make him happy? Avery wanted to, very much.

A knock sounded on the door and the two women glanced at each other.

Pepper lifted a brow. "Expecting anyone?"

"No." She stood. "Rowdy said the other ladies in the building sometimes pester him."

Pepper went back to looking at books. "If that's who it is, tell her to get lost. He's taken."

Thinking she just might do that, Avery started for the door.

"But make sure before you open it."

"Of course." She went up the short stairs and to the door. Rowdy didn't have a peephole in the door, so she called out, "Who is it?"

"Avery?" Meyer said. "Your mother insisted I bring her by for a visit."

Oh, wow. Her mother was here? Thinking that something had happened, that her mother might have gotten bad news during a checkup, Avery turned the locks and swung open the door.

And there stood Meyer. Instead of her mother being at his side, he'd brought Fisher.

The enormity of the ruse hit Avery like a sucker punch. She drew in a breath, surprised, angry—and a little fearful.

Before any one emotion could claim the lead, Meyer pushed his way in—which forced her to back up. In her nervousness she almost fell down the short flight of stairs.

Fisher shot out a hand and caught her arm. He wore a dark scowl and what looked like confusion.

"What the hell is this, Meyer?" He didn't release Avery when he said it, but he did shove the door shut.

Avery had just enough awareness to notice he didn't lock it. With any luck, she'd get a break and she could run out—if Pepper could follow. No way would she leave Rowdy's sister behind. But maybe she could go for help. If she made it to the street—

"Come on, then." Meyer gestured for them to go down the stairs. "Let's all get cozy."

Hand still squeezing her upper arm, Fisher took in Meyer's expression, then turned to Avery with clear displeasure. "You heard him." He dragged her along as he went down into Rowdy's apartment. "So this is where you've been staying?"

It occurred to Avery that Pepper was out of sight. Fisher and Meyer were both looking around, but they didn't see her. Had she ducked behind the bookshelf? Under the bed?

Lord, please don't let her be as fearless as Rowdy. Never would she forgive herself if anything happened to Rowdy's sister.

Anxiety left her mouth dry and made her heart race. "What are you doing here?" She'd hoped to sound in charge, confident and courageous when she spoke, but the words came out breathless and shaky.

Bemused, Fisher said, "I have no real idea."

Though he held her arm too tightly, his thumb

brushed over her skin, and that ramped up her fear factor even more. She'd rather Fisher abuse her than get amorous.

"What do you mean, you don't know? You came here."

He shrugged. "Meyer told me we were meeting a thug who would discourage your lover. I'm as surprised as you are by his plans."

"You were balking at the idea of chasing her," Meyer explained. "I had to take matters into my own hands."

"This changes nothing." Fisher held on to Avery when she tried to wrench away. Forcefully, he pressed her into a chair at the kitchen table. "I don't mind getting a little revenge, but she's used goods now and no longer appeals to me."

"Used goods?"

"You've been fucking a broken, low-life brute. Do you have any idea how that repels me?"

"Good!"

"No, Avery, don't be that way. He'll change his mind." Meyer paced to the windows to look out. "Once your bodyguard is gone, Fisher will see again how perfectly suited the two of you are."

"You're insane," Avery whispered. "I'm not going to listen to this." She started to stand.

Fisher slammed her back down in the chair. "Be quiet." He stepped behind her, both hands on her shoulders close to her neck. He tightened his hold, keeping her locked in fear. "In this instance, Meyer, I have to wonder if she's right."

"She's wrong!" He jerked around to face them—a gun in his hand.

Ohmigod. Even if she got away from Fisher's hold,

she'd never make it to the door in time to get out, not without being shot. Knowing Pepper was somewhere in the room only amplified her fear. If she was even half as daring as Rowdy, she might try to rush Meyer. And if she did, he very well might kill her.

"Meyer." Fisher's tone held a new edge. "Just what are you doing?"

"I'm setting things right. Sonya wants her home, so home she will be. Now, do your bit, damn you."

From the corner of her eye, Avery saw a shadow move. Pepper. No, no, no.

"My bit?" Fisher asked, thankfully keeping Meyer's attention.

"You're an abusive ass, Fisher." Meyer pulled out a chair opposite them and sat down as casual as you please. He crossed his legs and rested his gun hand on the tabletop—pointed toward them.

Avery had the horrible suspicion that Fisher stood behind her so that she could be his shield. The miserable coward.

"I don't know what you're talking about," Fisher said. But Avery heard the lie in his voice—and so did Meyer.

"I've known it for years. The women you've paid not to prosecute. The women you've hurt."

Out of sheer surprise, Fisher's hands loosened. "I don't know where you heard such lies, but I assure you—"

"Please. Where women are concerned, you're a masochistic prick." Meyer shrugged, uncaring. "I've convinced Sonya otherwise, of course. I've not only played up your good deeds but I've painstakingly covered the tracks of your ill repute."

"Why?" Avery whispered. This man knew that

Fisher had tried to rape her. He was saying Fisher had done so to other women. Rage crept in around the hurt and fear. "Why would you do that?"

As if it explained everything, Meyer said, "He comes from a good family. He has the respect of the community, is well looked upon by the press. He produces excellent business results. My colleagues love him. And your mother is fond of him."

Fisher shook his head, but he didn't deny any of it. "Damn, Meyer, I don't know what to say."

Meyer waved it off. "I have my own investigators, you know. They've made sure you haven't left any messes behind. That fuckup with Avery...it was touch and go, especially where her mother is concerned. But I managed to convince Sonya that you were an innocent pawn and that Avery was just upset over losing her father and her mother marrying me. I was very sincere, very *hurt* over the slight Avery dealt me with her attitude. I played the loving stepfather to a T." He grinned. "I assured her Avery would return home where she belonged after she got the wildness out of her system. But it's gone on too long, and Sonya has suffered too much. So now you'll do what needs to be done."

"That being?"

"Sonya wants her daughter back. As long as you get Avery to toe the line, I have no qualms how you do it." He looked Avery in the eyes. "Maybe get her pregnant."

"Go to hell!" She struggled away from Fisher, and he barely caught her, jerking her around with her back to his chest, locking his massive arms around her. "You won't touch me!" she insisted while fighting him.

Fisher laughed. "I'm touching you now."

She could feel him growing hard. Revulsion made her stomach pitch and she gagged.

"Don't," Fisher said near her ear. "You will regret it if you vomit on me."

Through locked teeth, Avery said, "You will regret it more, I swear to you, if you do this."

"A challenge," Meyer said with anticipation. "Go on, then."

Fisher stalled. "Here?"

"Yes." He settled back in his chair. "I believe I'll watch."

Fisher gave a disbelieving laugh. "No, I don't think so, Meyer. Having an audience is not my thing."

"That's unfortunate, because I'm finding it might be mine." Meyer aimed the gun. "And you will do it, or lose everything."

She could feel Fisher's breath on her temple, the bellowing of his chest on her back. Instead of outright refusing, he said, "What if her junkyard dog returns?"

"I'll handle the crude bastard. Don't worry about that." Meyer showed his teeth in a sick smile. "He's as good as gone."

Terror gave Avery courage. Rowdy could return at any minute, so she knew she needed to do something now, even if it got her shot. In fact, a gunshot would maybe alert others. It'd give Pepper a chance to escape. And it would bring the police, maybe even Logan and Reese.

Rowdy would be safe—and at the moment, that's what mattered most of all.

CANNON DETESTED INDECISION. He was out jogging—part of his conditioning—and he'd just so happened to be going past the bar when he noticed the men heading into Rowdy's apartment building. He recognized one of them as the man who'd visited the bar.

The other guy... He had a bad feeling.

Being that he wore sweatpants and a long-sleeved shirt with running shoes, he didn't have his wallet or cell phone on him. He couldn't call Rowdy to verify things were copasetic.

Should he go up to Rowdy's apartment to check on them, even though it seemed like ridiculous overkill to get bent out of shape over two clean-cut visitors? Rowdy could sure as hell handle himself.

Still...

"Screw it," Cannon said aloud and, choices limited, jogged toward the family-owned restaurant less than a block away. He'd use their phone to call Rowdy and then he'd decide what to do.

WITH SEVERAL PURCHASES on the seat beside him, Rowdy drove toward Avery's apartment. He'd thought to take his time, to use up a few hours while he thought things through.

Instead, he'd rushed, grabbing what he knew he needed, because he missed Avery. He kept thinking of how stoic she'd looked when he mentioned her cutting back at work.

She read him so easily, knowing without him saying it that he wanted her to return to her safe, cushioned life.

Only...he didn't. Not really. He wanted to keep her close.

He wanted her forever.

Would that be fair to her, though? She said she loved him. Could she really be content as the bartender in a neighborhood joint, living on a budget and married to a man like him?

Marriage.

He swallowed hard, for the first time in his life letting himself consider it—

When his cell rang, he was actually glad to have a new focus. Seeing it was Pepper, he answered with, "What's up, kiddo?"

Instead of anyone replying, he heard background noise, like that through a speaker. At first the conversation was indistinct, and then he recognized Avery's voice.

"This isn't happening, so you can both forget it."

A man said, "Can't you shut her up?"

Meyer.

And Fisher's voice, strained, replied, "I can, but I'm thinking we should go somewhere else."

"Can you imagine the fuss she'll kick up if we try to drag her out of here? Besides, how can I get her boyfriend if we're not here when he arrives?"

A dozen emotions slammed into Rowdy, but overriding everything else was the pounding urgency to protect Avery.

With only a glance in the rearview mirror he made a sharp U-turn, sending the car into a skid before it righted itself back in the direction of his apartment. Brakes squealed, horns blared. He pressed his foot to the accelerator. "I'm on my way," he whispered, just in case Pepper could hear him.

He turned his phone on speaker and laid it on the seat so that he could use both hands to drive.

His eyes went dry and hot, his throat so tight he couldn't swallow. Every muscle tensed as he maneuvered the road, speeding up to pass a van, then punching it once he found a clear spot on the road, going well over the speed limit.

He heard Avery gasp, heard her cursing Fisher, calling him some choice names. Meyer demanded that she be quiet.

A slap.

He squeezed the steering wheel; for right now, she was okay, fighting back and more angry than terrified. He had to tell himself that or he'd drive through the front doors of his building.

It took him less than ten minutes that felt like an hour before he saw the building. Slowing, he pulled down an alley before he got too close.

He would park behind the bar and cross over on foot, just in case Meyer or Fisher watched the road. He needed to call...well, maybe not Logan. He was a good cop, but with Pepper involved, would he be able to keep his head?

Reese, then. Except that he'd have to hang up on Pepper to do that. He slammed the car into Park at the back of the bar and, praying he wouldn't be too late, picked up his cell.

Cannon stepped out of nowhere, covered in sweat, almost like he'd been watching for him.

"I tried to call," Cannon yelled. "As soon as I saw you, I ran to catch up." He sucked in a deep breath. "Two men—"

"Keep it down." Rowdy opened the car door and lifted his cell. "My sister is on the line." And so that Cannon would understand, he added, "She's at my place. With Avery. I think she's hidden. She called so I could hear it all, so I'd know what was going down."

Cannon clenched his jaw. "The two men?"

"Avery's stepfather and her bastard ex." Rowdy opened the glove box and got out a tactical knife in a sheath. He shoved it into the waistband at the small of his back. "Anyone else?"

"I only saw those two go in." Cannon watched as Rowdy pulled his shirt over the knife. "You have a gun?"

"Yeah." He left his car and started down the back alleys, going one alley up from the apartment building. "It's in my apartment."

"Fuck." Cannon kept pace beside him. "Now I know why I couldn't reach you."

Rowdy put the phone to his ear to listen a moment. Some arguing, but still nothing from Pepper. "Long as I keep the call open, I can gauge the best time to move in."

"I called your buddy, the cop."

"Reese?"

"Yeah."

Rowdy nodded. "If he gets here, let him know what's going on."

"Jesus, Rowdy. Shouldn't you wait?"

"They're going to rape Avery."

Cannon shoved a hand through his hair. "Mother-fuckers…"

Rowdy looked at the windows of his apartment. The angle would make it tough for anyone to see him now. He peeled off his jacket and tossed it toward Cannon. "Mostly they want to kill me." He met Cannon's appalled stare. "When I show up, that'll buy Avery some time."

"I'll go with you."

"No. You stay here and watch for Reese." Done discussing it, Rowdy jogged across the street and, praying he'd be in time, he went into the building and up the stairs.

He found the door unlocked and quietly slipped it open enough to slip in when the time was right. Flattened on the wall outside the door, he listened in, and he prepared himself.

One way or another, he would get both women out of there safe. If it meant killing Fisher and Meyer, he was fine with that.

And if it meant dying himself, it was a price he was willing to pay.

Just please, God, let Avery and Pepper be okay.

AVERY REFUSED TO give Fisher the satisfaction of cowering, or flinching in pain, even when she thought he might break her arm. She just glared her hatred at him, infuriating him.

"You think you're a little toughie now, is that it?"

"No. I'm still me, Fisher, still a woman who is utterly repulsed by you."

"Yes, you're a woman." He cupped her chin, forced her face up. "And I'm the man who will tame you."

She gave him a twisted smile. "Poor, pathetic Fisher. I've had a real man, and I know the difference. You're nothing."

He drew back to slap her again and a noise sounded by Rowdy's bed.

Meyer said, "Wait." Leaving the table, gun held out, he moved to investigate.

Hide, Pepper. Avery held her breath. *Please, please, hide.*

Fisher caught her hair and turned her toward him,

jerking her face up close to his. Through stiff lips, he hissed, "He is insane, you stupid bitch."

"You both are," Avery told him just as quietly, "if you think you're going to get away with this."

"Of course we won't, so stop trying to goad me so I can figure out how to get us out of here."

Right. He wanted her to believe he'd help her? Avery knew Fisher was not the heroic type. Meyer wouldn't let her leave, and she didn't care if Fisher got out alive. She cared about Pepper, about Rowdy.

Somehow she had to save them both.

Fisher pulled her head back farther, then glanced at Meyer. While he was distracted, she tensed—and brought her knee up hard into his groin.

For a split second, he looked merely stunned that she would do such a thing. Then his eyes widened, his mouth went slack and his hand loosened from her hair.

He wheezed, "Goddamn you, Avery—" and collapsed to his knees.

Avery tried to rush Meyer, but he said, oh-so-calmly, "Do it and I'll kill her."

He had his gun trained on Pepper, who had hunkered down on the other side of the bed. Avery froze.

"Come out, then," Meyer said, gesturing with the gun. "Hurry it up before I lose my patience."

Avery clenched her hands into fists. "Don't you dare hurt her, you bastard."

Pepper curled her lip, flipped her hair back and stood straight and tall as if she hadn't been hiding from a madman and a pervert. She walked past Meyer with no regard for the gun aimed at her.

Meyer laughed, but the laugh held no real humor. He followed Pepper toward the table. "Who are you?"

"I'm Rowdy's sister."

"The devil has a relative? Interesting." He pulled out a chair for her. "Sit down. Both of you."

"So you can shoot us?" Pepper narrowed her eyes and walked to the other side of the table. "No, thanks."

She had her back to the kitchen, facing the bedroom area. The door to leave was to their right.

On the floor blocking the way, Fisher showed signs of life.

Meyer lost his patience. "Get up, Fisher. I've had enough of your vacillating. If you can't play your part, then you're useless to me."

Fisher struggled up, his hand to his crotch.

"There are too many people here," Meyer decided as he corralled them in the kitchen. "It's getting impossible to keep track. So who should go?"

"You," Pepper said.

Very slowly, trying not to push Meyer into a hasty move, Avery stepped in front of Pepper. She gave her a warning look, and to her surprise, Pepper subsided.

With cool command Avery faced Meyer. "You won't hurt her," she stated. She pressed back against Pepper, pushing her farther into the kitchen. If anyone started shooting, she could maybe get behind the fridge, or the stove. Or she could possibly grab a kitchen knife… something, *anything,* was better than being a standing duck.

"You think not?"

"If you even try," Avery promised him, "you'll have to kill me, too, and then what will you tell Mom?"

"That you ran away for good?"

Avery shook her head. "She's believed a lot from you, Meyer, but she won't believe that. She knows I love her and she knows I'd never leave her for good, especially not now, while she's being treated for her cancer."

"You didn't care before."

"I didn't know she'd been sick. But now I do. She and I have talked. We've mended things." Avery crossed her arms and looked at Fisher, seeing him as the weaker link, as insane as that seemed. If she could just keep them talking, maybe she could think of a way out of this. "Why were you hanging around the bar again?"

"I wasn't. As I told Meyer, you lost your appeal when you started sleeping around with a bum like Rowdy Yates."

Avery put a hand back, letting Pepper know not to react. "Rowdy knows it was you, Fish." Adopting Rowdy's nickname for him worked; Fisher bunched up in impotent rage. "He's told his cop friends, and even now, they're checking up on you. If anything happens to either of us, you'll be one of the first people they come after."

"That low-life ruffian is friends with law officers?" Meyer chortled with credible humor. "I don't believe that nonsense."

"It doesn't matter, anyway," Fisher insisted. "If you'd fallen back into my lap, Avery, then yes, I would have taken advantage by sleeping with you."

"You mean raping me?"

He gave her a flat stare. "But do you honestly think I'd marry you after you slept with a bar owner?" Fisher shook his head. "Not likely."

Fisher might not have noticed Meyer's anger over that disclosure, but Avery saw it, and worried for an imminent explosion. "Then why were you hanging around?"

"I already told you that I wasn't." He scowled at Meyer. "Was it you?"

"Yes, but it no longer matters." Using the gun, Meyer waved away the importance of the question. "The mayor is my friend. The police commissioner is a friend. I can discredit two low-level detectives without even trying."

"Maybe not this time." Again Avery backed Pepper farther into the kitchen. "Rowdy's sister is married to one of those detectives."

Fisher blanched.

"He's a good cop," Pepper added. "The best."

Avery nodded. "He will never let it go if anything happens to her."

"Meyer," Fisher said, easing closer to him. "Let's think about this. There's no reason to make matters worse." Casually, he came closer still. "I'm sure Avery can be reasonable."

"Of course," Avery said.

Fisher was only a few feet from Meyer now. "And the cops," he suggested, "can probably be bought. Between us, we have more than enough resources to make this…breach in good judgment go away."

Pepper said nothing, thank God. Neither Reese nor Logan could be bought, but if Fisher convinced Meyer otherwise, maybe he'd let them go.

Meyer narrowed his eyes. "I think it's better if they all go."

Fisher looked apoplectic. "You can't be serious."

"The girl, the cops." Meyer shrugged. "If you no longer want her, what does it matter?"

Avery tsked. "That's an awful lot of deaths adding up. Hard to hide that many bodies."

"It'd be impossible." And with that, Fisher lunged for Meyer.

It was ludicrous, given that Fisher was so much bigger, younger, faster, but Meyer had insanity on his side.

He squawked—and managed to shoot Fisher in the leg.

The noise was deafening, almost stopping Avery's heart. Pepper, damn her, took advantage of the confusion and separated from her.

Fisher went down to the floor with a sharp cry, blood pumping steadily from his leg to form a quick puddle of red gore around him.

Wild-eyed and heaving, Meyer shouted, "Goddamn it! Now look what you made me do." Straight armed, his hand shaking, he took aim at Avery. It felt like everything inside her shut down in that instant.

Pepper yelled, "No!"

And into the chaos, the front door slammed open.

Rowdy went down the steps in one leap. He looked larger than life, confident and in control.

He stared only at Meyer, his gaze so focused and so lethal that Avery's knees almost gave out.

CHAPTER TWENTY-FOUR

"YOU DIDN'T LOCK the door," Meyer said to Fisher in confusion.

"I have my own key," Rowdy reminded him, calm, even. "I would have gotten in anyway."

"You knew we were here?"

"I've had you watched, both of you." Not exactly true, but a lie didn't bother Rowdy if it got him the desired results—which in this case, would be the upper hand. "You can still leave."

Meyer shook his head. "No. It's too late for that."

"It'll only be too late if you hurt anyone else." Arms out to his sides, Rowdy advanced on Meyer. "If you want to leave now, I won't touch you, I swear."

Meyer laughed. He looked at the women, then back at Rowdy and he laughed some more. "You think it'll be that easy?"

He didn't dare look at his sister or Avery. If he did, fury would take over and he'd be on Meyer, gun or not, in seconds. "I think you value life. I know you love Sonya."

"My Sonya."

"Think of her, Meyer." Rowdy counted on Avery's mother being Meyer's one weakness. "Where will she be if you die today? If you go to jail for life?"

"She's all I've ever thought of!"

"Good. That's good." Sanity was such a fragile thing. Had Meyer always been nuts? "You know she loves you, too."

"She wanted her fucking daughter back," Meyer spat. "But Avery was too selfish—"

Adrenaline pumped through his blood. *"Look at me, Meyer."* Rowdy steadily approached. "That's over now. Avery understands how much Sonya needs her. But she needs you, too."

"No." Meyer caught Pepper trying to stray closer and his face contorted in rage. "Stupid bitch, you will back up right now."

Pepper froze.

"She's not going to do anything, Meyer. You have the gun. Now look at me."

"I will when she backs off."

Instead of Pepper doing the reasonable thing, she held her ground. And Avery, damn her, crowded in next to Pepper.

Rowdy had lost far too much in his life. He would not lose Avery or Pepper. "Meyer, does Sonya know where you are?"

"She hasn't a clue." He eyed the women. "She's so busy being stoic, pushing forward with a smile intact. She's beautiful."

"Yes, she is." Rowdy only had a few more feet to go. Then he'd be close enough to rush Meyer. "Beautiful and smart and kind. You're a lucky man."

"You're not." Meyer eased the gun from Avery to Pepper and back again. "Which one should it be, Rowdy? Your little sister or your lover?"

Fisher said, "Jesus, Meyer." Face pale with pain and blood loss, he squeezed his leg. "Let it go."

"You are a disappointment."

Fearful, Fisher glanced at Rowdy, but Rowdy looked only at Meyer. "I want you to put the gun down." *Put it down before I jam it down your goddamn throat.*

"Not until you choose."

Holding on to the pole, Fisher tried to stand. "We're not getting out of here if you don't stop. Let's go now."

"We have nowhere to go," Meyer told him.

"I could use a fucking hospital!" Fisher got mostly upright, slumping against the pole. "Be reasonable."

"You're not as smart as I thought, Fisher. There's no cleaning this up. I know it even if you don't. So let me have my fun. I'm not going down without taking one of them with me." He smiled. "I'll be generous, Rowdy. You can keep one. Which is it to be?"

Before Rowdy could come up with a reply, Avery stepped forward. "Let Pepper go."

Rowdy's heart stalled. In his head, he whispered *no.*

Then his sister joined Avery. "Screw that. I'm not going anywhere. Let Avery leave."

Cursing low, Rowdy gave up subterfuge and strode forward. "You won't hurt either of them, you miserable fuck. Before you get off a shot, I swear to you, I will rip out your twisted heart."

Just a few more steps, Rowdy thought. And then he'd be close enough to jump the bastard.

Meyer must have realized it, too. Panicked, he turned the gun on Rowdy. "Stop!"

Relieved to again be the focus, Rowdy kept going. "Fuck you." If Meyer didn't manage a killing shot, Rowdy would disarm him. Either way, Pepper would know to react. She and Avery would find a way to get safe.

Meyer took aim, his finger squeezing the trigger.

Rowdy braced himself, ready to lunge—and a bullet hit Meyer in the chest. For a split second Rowdy stared, dumbfounded, as the force of the shot sent Meyer stumbling backward. He tripped over one of the kitchen chairs and landed flat on his back, a blood blossom expanding over his shirt.

On instinct, Rowdy launched himself at Avery and Pepper, hastily pushing them both to floor behind him. He had no idea who had fired the shot, if Fisher was now armed, as well. He twisted to survey the danger.

Reese stepped in, gun drawn as he searched the scene. "Rowdy? Are you hurt?"

Rowdy drew a breath, still with a death grip on Avery and Pepper. "No." He sounded hoarse, and took a second to breathe. He stroked a hand over Avery's hair, ran his other hand over his sister's back. "Fish is bleeding like a stuck pig, but we're okay."

Logan, the one who'd taken the shot, came in next, his gun still at the ready. He went straight to Meyer, disarmed him and then said, "Pepper?"

Cannon stood in the doorway, taking in the destruction.

Safe. They were all safe.

Rowdy was still hugging Pepper on one side, Avery on the other, when Pepper struggled away from him and ran to Logan.

Logan caught her up with one arm, squeezing her hard. For only a moment, Logan closed his eyes in relief.

He'd misjudged him, Rowdy realized. Logan was a cop through and through, and no matter how personal things might get, he had a cool enough head to do what needed to be done.

Pepper stuck her face in Logan's neck and damn,

the way her shoulders jerked, Rowdy thought she might be crying.

A suffocating pressure squeezed his chest. He'd never felt anything like it, but now, knowing Avery and his sister were both okay, it should have eased.

It didn't. It got worse and worse, painful, frightening.

Until Avery gulped in air, once, twice, then gave a soft sob. Everything inside him turned to mush. He pulled her up and into his lap, cradling her close. "You're not hurt?"

She shook her head, her hands on his face, big tears tracking down her cheeks. She had a bruise on the left side of her face.

"Who did this?" Rowdy asked, brushing gently with his thumb.

She shook her head, letting him know it didn't matter. Not now. "You scared me so badly."

"Oh, babe." He pulled her in, kissed her forehead. "Scared doesn't even begin to cover it."

Going from soft and shaken to furious in a single beat, she slugged him. Hard. Right in the shoulder. "What the hell do you mean, Rowdy Yates, daring that maniac to shoot you?"

"I didn't." Not really. His only thought had been to keep Avery and Pepper safe.

Suddenly Pepper was back, her expression mean as she dropped to her haunches to give him a shove.

Rowdy almost toppled backward. "What the hell, Pepper."

"You bastard!"

Rowdy stared at her. Never had his sister cursed him.

She reached past Avery, who still sat on his lap, to grab his ear. "You could have been killed!"

"Jesus." He caught her wrist—gently, because he loved her more than life—and freed his ear. "He was going to shoot you."

"I wouldn't have let that happen," Avery said around another sob.

"And you!" He pulled Pepper down beside him again so he could give his attention to Avery. "I had it under control, honey. You should have stayed back instead of—"

"Doing what *you* did?" She struggled up and away from him. *"I love you, damn it."*

Rowdy stared up at her. Half the neighborhood had probably just heard her shout.

"He'll live," Reese said as he checked on Fisher. "But he probably won't be walking anytime soon."

Cannon came to stand by Avery. "Ambulance will be here soon. I can already hear their sirens."

Rowdy thought about sprawling back on the cold floor, taking a minute to get himself together, to come to grips with all he felt. Avery stood there heaving, Cannon looked expectant, his sister openly cried while clutching his arm and Reese and Logan were handling everything.

But it was his apartment, so he manned up and stood, then pulled two chairs away from the table. "Sit down," he said to Pepper.

"We're going to talk about this," she insisted. "About this warped way you have of putting yourself at—"

"Sure, kiddo." He got her to sit, then messed up her hair. "Whatever you want."

"And don't you patronize me!"

"Wouldn't think of it." He glanced toward Logan, but his brother-in-law looked carved from stone—probably his way of keeping his shit together until he got done doing his job. Rowdy leaned down to Pepper's ear. "I think he needs a little comfort, kiddo."

"He needs to work first," Logan said. "She can comfort me later."

Yeah, he didn't want to know about that. Rowdy didn't quite look at Avery yet, but in every fiber of his being, he was aware of her standing there, shaking, upset. "Do you need me for anything?" he asked Logan.

Reese glanced up at him, then at Avery. "At the moment? No. But don't take off."

Where the hell would he go?

Because Cannon looked like he wanted to help, Rowdy said, "Get her something to drink, okay? Stay with her until Logan finishes up."

"Sure." Cannon rubbed the back of his neck. "Jesus, what a mess. Tonight, whatever I can do to help out at the bar, just let me know."

"Thanks." Rowdy gave one last kiss to the top of Pepper's head. "You did great, kiddo."

"My phone is still under your bed." Bracing her feet on the edge of the chair, she pulled her knees up and wrapped her arms around her shins. "It was the only way I could think of to let you know what was happening."

"It was perfect."

"*She's* perfect," Logan said. Then he announced, "This one's dead."

Rowdy glanced toward Meyer, and his only thought was of Sonya. She'd have Avery in her life to help her through the loss, and personally, he thought that was more than the woman deserved.

Preparing himself, because he knew it wasn't going

to be easy, Rowdy turned to Avery. She was a terrible crier. Mascara tracks ran down her bruised face and her nose was already redder than her hair. Her skin had turned blotchy, her eyes swollen.

God, he loved her.

He stood there, staring at her, drinking it in, accepting that he loved her and that no matter what, he needed her. With him. In his life. A part of him.

Day in and day out, whatever life dealt.

She wiped her tears, sniffled. And waited.

She'd been waiting on him for so long that he felt like a complete and total bastard. And a coward.

In two long strides he reached her and drew her in. That got her sobbing pretty good again. She clutched at him, forgetting his stupid stitches, his injury, as she burrowed closer.

"It wasn't you," she told him brokenly. "This happened because of me. Because of my life."

"Yeah, I know." He'd been so worried about Avery deserving more than he could give her. He didn't want her put at risk because of him, because of where he lived and the business he owned, the associations he'd made.

"It was my background…and it endangered you and your sister."

"Shhh."

From the kitchen table, Pepper said, "Avery?"

Avery drew a gulping, shuddering breath, then said, "Yes?"

"Cause a scene."

Half laughing around her tears, Avery squeezed him close again.

Rowdy had no idea what that exchange meant, but

he picked her up and went to the couch. On the way, he managed to kick Fisher, who groaned weakly.

The prick.

Avery sniffled another laugh. "Did you do that on purpose?"

Amazing, unique, wonderful Avery. He didn't know any other woman who could find humor in the situation. "If he wouldn't get more blood all over my apartment, I'd take him apart for slapping you."

"I'd help you."

"Maybe we'll get our chance yet."

"I was so afraid," she said, her voice going high and thin again. "But…but I tried to hide it from him. I wanted him to know what a sick and weak…*nothing* he is."

"I heard." Rowdy rubbed his face against her hair, his heart so full that it hurt. "Pepper called me. I could hear you talking. You were incredible." He hugged her tighter. "I'm so proud of you."

"Proud." She wiped her eyes on his shirt. "Great. I feel so much better."

Sarcasm at a time like this was almost as amazing as the humor. Rowdy couldn't take it a second more. "And I love you."

She went perfectly still, then jerked back to see him.

Rowdy touched her face, so blotchy from her crying jag. "I love you so damn much, Avery, it scares me. But losing you scares me more."

From the kitchen table, Pepper said, "There, you see? My brother is a very smart man."

Cannon said, "Yeah, I know."

Paramedics arrived along with some unis. Reese and

Logan ran the show, so Rowdy didn't have to do anything but hold Avery.

When she sat there staring at him, he asked, "What did my sister mean about you causing a scene?"

Her eyes were round and watchful, as if she didn't quite believe him yet. "I told her if you asked me to leave, I wouldn't. Cause a scene I mean."

"But Pepper likes you enough that she'd want you to, huh?"

Pepper chimed in, saying, "I love *you* enough, brother, that I wanted her to do what was right for you." Then she thought to add, "But yeah, I like Avery a lot, too."

Rowdy smiled, easing Avery's untidy hair away from her ravaged face. "Do you want to go in the bathroom?" He kissed the corner of her mouth. "You're kind of a mess."

She slugged him again, but she was smiling. "Yes, please."

Again, he lifted her.

One of the EMTs asked, "Is she okay?"

He waited, but Avery didn't answer, so he said for her, "She's just upset because I love her."

"Rowdy!" She kept her face tucked in close, hiding.

He grinned as he carried her into his bathroom and sat her on the side of the tub. He rinsed out a washcloth in cold water, handed it to her and then splashed his own face.

His hands were shaking.

"You really love me?"

Such a small, uncertain voice. "Yeah." He dried his face and sat on the tub beside her. She'd missed much of the mess, so he took the cloth from her and tried to help remove some of her ruined makeup. "I really love you."

She inhaled.

"Will you marry me, Avery?"

Her lips started to tremble again, so he kissed them. Just a soft kiss at first, but this was Avery and soon he had a hand in her hair, holding her close while he reaffirmed that she was safe, and that she was his.

Logan tapped at the door, then pushed it open. "You're both okay?"

"He loves me," Avery said. "We're going to get married."

Logan half smiled. "Congratulations."

"Thank you."

Her formality was as unique as everything else. Rowdy couldn't stop touching her, and he knew he'd never stop loving her.

"I hate to do this right now, but we need to talk to each of you. Alone." Logan held on to the doorknob, his gaze sympathetic. "And Avery, as next of kin, we need to let your mother know that Meyer is gone."

She nodded.

Rowdy said, "We can do it together."

Avery straightened her shoulders. "May I wash my face first?"

Logan said, "Sure. No problem." He stepped back out of the room.

Rowdy stood with her. "We'll take the day off. Cannon can handle things tonight. Tomorrow—"

"Tomorrow," Avery interrupted, "I'll return to my job as your full-time bartender."

"I've been thinking about that," Rowdy told her. "We can talk about it more later, but I'd like you to be a co-owner in the bar." He held up a hand to stop her protests. "As a co-owner, you can continue to bartend if that's what you want. But you already help in every decision there is."

"I don't have any money to buy in."

His mouth quirked. "You give a lot of your time, and you give great input. Together, we'll go over finances."

"Together." She let out a happy sigh. "Okay, yes."

Rowdy kissed her red nose, her stubborn chin and her soft mouth. "God, I love you, babe."

"This started out as such a bad day."

He had to laugh. "Your face is bruised, there's a dead man in my apartment and another who, with any luck, will not only be ruined, but will do some serious jail time."

"But you love me," she said. "And that makes it a very good day."

MARCUS HUGGED ROWDY'S KNEES, then ran out to the yard with Cash racing behind him. They were due to get snow at the end of the week, but today the sun was bright enough to warm the coldest heart.

Rowdy stood in the doorway, watching the kid climb into the tire swing. Avery's mother, bundled up in a hooded white sweatshirt, gave the tire a push to get Marcus started, then laughed when Cash ran back and forth in excitement. Avery hugged her mother's arm.

Hard to believe how things had rolled out. Thanks to Sonya's insistence, Meyer had written Avery into his will. He shook his head. He didn't want Meyer's money, but Sonya insisted. It meant a lot to her, a way to alleviate some of her guilt over how gullible she'd been, how she'd so unfairly misjudged Avery.

And so they'd agreed to take the money—which they would invest into a community project Cannon had started for at-risk kids.

It felt good. Hell, his whole life felt blessed now that Avery was in it.

Nothing seemed impossible anymore.

Behind him, Pepper said, "He's pretty darned cute, isn't he?"

"Marcus?" Rowdy drew her into his side and kissed the top of her head. "Yeah, he is." A month with Alice and Reese had already made a difference. Marcus wore clothes that fit, and while he was still a skinny little dude, he looked healthier, happier. A lot more secure. He had nightmares, and he still distrusted his good fortune, but things were getting better, little by little. "He's really coming around."

"Love will do that to a person."

Amen. "You and Logan ever think about having kids?" He kind of liked the idea of being an uncle.

Pepper floored him when she said, "Yeah, we've talked about it."

"No shit?" He looked down at the kid sister he'd spent a lifetime protecting. She was the one person he'd thought would always be the center of his world. He still loved her like crazy, and he'd still die for her.

But the love he felt was no longer so...desperate.

"No shit," she replied with a grin. "Can you see me all round with a baby?"

"Yeah, I can." She'd be beautiful, no matter what. "You'd make a great mother, kiddo." Fiercely protective, nurturing and she'd raise the kid to be strong, like her.

"We want to wait another year or two," Pepper told

him, then snuggled in to his side again. "But after that… we'll see."

When Avery started toward the house, her long red hair teased by the breeze, Pepper said, "She's really something. I can see why you love her."

"Yeah." Every day he found more and more reasons.

Grinning, Pepper hugged him tight. "Dinner will be ready in a few minutes."

"Thanks." He opened the patio doors to greet his soon-to-be wife. "How's your mom?"

"Doing better." She turned her face up for his kiss.

Rowdy was happy to oblige. He touched his mouth to hers, then whispered, "I love you." The words that once felt so impossible to say were now impossible to keep to himself.

"I love you, too." She settled beside him with a sigh. "Marcus and my mother get along really well. She wants to spoil him." Avery winced. "I hope Reese and Alice won't mind too much."

"We'll talk to them, see what they say. But I think it's good for Sonya to have a different focus now that Meyer is out of her life."

"She wants to throw us a big wedding."

Rowdy blanched, but only for a second. "Is that what you want?" Because if a big society wedding would make her happy, he'd throw on a monkey suit and play along.

"No." She grinned up to see him. "I want our family and friends there, and I want the pretty white dress, but most of all I want you." She ran a hand over his abs, something she often did. "If you want to wear your jeans, I'm okay with it."

Rowdy had to laugh. "How did I get so lucky?"

"You hired the right bartender to run Getting Rowdy. That's how." She hugged him tight.

"I've been thinking about the name of the place."

"It's already established, so you can't change it," she warned him.

"It's already changed. I had the sign painted."

"Without talking to me?"

Her umbrage amused him. "It's still Getting Rowdy, but at the bottom, in smaller print, it now says, With Avery. Because honest to God, honey, the bar wouldn't be the same—I wouldn't be the same—without you."

Her smile came slowly. "Well, since I'm now officially the only woman getting rowdy with you, it fits."

* * * * *

*Read on for a sneak peek of FIGHTING DIRTY,
the newest* ULTIMATE *novel from*
New York Times *bestselling author Lori Foster...*

Sitting alone at the bar, drinking a freaking lemon water, Armie Jacobson only half listened as Miles and Brand talked about upcoming fights at the table opposite him. Women tried to get his attention but he didn't have any interest. He'd put up a good front, given it a shot several times, and he'd probably convinced everyone with his bullshit, but the truth was that he hadn't had any real interest in a good long while.

Not since that day he'd finally tasted Rissy—Merissa Colter.

His gaze went to the small hallway in Rowdy's bar. Dim and narrow, it led to an office and the johns. Months ago he'd caught Rissy there, and for a few minutes he'd lost the fight. Mouth on mouth, tongues playing, damp heat and a firestorm of sensation. Remembering, he closed his eyes and gave in to the surge of molten lust. God Almighty, she'd tasted good. Felt good. Fit against him perfectly.

An elbow to his ribs got his eyes open again. Instead of one of the guys, it was Vanity, Stack's wife, who slid onto a stool beside him. "What?" he asked.

"You tell me," she said, her gaze unwavering, her nails tapping on the bar counter.

Gorgeous beyond words with long blond hair, a killer body and an angel's face, Vanity was still one of the most down-to-earth, kindhearted people he knew. "Is that supposed to make sense to me, Vee?"

"Yes. You're moping and I want to know why."

Stack stood behind his wife and braced an arm on the bar. "It's the upcoming fight," Stack predicted. "He's getting cold feet."

"No way," Justice said, taking a seat behind Armie.

Armie looked back and forth between them. "Sure, join me. Make yourselves comfortable."

Vanity patted his arm in a pitying way. "We don't stand on formality, not when we see a friend moping."

"I'm not moping," he denied. God, he was *so* moping.

Justice laughed. "I've watched five different women hit on you—and you made excuses to all of them."

"Seriously?" Vanity asked Armie. "Are you off the market?"

She looked way too pleased by that notion.

Stack laughed. "That's even more ridiculous than my gibe about him having cold feet."

A brunette approached the bar and Armie swallowed a groan. Of course he remembered her, but he pretended he didn't.

Because he was a dick like that.

"Armie?" Ignoring the others, she trailed a finger up his arm and over his shoulder. "I'm free tonight."

"Yeah?" Armie looked at Justice. "So is he. You two should hook up."

Justice straightened. "Gospel truth, ma'am."

The brunette's eyes narrowed. "I was talking to you, Armie."

"And I handed you off. Take it or leave it."

Vanity slugged him.

Stack coughed.

Justice just looked hopeful.

The brunette asked expectantly, "Will you join us?"

"No!" Justice said quickly. "He won't."

Armie looked at the lady's pout, Vanity's disapproving expression, Justice's appalled frown, and he had to laugh. "If you'll all excuse me?"

Paying no attention to questions, he threw some bills on the bar and took off. Halfway toward the door, Miles called out to him.

Armie kept going.

Two women tried to waylay him, but he pretended not to notice. Once outside, he sucked in the cold evening air, but it did nothing to clear his head. And suddenly, without looking behind him, he knew Cannon Colter was there. "Shit."

Cannon laughed. "You're okay to drive?"

Working to clear all emotion from his face, Armie turned to his friend. "Can't get drunk on nasty lemon water, now can I?"

"Is that what you wanted to do? Get drunk?"

No, he wanted to drag Merissa to bed and keep her there until his blood no longer burned and lurid thoughts of her cleared out of his brain. He popped his neck, shook his head and said, "I don't know."

"It's not the fight." Folding his arms, Cannon leaned back on the outside wall of Rowdy's bar. "I know you too well to think you're concerned about Carter."

"I'll either win the fight or not. I'm prepared." Armie shrugged, showing his indifference. He never thought in terms of winning or losing. Just winning. And to that end he did what he needed to do to ensure success.

"Everyone assumes there's added pressure because

you'll be in the SBC now. But again," Cannon stated, "I know you better than that."

"A fight is a fight," Armie confirmed. "The size of the crowd—"

"Or the size of the paycheck?"

"—doesn't matter to me."

"I know." Cannon lifted a brow. "So you want to tell me what's eating at you?"

A bad case of desperate lust for your little sister. Not something he'd ever share. Rather than deny the problem, Armie shook his head. "I'll deal with it."

"By avoiding sex?"

He jutted his chin. "Who says I am?"

Cannon didn't blink. "Man, I know you. Better than anyone. You thought I wouldn't notice when you went cold turkey?"

That so shocked Armie that he took a step back. He couldn't think of a single thing to say. If he tried to blame it on fight preparation, Cannon would just laugh at him again. "I don't suppose you'd butt out?"

"Sure. If that's what you really want." Cannon straightened away from the wall. "But if you want to talk, if you need anything—"

"I know." Once, a lifetime ago, Cannon had been the only person to back him. Against all odds and ugly accusations, he'd stood with Armie and never, not once, showed a single shadow of doubt. Uncomfortable with the idea of ever again being that needy, Armie flexed his shoulders and said, "Thanks, but it's fine."

"I know that." Cannon squeezed his shoulder. "You just need to start believing it."

Armie glared at his friend as he went back into the bar. He didn't need that melodramatic crap heaped on him. Breathing hard, he looked around at the moon-washed blacktop, the frost-covered bus bench, then up at the inky, star-studded sky.

What was Merissa doing right now? Was she with another man—as he'd suggested?

It was what he wanted, what would be best—for her—but at the same time… Jesus, it tortured him.

After the life he'd led, the background he'd overcome and the physical ability he'd gained, he wasn't afraid of anything or anyone, except Merissa Colter's effect on him. That scared him all right. Bone-deep, heart-sucking fear…

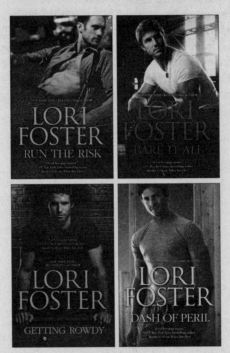

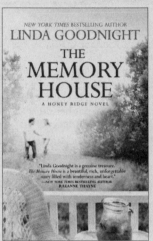

Turn your love of reading into rewards you'll love with
Harlequin My Rewards

LORI FOSTER

78905	WHEN YOU DARE	___ $7.99 U.S. ___	$8.99 CAN.
77816	HOT IN HERE	___ $7.99 U.S. ___	$8.99 CAN.
77761	BARE IT ALL	___ $7.99 U.S. ___	$9.99 CAN.
77708	THE BUCKHORN LEGACY	___ $7.99 U.S. ___	$9.99 CAN.
77695	RUN THE RISK	___ $7.99 U.S. ___	$9.99 CAN.
77656	A PERFECT STORM	___ $7.99 U.S. ___	$9.99 CAN.
77647	FOREVER BUCKHORN	___ $7.99 U.S. ___	$9.99 CAN.
77612	BUCKHORN BEGINNINGS	___ $7.99 U.S. ___	$9.99 CAN.
77582	SAVOR THE DANGER	___ $7.99 U.S. ___	$9.99 CAN.
77575	TRACE OF FEVER	___ $7.99 U.S. ___	$9.99 CAN.
77444	TEMPTED	___ $7.99 U.S. ___	$9.99 CAN.

(limited quantities available)

TOTAL AMOUNT	$ _____
POSTAGE & HANDLING	$ _____
($1.00 FOR 1 BOOK, 50¢ for each additional)	
APPLICABLE TAXES*	$ _____
TOTAL PAYABLE	$ _____

(check or money order—please do not send cash)

To order, complete this form and send it, along with a check or money order for the total above, payable to HQN Books, to: **In the U.S.:** 3010 Walden Avenue, P.O. Box 9077, Buffalo, NY 14269-9077; **In Canada:** P.O. Box 636, Fort Erie, Ontario, L2A 5X3.

Name: _____
Address: _____ City: _____
State/Prov.: _____ Zip/Postal Code: _____
Account Number (if applicable): _____

075 CSAS

*New York residents remit applicable sales taxes.
*Canadian residents remit applicable GST and provincial taxes.

HQN™
www.HQNBooks.com

PHLF0216BL